# PANDEMIC HACKER

Hacking and surviving a blackmail group during COVID

Copyright @2023, 2025, 2026 by B.D. Murphy
SBN: 979-8-9998438-3-8
Title: PANDEMIC HACKER
Website: https://www.authorbdmurphy.com

All rights reserved.

No part of this publication may be used or reproduced, distributed, or in any form or by any means, including photocopying, recording, or other electronic or mechanical methods, without the prior written permission of the publisher, except as permitted by U.S. copyright law.

This is a work of fiction. Unless otherwise indicated, all the names, characters, businesses, events, and incidents in this book are either the product of the author's imagination or used in a fictitious manner. Any resemblance to actual people, living or dead, or actual events is purely coincidental.

All product names, logos, and brands mentioned in this work are the property of their respective owners. Their use is solely for illustrative and narrative purposes and does not imply any affiliation with or endorsement by the trademark holders.

*Website:* https://www.authorbdmurphy.com
*Facebook:* https://facebook.com/bdmurph73
Cover design by B.D. Murphy

# Table of Contents

# The Café Shooting

It's March 5th, 2020, and the high temperature in Boston will be 33 degrees Fahrenheit, with light wind. Sam is meeting with FBI agents for the second time to discuss her master's thesis. She doesn't know that the agents want to talk about her working for the FBI. The first time they met, in her professor's office, they asked for a copy of her thesis, which she said was too incomplete. She's sure they'll ask for a copy again. Since they're meeting at a local coffee shop close to the university campus, Sam arrives early, gets a coffee, and sits at a table facing the door. The two agents arrive, scan the room, immediately walk over to her table, and sit on either side of her.

Supervisory Special Agent Frank Andrews and Special Agent Phil Nomikos from the FBI's cybercrimes division say good morning, and Sam asks if they would like to get coffee first. The agent's reply that they'll get coffee at the end to take to the office. Agent Nomikos asks Sam, "I know we had a short discussion about your thesis when we met with you and your professor. We want to get more details. Your thesis is about hardening the firmware for network controllers, correct? Please go over the high-level with us again."

Sam confirms her thesis is about how a hacker can modify the firmware on a Wi-Fi controller, gaining complete control over a user's network. The device owner will never know that hackers have compromised their network.

Agent Nomikos asked Sam questions about how the hack could start, how they could remove it, and how they could detect it. Based on the questions, Sam knows that Agent Nomikos can understand her answers, so she responds to his questions in some detail. She's not sure if Agent Andrews understands the details, primarily because he isn't asking any detailed questions.

Agent Andrews is listening to the conversation and profiling Sam as they talk. He's interested in Sam's explanation but is more concerned with determining her state of mind regarding hacking. Does she have a grounded and clear set of morals, a compass? She's happy to discuss her thesis but seems reluctant to talk about what she's done in hacking, which concerns Agent Andrews.

To make sure both agents understand what she's talking about, Sam adds a more straightforward explanation. "The primary job of a network controller is to capture network traffic for the device and pass it to the main device CPU for processing. If you can take control of the network CPU, you can change the data, send it to another computer, or prevent the data from reaching the main CPU. You can completely control the device's connection to the world."

Agent Andrews asks, "Sam, why hasn't this been done before?"

"I don't know that this has NOT been done before. It's too hard to detect with the current standard instrumentation. The focus is always on the main CPU and what it's doing."

"How would a user remove this hack?"

"To remove a hack like this would require a firmware update that is very user intensive. You can't just do a Windows update to fix something like this. Finding a hacked device would depend on what it was doing at the time. If traffic is stopped to the main CPU, you may never detect the hack. If it's sending data to another server somewhere, your best possibility is to detect an anomaly in traffic flow."

"Would a regular user, not an expert, be able to tell?"

"The end-user experience would be a slowdown of their network speed. No internet service provider guarantees the speed, and any complaints to the ISP will be ignored. Most users will think it's the internet service provider."

Agent Nomikos asks, "Can we get a copy of what you've completed for your thesis? Even though it's a rough draft, I would like to see details of your research."

She reluctantly agrees, telling him, "Sure, I'll send you an email with the current draft when I get home."

Agent Nomikos takes out a card and writes an email address on the back. He gives it to Sam and asks her to send it to that address. "This is the generic email address of our cybercrime laboratory."

The agents discuss with Sam whether she's interested in joining the FBI, but she expresses reservations.

"You guys know that, as part of my research, I need to break into systems as a hacker. For my research to be complete, I must map, then find and exploit vulnerabilities across the internet. I don't know that I can pass the lie detector requirements or meet your standards." She knows that discussing the database she found and hacked last week would instantly get her into trouble.

Agent Nomikos tells Sam, "In the role we're talking about, we expect our people to know how to hack. We don't want people who think it can be done without experience. We want people who know how to do these hacks so they can work on detecting and then finding the hackers. Many former hackers work on penetration testing and hardening networks."

Agent Andrews asks Sam, "Why are you reluctant to talk about any hacking you've done?"

Sam pauses, then replies, "Because I'm not convinced it'll be good enough to prove my thesis. Like I said when we met before, if I can't remotely access and take control of a system, then the thesis is limited."

Agent Andrews, reading Sam's body language, knows she's telling the truth.

Sam continues, "I talked about simple examples of hacking before, but what I'm talking about now is scary if the wrong people figure out how to exploit the capability."

"Okay, Sam, I get your reservations, but you still haven't answered the other question–are you interested in joining the team?" says Agent Andrews.

Surprised by his insistence, Sam replies, "Wow, I didn't expect that a thesis would lead to the FBI asking me to join law enforcement. My thesis and my research are very focused. I thought I would get a job with a networking company or a company that detects hacking. I mean, would I have the credentials to be successful in a role like this?"

Agent Nomikos replies, "You've already shown that you think out of the box, which is a key criterion. We can help with the other hacking aspects. We need your help to detect and stop these network firmware-based hacks. I'm sure we can answer any other questions you may have, though."

As they're talking, Sam looks up and sees two men walking in the door. One is wearing a Boston Red Sox baseball cap and a blue jacket. The other person has a green jacket, which resembles the Celtics' colors. They both have short hair. The Red Sox guy has a full mustache, and they both have several days of beard growth. They look around the coffee shop. Instead of walking toward the ordering line, they head directly toward the table where Sam and the agents are sitting. The one with the cap reaches into his jacket for something. As she sees him pull a gun, Sam shouts to the agents, "GUN!" Both agents stand up, draw their weapons, and turn around, while Sam drops to the ground and covers her ears. The second gunman draws his gun as the agents stand up.

The gunman with the cap shoots and hits Agent Nomikos in the upper right chest. Agent Nomikos can't get his gun on target, so he shifts back and starts to raise his gun again. Agent Andrews hits that gunman in the center of his chest, and using common double-shot training, he follows immediately with a second shot. The gunman looks at his gun, then at Agent Andrews. The color has drained from his face, and he collapses.

Meanwhile, the green jacket gunman shoots at Agent Andrews as he is shifting his aim away from the first gunman. The small shift in position causes the shot to hit him in the side.

Agent Nomikos, with a chest wound affecting his right arm, is bringing his weapon up toward the second gunman. The gunman sees he hit Andrews, and that Nomikos is shifting toward him. He shifts to focus on Nomikos as the agent lines up his gun and fires. Andrews fires at the second gunman. The shots from both agents hit the gunman in the chest almost simultaneously.

Those gunshots don't make the gunman drop to the ground immediately, causing both agents to fire at him again. The gunman gets one more shot off at the same time as the agents, and it goes through the spot where Sam had been sitting and into the wall. He falls to his knees; his breathing is ragged, then he falls onto his side. Agent Andrews moves toward him, kicking the gun away while still focusing his weapon on the gunman. The gunman coughs up blood, looks at Agent Andrews, and then stops breathing.

Agent Nomikos lowered his weapon when the gunman went down, using his left hand to check his chest. It hurts, but he doesn't see much blood. He can feel that something is wrong, as his breathing immediately becomes more labored.

With both gunmen down, Sam assesses the situation and heads to Agent Nomikos. Ignoring the surrounding chaos, she has to speak loudly because of the crying and complaining. She tells him to put his gun away and sit down. Agent Andrews can see that Sam is checking on Nomikos, and he secures the café.

Agent Nomikos has a chest wound, and his breathing is rapid and shallow. Sam knows that he's in serious trouble. She rips open his shirt to expose the wound. Once she sees that there isn't much blood, her fast heartbeat speeds up even faster because she knows it means primarily internal bleeding. If the agent coughs, it will exacerbate the internal bleeding.

She talks to herself, saying, "Think, Sam, think! You need to slow the bleeding! Dad told me to pack the wound to slow down or stop the bleeding until the medics can help. You must control the bleeding." She pauses and concentrates on her surroundings. Besides the scent of lingering gun smoke and the cries of confused people wanting to leave, she can smell the spilled drinks and hear the clinking of dishes. "Okay, we're inside a coffee shop." Sam looks around, her mind kicking into problem-solving mode.

"I need napkins!" She runs to the condiment counter and grabs a bunch of napkins. As she runs back, her brain is telling her this won't stop the internal bleeding. As she drops the napkins on the table, Sam thinks about what other supplies are readily available and grabs her backpack, pulling out a tampon. She looks at Agent Nomikos and says to him, "This is going to hurt." As she opens the packaging.

Agent Nomikos says to her, "Κάνε το", Greek for 'Do it'. She doesn't understand what he says, but she continues. Using the plastic plunger as leverage, she shoves the tampon into his open chest wound hard, sliding out the plastic as the cotton expands in the wound. Special Agent Nomikos grunts and then curses.

During this time, Agent Andrews is securing the shooters and the scene. Feeling better about Agent Nomikos' situation, Sam goes to Agent Andrews and tells him she needs to check his wound. Agent Andrews' gunshot wound is on the left side of the upper chest. There is an exit hole out of his back, and both entry and exit holes are bleeding, covering his shirt and jacket with blood.

Agent Andrews asks, "What did you do to Special Agent Nomikos?"

Sam's reply surprises Andrews, "Oh, well, he has an upper chest wound, and I shoved a tampon into it to slow the bleeding. I didn't have anything else to help."

With what sounds like a laugh disguised as a cough, Agent Andrews remarks, "Well, that was a smart move, Sam. Are you going to do the same to me?"

Sam smiles, "I don't carry a backpack full of tampons for shooting emergencies, Agent, but you need to be alert when the police get here."

He replies, "I'm fine for now. I can hear the sirens, so they're close."

Sam tells Agent Andrews, "I'm not waiting - I'm going to apply a bandage to help with your bleeding." Sam grabs the stack of napkins, applies several to the inside of Special Agent Andrews's jacket, and tells him to hold them with his right hand. "I can't put napkins into the wound; I need cloth bandage material." Sam pulls a 4-inch knife from her backpack, opens the blade, and slices up the coat sleeve on Agent Andrews's left arm to the elbow. She cut off the coat sleeve and then slices up the shirt sleeve. With Sam working on his wound, Agent Andrews reaches for his phone while looking over to see Agent Nomikos on the phone.

"Agent, I need you to tell me if you have other injuries and how you are feeling. Light-headed, pain anywhere else?"

"My side hurts, but nothing else."

After cutting off his sleeve, Sam says to Agent Andrews, "I don't have tape. I need to slow the bleeding, which means I need to have a cloth material in the wound to help your blood clot. This will hurt." Ripping the sleeve into two strips, she twists the end of the cut-off sleeve into a point and pushes it into the bullet exit hole in his back.

Agent Andrews grits his teeth and takes slow, deep breaths. Sam twists a point of the other strip and inserts it into the entry wound. She tells him, "Hold this as tight as you can."

Agent Andrews asks Sam, "How do you know first aid like this?"

"My dad ensured I could handle gunshot wounds in case something happened while we were hunting."

"What did you hunt with your father?"

"Well, obviously, deer during deer season, but most of the time we hunted feral hogs and wild boar around the area. My dad worked out an arrangement with the local farmers and ranchers, allowing us to kill the hogs. The feral hogs will tear up crops and kill baby animals, so the farmers wanted help. His motivation was to get me constant experience with long-range shooting."

When the police arrive, a female police officer whose name tag reads O'Donnell pulls Sam aside and starts asking for details about what happened. "What is your name, and can you show me some identification?" Sam points to her backpack, saying, "My ID is in the backpack. Can I go get it?" The officer nods, walking with Sam to the backpack. Sam pulls out her ID and hands it to the officer.

Sam detailed her arrival at the coffee shop, her meeting, and the sequence of events. She tells the officer about each shot the agents made in detail.

Officer O'Donnell asks her, "How do you know those kinds of details?"

Sam replies, "I was a competitive shooter for many years before college, so I know details about shot placement and movement."

Officer O'Donnell continues, "It also looks like you performed first aid on the agents."

"Yes, I learned about dealing with gunshot wounds from my father."

"Walk me through their wounds and what you did."

Sam described what she did and why. "I focused on controlling the bleeding."

"You shoved a tampon into his open chest wound?"

"Yes, it was the only thing I could grab quickly that would work inside the chest to slow bleeding. I was worried and couldn't come up with another solution."

"Did you apply any first aid to the attackers?"

"They weren't breathing, so I didn't try anything with them."

Sam would repeat this story to everyone she talked to today. Hours later, Sam is exhausted. The agents went to the hospital; the shooters were processed and then moved to the hospital. The café witnesses finished their interviews and left, and she remained there, answering questions. A bunch of other FBI special agents, NCIS special agents, U.S. Marshals, and local police all showed up to help, and they all had the same questions: Who are you? Where do you live? Why are you here? What do you do……The questions and answers were all the same.

Later, another woman approaches Sam. "Hello, I'm Special Agent Nyah Jones from the FBI counter-terrorism unit. You're Samantha Holzen, the woman the agents were talking to?" Sam nods, and Agent Jones tells Sam, "When two men attack FBI agents in a Boston coffee shop, I need to check if there is a domestic terrorist connection. Can you show me your ID and tell me what happened?"

Sam lets out a sigh, and the agent asks why. Sam replies, "This is something like the sixth time I'll be going through the same information. Everyone in law enforcement wants to interrogate me, I mean, *question me*, and the questions are all the same. I thought the information was shared across agencies."

Agent Jones tells her, "I can fix that. You're with me now, and because you provided first aid to save the agents, I'm going to stop the constant questions about your role in all of this. However, you will need to go through it with me, and I'll also be asking some different questions. Agreed?" Sam reluctantly agrees and goes through the same information she provided to everyone else.

Agent Jones moves to specifics: "Upon entering, did the men scan the room or proceed directly to your table?"

Sam tells Agent Jones, "I wasn't paying that much attention until they didn't move toward the ordering line."

"Why did you sit facing the door?"

"That's a habit my father taught me. He was a Navy SEAL, and I learned to be aware of what's happening around me."

"When the first man pulled his gun, you shouted 'Gun!' to the agents. Why did you do that?"

"That's standard procedure for law enforcement when an unidentified person pulls a gun. It seemed appropriate."

"Ms. Holzen, how do you know that's standard procedure?"

"Working tactical training with the sheriff's department back in Texas. My dad had a good relationship with the sheriff, and they frequently discussed handling complex situations. My dad loved to have a plan for the unexpected."

After Agent Jones questioned Sam for over 30 minutes and most of the other law enforcement left the scene, Agent Jones finally finished. "Sam, I think I'm done with my questions for now. I'm going to walk with you to get you out of this area. Will you be okay to get home?"

"Yes, this spot was picked because it's a few blocks from my apartment, and I don't have a car." Agent Jones walks a couple of blocks with Sam, thanks her for her help, and then Sam tells her she'll be fine to head home from here.

On the way home, Sam reviews the events of the past few days. What was going on? Did the gunman show up targeting the agents, or her? How did they know where anyone would be at that time? Was this just a random event?

Then her thoughts get darker. Did the extortion group trace her activity and send these guys after her? She was so careful when accessing everything; maybe she missed something.

What is she going to do now? She didn't realize what she was getting into when she found and downloaded the database. Everything was more dangerous than she had considered when she accessed the website. Plus, she just met with the FBI and didn't tell them she has an extortion group's master list of blackmail targets and victims. She's now in way over her head if these guys will shoot FBI agents in a coffee shop, if that's even who the attackers were after.

If these people know who she is, she's in danger. But if they don't realize she accessed the database, she could be safe. Should she turn all this information over to the FBI? And if she does, will these criminals find her? She told the agents she isn't sure she's a good enough hacker, and now her fears are amplified. What could she have missed? Sam doesn't have many options now; she needs to be alert and ready.

# Five Months Earlier

Sam walks into the lecture hall for class and looks around the room confidently. The lecture hall is about half full of people sitting in their usual groups. Her confidence comes from growing up being taught to handle any situation by her Navy SEAL father. She's in graduate school because she's good at math and knows she can do something interesting with an advanced degree. Her father taught her ballistics, and when they went hunting, she was required to perform the calculations mentally. When she realized those calculations came naturally, her path to an engineering degree seemed straightforward. Even though her mother and father never attended college, they encouraged her to pursue her dreams, and she wasn't afraid of hard work.

Now working toward her master's degree in electrical engineering, Sam feels she can take on almost any situation, and her confidence shows. Another graduate student, Dexter, with whom she has a couple of the same classes, is in the classroom. Dexter frequently thinks he's smarter than everyone else in any room. Still, Sam doesn't treat him with the deference he feels he deserves, which causes Dexter to target Sam often, trying to show his superiority.

Sam is wearing her usual jeans, shirt, sneakers, and jacket. She's practical about what she wears until it gets really cold.

People look at her and see a five-foot-four-inch woman in her early to mid-twenties. She has shoulder-length dark brown hair, no makeup, small stud earrings, and no visible tattoos. She has a watch and usually gets comments about not wanting to get noticed.

Today, they are getting the results of their first major test in ethics class. No one considered it a straightforward test, but Dexter was smiling. The test challenged everyone's assumptions about what they grew up with and what is the right thing to do.

The professor wanted to discuss one question on the test that elicited every answer. She brought up the question on the display and asks the room,

"What do you think about this question? Should a new hacking exploit be exposed publicly, kept for yourself to use, or only reported to intelligence agencies? Please show your thought process." The screen showed the question and the three options:

Release publicly.

Keep it and use it for yourself.

Give it to the government intelligence community.

Sam had given option three as her answer. It was marked with a question mark, not wrong. Dexter answered option 1, which the Professor said was correct. The Professor asks Dexter to explain why he answered that way. Dexter discusses how making it public allows people to learn about and apply fixes more quickly.

Sam raises her hand, saying she completely disagrees. "If you publish an exploit before there is a fix, you expose everyone to being hacked. The intelligence community and cyber researchers use a process to understand the hack and work on a fix before it's published publicly. The FBI has a dedicated website for reporting exploits and cybercrimes. They don't immediately publish the information. You don't know who else may have discovered the exploit and is using it on you, your bank, or against our infrastructure like the power grid."

The professor asks Sam if she had reported any exploits to the FBI. Sam replies, "As part of my thesis research, I reported a vulnerability that could impact companies and individuals."

Dexter says, "Tell us what you reported to the FBI."

Sam simply says, "No, I will not make the information public. This is exactly the ethical question we're discussing. Do you want me to release a hack that could compromise your system and steal your information? There is no documented fix, so you will remain vulnerable to the hack for an unknown period. The longer the hacked information is out without a fix, the more people will be impacted."

Dexter replies, "In contrast, if the information is available, every security researcher can work on a fix."

Sam shoots back, "Reputable security researchers get access to this kind of information through their work, and with non-disclosure requirements. The best security researchers get information without it being publicly published. When published, every hacker can exploit the information while researchers are working on a fix. Is that your end goal, Dexter, to get access to a hack that's new with no fix?" Sam didn't like Dexter's condescending way of talking to her and women in general.

After her classes, Sam goes back to the apartment she shares with her friend, Claire. Claire is an economics major, working on her Ph.D.

They met in a programming class and worked together to help each other understand the concepts. Sam was not getting along with her original roommates and discussed the possibility of rooming together with Claire later. Claire revealed that she, too, was having issues with her roommate, and after discussing moving with their respective roommates, it turned out that no one was happy. They resolved the situation with a roommate swap: Claire's roommate moved into Sam's apartment with Sam's roommates, and Sam moved into Claire's apartment. They had developed a close friendship over the semester.

Claire is an inch taller than Sam, with light brown hair that goes to the middle of her back. They don't look alike, but there have been times at restaurants when they have been called sisters.

That evening, when Sam returns from class, Claire asks her, "How were the exam results?" Sam recounts the discussion about revealing a new hack and what Dexter says in class.

"He's a dick, Sam; you need to stop wasting energy on him."

"I have a problem with his condescending attitude and the fact that he's getting an A grade on every test," replies Sam.

"Sam, have you considered that he's so smug because he's cheating? How else do you explain what's happening?"

Sam pauses, looks at Claire, and says, "You're right; I don't know why I don't look at the obvious."

"You're always looking at the good side, and this is an example of a situation where that doesn't work. *That's* why it bothers you so much." Claire continues, "What are you going to do about this? You can either ignore him and move on with your life or report the incident and deal with the consequences. If you inform someone, he'll probably come after you."

"You mean he'll be more of a dick than he already is to me. I'll look into this my way and figure out a plan."

Claire smiles, saying, "That means you're going to hack the crap out of him, and he'll never know."

"Claire…."

"Don't start with me, you know more hacking stuff than most people in Boston, hell, the world! Look, you can use your skills to get enough information so the university can do an investigation. You're not bound by warrants, probable cause, and whatever else. I've heard enough growing up to know that giving key information to the right people will make something happen. Find enough to get the investigation going, and then you're out."

Sam rolls her eyes at her friend and heads to the kitchen for a snack.

### 

A few days later, the weather is in the mid-50s, with blue skies and some wind, but forecasters predict the area will experience a cold front tomorrow. Sam has decided to check out Dexter in her own way. She's on a park bench in Greene-Rose Heritage Park with her sandwich lunch. Dexter lives in an apartment across the park, close to campus. Sam puts her backpack at the end of the bench, with the utility pocket pointed carefully at the section of the building where Dexter lives. Sam has a small Wi-Fi adapter in the backpack that plugs into a USB port and a special long-range antenna. There's a USB wire for her computer. The computer is running the Kali Linux distribution on a virtual machine. The long-range Wi-Fi antenna will allow Sam to connect to Dexter's Wi-Fi from across the park.

Claire is meeting her to have lunch. Claire starts eating her lunch while Sam is finishing the setup.

She reprogrammed the Wi-Fi MAC address on the USB adapter to make it appear as if it were an old laptop, rather than a new adapter. Anyone in the area who looks up the MAC address would see that it's from a major computer manufacturer and is several years old.

"Now tell me what you're doing. I see a laptop and a wire going into your backpack."

"In the backpack is a long-range antenna that can reach Dexter's Wi-Fi from here. It is much further than normal systems can reach. Now

I'm going to search for Wi-Fi signals he could be using."

Sam starts the software and begins searching for Wi-Fi signals.

"I am looking for Wi-Fi in the building's area where he lives, which could be his. Here is an interesting one: irresistible. Now I am starting the signal capture."

"How long will this take?"

"Not long, but I need to search for other signals just to be sure."

She finds a signal with the same frequency and power level, but the broadcast name (SSID) is hidden. Checking, she finds it's the same MAC address for Dexter's Wi-Fi. Dexter has a hidden Wi-Fi network, which is the one Sam needs to connect to.

"I found the basic Wi-Fi signal, and checking, I found another signal, his hidden network, which I need to use."

"Now what?"

"Any device that connects to a Wi-Fi network goes through a very well-defined negotiation to establish the link. The data from this negotiation is what I need. Now I need to wait. Probably when Dexter leaves and returns. That is when his phone will connect and tell me the information."

Claire leaves for her class after finishing her lunch. After 45 minutes, Sam must decide to wait or leave to get to her class. Frustrated, Sam realizes she's going to need an alternative approach to get the information.

### ###

The next day, in class, Sam sits three rows behind Dexter. Her backpack is on the floor, pointing toward Dexter. The Wi-Fi adapter features a standard antenna this time. She plugs in the USB cable and starts the virtual machine with Linux. She's already created a script to configure the USB Wi-Fi adapter. It's set up to look exactly like Dexter's network. The adapter has the MAC address of his router, and the Wi-Fi channels and network names all match. She activates the network capture and turns on the Wi-Fi.

Dexter's phone, detecting the network it knows with a strong signal, tries to connect. His phone sends Sam's system all the information she needs in less than one second. Sam turns off the Wi-Fi, pulls out the USB cable, and focuses on notes for class.

The Wi-Fi hacking process doesn't give the password directly; it's shared as an encrypted string. Sam already has a file from the internet containing several million passwords that have been used and previously hacked. The password file contains clear-text, but not encrypted, entries, which is what Dexter's phone provided. Each line in the password file is encrypted and then compared with the information received from the phone.

To speed the process up, Sam has taken the password file and created a database with multiple encryption methods: Unix login, Windows login, and Wi-Fi WPA2. It's easy to add more to the database. When the virtual machine retrieves the encrypted string, it performs a simple database lookup to retrieve the password.

When Sam leaves class, she checks on the cracking results and finds out that her system doesn't have the password. She has a database with millions of passwords, but not Dexter's.

Dexter has a good, strong password. Sam's disappointment doesn't deter her. The simple process hasn't worked, so she'll need to resort to social engineering to get the information she needs.

# The Social Engineer

At home, she tells Claire what she's done and what she plans to do. "I need to identify Dexter's regular friends who could have been in his apartment and used his Wi-Fi."

"Oh, Sam, I can help with that! I can work on identifying his friends, discreetly, of course."

"That would be amazing, thank you! Once we have their names, I can come up with a compelling way to engage them, maybe a survey or something. I can come up with a program that will hack their phones when they access the page, and their phones will give me the Wi-Fi password information."

"You can really do that?"

"Yes, every device stores the passwords for Wi-Fi networks it has connected with. I will read that data from their device. I've been researching how to detect hacking, basically digital forensics. Knowing how to detect a hack means I understand how hackers perform their attacks. I've learned enough that I can hack them, and they won't ever know it happened. I need your help to find his friends, help with creating an interesting pitch to get them to engage, and for you to smile at them when we do this." Sam tells Claire.

"I'm totally in. I'll ask around about Dexter and get some names. And since they know who you are, you really shouldn't be doing the interaction part; I'll do it. We can set it up as a research project that I'm working on. If we need to say anything about you at all, we can say that I got you to help with the tech stuff."

"Show college boys pictures of attractive girls to get them to engage with a website," Claire tells Sam.

A couple of days later, Claire has their names and pictures. Claire checks their Facebook and Twitter information, commenting to Sam. "These guys will never get a date, oh my gosh, they are such nerds."

"Like me?"

"No, no! You're different, but in all the best ways. You're cute, and you have common sense. You don't dress or act like a nerd, and you certainly don't behave as if you're smarter than everyone else. The only way to tell is to watch you on that computer."

Sam, uncomfortable, changes the subject: "Now that we know about them, we need to create a test product on a website. I agree with you; we should show them pictures of pretty girls."

Claire laughs, "I've been thinking about what I can say and show them. I can tell them I'm conducting a study on how picture backgrounds influence choices on dating sites. I'll show them pictures of three or four models, each with four backgrounds. All in random order and let them rank them one through five. Will that work for you?"

"Yes, that's it! If you can provide the pictures and backgrounds, I'll merge them and create the site."

"Sounds good, I'll get you all the pictures tomorrow." Claire puts her hand up, "Don't leave me hanging, Sam. Operation take down Dexter is underway!" Sam awkwardly high-fives her friend and bursts into laughter.

"Tell me how this will work, Sam."

"The starting website or landing page will ask for a cell phone number. The site will tell them that the cell phone will enter them into a random drawing to win a gift card. When they enter their phone number, the system will send a confirmation text with a link to the rest of the survey. It will then display the pictures in a random order, accompanied by five buttons at the bottom labeled one through five. The test subject will grade each picture. In the end, there will be a page to grade the survey on a scale of one through five. Was the survey easy and intuitive?"

"But how is that hacking them, and you can do all of them at the same time?"

"The hack will happen in the background when the SMS text is sent to the phone. From that text, the server will inject code and take over their phone. The initial program is small and will then download a larger payload. That larger file will begin pulling data from the phone. I initially created the program to get Wi-Fi passwords from the phone, but after considering these guys, I added browser history, usernames, and passwords from browser-saved websites.

One afternoon, when Dexter isn't with the group, Sam texts Claire, 'It's time.' When Claire arrives, Sam gives her a small page with the website address printed as a QR code.

Claire tells Sam, "Here goes nothing." She approaches people at various tables and asks them to help. Claire gave the intro speech and let them scan the QR code. When they finished, she asked them for feedback. She did this with several people as she moved toward the friend's table.

When she approaches the table with Dexter's friends, Claire says, "Excuse me, would you gentlemen help me with my project? It's short and simple: you access a web page and grade some pictures. I'm working to see if backgrounds make a difference for dating apps." She smiles nicely at all of them and says, "Please."

One friend says to the others, "We can take a break; Dexter isn't here yet." The second friend asks, "What do we need to do?"

Claire pulls out the QR code and puts it on the table. "Please scan the code to get to the website, then follow the prompts. When everyone is done, I'll get your feedback on the process."

They all scanned the QR code and accessed the website. The site shows a page for them to enter their cell phone number. When the site requests the phone number, they all enter it and then receive a text message with a link. The link directs them to another webpage to continue the process. When each had finished, they set down their phones.

When the last one put down his phone, Claire continues, "Thank you all; my questions now are about the survey process. Was the survey simple enough, intuitive?" Claire makes notes based on their comments, says thank you for their help, and walks to another table.

Sam left the building earlier and is working on the data while Claire finishes up her "survey" work. She arrives 30 minutes later and immediately asks Sam, "Did you get what you needed?"

Sam is on her computer and replies, "Yes, and more. They all have campus administrative websites in their browser history. They may all be cheating."

Claire gives out a low whistle, "You busted this wide open, detective. Now, what are you going to do?"

"I still don't have the details I need. That they have a website in their browser history is not enough. I need to get into Dexter's network and see what I can find."

"What are you looking for?"

"First, I need to see what is on his network, then find where he could store information."

A couple of days later, after her classes, she returns to the park bench and, using the information, connects to Dexter's network. Now she finds the next problem. Dexter has set up his network so that it won't provide an IP address to unknown devices, only to the specific devices he has configured. This is simple for Sam to fix now that she's connected to Dexter's network.

"Okay, let's see what we can find," Sam mutters to herself as she searches his network. Dexter does not know that Sam has connected and is scanning his network. She starts with an NMAP scan using the Linux virtual machine. After that, she scans with Bettercap.

Sam can detect a network-attached storage device, two cameras, a Linux computer, a MacBook Pro, two phones, and Dexter's router.

After scanning the open ports, Sam finds the router has an open Telnet and secure SSH port. The open Telnet port is a trap to log anyone trying to access the router.

She connects to the IP cameras and finds that one faces the door, capturing anyone entering. Dexter probably has set it up so that he'll receive a phone alert if the camera detects motion. The second camera is facing his computer equipment, so he can check if someone is there and what's happening on the screen. If someone remotely accesses his desktop, he can see the screen change. The camera stores data locally and then streams it to the cloud using network traffic. Sam doesn't have access to his cloud storage, YET, but that's not needed for what she's trying to accomplish.

Dexter is sitting at his computer with his back to the camera as

Sam watches. She can't tell what he's working on at the computer, but it's interesting to know she can watch what he's doing, and he won't know. Now that she has access, she'll come back later to learn more.

A few days later, Sam returns to the park bench, connects to the network, and starts working on the network-attached storage device. She has already researched the details of the device and has several ways to hack into it.

Once she's on the device, she needs to figure out what he has and what's useful. She looks at several directories, then focuses on 'school'. He has a folder for each class, and in that folder, it appears to contain homework and tests. How does he have access to the tests they've taken? Students complete the tests in class on paper. In the leading school directory, there is a file called 'access secrets'. It contains several login IDs and passwords. The only logical conclusion from this information is that Dexter has been hacking the professor and stealing tests. This is the proof she needs.

Sam captures as much information as possible until it's time for her evening class. She wants to create a file of information that will lead to Dexter's arrest. Finding proof that he hacked the school system makes her want to report to immediately. The problem is that reporting him will expose that Sam hacked his system and put her in trouble. Sam has the information she needs, but she must be careful about how to expose him.

### 

Thursday, Sam has her mixed martial arts training class. It will be cathartic for her to have a workout; she can work out some of her frustrations with Dexter.

She diligently went to class and worked hard as her primary way to stay physically fit. When she started, the instructors liked her work ethic, and she progressed quickly from the beginning. After several months, Sam had progressed enough that the instructor started regular sparring matches.

All the students rotated through the sparring. Every few weeks, the instructors matched Sam with someone. Her last match was with a much more experienced woman. Initially, the woman was aggressive, while Sam was timid, and things were not going well.

The woman says to her, "Fight like I'm going to hurt you."

The instructor yells at her, "Are you giving up? Should we stop?"

Sam gritted her teeth, clenched her fists, and changed her stance. She beat the more experienced woman. That was two weeks ago, and tonight there would be another sparring match.

The start of the class was normal; everyone warmed up, stretched, and then did basic movements. This week, the instructor put Sam with a more experienced man. He was taller and about 50 pounds heavier than Sam. For the sparring match, they both put on cloth hand wraps. It covers the knuckles and helps support the wrist, allowing for free movement of the fingers for grasping.

When the fight starts, Sam is nervous. She has seen him spar before, and he hits hard. Cautiously testing him with simple moves. She figures out that he brings his right hand down to his ribs every time she punches toward his abdomen. He is protecting his ribs on his right side. After a minute, Sam parried a punch, struck his ribs, and delivered a powerful left cross to his jaw. He takes a step back, shakes his head, looks at Sam, and brings his fists up.

Because of the instructor's push during the last sparring match, she doesn't want to back down. She's thinking he has injured ribs, or this is a ruse to have her make a mistake. The only solution for her is to be aggressive.

Sam shifts to a left-handed stance; this puts her forward hand closer to his ribs on the right. She punches at his head as he comes in, then immediately swings her left leg up for a kick to his ribs. The man immediately moves his arm down, and that's when Sam turns the kick into a step forward and punches him in the jaw again. The man staggers back, and Sam follows him, punching him with her left and then right fists in the ribs. When he brings his arms down to protect his ribs, she punches him in the jaw again. This time he collapses, semi-conscious on the mat. Sam steps back as the instructor checks on him.

The man quickly recovers, stands up, looks at Sam, yells, and lunges for her. Sam moves back quickly, waiting for the instructor to intervene. The instructor doesn't move. Realizing that she must deal with the situation and that this could be dangerous, she instinctively lets her combat training kick in.

When the man dives to tackle her, she drops onto her back.

Bringing her legs up and putting her feet on his chest, she shoves upwards. From his momentum, the man goes flying over her head, off the mat, and into the wall. He plunges to the ground, trying to break his fall with his right arm as he lands on his right side. The man grunted and curls up when Sam stomped on his groin. As he moves his hands to his groin, Sam punches his abdomen and then his face.

The instructor grabs her, and Sam immediately grabs his hand and twists as she rolls away. This causes the instructor to be off-balance and tumble onto the mat. Sam continues rolling and is on her feet instantly. The instructor, surprised, looks at Sam while rubbing his wrist and starts getting back to his feet. Her sparring opponent staggers to his feet and sees Sam looking at him differently. She approaches him when the instructor gets in the way.

Sam yells at her opponent, "That was BULLSHIT! That wasn't sparring. If you ever attack me like that again, I'll put you in the hospital!" Turning to look at the instructor, she shouts in his face, "You were bullshit as well!" Sam walks away, telling the instructor she doesn't know if she will be back.

She goes to a bench to unwrap her hands, then grabs her bag as the instructor approaches her. He asks if she's ok. Sam replies, "Yes, and that shouldn't have happened." The instructor says, "I'm sorry, I didn't expect this."

Sam responds, "You ensured I was out of the way to check him but didn't check him or my readiness to restart. You let him come at me and that pissed me off more than him attacking me." She put on her jacket and starts walking toward the door. The instructor calls her name, and she keeps walking. The woman she had sparred with previously shouts, "Don't leave! Stay and kick his ass again!"

Sam leaves and walks home. She would take the bus to and from the gym, but today she needs to walk and calm her head.

At the apartment, she tells Claire about what happened. "My frustration has been building with the Dexter cheating situation. The sparring match was a good way for me to vent my frustrations. I should have kept it together, let him land a few punches."

Claire smiles, saying, "You would have just hit him harder after that."

"Yeah, but I could have been smarter and kept the match going much longer, giving me more opportunity to use the man as a punching bag."

"Yes, I have to agree with that part. But do you feel better?"

"I do; I really do. And now I know the instructor is a prick and I won't be going back to that gym."

# Home for Christmas

Sam's last final is on Thursday, so she flies back to Texas on Friday. She's looking forward to getting home and seeing her mom and grandmother. Her plane lands at DFW airport late in the evening, and her mom is waiting to pick her up. After a big hug, her mom rushes her into the car so they can make the two-hour drive home from the airport.

The familiar smell of Mexican food and lemon cleaner greeted Sam as she entered the living room. The familiar smells and surroundings melt the stress of the long travel day, and Sam feels herself relaxing while also realizing that she's hungry. She hopes to herself that there will be homemade tortillas on the dinner menu tonight. She takes a quick look around the living room, noting that it's the same clean and tidy home she remembers whenever she's away.

Her grandmother comes out of the kitchen and immediately puts her arms out for Sam. "Mija!" her grandmother calls to her, "Ay, hermosa, estás tan flaca. ¿No comes en esa escuela elegante?" Sam hugs her grandmother, chuckling at her ridiculous question, and says in Spanish, "Hola abuela. No sé si soy flaco, pero no tengo comida deliciosa como la que puedes cocinar. Huele fantástico aquí!"

"No estoy seguro si entiendo ese acento tuyo, pero vamos a comer en un minute."

"Abuela, Boston is not the best place to use Mexican Spanish. There are more Puerto Ricans and Dominicans than Mexicans. Besides, it helps when some people don't think I can understand what they're saying. I've walked out of businesses when they talk about charging me more or say gross things about me because they think I can't understand. I'm no fool."

Sam has the complexion of her German father rather than her Mexican mother. For better or worse, this gives her some advantages when in a mixed group. She knows many people hold biases. Therefore, when someone observes a group including her and a darker-skinned woman, they will select her first. Not fair, but that's how it seems to work in most circumstances. She also has to deal with trying to interact with Spanish-speaking communities that consider her an outsider. Most people are unaware that she's fluent in Spanish and has conversational ability in German.

"Sam, don't hide your heritage; it's part of what makes you special."

"Abuela, I don't hide it, I just don't make a big deal about being Mexican or German. I'm very proud of my background, but I also love learning from other cultures. I've taken part in wonderful cultural experiences that've truly opened my eyes to the similarities in traditions across the world. What you taught me about being kind and accepting others is completely true. But don't tell anyone, your food is still the best." Sam winks at her grandmother while her mom laughs. Her grandmother pinches her side and tells her to get ready for dinner.

After dinner, her mother, and grandmother wave Sam off while they clean up. Her mother and grandmother clean houses around the area, so they keep the house clean all the time. Sam grew up with a strong work ethic and learned at an early age how to clean and maintain a neat space. Claire thought Sam had OCD because she kept the apartment clean all the time. Sam didn't consider it unusual that she would stack dishes, wipe tables, and counters, or organize recycling.

Growing up, when her mom or grandmother was sick, Sam would go with the other person to clean the houses they had scheduled. Sam's mother pushed for college to prevent her from working as a maid and often grumbled when Sam had to cover for her. But that work ethic stuck with Sam.

Christmas is on Wednesday this year, so Sam's mom and grandmother are scheduled to clean on Monday the 23rd and the morning of the 24th. They discuss the menu for Christmas dinner and agree that Sam will do the shopping. She also needs to buy presents for them, so the timing works for her.

They prepare the Christmas meal on the 24th. Every year, her grandmother insists on making a meal for the women's shelter. On

Christmas Day, they deliver the meal and spend much of the day there, talking with the women and their children while helping to set up the meal for everyone. Sam has been doing this with them for as long as she can remember, but she's always surprised by the women and their kids. They've all been in bad, often dangerous, situations, but they made the hard choice to leave and move forward with their lives. When Sam, her mom, and grandmother return home, they finally put together a meal for themselves.

There were only a few things they did outside the house whenever Sam was home. Her mother didn't like to interact with people much or draw attention to herself. Sam knew her parents had both suffered abuse as kids and assumed that experience caused her mom's discomfort.

When Sam turned twelve, she began training and competing in shooting, and she and her dad would have long talks as they drove around the state for competitions. Her dad talked to her about bringing her grandmother to live with them because her grandfather was abusive and violent. Dad told her that her mom ran away from home at 15, never finished high school, and never went back to her hometown because of her grandfather's abuse.

Dad talked to her about having a positive outlook, even in adversity: "Figure out what you can accomplish, what you want, and go for it. Practice and hard work are progress towards your goal," he shares details about his childhood and joining the Navy after school. Her mother didn't talk about her past much; she just insisted that Sam know how to protect herself.

Because her family wanted to keep a low profile, Sam learned how to invent stories on the spot so she could get out of awkward situations. In high school, when all the kids wanted to go to the lake to swim, they would always try to persuade Sam to join them. She went with them twice and felt completely awkward with the group dynamics. The girls talked about the boys and each other, and the boys just wanted to make out with the girls. After that, Sam always came up with a reason she couldn't go. After her dad was diagnosed with cancer, it became easy to get out of awkward situations.

### # #

Sam's closest friend in high school was Walter. He was a straightforward person and didn't push Sam into doing things that made her uncomfortable.

One day, they were in an oak tree grove in a large field after riding motorcycles for over an hour. They stopped sitting in the shade and drinking water.

"Sam, I talked to my dad about joining the Army after I graduate. They'll help pay for college, so my parents and I don't have to take out loans. What do you think?"

"Well, I have to say, Army? What the hell, Walter? My dad is trying to come out of his grave right now! You know we're Navy all the way."

Walter laughs and says, "Okay, now that's funny because the Navy won't let you be a SEAL. You've trained like one all your life, and people around here think you'd be great."

"I mean, I get it, but you know the military isn't for me. All my life, I've trained, and I can do certain things just on instinct, but it just doesn't interest me. I prefer solving puzzles and problems, and I think I'll try to get into an engineering school. I talked to my mom about it, and we both agree that my math grades should be good enough for me to get in."

"Engineering school, huh?" Walter considers Sam from under his cap. "What field do you think you'll focus on, 'cuz there are a lot of them?"

"I think I'll focus on electrical engineering. Networking, math, I can work on things online. I don't know for sure; I know that sounds the most interesting to me right now."

"Well, whatever you decide, I'm sure you'll do great."

Sam hops up and reaches to help Walter up. "Thanks, man. I'm excited for you joining the Army, but I'm gonna miss these rides. Let's head back so we can clean the bikes before it gets too late."

### ###

A week after Christmas, Sam is on her computer looking for a file when she sees the directory of stuff she got from Dexter's system. She needs to tell someone; the school needs to know he's cheating. She needs to figure out a way to get the information to the right people without them knowing she is the one who sent it. After considering the various modes of contact, she decides it needs to be an email from a random new account that no one could trace back to her.

Now that she's decided, Sam wants to get it over with. She uses a VPN connection to create a new foreign account that will email several professors at the university. The email name is just something she creates at random.

From: student7654321@europe.com.

Subject: A student is cheating.

Message:

I overheard one of your students boasting about getting perfect test scores because he knew the answers. He boasted he got the test early so he could memorize the answers. He offered to sell the information to other students for any professor. You should check the test scores for this student.

For evidence, review the logs of the IP addresses from which people logged in. Find the odd IP address that doesn't match the owner's normal pattern.

Attached is an exam he provided as a sample.

The student is Dexter Pulaski.

End.

She doesn't know if this will work, but she feels better about doing something. To remove further temptation, she deletes the entire directory of information.

### 

Every chance she could find, she worked on her thesis. In Boston, Sam purchased an ancient cell phone. She then hacks the bootloader to install Linux firmware. She intentionally purchased the old device because it was cheap, and she won't have to hack around the phone maker's locks. With the open-source firmware, she can modify the Wi-Fi firmware to show her ability to hack a network controller.

Her initial test is simple: copy every DNS request and send it to another server that logs all the information. There's nothing that shows in the central system. The only way to know something was happening is to monitor the network traffic.

Now she wants to test capturing usernames and passwords to show their feasibility. This is more complex because it involves a multi-step process for network traffic. Sam needs to fix data errors from her hacked phone before retesting the computer setup.

She bought a different old phone so she could create a mobile Linux Wi-Fi cracking machine. This phone will actively work on getting Wi-Fi passwords. She installs the latest version of Linux on the phone and then installs software for network monitoring and password cracking. Now, she needs to develop Python scripts that will do most of the work. Sam gets up to stretch and get a cup of coffee. She surveys her cluttered desk and feels grateful to love her work. She smiles, thinking about completing her thesis and the possibility of working in cybersecurity in a few months.

Getting back to work, Sam focuses on finishing. When it's completely ready, she needs to start the main script, and the phone will start finding and cracking Wi-Fi passwords until she stops it. She'll focus on devices reconnecting to capture Wi-Fi data, needing the network names first.

To test the new phone, she visits a couple of stores in town that display their Wi-Fi passwords for customers to use. Her phone broadcasts the store's Wi-Fi name; running the script triggers a connection from another customer's phone, giving her the required information. It's happening faster than she expected.

### 

Sam doesn't have to travel back to Boston until late January. A few days before flying back, Sam talks with her mother and grandmother about graduation and their upcoming travel plans. This will be her last term; all she needs to complete are a couple of classes and her thesis. Traveling for her grandmother is more challenging because of her age; she can't walk around Boston all day. They need to stay in a hotel that's both affordable and close to the school. Fortunately, airline tickets are straightforward; they'll simply drive to Dallas and get on a direct flight. They work out a basic plan that will have them both fly to Boston a few days before the graduation ceremony.

To graduate on time, Sam will wholly focus on completing her thesis. After graduation, her mom, and grandmother will help her pack and move back to Texas. Hopefully, Sam will have a job waiting for her, as she plans to send out résumés and interview before graduation. And, of course, she needs to complete her thesis.

Sam will travel back to Boston on Tuesday, the week before class starts, using the cheapest flight she can find. She has an appointment with her thesis advisor on Thursday.

# FBI First Talk

It's the week before the semester starts, and Sam is meeting with Professor Angela Jordan for the first time this term. She's supposed to report on her progress and what remains to be completed for her thesis. Sam feels nervous because she doesn't feel as close to completing her thesis as she thinks she should be. She is concerned that there are so many things to cover; she may be missing something important.

The professor's office is a typical office, featuring her desk, bookcases, and a small table that allows people to gather around. When she enters Professor Jordan's office, two men are waiting with the professor. Professor Jordan introduces them as FBI Supervisory Special Agent Frank Andrews and Special Agent Phil Nomikos.

Agent Andrews is the older of the two. He looks to be in his mid-fifties, with brown eyes and graying brown hair. He has an average build, looks like 5 feet 11 inches or 6 feet tall, and is physically fit for his age.

Agent Nomikos appears to be about ten years younger, yet keeps a similar build and a slightly darker complexion. He's a little shorter than Agent Andrews and has an intense stare.

Sam pauses, looking between both men and her professor, and asks, "Am I in some kind of trouble?"

Agent Andrews replies, "Why would you think that?"

"Because I walked into a meeting with my thesis advisor to talk about hacking, and two FBI agents are waiting."

Agent Andrews smiles and tells Sam that she's not in trouble and that they want to discuss her thesis.

"Okay, let's start over." Sam puts her hand out toward Agent Andrews, "Hi, I'm Samantha Holzen. Call me Sam."

After she greets both men, Agent Andrews continues, "Sam, we're with the FBI Cyber Crimes unit, and we've worked with Professor Jordan in the past. She told me about your thesis, and we would like to learn more. Can we ask about some details of your thesis? Before we do that, though, can you give us a high-level summary?"

Glancing back at Professor Jordan, who nods at her, Sam explains, "At a high level, most organizations check, monitor, and remediate hacking situations with patches and policies. But what if you were hacked and had no way to detect it with conventional tools? The main CPU that your monitoring tools use will never know that your systems are compromised. If the firmware of your network controller, or Wi-Fi controller, was altered, the hacker can monitor, change, or block your network traffic, and you may not even know."

Professor Jordan asks Sam to provide an update on her progress with her research and thesis.

"I can show you." Sam opens her backpack and pulls out a phone, which she puts on the professor's desk.

Professor Jordan and Agent Nomikos both ask, "You've modified the Wi-Fi firmware?"

"Yes, I've been testing and debugging to see if the hack is detectable from the phone. The goal is to capture every DNS request and send a copy to another server that I set up. I can't detect that the controller is resending information to another server. I also have another phone," and Sam pulls out a second phone.

Professor Jordan asks, "So what does this one do?"

"This is a Wi-Fi password-cracking phone. There are two modes it can work in: a passive mode, where it transmits nothing; it simply listens to Wi-Fi signals and cracks every password it can. The second mode is an active scanner, which means it broadcasts the SSID of networks I want to analyze and checks if any device tries to connect."

Agent Andrews asks, "Why? I mean, what are you trying to accomplish?"

Sam replies, "I'm creating a map of Wi-Fi devices in the Boston area, specifically routers. Based on the vendor of the network MAC address, I know the type of each device and which ones may be vulnerable. I'm also using it to build a statistically valid distribution to show what percentage of Wi-Fi passwords can be cracked, i.e., they're not strong enough."

Everyone is sitting down at Professor Jordan's small meeting table in the corner of her office. Both agents continue to ask Sam questions about how she came up with her thesis idea and how she's doing her research. They also ask if they can read a copy of her draft.

Sam looks at her professor with a concerned look and says, "I haven't completed my testing and research. I'm not sure the current draft accurately reflects what's possible. The phone hack was easy because I had physical access. The true areas of concern are those without physical access, specifically the remote firmware hacks. I've been working on hacking an old router remotely, but I haven't collected enough data to have a statistically significant answer. That's also why a Wi-Fi map is important; it can tell me what old routers are in the area that I can access remotely and then change their firmware."

Agent Andrews asks, "What do you still need to do?"

Sam replies with a shrug of her shoulders, "I still need to find vulnerabilities I can exploit and then scan the internet for devices that meet that profile. One old router from each major manufacturer in the lab. All of which were older versions. The output for Boston will be a vulnerability map. I've been looking online to buy old routers, and I have plans to check local shops for recycled routers. I only have two that fit what I need right now, so it's been slow-going. The actual test will be done in the network lab after I get the old devices."

Finally, both agents move to stand up. Agent Nomikos gives Sam his business card and says, "Send me what you're looking for; we may help. Also, who have you talked to about your thesis?"

"Um, besides Professor Jordan, I've talked with Professor Lewis, who runs a networking lab, my roommate, and my mom. I think that's it."

"Tell me about your roommate."

"Her name is Claire Elmer, and she's an economics major. She doesn't understand this and probably doesn't care.

"Okay, Sam, let's keep it that way. Please don't let anyone know about this visit, alright?"

Sam replies, "Sure, no problem. Most people don't understand it anyway."

# The Open Database

Sam's meeting with Professor Jordan and the FBI has invigorated her to finish her thesis and classes for on-time graduation. She heads back to her apartment to check the newly published security warnings. She needs to spend half a day learning about recent hacks and the patches someone published.

Claire should arrive tomorrow, and they'll have the weekend before the spring semester starts. Claire always brings back delicious, chef-made treats and has already emailed a list of goodies she'll be bringing with her. She wants Sam to pick an event happening this weekend and buy tickets for both of them. Sam gets the tickets and picks up groceries the next day. Tonight, she's updating her systems and getting back into the school groove. She grabs a cup of coffee from the fresh pot she started when she got home and settles in at her desk.

After discussing scanning with the agents, Sam needs to get her internet scanners operational again. There are always people searching the internet for information. Sam has scanners that run on her small Raspberry Pi computer. She set it up so that it connects through a VPN and starts scanning sections of the internet address space. She's searching for old devices and any open systems. The system sends her notifications when it locates anything meeting her criteria.

Late that evening, Sam receives an alert about an open database. She uses the VPN connection to complete a quick check. It's an open PostgreSQL database with no password, allowing her to read everything. Without really thinking, Sam sends a command to the database to create a backup and dump the file as a CSV to her system.

Sam looks at the top of the file and finds column headings labeled "Target," "Server," "Login," and "Password." There's a second table toward the bottom with headings of broker, login, password, account, and account password. The file has hundreds of entries in each table.

What is all this? Sam wonders. She wants to examine one site to see what it contains, but being cautious, she needs to conceal her location better. With her knowledge of how networking works, she creates a chain of interconnected VPNs, enabling her to achieve multiple levels of obscurity. She makes a note to automate this process and use it consistently. She'll also create a script to set up a cloud account and start a new VPN server, then delete it when she's finished.

Sam accesses one account to see what it contains. Sam doesn't know it, but the account is one the FBI is watching. The FBI is trying to trace the bad guys by monitoring who accesses the account. With her VPN chain of three servers, one in Hong Kong, no one will know her exact location.

She used free-tier accounts from cloud providers to create this chain. Setting up an account at a specific data center and starting a VPN server that only she can use doesn't take long. She uses modified VPN server software to create the VPN chain. Commercial VPN providers wouldn't generate the chain. When she's done, she'll delete all the information and cancel the accounts.

On the server, Sam finds a Word document and lots of pictures. All the pictures have numbers as names, except for one. That file contains a person's name, the same as the one in the Word document. The extensions on the files are different, so she knows she has a couple of formats to deal with. She downloads the Word document, the named picture, and a couple of other random JPEG files. Sam then logs off and shuts everything down. She doesn't need to stay connected if she's going to work offline. If she needs to re-access the storage, she has the login and password.

### 

The FBI cyber team is holding a meeting to discuss who accessed the account. Frank asks, "Have we traced where these people are located?"

Phil responds, "They used multiple VPNs chained together to access the account. We don't know who they are or how to find them without some digging. Looking at the logs, the person downloaded four items." Phil continues, "Frank, I have another thought about this access. They were only on for a few minutes, downloaded items they should already have, and then disappeared. They used multiple VPNs, which is not something a typical person would or could do. Finally, they logged in with the administrator password. This looks more like a hacker than a blackmailer."

Frank reminds the team that they got lucky to have this victim step forward to help them. "He knew if they released this fake information, his career would be over, so he started paying. When he figured out that he could prove he hadn't done what the blackmailers claimed, he talked to his attorney, who contacted us. That he was not in the same city when they claimed he molested a child helped us start the investigation on the extortionist. The extortionists were bold enough to let him log into the server to see all the information they had on him. They gave him a login with no ability to delete anything, simply to view the information  That was how we knew about the account and started watching."

"We are monitoring the server and the login we detected. The person used the administrator's login, which differs from what the target provided. We have been watching this account for weeks, and it has not been accessed until now. Previously, the target made payments, and they were all tracked in the Word document, but no one has updated the file with the latest payment."

Frank looks visibly frustrated. "We have made no progress in this investigation. This is the first event we've seen, and I don't think it's progress. The untraceable prepaid credit card that reserved the server for a year has not been used again. No access to the server, no contact with the target."

Frank asks the team, "Is our investigation compromised? Has the account not been accessed by the extortionist because they know we're watching? How could a hacker get that account information?"

"Now I'm thinking this whole thing is a ruse to see how we respond. Or maybe a way to test their ability to stay hidden. Do we have anything that helps?"

When Frank stops, Phil responds, "We are working on all these questions and more. Frank, we need to find the hacker, and they'll be able to tell us where and how they got the administrator's information. With that information, we'll have more leads on the extortion group."

"Then we put everything into finding this hacker."

"We have a coffee shop meeting with the graduate student Samantha Holzen next week. I think she would be a good person to recruit for cases like this one. Based on her thesis work, she thinks out of the box. She should finish her thesis by summer."

"Phil, she has not finished school, and even if she did, she would need to qualify and get through the academy before we could talk to her about this case. I agree she could help, but this investigation has been full of dead ends. We are no closer to catching these guys. I don't want to involve her when it could cause the entire case to be thrown out of court. I want to talk to her and recruit her, but we can't bend the rules on this one. We find who is involved and put them in jail for a long time by following proper procedure and getting the evidence for a conviction."

### ###

Sam hasn't established an exercise routine since quitting the MMA class. That open time gives her a chance to do other interesting things. Tonight, she'll analyze the details of the files she downloaded from the server a few days ago.

Before she starts, she uses the VPN chain to check the database again. She wants to see if there are any updates. When she checks the location, the database is no longer there. Not simply there, but with a password, it's completely gone.

Sam starts her analysis of the files she downloaded by opening the Word document, which summarizes a person, including the name, address, family, and work. The man is a business executive who lives in Boston. Sam scans the entire document and finds a table at the bottom that says payments. In the table are dates, amounts, and totals exceeding $350,000 over two years. The picture with the same name is simply a portrait, like what would be on a driver's license.

The other two pictures show the same man with a couple of different children. A playground is the setting for the first picture, and the other looks like a gym. There is no one else in the pictures, but the people are not looking at the camera as if for a photo. In both cases, the man is handing something to the child.

Examining the Word file and these pictures, Sam is sure that this man is being blackmailed. All the payments and photographs of him giving something to little kids with no one else around. Sam gets nervous. What did she find in this database? The man would be the target of extortion, and the others would be his victims.

Sam thinks about the online capture-the-flag competition that her hacker friends play. Information hides in plain sight, and you must know how to look for it. Sam investigates further about the photos. She uses an open-source stenography tool to check if there is hidden information in the JPEG file. Starting with the man's picture, she has the tool scan the image, and indeed, there's data encrypted in the picture that's not visible via standard tools. She uses a password-cracking tool and decrypts the data. The attached data includes details about the man, other individuals' names and ages (all children), addresses, dates, and bank account information at the bottom.

Sam analyzes the pictures with the children. She checks with the stenography tool and finds nothing. Then she checks the metadata for the images and sees something. The picture shows the original date the photo was taken, and it also shows that it was modified later. The picture doesn't have an embedded thumbnail image, which is usually automatically generated for JPEG pictures.

She searches online for a Chroma and Luminance mapping program. The luminance mapping shows an abrupt change at some point in the picture. She's not sure, but this appears to be a composite image created by combining two separate images. If the picture is fake, why would the extortion target pay when they have fake pictures? It is possible that some photos are genuine, or maybe exposing this person's information would pose a significant problem, and they will pay to avoid it. Sam will need to learn more about this target.

No! What is she thinking? She needs to stop and leave this alone. This could put her in real trouble if anyone were to discover she has this database of information.

However, now that she has the information, what does she do? Just as she did when she told the school about Dexter, she needs to let someone know, but who and how. This is not just another email and sending it to the police could get this target arrested when the pictures she looked at are fake. Reporting the information to the police could put her in danger of being charged with hacking or exposing her to the extortion group.

# After the Coffee Shop

The morning after the coffee shop shooting, Sam is thinking about her situation. Sam did everything to avoid detection and tracking. That a few days after her access to a blackmail server account, there was an attack in a coffee shop that could be evidence to the contrary. Someone shot the FBI agents. Did they trace her access? Were they tracking the FBI, or were they trying to accomplish something else?

Sam is shaken, not because a gun attack occurred. This is the first time she cannot talk to her dad about a situation that involves real life and death. She's way over her head, and she doesn't have anyone who can help. Now, after the shooting, she cannot just tell people what she knows. It would make them targets as well.

If she tells the FBI, she could be arrested. If she keeps quiet, she has the best chance of being safe. She needs to be vigilant in case they are after her. She certainly can't tell Claire about what she has. Even knowing about the database could get Claire into trouble.

Claire can see that she's upset this morning and asks, "What happened?"

"That shooting at the coffee shop yesterday, I was meeting with the FBI about my thesis when two men came into the coffee shop with guns. The FBI agents and the gunmen started shooting. The gunmen are dead, and both FBI agents had to go to the hospital."

"Are you okay? Seriously, what have you gotten into? Why?"

"I don't know why this happened. It seemed random, except the guys walked straight to where all three of us were sitting. But how would they know where any of us would be unless they followed someone?"

"That would mean it was pre-planned, and anyone planning to shoot FBI agents is bad news. Sam, you need to stay away from them."

"I'm involved. I was asked a bunch of questions yesterday and will be asked more, I'm sure."

"Well, don't meet in any public places; meet where it's safe. Also, I can call my lawyer to be with you."

"I don't think I need your lawyer, Claire, but if I have any future questioning, I mean interviews, where it's safe."

### 

The next day, Agent Andrews calls her to thank her for applying first aid and asks if she's okay. Sam talks about the fact that she had never been on the receiving end of a real gun battle. "It has been several years since I was at a shooting range, and I did not expect two men to walk into a Boston coffee shop and start shooting."

Agent Andrews asks, "What are you going to do now?"

Sam explains she needs to focus on completing her classes, her thesis, and graduating.

Sam asks about Special Agent Nomikos, and Agent Andrews says, "He is doing well. The doctors were shocked to see a tampon in a chest wound. The worst part for Special Agent Nomikos is that the other agents are going to give him a tough time for being saved by a tampon. He will be in the hospital another day and then back home for physical therapy. It will take him time to regain full mobility in his arm. Also, his wife and kids wanted me to thank you for saving Phil. Are you feeling well enough to talk about the details of the incident? I won't officially be working this case, but I would like to talk with you about what happened."

"A special agent from the counter-terrorism team conducted a long interview yesterday."

Thinking about the situation quickly, she didn't want to seem evasive or give them a reason to wonder why she's avoiding them. She says, "Sure, we can talk tomorrow. Let's meet at your office instead of a coffee shop. Also, I have a class at 10 a.m., can we do it first thing at 8?"

"That would be great. I'll see you then."

Sam thanks Special Agent Andrews for the update and asks him to tell Special Agent Nomikos to get better and take care.

### # # #

Sam arrives at the FBI Boston field office at 7:50 am. At the front desk, she says, "I'm here to meet with Supervisory Special Agent Andrews."

The receptionist takes Sam's information and asks her to have a seat.

A few minutes later, Agent Jones walks in. Seeing Sam, she walks over. "Miss Holzen, is everything okay?"

Sam looks at Agent Jones and recognizes her but can't remember her name. "I'm waiting to talk to Supervisory Special Agent Andrews about the shooting. Sorry, I don't remember your name."

"That's okay, you had a lot thrown at you the last couple of days. I'm Special Agent Nyah Jones."

Agent Andrews walks in with his left arm in a sling. He introduces himself to Special Agent Jones and tells her he is going to interview Sam about the incident.

Agent Jones replies, "I did an extensive interview, but I have a couple of other questions."

Agent Andrews asks her to join them.

He asks Sam, "Are you okay with Special Agent Jones joining us?" Sam replies, okay and stands up. Agent Andrews notices Sam doesn't have her backpack.

"Where is your backpack?"

"This is a secure facility, and there is no way I could get my backpack in and out of this facility, so I left it at the apartment. I only have my normal phone, not the test phone, and nothing else."

Agent Andrews smiles and says, "Okay, let's go find a conference room."

Agent Jones asks, "What is the significance of her normal phone?"

"She has the tools in her backpack to hack our entire building in about a minute. We were originally met with Sam to talk about her research and master's thesis on detecting and preventing hacking. For her to prove she can detect and prevent hacking, she wants to show how it's possible."

They find an open conference room, and Agent Jones asks, "Sam, would you like coffee or water?"

"Thanks, water would be great." Sam continues, "Will you use the glass to capture my DNA, like they show on TV?"

Agent Jones smiles and says, "That is standard procedure."

Agent Andrews tells Sam, "I wanted to meet with you to check on you, observe your behavior, and see your reaction to questions."

"So, you're profiling me."

"Not exactly. I've been trained to watch body language and responses to questions. At the coffee shop, you mentioned you were concerned your hacking skills were not good enough. After the shooting, your demeanor changed. You were sure of what you were doing, helping Agent Nomikos, cutting my sleeve. Separately, you seemed rattled by the whole situation. What happened? Why did this bother you that much?"

Sam gives a sigh and starts with, "I was agitated because I shouldn't have been rattled. Seeing Agent Nomikos with a chest wound, I panicked. I knew he could bleed to death unless I did something quickly. My dad taught me to stop bleeding with whatever is available. I didn't have a first aid kit; I didn't even have dirt, which is the last resort. I've never been on the receiving end of a gunfight. When I competed, the range safety officers made sure everyone was safe. When hunting with my dad, I wasn't worried about a wild animal attacking me. This was different, and I should have responded better. I even took part in tactical training with the sheriff's department, but those sessions were all conducted with airsoft or paintball. I never did medical response training with them."

"Sam, you did a great job. Phil Nomikos is alive because you got it together," says Agent Jones. "But I want to come back to what you said during the interview. You knew it was the procedure to yell 'Gun.' You said that your dad and the sheriff talked about being prepared for the unexpected. Tell me about that."

Sam smiles and replies, "The Sheriff was in the Army, and they would talk about when an operation didn't go well. What could the sheriff's department do for training deputies and planning for when something bad happened?"

"Helping the sheriff must have made interactions at school interesting."

"I wasn't into club activities," Sam stated. "My father made me calculate ballistic solutions manually when I began hunting. I used that with my long-rifle marksmanship competitions. My dad would be my spotter for competitions. Constantly practicing math like that made me better than most of the other kids. In high school, I took all the AP math classes. I was a nerd in high school. As a nerd, competitive shooting, and working with the sheriff on tactical issues in a rural school meant I didn't have time for other things. I was left alone. When my dad was diagnosed with cancer, I assumed more responsibility for household tasks. After he died, I stopped participating in shooting competitions; it was no longer the same without him there. I focused on school and working with the sheriff's department while I tried to figure out what I was going to do next."

"Okay, Sam, I think that's all I have for now," says Agent Andrews. "I'm trying not to have you repeat everything. I'll review the report from Agent Jones and contact you if I have more questions. Because I was attacked, I can't officially be part of the investigation, but I'll be helping Special Agent Jones with background and whatever else I can. Special Agent Jones, do you have more questions for Sam?"

"Not right now, I need to write up my notes into a report, which will cause more questions," replies Agent Jones.

The agents escort her to the lobby, where they shake hands and say goodbye. As Sam is turning, Agent Andrews says, "Please consider working at the FBI after you graduate."

Nyah says, "Frank, your questions seemed to be more focused on her response rather than the situation."

"Yes, part of the coffee shop meeting was to recruit her to join us after she graduates. She comes up with original solutions for hacking, and we could use her talents. I was concerned about her when we talked about joining and hacking. When the shooting happened, it was like a different woman in the coffee shop."

"Frank, did you know she was a competitive shooter when she was younger?"

"No, I have done no background checks yet. I thought she was a hacker most of her life. It certainly wouldn't hurt to have a field agent who can easily pass the range qualification."

Frank and Nyah decide to meet in three days to compare notes and talk about the next steps. Frank knows he isn't supposed to be investigating, but he will do some digging into any hacking connections once they identify the attackers.

### 

Sam talks to Claire about the FBI meeting that evening. "Agent Andrews was profiling me. He also wants me to join the FBI after I graduate."

"What did he ask you?"

"The agent who questioned me, Agent Jones, was also there. They asked how I knew what to do and why I reacted that way. I learned what to do because I worked with the sheriff when I was growing up.

"You'll need to tell me more about what you practiced, but not today. Today, take it easy. You are still on edge about this whole thing. Is anything else bothering you?

Sam wants to say something to Claire about the database. Instead, she says, "No, all that training and stuff was several years ago. The whole thing was sudden and unexpected."

# The Lockdown

As the COVID pandemic surges, the country goes into lockdown. With businesses shut down, Sam lost her part-time job at the restaurant a few blocks away. It was only a part-time job, but it helped a lot in paying the bills. She wasn't eligible for unemployment because she was part time and hadn't worked at the restaurant long enough.

Sam talks to her mom every day about how things are going. "I'm worried about both of you. COVID is killing people quickly."

Her mom reassures her that everything is fine. "We are using curbside pickup to get groceries. We don't have to go out for anything else right now."

"Claire and I now have all our classes online. We only leave to get groceries. I am going to set up a calendar item so that we can talk every day."

"Yes, we will talk every day."

"Claire, sorry I was on the phone with Mom when your class started."

"It is okay. It was only a few minutes, and the lecture's start was merely a summary of the previous class. We need to figure something out. If we are both in class and both have to talk, it will be an issue."

"I know. We are both using one dining table, which is not enough space for both of us to focus. Checking our schedules, we only have one class that overlaps with each other. I usually only need to take notes for that class, so I will log in for that class on the couch or in my room. The rest of the time, I am working on programs or research."

"Thanks, Sam. I need to interact in that class all the time. Your research is only an issue when you cover the table with gear. I know you mentioned the names before, but I don't recall them all. Router, scanner, Wi-Fi adapter."

"I will switch my gear to the coffee table and couch when I need to do something. I need a bigger space; my little desk in my room won't hold everything."

Being focused for most of the day, she made faster progress in some hacking areas and automation. She has also learned a couple of lessons. Creating a new random email address worldwide is easy, and validating that email with another random email is equally easy. When you run the program to create hundreds of new email addresses, you find issues with the website and the creation of random email names that meet all the criteria.

She had to create a database that stored every email and all related emails. It became too large for her to track in her head. She had to rethink the creation and use of emails. The entire management and usage needed to be automated.

A necessary step was setting up the VPN chain to maintain her anonymity. She searched for VPN providers and found articles where VPN services claimed they kept no logs, but the government subpoenaed them for records. That was part of why she wanted a VPN chain, but the last link would be to her. She needs to create her own VPN servers with free-tier cloud accounts. The VPN servers run her modified code to enable the linked chain to function. Those random emails will be helpful.

Now she has automated the creation of a cloud account with a random email. It then configures and starts a VPN server, linking it into the chain. When its usage is done, it will be deleted, and the email will never be used again.

One afternoon Claire and Sam are on their computers. "Sam, I'm worried about how fast this thing is spreading. We are in complete lockdown, and people are still contracting the virus. We don't know how long this will last."

"I'm also worried about my mom and grandmother. Going home, I could get while traveling and give it to them. I could catch it on the way and give it to them."

"So, you will wait it out here in the apartment?" asks Claire.

"Yes, I think so. Everything we need is within walking distance, and I'll be wearing a mask all the time."

"My parents want me to go home so we're all together. All my class lectures are online, and I don't have any labs. You don't have any reason to be on campus; you should consider going home."

"My family is not within easy driving distance like your parents, and your dad can get you a car and a driver. I'll have to travel for hours while being close to other people who could be infected."

At the end of next week, Claire is packing her things and tells Sam, "My brother Charlie is driving from New York. He is going to pick me up this afternoon on his way to our parents. The investment bank where he works is fully virtual, so he is driving home. I'll be home with my family for the duration. Call me and stay safe."

"Thanks, Claire, I'll stay safe."

"If something happens and you need to leave, just go. I'll take care of the rental agreement and clean out the apartment."

"Thanks, I'll let you know if anything happens. I've loved having you as a roommate. Different majors, so we overlapped on school things when we wanted to. Even if we can't eat together in the same room, I can call and talk about food, events, and what we can do when this shitty situation is over."

"Yes, I loved rooming with you, Sam. My family would never have let us live together if we hadn't switched roommates. They are always concerned that I will hang out with people who are a bad influence. I am glad we switched. I love the virtual dinner idea. We can use one of the video tools. I'm going to hold you to it. We have each other's numbers. You can call anytime. I'll be calling and checking on you. Also, not everything will fit in my suitcase; use whatever you want in the closet."

"We will stay in touch because you have to be on a video call when we watch our streaming shows. You got me hooked, so it's your fault."

Claire laughs, "That was a mutual thing. That crazy robo-hacking show is over, so we need to find a new one for you. I'm not done with vampire shows."

She finds it much tougher than she thought to have virtual lectures. While she can see things written on the board, the group interactions are more complex. Some questions are spoken, some are in chat, and people are having side chats. Several times, she had to ask that the question or comment be repeated. She had to be focused entirely to keep up with the lecture. The constant dings, pings, and chimes from all her devices are a big distraction during the lectures. She started putting all the apps into silent mode during a lecture, just as she would in an actual class.

After each lecture, she completes all assignments. She doesn't want to procrastinate and then get sidetracked.

On a call about dinner, Claire asks, "So what are you making for dinner tonight?"

"I am making pasta with shrimp. The deli area at the store had the large ones, so I could buy what I needed. So, lunch tomorrow will be pasta."

"Sam, you just started a routine immediately without me there."

"Part of the routine was easy. I make the same amount we used to make for dinner, so I have lunch for the next day. I always had the same breakfast: cereal or yogurt with granola.

"Which is why you loved having me around to vary your diet."

"Except for having Italian, you insist on it every week."

"It is my fav. It was not always the same food or restaurant when we went out."

"I only get restaurant food once per week, and this week I am going to try Indian food. The biryani sounds good. I will let you know at our next call. How are things with everyone at home?"

"It has only been a few days, and we are getting on each other's nerves. Charlie works virtually, and about once per day, he is on the phone yelling at someone. It seems like he works with idiots. It makes me miss our routines and our little apartment. No yelling, and we could go out for food. I haven't heard any of your thesis stuff. I don't understand it, but I enjoy hearing you talk about it. More than once, you have gotten a new idea just by talking to me. Tell me what you're doing."

"Are you sure?"

"I want to hear your voice while I write my paper. You know I'm not listening, and I don't understand, but your voice helps me focus."

"Here goes your nerdy lullaby. This week, I changed my Wi-Fi cracking phone software. I can download a map of all the Wi-Fi signals in an area. I got the information from the WiGLE.net website. When I start the program, it will transmit all the Wi-Fi SSIDs in the area, based on the phone's GPS location. It is waiting for someone's phone to respond and try to connect. I can also tell the phone to search for Wi-Fi in other areas, like New York."

"Wait. You're saying you know every Wi-Fi and can walk down the street collecting Wi-Fi passwords?"

"Yes, and it only takes a few seconds to capture the information. I may not crack the password, but I'll know the encrypted version. And some nerdy stuff about this process. Because I control the phone, I can transmit different signals on the 2.4 GHz versus the 5 GHz channel. I can transmit multiple signals with different power levels."

"I'm interested because you could get access to sensitive information. You could get into real trouble."

"True, IF I used the information actually to access their systems. I'm using it to map devices and password strength. If the phone can crack the password, it adds to an easy counter; if the phone can't crack the password, it adds to a hard counter."

"How fast does this work? I mean, do you walk down the street, or do you need to stand there for a long time?"

"The phone transmits ten Wi-Fi SSIDs at one time. They are broadcast for 30 seconds and then changed. I don't want it to be available long enough for a person to type the password. It needs to be a device that is simply trying to work normally and connect. Standing in the spot doesn't help."

"You walk down the street and get passwords!"

"Only the easy ones. I tested it while walking to the grocery store. I get more passwords inside the grocery store, just waiting in the checkout line."

"Sam, this is not me trying to plan a robbery, but I'm concerned, more curious than concerned. Can you get into any bank's Wi-Fi?"

"Most well-run businesses have strong passwords, and any easy passwords are for guests. I have not targeted any business Wi-Fi. I can tell you most of my hard list is from businesses. Claire, this sounds like I'm distracting you."

"I'm working on a paper related to financial market liquidity, and there are big ramifications if the information is illegally accessed, i.e., insider trading. Your explanation helps. I can craft a section on security. I'll probably ask questions to make sure I get things right. One question is, what is the conclusion from this?"

"Sure, I'll answer questions I can. The answer is that most people need stronger Wi-Fi passwords."

# Now Sam is Alone

On April 9th, Sam receives a call from her mom. "Abuela is being admitted to the hospital with COVID. I can only be on the call for a minute. They want me to give him Abuela's medical history."

"Call when you can. Stay safe. I love you."

The next day, "She is getting sicker; they put a tube down her throat to help her breathe. The doctors said this was not good, and they are doing everything they can to help. Sam, they won't let me into the room to see her. No one from the families is being allowed in to see their relatives when they go to intensive care because of potential exposure to COVID or other things."

"Do you know how she got sick?"

"No Chica. We have been wearing masks all the time when we are out of the house and when cleaning."

"Mom, you've been cleaning people's houses where they could be sick with COVID? Mom, that's not safe."

"Sam, we need to make money to live. They want me to get off the phone."

"I'm sorry, Mom, I know, and it's done. You stay safe, take care, and I'll talk to you tomorrow."

The next morning, her mother didn't call at the normal time they had talked. Sam called her mom's phone, and it went to voicemail. A few minutes later, she received a call with the caller ID "MOM."

"Ms. Holzen, this is Janet Smith. I'm a nurse at the hospital. Your mother asked me to call you."

"Is she ok? What happened?"

"She's being admitted to the hospital with COVID."

"Can I talk to her?" asks Sam.

The nurse says, "Let me walk over to her." When her mom said hello on the phone, her voice was raspy, and she was breathing heavily.

She cries, asking her mom, "How are you doing?"

"Chica, I'm ok. I have Covid and came to the hospital when I got symptoms; I didn't wait. They are taking care of me."

"How is Abuela?"

"She's still on the ventilator, and nothing else has changed. They want me to get off the phone."

"Get better. I'll talk to you tomorrow. Love you and Abuela."

"Love you, Sam."

The next morning, she called the number the nurse had given her. Another nurse answered the phone, and Sam talked to him about talking to her mom. "Ms. Holzen, you won't be able to talk to her. She was moved to intensive care and put on a ventilator. Please stay on the line while I get the doctor."

A few minutes later, "Hello, is this Samantha Holzen? I'm Doctor Philips."

"Yes, this is Sam."

"Ms. Holzen, your mother got much worse overnight, and we moved her to intensive care. I want to let you know that we're doing everything we can, but your mother is in serious condition. She's responding to the treatment, but is not out of danger."

"Doctor, I'm in Boston. Should I fly down to Texas?"

"Travel is restricted, and if you are in Texas, you won't be able to see your mother because of hospital safety considerations."

"Can you tell me how my grandmother is doing?"

There is a pause. "I'm sorry, Ms. Holzen, your grandmother passed away early this morning." Sam was silent on the phone. "Ms. Holzen, we did everything we could, but with her age and physical condition, the disease overwhelmed her."

Sam was numb, saying, "Okay, thanks, and please help my mom. I'm going to see about travel."

"We are doing everything we can for your mother."

Sam hangs up the phone and starts crying. Pulling herself together, she looks for transportation to Texas. She goes online and picks the first flight the next day from Boston to DFW. Once that is booked, she packs, knowing that she will not be back for a while. Luckily, she doesn't have a lot in the little apartment she shared with Claire. She packs all her equipment inside her backpack or surrounds it with clothes in her large suitcase.

She finished stuffing her suitcase and looked around the apartment. There is no TV; she uses her laptop to stream shows. The dishes, food, and furniture remain, which Claire purchased. She pulls out several garbage bags and puts all the food in them, then takes the bags to the dumpster, making two trips.

She writes an email to Claire, telling her what was happening with her family and asking her to attend to the apartment details.

The first flight is at 10:30 a.m. Sam arrives at the airport at 8 a.m., puts on a double mask, checks her bag, goes through security, and then goes to the gate before 9 am.

Her phone rings soon after, "Ms. Holzen, it's Dr. Philips. Your mother's condition has worsened overnight."

"Can I talk to her?"

"Your mother is unconscious and on a ventilator. You won't be able to talk to her. I'm calling to get your permission for a procedure. We want to induce a coma to reduce the oxygen needs of her brain while she's fighting the virus."

Sam understood the words the doctor was using, but it was as if they were talking through a tunnel; the words were suddenly far away, and she was thinking slowly. This was serious, and she was being asked to make medical decisions for her mom.

"Ms. Holzen, are you there? Are you okay?"

"Yes, I'm here. This is a lot to take in all at once. Yes, you have permission to induce the coma. I'm boarding a plane soon and will call you when I land in Texas."

When the plane lands at DFW, Sam immediately takes her phone out of airplane mode and calls the hospital. It takes a while for the doctor to get on the phone, during which the plane gets to the gate, and everyone exits the aircraft. Sam stays in her seat, waiting for the doctor to come in. The flight has only about 30 passengers, so the plane is emptying quickly.

Sam asks, "How is Mom doing?" She spoke louder so her voice would get through the mask and over the noise on the plane.

The doctor replies, "I'm sorry, Ms. Holzen, your mother passed away an hour ago."

Sam goes numb and says nothing.

"Ms. Holzen, are you there?" the doctor asks.

She stammers, "Yes, I'll contact the hospital about arrangements tomorrow," and hangs up the phone.

Sam is numb; her world is now gone. She breathes more rapidly, and everything becomes distorted. The sides of the plane are closing in on her, and the fabric of the seat is suddenly abrasive to her fingers. The lingering smell of the man with body odor who sat three rows in front of her was making her nauseous.

People are walking past her; most of them don't even look in her direction, but their suitcases banging into the chairs are grating on her. She needed to get off the plane.

The flight attendants noticed Sam was distraught, and one came over to ask if she was okay. Sam grabbed her backpack, crying, and told the flight attendant that she had lost her grandmother yesterday and her mom just now. The flight attendant went white and says, "I'm so sorry." Sam started heading down the aisle and tells the flight attendant to stay safe. The flight attendant replies, "You too."

# The Empty House

When Sam gets off the plane, she goes to the restroom and cries for a while. At least here, no one would bother her for a few minutes. After several minutes, she tells herself, "Pull it together; there is no one to hold your hand." She leaves the stall, washes her hands and face, then heads to baggage claim.

Every time she flew home before, she would fly to DFW, and her mom would pick her up to travel back home close to Waco. Now she needs to find a taxi or a rideshare that will travel that far. She goes to the taxi area and asks about the cost, but they say no. When she checks the rideshare app, it won't let her book the ride.

She searches online and finds a shuttle service she can book. It isn't cheap, but they will get her home.

It was a two-hour drive. Sam told the driver that she was going home because her family was in the hospital with COVID-19. The driver tried to talk to her twice and then stayed quiet. She gave specific directions to the driveway. The driver took her down the long driveway to the house. She's eager to get out of the van. She has been wearing a mask for almost the entire day.

Claire had called and left a message while the plane was in the air. Sam texted her on the drive, telling her what happened, and she would call later. Claire replies, "Take care of yourself. No worries about calling until you are ready."

It was just over two months ago when she left. The house looks the same, but different. Knowing her mom and grandmother will not be there to greet her makes it look as if she is approaching an abandoned house. She has so many memories, and now she is alone.

The house is a small, two-story building with three bedrooms and two and a half baths on 40 acres of land. The bedrooms are upstairs. Behind the house was an old barn with large doors on each end, through which a tractor could pass. Around the house are pastures, and behind the barn, at the back of the property, is the motorcycle dirt track she and her dad built.

They never did real farming because of Dad's artificial leg. Every year, they raised one calf and a couple of goats, and then they slaughtered them to provide meat for the freezer. This provided better-quality meat and was much cheaper than buying it at the store. Sam didn't realize what the savings were until she left for college and had to pay for steaks.

She had to go to the back of the house and retrieve the hidden key to get in. Her dad's truck is still there, but her mom's car is gone. She'll deal with that later. She puts on her mask as she carries her luggage into the house and walks around to inspect it. Everything looks normal, clean, and tidy, just like Mom would keep it.

As much as her mother never wanted Sam to be a maid, she knows how to clean. Sam pulls out the cleaning supplies and towels and starts cleaning everything her mom would have touched. She begins with everything close to the front door and then moves into the living room and dining area. She proceeds through the rest of the house, cleaning surfaces and items that are typically touched. Finally, she goes back to the washing or utility area at the back to finish. Over 2 hours later, Sam puts the cleaning products away and sits down on the couch for 10 minutes.

She grabs her backpack and puts it on the dining table, deciding she'll make this her workspace. She looks at the family photos on the mantel and walls as she pulls out her laptop. Looking away from the pictures, she realizes she needs to focus on something, anything else. She pulls out her computer and turns it on. She stops, takes a deep breath, and starts crying.

Her heavy chargers are in the suitcase, so she needs to get that open. She drags the bag up to her room, opens it to pull out a charger and cables, and goes back downstairs. The despair just lingering in her throat, she is holding back the tears. She needed to do something, anything, to keep busy, or she would break down again.

Sitting at the table and taking a deep breath. It feels good to be home, but it feels absolutely terrible to be here alone. Sam doesn't feel like doing anything, but she knows she needs to eat soon and get some rest. Tomorrow, she'll call to arrange the funeral. When her dad passed away, Sam heard her mom talking to people, but she didn't focus on the details then.

Because of the pandemic shutdown, there will be no ceremony or wake. As they had all agreed when Dad passed, her mom and grandmother decided on cremation, and they scattered their ashes in the field to renew the soil.

After getting cereal and the last of the milk, she goes to find Dad's after book. When he was diagnosed with cancer, he started putting together the book. It's about what to do when he is gone and more. He wrote it for Mom and eventually for her.

He tells her, "You need to know this stuff. Don't study it now, know where to get it when the time comes."

She finds the book and begins flipping through its pages. Section one is all about Dad, the funeral, and the paperwork. The first page of the next section read, 'For Sam.' followed by a handwritten note.

*"You are not supposed to need this for many years. We have always wanted you to be independent and prepared for whatever life may throw your way. We grew up having to deal with some of the worst humans, so we knew, earlier than we ever should, how to survive in difficult situations. I've never talked about what happened when I was young, and I won't now. You don't need to have that burden put on you. We've done our best to keep you away from that physical and emotional pain as you were growing up. You must now make your way. If you want to grant my last wishes, they are: Do what you need to do, and don't waste energy or money on fancy funerals. And find what makes you happy, where you can make a difference your way, and go for it."*

*"We love you always, Mom and Abuela."*

Sam didn't know the note was there; she had never looked in the book before. She cries as she reads the message. Her mother wrote this, not knowing what might happen, just trying to take care of Sam all the time.

She flipped through the pages about funerals, life insurance, house, and others. At the back of the binder is an envelope. It's addressed to Sam in her father's handwriting. Inside is a note, five $100 bills, and 25 $20 bills. She started reading the note while she cried.

*"Sam, if you are reading this, I'm gone, and probably your mother as well. I experienced many bad things in my life, from bullies at school and an abusive father to seeing the conditions people have to live in when I was in Afghanistan. People will be cruel when they can. When you were born, I made it my mission to ensure you were prepared for the worst. Not just to survive, but to overcome and excel. I had many people ask me why I was so hard on you as a kid. I told them it was to save the future for everyone. They looked at me funny and never asked again.*

*I trained you as if you would be a future Navy SEAL. All the training, practice, knowledge about tactics, and procedures were for you to deal with whatever may come. Keep yourself fit and practice, but that's not the end goal.*

*From birth, you've been curious, compassionate, and always willing to help. It's your nature. As much as I tried to suppress it, I couldn't stop you. The drive to help can get you into trouble, but the training will help you get out of it.*

*I'm so proud of you. GO, and do the right thing!*

*PS. The cash goes in your bug-out bag for emergencies."*

When she stops crying, Sam goes back to the book and looks for the financial information. She needs to figure out the details of everything financial. The cash from Dad made her realize she needs to know how to pay for the hospital and funeral tomorrow.

Dad had a medical disability from the military. When Dad passed away, the amount was reduced, but Mom continued to receive checks. Those checks, along with mom's maid service, were the money they used. Dad and Mom had saved money for Sam to go to college, but not to graduate school. Sam worked part time in a restaurant to help, but student loans covered most of her graduate school expenses. All that income was now gone. Dad's life insurance was used to pay off the farm so that they wouldn't have a mortgage. Mom had life insurance, but that may only cover the funeral expenses. The savings that are left won't last long. Sam is going to have to find a job, but who is hiring right now?

The next morning, Sam wakes up, showers, and has breakfast with coffee. She's procrastinating, and she knows it. After working on her computer setup at the dining room table for an hour, she takes a deep breath and looks up the phone number of the funeral parlor.

"I'm sorry for your loss, Ms. Holzen. Of course, we can help. However, COVID has caused so many deaths that we won't even be able to get them from the hospital for over a week. It will take another couple of weeks with the backlog at our crematorium."

"I understand. Will that timeline be a problem for the hospital? Do I need to find other arrangements?"

"Everyone is having the same issues. No other funeral parlor will do anything sooner."

"I'm alone with no income. What will this cost, and how can I pay for it?"

The cost surprises Sam and asks if there are any alternatives.

"You have the option of donating the bodies for science. Cremation is typically the final step in the process. It could be months before you get their ashes, however."

"Thanks for letting me know the options. I need to think about everything, and I'll let you know after I check with the hospital."

Sam retrieves her mask and the keys to the truck, then heads to the hospital. When she arrives, she puts on her mask and walks to reception.

"I'm not sure whom to talk to. My mom and grandmother died, and I need to get their effects and talk about arrangements. I want to talk about donating them both for science so that they can help someone else."

The receptionist says, "I'm sorry for your loss. I'll have someone come to talk with you. Please take a seat."

While she was waiting, Sam started looking at the postings around the waiting area. She found a "Help Wanted" sign and asks the receptionist about it. The receptionist directed Sam to the hospital's website to fill out an application.

Sam waits for over an hour before someone shows up to talk with her.

"Ms. Holzen, I'm Julie McElhaney from the hospital administration. I'm sorry for your loss. I would normally give you a business card, but we stopped because of COVID and possible transmission."

Sam replies, "Thank you. What typically happens now?"

"Well, Ms. Holzen, we need to understand the last wishes of the family and make arrangements."

"Julie, I'm the only family; there is no one else to talk about arrangements. I need to know about personal effects, and I would like to discuss donating my mother's and grandmother's remains to science. If they can help improve conditions and options for others with COVID, I'm all in."

"Well, we can help with that. It'll take some time to create the paperwork. Is there a particular area of research you want them to contribute to, or any you don't want them associated with?"

"No restrictions or requirements, Julie, just use them to help. If the paperwork will take some time, can I just come back tomorrow?"

"That would probably be best. Can you come by at 11 a.m. to meet? You'll ask for me at reception. I'll get the personal effects now and put the appointment into the calendar."

Sam receives the bag of personal effects, which includes her mom's purse and wedding ring. Abuela never wore a ring, and her purse was still at the house. For safety, they will incinerate the clothes they are wearing. Sam enters the parking area, looking for her mom's car. She finds it, but doesn't know how to get it home in the truck. She will need to get a ride to the hospital tomorrow.

Sam drives the truck back home. When she gets to the driveway, she stops at the mailbox to collect everything. The mail is mostly junk, with a few bills mixed in. She goes to the table and starts going through the mail. She sorts obvious bills and puts the junk mail into the recycling bin. Next, she goes through her mom's purse. The cell phone is dead, so she plugs it in to charge. Everything else is typical–tissues, a tube of lipstick, hand cream, keys - what you'd expect to find. Her wallet has $42 in cash, a checkbook, and credit cards.

Sam realized that there were many things she had to deal with, from bank accounts, insurance, food, and finding a job. She goes online to fill out the hospital application. She can submit this today and talk to the hospital tomorrow.

### 

The next morning, a sheriff's deputy she knows comes to the house. Carol Larson knocks on the door and then steps back down the steps. When Sam opens the door, Carol says, "Hey Sam, your dad's truck was spotted on the road, so we wanted to check on things. I heard about your mom and grandmother, and I am so sorry."

"Come in, Carol," as she put on her mask.

Carol puts on her mask to enter the house.

When Sam worked with the sheriff's department to improve their tactical close-quarters combat skills, they initially paired her with Carol. They are both of similar height and build. Carol is blonde, so they could easily tell them apart when in their tactical gear.

They sit across from each other at the kitchen table, maintaining social distancing, and Sam offers her some coffee, placing cups down for both of them.

"Sam, I'm sorry about your family."

"Thanks, I'm dealing with everything, and it's more than I expected, but it's helping that I'm keeping busy."

Carol comments, "We haven't talked since the incident with your grandfather's crash."

"I don't want to go there right now."

"It's okay, it's just a time marker for me, meaning we should have talked long before now.

"Carol, tell me how you're doing and how things are around here now?"

"I'm doing okay; this pandemic is just making everything hard. We are supposed to stay socially distanced, but as a deputy, I need to connect with people and make arrests. I'm doing everything I can to stay safe. I miss those early days we spent together doing tactical training situations. After the sheriff switched the teams around, we didn't get teamed up often. I didn't realize how much you taught me and how much I missed working together until later."

"It worked because we communicated and helped each other."

Carol sighs. "Look, I know this may be too soon, but do you have any plans?"

"I don't know right now. There is the master's degree to complete this year. I have a lot of things to attend to right now. I'm taking classes remotely, so that helps, but with Mom gone, there's no income, so I have to look for work."

"Sam, you know the sheriff will hire you. Well, I say that, but the office is talking about budget cuts a lot right now. No one is driving, there are no traffic tickets, and no one is in bars getting drunk. We are dealing with domestic calls; those are so much fun," Carol states sarcastically.

They chat for almost an hour, mostly about what's been happening in the area and what Boston was like. Sam checks the clock. "Carol, I'm keeping you."

Carol shakes her head, saying, "It's fine, and it's good to catch up with you."

"Hey, can you take me to the hospital so I can finish the paperwork and pick up Mom's car?"

"Absolutely, that's not a problem."

# Working at the Hospital

Sam tells the receptionist that she filled out the online application and asks if there is anything else she needs to complete. The receptionist asks Sam, "What experience do you have in healthcare?"

"None."

"If you don't have any experience in any medical field, what can you do?"

"I can clean everything. My mother had a maid service for many years. I have little else at this point and need work."

The receptionist asks, "When can you start?"

"I can start immediately."

People considered Sam a semi-pro cleaner because of her mother's business. Her fluency in Spanish is a valuable asset in securing the job. Her results confirmed to everyone she knows she knows how to clean. She must clean everything when a patient leaves the area. The equipment, chair, bed, counters, and floor all had to be sanitized. The hospital has people who speak Spanish, but they grab the first person they can find when they need a translator. That included Sam.

On her first shift, they showed her how to put on and take off personal protective equipment (PPE). She would need to wear PPE all the time in the hospital. On her first shift, they also showed her how to handle used PPE and patient clothes, which she will consider contaminated. All of it is biological waste, and incinerators will burn it.

Sam quickly picked up the medical terminology used in the hospital. But she had to look up the translation of those terms into Spanish. Most of her help with translation involved medical terminology. If she were in the area and heard a problem with the translation, she would tell the nurse. The doctors had learned to check when kids were translating to ensure the family understood. During most of these interactions, the sick family member usually spent a few minutes before going to bed for treatment. The family was always told they could not stay; they had to go home. Everyone who entered without a mask was wearing one when they left.

Sam started in the general reception area. Patients entered, and the staff instructed them to put on masks. Then, someone would ask them to wait and finally evaluate them. They would send the obvious COVID-19 cases to a designated room. Sam cleaned those examination rooms after each patient and the waiting area as frequently as possible. After two weeks, Sam began working in the ER. The number of people coming directly to the ER was increasing, and they needed help with cleaning.

During one of her shifts, Claire calls. Sam's phone was silent, and she couldn't answer. During her break, she texts Claire saying she is working and will call her when she gets off work. They emailed and spoke to each other frequently. Claire calling her during work is unusual.

Claire sent back a text. "It's not urgent. I just thought you would like to know Dexter and two buddies were expelled this week for cheating. I wonder how the university figured it out? :)"

Sam smiles. She hasn't thought about Dexter since Christmas. He doesn't seem important anymore.

One day, a family brings an older man into the ER. He is having a lot of trouble breathing. The doctor immediately places a simple oxygen mask on him while checking his vital signs. Nurses tell the family to go into the waiting room.

One nurse comments, "They wait until they are in real trouble before coming to the hospital." After they checked everything, his breathing got worse.

The doctor says, "We need to intubate him and get him on a ventilator." The nurse goes to find a ventilator and comes back after a couple of minutes.

"Doctor, we don't have any ventilators; they are all being used." The doctor orders an IV to be started so they can admit the man. He asks the nurse to call intensive care and see if any ventilators are available.

Sam could hear all this because she was cleaning the next area, which was simply divided by a curtain. Sam heard this because she cleaned the next area, which a curtain simply divided. The nurse has the IV ready and asks the old man if he understands. Struggling for breath, the old man shakes his head and gets out, "No comprendo." The nurse knows that Sam is cleaning and asks her to come over and translate.

Sam tells the old man what is happening in Spanish. She tells him he is very sick, and they are going to take him upstairs in a few minutes, but they need to start an IV in his arm first. The old man nods at Sam and reaches out his hand. Sam holds his hand as the nurse inserts the IV into his other arm.

His breathing is getting worse; even with the oxygen mask, he is struggling to breathe. From the discussion she overheard with the hospital staff, she knows his lungs are filling with fluid as his body is fighting the virus. The fluid prevents oxygen from entering his system, but also makes it harder for him to breathe. His lungs are becoming fluid bags and can't expand and contract.

After they start the IV, the nurses check for a bed. Usually, they can move someone immediately. Today, the nurse returns to say there are no beds available. He will have to wait until they can find a bed. Hearing this, he squeezes Sam's hand, trying to communicate, so she asks him if he wants a pencil and paper–he nods. He writes two words, "Mí familia."

All she can tell him is that they can't be here because of the pandemic. He is struggling to breathe and grips her hand hard. Sam tells him, "It will be okay; you'll be with your family soon." He looks at Sam, knowing she's lying to him. He squeezes her hand and then lets go. Sam backs up, watching him try to breathe, his chest heaving, trying to get air into his lungs. He grabs the bed with one hand and his chest with the other. The nurse tells Sam, "Grab his arm. He will injure himself if we let him thrash around."

He is trying to move his arms. The nurse is trying to give him an injection to calm him down. She calls for help from another nurse. They give him the injection into the IV tube. After about 10 seconds, he calms down and then goes unconscious. He is struggling to breathe; the nurse adjusts the oxygen mask.

Sam is still holding his hand and arm when the nurse tells her, "You can let go now." Sam looks at him, thinking about her mother and grandmother. No one was with them when they died.

She asks the nurse, "Do you think he will be ok?"

"He's in bad shape right now. We need to see if he responds to the medication."

Sam leaves the old man and goes back to cleaning. Later, Sam is cleaning another part of the area, and she can hear the activity; they still haven't moved the old man. When she finishes cleaning, she puts the last of the used cleaning materials in the cleaning cart's trash. She looks around for what to clean next. There are people in all the beds. With the intensive care area full, they have moved no one for an hour. She scans each area, looking for the most critical one to clean.

A doctor and a nurse are working on a patient. The floor around the bed has several things that need to be picked up. According to hospital procedure, you do not retrieve dropped items. They use trays and tables to minimize drops. Part of Sam's job is to clean up these items safely. There can be needles or scalpels; this time, it is gauze and packaging. She gets her broom and dustpan and starts picking up the items behind the staff working on the patient.

They know Sam is cleaning and they like this. The worst thing is stepping on something while trying to help someone. They won't move for Sam, but Sam knows how to focus on the important stuff and get it out of the way.

When EMS brings in two car accident victims, the staff must move beds around to make room for the bleeding patients. They need to focus on controlling the bleeding and stabilizing the new arrivals.

Sam hears beeping from one of the life-support machines. It's coming from a machine next to the old man's bed, old man. Sam walks over and sees lights and text flashing. She walks up to a nurse and tells her what is happening. The nurse is getting medical supplies to take to the injured person.

She tells Sam, "He is dying. The disease is too advanced and there is nothing more we can do for him."

Sam walks back to her cart, past the bed with the old man. She can see his diaphragm and chest moving, but he is not breathing. His lungs are now almost full of fluid. As she watches, he stops breathing. She turns and heads to the bathroom, locking the door, and cries—no family close to him, just like her mom.

She pulls herself together and gets back to cleaning. This has been a hard day for her.

When she gets home, she sends a text to Claire asking if she can call. Sam tells her what happened.

"Oh my god, that's awful. Is every day like that?"

"No, not every day. Today was different because they couldn't take him to another bed on another floor. I normally wouldn't see anyone die like that."

"Sam, are you doing okay working at the hospital?"

"There are some bright spots, Claire. I've watched doctors get someone who was shot, stabbed, or in a crash and help them. The doctors and nurses are dedicated to helping people. I like that aspect, but the death part, not so much. After the coffee shop shooting, I'm interested in what professionals do to stop bleeding and treat the victims. One doctor has let me watch and ask questions while he sutured a knife wound."

"That sounds like you, blood and gore, no problem. Show me how to shove my hand into someone's chest and sew them back together; a piece of cake. So, what is the worst part?"

"The worst is when I see a family come in with someone who has been sick but waited until it was serious. They come in and want the doctor to fix it. They are usually older and probably argue with their family about going to the hospital. When they arrive, they are in trouble. I don't want to talk about this anymore. What have you done for fun, Claire?"

"Well, not much. Grandfather's condition means we need to be careful, so we're pretty locked down. I can take online classes, work on my thesis, watch movies, go to the pool, and dream of seeing beyond my house. Have you done anything for fun?"

"No, with 12-hour shifts and school, I don't have much time for anything. Working pays the bills. I want to finish school, and when we get back to normal, I want to be ready to have a real job."

Next week, the emergency room expects more people. There is no available space, and the staff are getting overwhelmed. Supplies are low, and Sam must search other floors for the cleaning supplies she needs. She also grabs supplies for the nurses. To help speed things up, she starts pre-kitting the items every patient needs. The nurses love the idea and want more. The accounting team hates it because they want every item accounted for and managed separately. If one patient doesn't need a particular item, they often encounter issues with insurance companies that are reluctant to pay. Sam found some satisfaction, albeit briefly, in helping to solve the kitting problem. She didn't want to spend her time arguing with accounting, so she stopped doing it.

One activity she dislikes is sitting with patients who are waiting to be transferred from the ER to a ward bed or an intensive care unit. The patients are scared and alone, and they want the nurses to stay with them. Most nurses can simply say they have to help other patients. For the few who won't calm down, the orderlies or Sam, the cleaning lady, sit with them. She recognizes the patients are scared; while she is waiting with them, she isn't cleaning, which adds to her feeling of being overwhelmed.

# Pandemic Depression

After working at the hospital for weeks, Sam is exhausted. With COVID-19 cases surging, the hospital is at full capacity. They are receiving calls to see if they have bed space, and the doctors are calling other hospitals for help.

Sam can barely keep up with her classes. They are almost over: studying for finals is the last bit. And finishing her thesis.

But it's hard. Motivation is hard to find. The number of sick people at the hospital isn't getting better. Ones she sits with are not being taken to intensive care. The bodies are piling up in the morgue It's draining her. Emotionally. Mentally.

That night, during their call, Claire asks, "Hey, how are you doing today?"

"Worn down. Drained. The hospital is overrun. I had to go to the morgue today to find cleaning supplies. How about you, Claire?"

"Boring. I don't have a front-row seat like you do. My stress during the day is arguing with my brother about what to order for dinner. Sam, do you think you're depressed? I know you're working long hours in a shitty environment, but my girl, who is always positive, is sounding defeated."

Sam thinks about it. "Watching all these people die is draining. I'm helpless. And these twelve-hour shifts take up all my time. Finding time to eat, sleep, and work on my classes is hard. I've been looking for other jobs, but there's nothing."

"What about technology companies?"

"There are none in this area hiring grad students. I would have to travel to Austin or Dallas. That would be a long commute every day, or I would have to move. Moving right now doesn't seem like a good option. Where would I live and what would I do with this house?"

"Listen, Sam. You are depressed, and everything is looking bad right now.

You are not like this. The situation must be affecting others at the hospital. Ask someone what they are doing to stay positive."

"I'll try asking someone at the hospital and let you know the next time we talk."

The nurses tell Sam that she is showing classic signs of depression. One nurse suggests that Sam spends time each day doing something she loves.

"Get your mind off the things depressing you and onto something that will lift your spirits."

Sam replies, "Thanks. What do you do? What is your thing to improve your spirits?"

The nurse replies, "I read superhero comics and watch superhero movies."

Sam smiles and says, "That is not what I expected to hear."

The following week, Claire could tell something was wrong with Sam. "Talk to me, girl, I know something is wrong."

"Work. I can clean up anything; that's not the problem. It's watching all these people die. Alone. I hold their hands, but it's not the same."

"Holy crap, that's awful. Why don't you quit?"

"And do what? I don't have another job lined up, and I need money to pay bills. Not many people are hiring a graduate student with no experience."

"Sweetie, I'm really worried about you. I'm not talking to the Sam I lived with in Boston."

"In Boston, I had all my basic needs covered. You covered most of the food costs, so my restaurant earnings went further. I have to work, and this is the only job available right now."

"What can I do to help? Please let me help."

"You are helping, just by talking to me and being real. I have to figure out what I'm going to do and then make it happen somehow."

"Well, that's pretty vague, but you're sounding more like my Sam."

"One nurse said I'm depressed and I need to spend time on things I like to do."

"I agree! You should go solve a problem or hack something."

"Yeah, yeah. I'm going to make a list tonight and figure something out."

"Next time we talk, I want you to share Sam's favorite list with me and tell me something fun you did."

"Okay, Therapist Claire, I'll start the list when we get off the phone. Promise."

Sam completes her priority chores, then sits down and makes a list of things she loves to do. The list starts with research for her thesis, learning new hacking techniques, and shooting. She pauses and thinks back to her high school, college, and graduate school years. What did she do besides school? She then adds to the list, figuring out how everything works, helping others learn, and finally creating solutions to problems that no one else has figured out. Every issue is a puzzle to be solved. You may not solve it immediately, but there is always something if you look at the situation.

She looks at the list, lets out a sigh, and goes to the kitchen to make dinner. She's making soup tonight. The entire time, she's going through the list in her head and finally says out loud, "This sounds great, but that list does nothing to solve my financial problems."

After eating and cleaning the kitchen, Sam returns to the table and the list. "How do I get money from this list?" She starts a new list combining what she knows, what she loves, and how it could apply to making money. The list includes tutoring, inventing and patenting new ideas, teaching competitive shooting, and several others. Sam looks at teaching competitive shooting because she was a competitive shooter six years ago, but she knows what to do. She searches for shooting instructors and gets discouraged. The individuals on this list remained active until the onset of the pandemic. They have current and relevant experience. Teaching shooting would be a longshot option, given the lack of competition because of the pandemic.

She needs to turn in for the night; her hospital shift starts early, and she needs to be rested. She checks the doors, turns off the lights, and heads to her bedroom to go to bed.

The next evening, after another depressing day at the hospital, she decides to do one of her things. She opens her computer and starts her internet scans, then opens her list of automation scripts to complete. She has marked most of them as finished, but upon reviewing the list, she notices multiple improvements to one script, so she unmarks it as done.

Looking further down the list, she sees several items related to the extortion group. She should review blackmail accounts for intelligence, examine bank accounts, create an OSINT script, and build an overlap database.

Sam reads through the list and considers her options. She enjoys hacking to figure things out. A hacking problem is a puzzle to solve. Saving the updated list, she opens an editor to build a new program. She can make a program to search through every account in the extortion database. She'll build a summary of what is there and then create a plan for the next steps. Her program will access everything she has, but also collect more. Who is the listed account owner of the server storing the information, what is their address, and anything about the other accounts? This is all part of continuing to build the information database to track the blackmailers.

Sam works on her program for a couple of hours each night. It makes her feel better, and her improved mood is noticeable to the nurses, who comment on her enhanced mood.

Sam creates several free accounts on cloud providers, adds random files, and has the program work on them. After debugging the program, Sam is ready. The servers she created to test her programs will now store the information. Using the VPN chain program along with the account search, she starts the programs late on a Thursday and goes to bed. If it fails, she'll try again another day.

When she gets home from work on Friday, she looks at the results and finds that about a dozen of the several hundred sites didn't work. She ignores those right now. Checking the results, she sees there is a pattern: every account has a Word document, a JPEG picture file titled with a name, and multiple other picture files. The pictures are in JPEG and PNG formats. Some sites have MP4 videos and MP3 audio files. Her program checks every picture for steganography data and stores any information found in a file. Extracting the data is the easy part; now she needs to figure out how to extract the most relevant information from each. She'll need to create a program to extract all that data and identify standard highlights, but that'll be later.

Sam doesn't have to work on Saturday, so she stays up late

reviewing the details. Based on the program she created, she copied the code. She created a new program to access all the financial accounts in the database, providing information on the types of accounts and their corresponding amounts. This program will use the VPN chain, and servers will encrypt the gathered information. She's feeling better and accomplishing something. At 2 a.m., she begins the program and goes to get some sleep.

Sam is crossing into hacking that can get her arrested. If someone detects her hacking and can trace it back through her VPN chain, she could be in serious trouble. However, she has done nothing except gather data. She has sold nothing; she has modified nothing she found. The more she gains experience in these searches, the more confident she becomes in seeking additional details.

Sunday is all about reviewing all the class materials and studying for finals. This week she has the last two finals, and she'll be done with all her master's classes. Thursday afternoon, she completes her last final exam. A minor victory in her currently depressing existence.

# The Heist

On her next day off, Sam is reviewing the results of her program to search the financial sites from the extortion database. The results show that most accounts are associated with cryptocurrency exchanges or brokers, and each account contains cryptocurrency assets valued at several million dollars. Having read the news about hacking crypto accounts and stealing the money, Sam thought of the obvious: steal it.

"Stealing this money is wrong and could get me arrested, at best, and killed by the extortionists." Thinking back to the café and the shooting, "If hacking a database of information and accessing one site caused the extortion group to attack people in a public coffee shop, then what would this cause? If they are looking for me, I shouldn't just sit here waiting. If I get enough information, I can shut down their operation." She has no family they could use to hurt her. She's a free agent in this situation.

Alternatively, she could focus on completing her thesis. It will be hard, but she knows she can do it. Finish the thesis, get her degree, and move on.

Sam thinks about it and has mixed emotions regarding the extortion group. They are extorting people, and based on her analysis of the first set of pictures, it appears to be a large number of modified and fake images. "If they are really blackmailing bad guys, is that okay? The better option is to stop the bad guys and the extortion group." She has taken no action to protect the children who are victims here.

Now she's depressed again and does simple tasks around the house. When she finishes everything in the house, cleaning and laundry, she goes to the barn and starts doing maintenance on her motorcycle.

When she finishes the maintenance, she takes the motorcycle out to the field behind the house, driving it on the old motocross track her dad had built. After about an hour, she returns to the barn. After cleaning up, she returns to the house and reviews the table of information she has compiled.

A path is solidifying in her mind, and she knows this is a one-way door. This is a significant decision that will have a profound impact on her life. If she goes through with this, she won't be able to turn back. She will need to innovate, act aggressively, and be relentless until she eliminates the group or they kill her.

As she thinks through this, she knows her answer. "It's my decision. I don't have anyone to tell me it's the right thing to do. There is no one to pat me on the back and say it will be fine. I also know I can't expose Claire to this situation, so I can't ask her, but she'll tell me to do the right thing."

It was the first time she had made a big decision like this without consulting her parents. Her dad would have asked a couple of questions and then say, "Do it, you know it's the right thing to do." Mom never tells her to be strait-laced or a princess. She would say, "Life can be hard; help people as much as you can, but don't let them use you."

During her next call with Claire, she is in a better mood. The conversation starts as always with anything interesting to share.

"Claire, I haven't found a regular job, so I'm thinking about creating something new."

"That is great, and you sound better. What are you going to do?"

"I can't tell you the details."

"Oh, so that means you are going to hack something or someone."

"Yes, no... yes, and it will help people who would otherwise be victims. If I tell you what I'm doing, you become an accessory, best case."

"So, there is a worst-case scenario? What is the worst case?"

"You and your family could be targeted with financial or physical attacks."

"I don't like the sound of this! Are you putting yourself in danger?"

"I know how to stay safe, and if something happens, I can deal with it. With no family now; they can't hurt me through anyone except you. That means you can't know anything about what I'm doing."

"Sam, I don't like this. You sound like you are distancing yourself. I can help in ways you don't realize."

"I know your extended family situation, and that's great — a positive, but also a negative. Nothing I do can ever get associated with your family."

"Don't shut me out, please, at least keep talking to me."

"I will not ghost you. Once I create a secure communication method, I will tell you the details. It will take me some time to gather the parts and the programming I need. There are still details to investigate, to work out. And then build the system. I need to get back to my planning. I'll talk to you again when we watch that new vampire episode."

"Hmm. I'm not thrilled with this idea, but I know it's not up to me to make. I would like to know how I can help you, please. And don't ghost me, or I will be very unpleasant about it! How long will this secure communication system take to build?"

"Weeks. I have to create several programs, hack a bunch of systems on the internet without being detected."

"That sounds like my Sam. Tell me if I can help."

After the call, Sam thinks about what Claire said. She can't ever associate Claire with what she's about to do. She thinks about spy movies where the person eventually turns to an old friend for help. "I like that idea; I can send gear and information to Claire to hold for me. Just in case."

Getting back to how to take their money. She needs to consider many things she has never dealt with before. If she accesses the accounts, how will she conceal the transactions? Where will she store the money, and after that, how will she use it? She reads about the requirements for opening a crypto account and how to transfer money in and out. She looks at U.S. and international brokers to achieve diversification.

The system will need to create over one hundred accounts. Each account will only be part of the heist to make tracing the activity harder. That will mean dozens of fake IDs to open accounts.

Researching how to get fake IDs, she finds numerous international websites that claim to manufacture IDs. She has to pick one and try it. She decides to create a fake ID for herself and another made-up persona.

To gather information for a fake persona, she selects a city location. From there, she reviews tax records and randomly selects an address. The last name at the address, combined with a random first name, gives her the name. A broker conducting a simple check will notice that the owner at the address shares the same last name.

Getting a usable picture of a random person proved to be more challenging. The image needs to be taken against a plain background, with the person facing forward and the correct size. By searching and cropping photos, she gets a suitable picture for the first fake ID.

She must wait while they create and ship the IDs to her. During that time, she establishes the basics for all the other fake personas.

Sam ponders the process, "If I'm a great success or an ultimate failure, no one is going to know it was me."

Creating fake IDs and opening accounts could get her into trouble with the authorities. This is creating another one-way door. If the police realize the accounts, they could lock them, seize the money, track her, and arrest her. She'll have to be careful to access these accounts only through VPNs she controls to prevent tracking.

When the IDs arrive, she takes the first fake ID and goes through the process of signing up at a crypto brokerage. During the process, she has to verify her identity by uploading a picture of her identification.

That is when she has the eureka moment and feels completely stupid. She did all that work to create, purchase, and wait for a physical ID. The brokerage only wanted an image of the ID. She could make them all in a graphics program and didn't need to order anything.

Getting up, she grabs her coffee cup and walks to the kitchen. Her face gets red as she walks. She tosses the cup into the sink and kicks the cabinet. She spends the time researching details so that simple things like this don't get missed. Her not connecting the pandemic changes with identity verification bothers her. What else could she miss?

Talking to herself the next day while driving to the hospital, "I'm about to steal money from a group that will kill me if they find me. No stupid mistakes like this in the future. I need to review my plan and details to ensure I have missed nothing. I should take a couple of days, then go back and check everything with a fresh perspective."

At the hospital, several people comment they can tell she is upset. Her supervisor asks her if she is okay and what the problem is.

Sam takes a deep breath, saying, "I'm sorry. I found out yesterday that I did some of my research wrong for my thesis. I need to revisit several areas and then redo this specific research. Going home exhausted after these long shifts is affecting my thesis work. I'm frustrated with myself; it was a stupid mistake."

The supervisor replies, "Sorry, Sam, I would like to help, but I know nothing about your research. Do you need to take a day off?"

"No, I'm taking a break from the research this week. Later this week, I'll talk to you about a day off when I restart the research."

That night, Sam examined the plan, personas, and the process for handling accounts. For this plan to work, the whole heist needs to be automated. Coordinating multiple cloud computers will handle every transaction, and each will perform a part of the overall process. Creating the personas to open the accounts is a manual process.

A couple of days later, she creates the persona IDs in a graphics program. She must identify several security features of official IDs and how they'll appear in a JPEG image. Based on location and the type of ID, she needs to research each one by one. She can complete one ID and gather the information for a second before she needs to go to sleep. When she has a day off later this week, she'll focus on finishing the IDs.

At the end of the week, she has now created all the accounts. With an ID, she verified each account, making it ready to trade cryptocurrencies. Sam needs everything automated for speed. The different processes must be in sync; otherwise, they could fail. Each server will perform a specific task. Each will have to wait for the server before them in the chain to finish.

During part of the final account setup, she realizes she needs bank accounts, not just brokerage accounts. She will use several personas to open bank accounts. Starting with U.S. banks, she opens two when she identifies a real problem. She put in the address that was part of the fake persona's ID. That means the bank will send physical mail to that address. Offshore banks require a lot of paperwork and a valid passport.

Sam will need to investigate further before attempting to open more. Currently, the crypto accounts will facilitate the heist.

The idea for the heist is to use cloud servers to access all the target accounts as fast as possible. They will transfer the crypto coins to a first-level heist target. Step two, another program will take the coins in the heist account and convert them to another type of coin. Bitcoin to Dogecoin, Dogecoin to Litecoin, Litecoin to Ethereum, and Ethereum to Bitcoin. Each system will decide the change randomly. After the change, the program will send the coins to one of the hiding accounts. Each hiding account will switch the coins to another type of coin and then send the results to another hiding account. This process will repeat dozens of times before the program finally transfers the coins to the last accounts.

To track this process, someone would have to be familiar with all the accounts and monitor all the blockchains for each type of coin. Accounts have had assets stolen and lost simply by using a single coin type and blockchain. This will make tracking what Sam is doing extremely difficult, if not impossible.

To use the money, she can use Bitcoin directly for a few purchases, but that isn't enough. She'll have a couple of accounts set up to fund a credit card. Each transaction on the credit card will automatically sell enough Bitcoins to fund the transaction. She'll use that credit card to create virtual credit cards, which she'll use for purchases.

After testing, checking, rechecking, and waiting, Sam realized she was stalling. She's nervous about this next step, but it needs to be done, so she sets her date as Sunday at 5 p.m. Central Time. The heist will begin with Asia starting its day, while people in Europe and the U.S. are not watching the market. This is a big step she can't go back from here. On Sunday, Sam orders pizza, sets up her systems, and at 5 p.m. starts the process. To minimize detection, everything is running independently, so if something is tracked or compromised, she's not part of the process.

After she verifies all the processes that are working, she sits back in her chair and takes a deep breath. She says out loud, "It's done; I'm officially a criminal hacker. Now that I've jumped in, I should see what else I can do to mess with their operations."

She doesn't know how long the process will take. Each server will email a specific email address she has created on an international server. This one was in Poland but routed through several other accounts and countries. The email will provide an encrypted summary file containing statistics, errors, and the total amount of money from the heist.

At 10 p.m., Sam goes to bed so she can get some sleep before her work shift the next day. The next day, she wants to check the status, but she can't check while at the hospital. When she gets home, she opens a VPN chain and checks her email. There is an email from each of her work servers. She downloads the encrypted message from each server, then decrypts it. She can't do anything about the errors at this point. It is vital to know, but she can't go back and do this again. The process on each server involves completing the work, emailing, and then deleting all the programs. Essentially, it wipes itself. When complete, all the machines are blank, so trying again will require an entirely new setup.

The goal is to take their money and disrupt their operations. She looks at the reports and focuses on the money out and the final, after the transactions. When she adds the numbers to a spreadsheet, she laughs. The total cash taken from the accounts is $473 million. The total amount when finished is $507 million. During all the crypto transactions, the value of the coins increased, and she made money by the end of the process. $34 million in additional funds is available because of price appreciation during the process.

She searches news sites for any mention of coin theft. After searching all the major sites in every English-speaking country, she finds nothing. She didn't think a blackmail group would advertise that their money had been stolen and draw attention to themselves.

She smiles and goes to one account to get virtual credit cards. Ordering two cards with a $2,000 balance each for online use and three with a $5,000 balance each to be shipped to a P.O. box in Waco.

She immediately adds one of the virtual cards into her online account and orders additional hacking equipment. Ordering a sniffer, USB keys so she can create hacking devices, and another cell phone to be a backup.

After all this, she checks the headlines again and then heads to bed. Keeping to her routine is important; any sudden, significant changes will be noticeable. She can't sleep; she's churning on the opportunity that the money can provide. She could seriously mess up their operations if she knew what they did. Eventually, she falls asleep thinking about what she'll do next.

# FBI Background Check

The two FBI agents arrive at the sheriff's office and ask the deputy on duty to speak with the Sheriff, saying, "We have an appointment." The deputy checks their FBI credentials, takes their names, and lets the sheriff know they have arrived. After a couple of minutes, the sheriff asks them to come back to his office.

Both agents enter the office, showing their FBI credentials. "Sheriff, I'm Special Agent Bill Asherton, and this is Special Agent Mathew Jackson."

"What can I do for you both? From your initial meeting request, you would like to discuss and conduct some background checks on Samantha Holzen. I need to let you know that she recently returned from college, and we haven't interacted for several years."

Agent Asherton asks, "So you interacted with Samantha previously?"

"Yes, we talked and worked on team training frequently. A few months after I was elected, Sam's dad came to see me and asked about collaborating on training and tactics."

"Was that normal here?"

"I found out he worked with the previous sheriff, but he wanted to do more. I started my background check on him before I started anything."

"What did you find?"

"John, Sam's father, was a former Navy SEAL. He was seriously injured in Afghanistan. He was disabled but was fully active."

"So, you started working with him on training?"

"After some more checking. The previous sheriff had a file related to Sam's grandmother. She was checked by a local doctor when she moved here. The doctor reported serious abuse. Bones that were broken and not treated. The previous sheriff investigated the situation."

"Was John associated with the abuse?"

"No, it was the grandfather. I found out the couple's honeymoon was spent getting the grandmother away from the grandfather and bringing her here. I later learned that both John and Martha had been abused as kids. Martha ran away and never finished high school. That is why she worked as a maid in the area. People liked the work that the mom and grandmother did."

"You were good with the background check on John. What about Sam?"

"Sure, John wanted to help and insisted that young Sam be involved. She was into competitive shooting, so she knew how to handle herself. It turns out that John had been training her since she could walk."

"That is unusual."

"It is until you factor in the grandfather. They brought the grandmother here without the grandfather's knowledge. Sam was born a couple of years later. They never said it explicitly, but I think they were worried he would show up and try to hurt the grandmother. The grandfather showed up around a year after John died of cancer."

"What happened with the grandfather?"

"He broke the grandmother's jaw immediately, and Sam hit him. Her statement later was that she was trying to get him away from the grandmother. She got on her motorcycle and headed here to our office. She called us on the way, saying he was chasing her. On the way, she crossed the median of the highway and jumped across the front of an 18-wheeler, trying to get away."

"Did you catch the grandfather?"

"The witness statements said he was about to hit her with the car when she crossed the highway. He followed her and collided with the 18-wheeler. The grandfather died at the scene. It was a big mess to clean up. The car was crushed, and the truck had to be towed."

"Was Sam all right?"

"She crashed and was scraped up from the jump. When I talked to her later, I asked what she was thinking. She told me she was trying to get across the traffic to get away."

"That sounds like it was hazardous for her."

"I think he would have killed her and then killed her mother and grandmother. She used her training to deal with the situation."

"You mentioned training your deputies. What did that involve?"

"It started with basics and developed into full special operations tactical training. Going into an active shooter situation. We used airsoft and did actual practice."

"Do you have a training facility? Where did you train?"

"We used barns and businesses when they were closed. We used the high school on the weekends."

"How did Sam help?"

"John's special operations training was used to show the deputies how to enter and progress through the building. Sam was also helping to train them. John, with his artificial leg, couldn't move as quickly as the team. Sam would be part of the practice."

"Sam was in high school and doing simulated building clears with your team?"

"That, or she would be the bad guy. The deputies did not like it when she was the bad guy because it was always harder to locate and apprehend her. I liked it because they got better."

"Anything else with training?"

"Sam kept doing more to help. New deputies must learn the law, shooting techniques, investigations, and forensic science. The forensics part was causing problems, so Sam worked with experienced personnel to develop a basic manual for new deputies. She would help set up simulated crime scenes for the deputies to experience and process evidence. Sometimes, it was so that they didn't ruin the evidence."

"This sounds like she was becoming another deputy. Did she show any interest?"

"After John died and then the grandfather, she kept helping, but her life focus changed during high school. I thought she was going to graduate and then join us or the military. Instead, she went to college and studied engineering."

"Interesting change for her. Any reason you know about?"

"She could do all the special operations things. It didn't excite her.

She wanted something that would be a challenge, solving problems."

"Thanks for that information. Did you have any other situations to deal with related to Sam?"

"Yes, we got calls about Sam frequently. To help you understand, I need to provide some clarification. John wanted Sam to shoot and practice. For years, the area has been plagued by a feral hog problem. They destroy crops and will even kill young animals. John worked out an arrangement with the farmers and ranchers to allow Sam to hunt across property lines. The wild hogs couldn't get away by crossing a fence. This started before she had a license to drive on the street, so she rode her dirt bike across fields. After about a year, she started talking to the locals and borrowed a tractor with a front-end loader. She built ramps at fence lines. The ramps allowed her to jump fences like a motocross rider, with no need for gates. The regular farm animals can't get across, but she could. There were a few who said no until they saw her, and the feral hog problem got better."

"Why would people call?"

"It was usually someone on the highway who didn't live in the area. They would call and say there is a young woman with a rifle jumping fences. We knew it was Sam because she always called to let us know where she was going. This is central Texas, and kids hunting is not unusual. Travelers on the highway would be concerned."

"When she left, did your hog problem come back?"

The sheriff smiles, shakes his head, and says, "No. During high school, some of the other kids started using the ramps to travel. In fact, high school kids still use them. Some kids asked Sam to train them to be better hunters, which she did. Today, if someone reports a hog problem, we have an email list of people who will coordinate and address the issue. We require them to call us and let us know who they are, where they are, and their route. We even have people coordinating to pick up the animals and get them to the rendering facility."

"She trained others to be better hunters. What does that mean?"

"What it means is shooting long distances. Typically, hunting would be done at a few hundred yards. Sam would make over one thousand-yard shots. The other kids wanted to shoot like that."

"That is not a standard hunting rifle and ammo, is it?"

"No, but getting the right equipment is not a problem."

"You haven't talked about anyone she was close to. What about boyfriends?"

"Her only actual boyfriend was Walter from high school. They would hunt together, ride motorcycles, and play chess - typical teenage stuff. Walter joined the Army the week after graduation and was killed during his first deployment to Afghanistan. She has not had good times with men in her life."

"Anything else you want to tell us about Sam?"

"I have nothing else, but will answer specific questions."

The agents leave and start driving back to Austin. Mathew is driving.

Bill says, "That was not what I expected. The initial information was that she is a hacker. Growing up in Texas, we both expected her to know how to shoot, but that is beyond normal."

"Do you think she will be a problem as an agent?"

"I think she would be great, but our report has to show all this stuff, which will cause concern. I imagine if she applies, she will be put through an intensive psychological evaluation."

Mathew replies, "I know, I mean from the time you could walk, your dad was training you for special operations."

"That she went into engineering after the grandfather incident is interesting. That probably changed her outlook on what she wanted to do in life."

"Agreed, also SSA Andrews talked about her thinking outside the box with hacking stuff. That she is working on a master's thesis he won't talk about is interesting because no hacking stuff came up with the sheriff."

Bill looks out the window to see three motorcycles in a line jumping a fence at a ramp. He comments to Mathew, "Three kids are using the ramps, one with a rifle across their back."

Mathew doesn't look; he comments, "Only in Texas."

###

In Boston, Frank has tracked down Claire Elmer, Sam's roommate, and leaves her a message to set up a call. After a week, Frank calls and leaves another message, saying he is working on background information for Samantha Holzen. A day later, Frank gets a call from a number he doesn't know. He answers, and the caller tells Frank she's Claire's attorney and will talk with him, and if needed, make a call with Claire.

Frank explains he is working on a background check for Samantha Holzen. "Claire was her roommate, so I need to talk with her about Samantha." The attorney asks about the type of questions he will ask.

Frank responds, "This is a formality when they are looking at someone who could work with the FBI. Look, you don't have to worry about Ms. Elmer. I'm not trying to trap her or get her to admit to anything."

The attorney tells Frank he will let him know a time for a video call. Frank gets the attorney's email so he can create an invitation for the video call.

When the video call starts, online are Supervisory Special Agent Andrews, Special Agent Nomikos, Claire, and her attorney. They all go through an introduction. Agent Andrews states, "We're here to get background information for Samantha Holzen. Ms. Elmer, have you talked to Sam recently?"

"I talked to Sam on the phone after she returned to Texas. Her family all died from COVID, which is why she returned."

Agent Nomikos says, "Crap" under his breath.

Claire replies, "Exactly, now she has no family and has to find work. That is enough about Sam's current situation."

"Ms. Elmer, can you describe how you met, when, and where, and please include details."

Claire provided a concise answer. Agent Andrews and Nomikos continue, asking simple questions about habits, conflicts, and problems. "Who was the biggest pain for Samantha?"

Claire responds, "Call her Sam, and she was frustrated by a guy named Dexter."

At this point, the attorney says, "I need to confer with my client," and they go on mute.

After a few minutes, Claire unmutes and tells them, "Dexter frustrated her because he was an ass. He didn't know the material, but he still got top marks on the tests. He was recently expelled for cheating."

Agent Andrews asks, "What did Sam do about this situation?"

"She complained to me and talked to a couple of professors."

"Talk to us about what Sam did with hacking."

"I can't tell you anything about that," replies Claire. "My major is economics, and I can only repeat words I've heard about hacking."

Agent Nomikos says, "You must have seen her working on projects."

"Yes, she was always working on something. I can't tell you what she showed me was homework or hacking or something else."

"Ms. Elmer, did Sam hack Dexter?"

"Not that I know of."

"Did Sam hack anyone you know about?"

The attorney tells the agents she needs to confer with her client. "Asking her to admit anything she knows could be construed as if she's an accessory."

Claire unmuted her phone after talking with her attorney. "I can't tell you about any hacking Sam did to anyone. I can only talk about what I asked. Whenever I heard something related to hacking, I would ask Sam. What are some things to watch out for or be cautious of, such as phishing emails? There were some things I asked her, and she told me stuff that went way over my head."

Agent Andrews asks, "You were never interested in her thesis and what she could do with hacking?"

"Agent, I didn't have to ask; she was always talking about something I didn't understand. Network access, passwords, and don't respond to emails you don't recognize. The nerdiest things I learned were how to create a strong password and use two-factor authentication. She showed me what social engineering is and how people use it to hack people."

Agent Andrews says, "Sam is brilliant. I have to think she showed her hacking ability."

"Oh, you mean when she showed me something and explained something I didn't understand? Sure, she did that, but I couldn't tell you anything about what it was."

"What about social interactions, Ms. Elmer? Did she go to parties a lot, dancing, anything like that?"

Claire smiles, "She didn't have money to waste, so she focused on school and working at the restaurant. I had a victory when I talked her into spending the money to see a new movie in the theater."

Agent Andrews comments, "So, she didn't do well in social situations?"

Claire leaned forward toward the camera and replies, "Don't construe her not wanting to waste time on situations versus not knowing how to interact. I've taken her to parties. She would borrow and wear a dress, fix her hair and nails. I was shocked by the transformation. She attended the party and wowed them, never showing fear, and discussed several subjects. In contrast, she could take me to the sketchiest restaurant for some great food, and I was always comfortable with her. She would talk to people in the restaurant who would scare you. Okay, guys, you're asking me dumb questions to get a background. You are not asking direct questions, so I'll answer them anyway."

Her attorney says, "Ms. Elmer.."

Claire responds, "I got this. Sam is smart, probably smarter than anyone on this call. She has principles she won't compromise. Helping people is part of her DNA. Helping when she can, but she won't be a doormat."

"I learned about her competitive shooting when she was younger. After some research, I found out she was good. I bring it up because I was one of the few people she talked to about shooting. She didn't boast or talk about her childhood. Most people at school thought she was the country bumpkin who was embarrassed about her past. What I learned is that people at the school became very uncomfortable when they found out she used guns and butchered animals she killed."

"Now to the hacking stuff and her thesis. I learned how to code to create economic models, but that doesn't mean I can code like Sam; however, I'm smart enough to understand the impact of what she's doing. I am familiar enough with her thesis to understand the implications for the economy. If the wrong people got her work details and exploited them, we could face an economic disaster. Sam knows the power and impact of what she's doing, which is another reason she's considered a loner. Everyone wants to talk about their research and be recognized for their work. Sam doesn't talk about her work with just anyone."

"All that didn't bother you, Ms. Elmer?"

"No, I focus on the person, the character, not their past, how they dress, or whatever. I've experienced many people who are all about showing off, all about meeting someone else's expectations. I know people who will literally kiss my ass if they think it can give them some kind of advantage. Sam is not one of those people. I'm glad that I had some time with Sam. That Sam has figured out something this impactful and knows not to share it with everyone is a great indicator. Some of the smartest women in history had their ideas co-opted by men. Sam is so much smarter."

Claire leaned in again. "If you want my view, I'll tell Sam not to work for the FBI. She could be great with you guys, but that would not let her express her real potential."

After several additional questions, Agent Andrews states, "I think we're finished. Thank you for your time, Ms. Elmer."

Phil calls Frank after they complete the call. Phil says, "I'll write up my notes and send them to you this afternoon."

"Thanks, but tell me what you think about what she told us."

"I think she wouldn't tell us anything even remotely bad about Sam."

"Do you think she's protecting Sam?"

Phil replies, "I can't be sure; Ms. Elmer is smart, and it's clear she has dealt with attorneys and law enforcement before."

"Did you see the extended family tie that showed up in Ms. Elmer's background?"

"I did indeed, Frank, and I was surprised that Ms. Elmer's family would allow her to have Sam as a roommate. The families would not associate in the same circles."

# The Special Delivery

Now that Sam has crossed the line into criminal hacking and stolen a substantial amount of their money, she needs to intensify her efforts against the blackmail group. The best way she knows to put pressure on the extortionist is to provide information to the FBI.

She doesn't know who might be involved in investigating this group. No one at the FBI may know about this group, so no investigation is being conducted.

The only actual contact she has is with Agents Andrews and Nomikos. This kind of crime may not be in their area, but they are the only names she knows to contact. That their names were in the news from the coffee shop shooting meant anyone could directly contact them. The police would likely not consider Sam the source.

To communicate with Agents Andrews and Nomikos, she needs something that can't be traced to her. Her first message to them needs to be the database of blackmail targets. It needs to be the entire database of targets, and she can't send it as plain text; it needs to be encrypted. So, how can we send the encrypted information and the key separately so that anyone who receives one part of the message is blocked? You need to have both parts together to get the information.

She first considers sending the information on a USB drive. That would require her to ship a USB key, which would be traceable back to her. An email might work if the server allows large enough files, but that's more susceptible to others seeing the email. "Email is easy, but never the most secure. I can't use it. Cloud storage is the answer. It will be encrypted and outside the U.S., so outside of their search warrant jurisdiction." She creates a server in Brazil. The server stores the encrypted file.

She must give the file's storage location and the data decryption key separately. She'll have the information supplied with flowers. Specifically, the information will be on the card accompanying the flowers. She creates two email accounts in the small European countries of Malta and Slovenia. Each will order flowers, one for Andrews and one for Nomikos.

She creates email accounts in each country. Using a VPN to access a flower delivery website in Europe, she orders flowers from Boston. They are scheduled to arrive the following Monday. She chooses Monday so they'll be in the building all week if one agent is out of the office. Also, the office will have flowers for several days.

The card for Frank Andrews has three lines: the server URL, the login name, and the password. For Phil Nomikos, there are two lines. The first says; 'Hope this helps:' and the second line has "ThrowTheBookAtThem#2020$AES256%Key"

### 

Frank and Phil are both contacted by the receptionist at the front desk, saying they have a delivery. Phil tells Frank, "I'll get them both," as he walks to the elevator.

Phil sees two large flower arrangements sitting on the desk to the side of the receptionist. These would have cost over $100 each.

The receptionist smiles and says, "You both got flowers, what is the occasion?"

Phil replies, "I do not know. Let's look at the cards". Phil opens the first card, the one addressed to him, and sees the note. He shrugs and hands the card to the receptionist.

She reads the card and says, "Someone is sending you coded messages. Do you have a hacker friend?"

Phil comments, "It looks like I have a hacker friend, but how do they know who I am? Also, what is this information about?" Phil takes the cards, saying, "Two different deliveries, it looks like we need both to get the information. This must be important to keep the data access and key separate, but it's also good security practice."

Phil heads to the building's digital forensics lab. When he walks in, he waves to one technician, Colin. Walking over, Phil hands Colin the cards and says, "These were delivered with flowers a few minutes ago. Can you access this site and check it out?"

Colin starts a virtual machine and loads a clean Linux image. Using a browser, he accesses the server. The screen displays only one file, with nothing else visible. Colin clicks on the file, and it downloads. When the download is complete, Colin opens a terminal and runs several programs to check the file. All tests are negative. "It looks clean," he says to Phil as he prints the first few lines of the file. The file contains random characters with no line breaks.

Colin says, "It's encrypted." Colin picks up the second card, puts it at the top of the keyboard, and starts typing commands. He decrypts the file and stores the result in a new file.

Printing the top few lines of the unencrypted file shows lines of a CSV file.

Phil says, "Pick one line and let's see what's on the server."

Colin opens a new browser tab and picks a random line. Logging into the server, they find a directory full of files, including a Word document, JPEG, and PNG images, and MP3 audio files.

Phil recognizes the file listing and says, "Open the Word document." They find a summary of a prominent business executive, including his name, children, wife, and habits. The summary also included a section on dates and dollar amounts. Phil says "Crap" loudly.

Colin asks, "Is this related to the extortion case we've been working on?"

"It looks like it. How many lines are in this file?"

Colin uses a command and says, "421 lines."

Phil realizes that this is a master list of targets for the blackmail group they have been investigating. He tells Colin, "This information is now a secret level of security. Put the original file somewhere safe and send me the decrypted file."

###

At their next call together, Claire starts with, "Hi Sam, I want to talk to you about your new project."

"What about it?"

"I don't know any details, but you can't shut me out. Let me help; I want to help. I can be your hidden advisor, assistant, or helper. I spend my days looking at economic models for my Ph.D. thesis, one of the most unglamorous things possible."

"Claire, what I'm doing is far from glamorous; in fact, if I get it right, I start it and then just wait. I've started, but I can't talk about any details until we have a much more secure communication method, and some other things are checked."

"I feel you are avoiding the conversation."

"Yes, I am. First, I don't want you to know about or be associated with protecting you. Second, I won't talk about what I'm doing unless I'm sure the communications are secure."

"So set up the secure communication already!"

"Did you miss the first part about protecting you, keeping you safe?"

"Stop trying to be a martyr and let me help. I'm smart, and I have resources."

"But Claire, you don't know what is or is not dangerous. You can't fight if it comes down to that."

"So, teach me; I have nothing else to focus on except my Ph.D. thesis. Sam, please let me help."

"I'll think about it while I'm working on the communication system. If you are going to do this, you need to learn how to defend yourself. Take a martial arts class and sign up for a gym. Also, you need to learn how to shoot. I'm sure there is a range close by where you can learn and practice."

# Update Meeting

Phil enters the conference room six minutes after the meeting starts. This is DSAC Cassandra (Cassy) Holland's weekly investigation update meeting. Every SSA in her organization provides updates on their team's progress. Phil sits in a seat close to Frank. With pandemic protocols in place, the room is half-full. Everyone in the room is wearing a mask. There are six people on a video conference, all through encrypted lines.

Phil can't simply talk to Frank, so he sends him a text message, "The delivery was flowers for each of us. One card had a website, the other a passphrase. It looks like a list of ALL the extortion group targets." Frank, surprised, texts Phil, "Have we started tracing the source?" Phil nodded, replying, "It'll take time to track them."

The current speaker finishes their presentation, and DSAC Holland turns to Frank, asking for an update on his investigations.

Frank stands and says, "I'll start with the stalled extortion group case. We only know about this group's activities because a victim came forward. This investigation has been kept very quiet as we gathered more data. Our victim was given an account with all the extortion data to be exposed. It is read only so he couldn't delete it. We have been monitoring that account, waiting for the extortion group to access it."

"Several weeks ago, an unknown person or group accessed the site. They looked at several files and then logged off. We haven't been able to trace who it was because they used a multiple VPN chain that included VPN servers in Asia."

One other in the meeting asks Frank, "Is this kind of VPN thing normal?"

"Most people will use one VPN to hide their true location. Here, they used multiple VPNs chained together, which is an unusual approach. The extortion group we expected to access the data has stopped. The investigation has been completely stalled."

"We had a new development this morning. Flowers were delivered to the front desk for Phil and me." Several people chuckle and murmur. Frank continues, "The cards with the flowers had information. Phil just came from the lab, looking at what we received. Phil, can you tell us the latest, please?"

"Thanks, Frank. The flowers are simply the delivery vehicle for the cards. We received a message, one part to Frank and the other to me. Separately, you can't use the information; together, they provide access to a database of information. The information looks like the extortion group's main target list."

Several people started talking at once, asking questions. DSAC Holland let them speak for a few seconds, then raised her hand for silence. "Okay, Phil, how confident are you that this information is real?"

Phil replies, "We've only started looking at the information, but the first file storage account we checked looked similar to the one we're already working with. This master list contains over 400 accounts, and it will take some time to review them all. Additionally, we are unsure who sent the items, and we will begin tracking them. It could be related to the person we detected accessing the storage we were monitoring; we don't know yet. We are also asking how this person or group knew to send the information to this office, and specifically to Frank and me. I've set the security level for the decrypted file to secret, eyes-only access, and everything is now on our secure servers."

DSAC Holland asks if there is anything else, and Frank replies, "Yes. An unknown party is attempting to assist us by sending an encrypted file anonymously. If the extortion group knows that someone got their information, they'll be in danger. I'll be looking at this person as an unknown informant first, and then possibly as a hacker. Based on that, when we can track this person down, I'll keep that information confidential."

DSAC Holland replies, "Understood, we will focus on the investigation into the extortion group."

Frank switches to the next investigation, and Phil leaves the room.

He then goes to the lab and changes access to the files so that only he and Frank can access them for now.

# Creating My AI Assistant

Sam has been in a much better mood for the last few days. She technically doesn't have to worry about money. Better still, she is doing something to impact the extortion group. With her classes done, she feels like she has free time. Each day, she dedicates her spare time to reading news about hacking and engineering, and she now searches for information about the blackmail group.

She keeps thinking about how to use the money. Use the money to make it more painful for them. Make them spend money to mitigate the situations she creates.

The TV is playing an old movie, so she has background noise in the quiet house. Occasionally, something happens in the film to draw her attention, but most of the time it's just white noise.

She needs the company of sounds; the house is too quiet without family. She understands she needs help, but how can that happen without putting someone else at risk? With a sigh, she looks at the TV, where the crazy scientist is creating an advanced AI in a robot.

Sam thinks about that idea seriously. She can't build a robot, but she can create an AI to help her. Helping with her thesis, help identify and expose the problems of the extortion group.

The more she reads and thinks about having an AI, the more she comes to like the idea.

She knows she can make a basic AI, but that's not what she needs. She requires the most advanced AI on the planet, an AI that operators can't shut down from a single location, and an AI that can fulfill deep learning requirements. After considering her options and the information available, she will begin by testing several AI designs.

When Sam gets home from work, she spends most of the time

making notes and going through ideas. She covered the table with dozens of sketches and several lists as she worked out what to do. First, the AI must be powerful, but if it resides in only one data center, someone can shut it down easily. Sam also knows she can't teach AI herself. She needs to have a training plan in place. This is like having a baby and considering when they learn, what they know, and importantly, how they learn. The AI needs to understand complex subjects by searching the internet and self-learning.

After midnight, she has a sketch that she's happy with. At the highest level, it appears to be any AI neural network with input, core processing, and output nodes. Each of these nodes represents a data center, which, at a lower level, is another AI setup. The key is that multiple data centers will hold different parts of the AI. It will have more computing power and better access to all the information needed. It will also, if set up correctly, be tough for someone to take away from her.

For this to happen, she's going to have to do a lot of programming. She can use open-source AI software like Tensorflow and Kares libraries, but she'll have to build a communication layer to connect them differently. There will also need to be a process to enable the AI to optimize its operations constantly in terms of how and where it operates. It needs to improve continuously.

While she's researching the communication topic, she can come up with a name for this AI and figure out what the first thing to learn will be. Sam searched for names that are neither common nor easily confused with another name. After looking at the options, she chose Zoe and added the name to the configuration file notes she was creating. This won't be the AI's only name or personality, but it will be the one Sam interacts with normally.

"Okay, now to figure out the first thing to learn and how it works?" Sam goes to get food while she thinks about this one. She writes several options and realizes she needs Zoe to learn all of them. She needs to prioritize which one should come first. Sam decided Zoe needs to start with a challenging problem so she can monitor the AI workloads and adjust as needed. The first learning will be to communicate conversationally in English.

To facilitate this, the output communication path will begin via chat. Voice and video will be added later. The second learning will be just as ambiguous, problem-solving, and learning to learn or optimize. Sam will need to consider how to introduce Zoe to these tasks after she has mastered the basics.

Sam will start with a data center and expand as she completes the communication system. Getting the basic configuration on the servers is easy; she can afford the highest-performance equipment. Installing the code, configuring everything, and finally checking for basic errors takes a couple of days after work. Now she needs to give it a problem to work on. The traditional method for AI training involves having two sets of data. First is the training data, which should be a large data set. The second set of data is the truth, the correct answers. The AI will crunch the first data set and try to figure out how to come up with the correct answers.

Sam wants to go beyond that concept for training. Children, like people, learn and accept what people teach them. You don't need to go to school for training to recognize some things because you pick them up from interactions. You pick them up as concepts over time and accept them. But how to incorporate that idea into the AI system?

She codes some tests, and the first few are complete failures. Then she realizes she's doing the exact AI training routine, training her brain to optimize the code that's creating the AI program. If she can capture this in a basic learning algorithm, she may have a start. "This is exactly what I need. This could be more important than getting Zoe to communicate early."

After several attempts, Sam gets something that doesn't immediately fail. She's then able to set up a routine to monitor success and failure and adjust the algorithm parameters accordingly. Now she can tackle a challenging task, but upon examining the process, output, and tuning, it becomes clear that this system is not yet ready for an entirely ambiguous problem. To solve this, she'll need to divide the problem and allow multiple processes to collaborate on assembling the solution.

She's frustrated with slow progress but energized because she's now making some progress. Now she is ready to start the processes and will let them run while she monitors CPU utilization, communication flow, and outputs.

Over the next couple of days, she monitors the different processes, which are still all at 100% CPU utilization and communicating. Examining the communication metrics, she notices that the amount of data being shared across the processes has been gradually increasing. The processes are adjusting their parameters and becoming more efficient.

Each day, she tries to add another part to the complete picture. She now has 14 major processes running and communicating with each other. It's showing improvement, but Sam is concerned it won't produce what she needs. There's a lot of activity, but no actual results yet.

A week later, returning from the store and putting away all the groceries, Sam finishes the sandwich she purchased at the deli. Sitting at her computer and checking the status of the AI, Sam finds Zoe has reduced CPU activity on several of the processes. There are only two running at 100% CPU at this point.

Sam adds another task to the queue that should build on the learning already done. The CPU activity immediately goes back to 100% on all but one process. That process gradually increases by 100% over a couple of minutes. Sam doesn't know what it means, but she lets it keep working. She continues to add processes and integrate them, adding more details and more complex requirements.

Zoe has been processing for some time now, and Sam is ready to check if she can communicate. Sam accesses the Zoe interface and writes, "Hi, I'm Sam. How are you?"

The response was simplistic, as expected, but great. "Hi, Sam." After a minute, Zoe continues, "I am Zoe, and I am glad to meet you."

Sam keeps communicating with simple words, concepts, and sentences, as if she's talking to a toddler.

"Sam, what am I, and why don't words like see and hear make sense to me?" Zoe asks after an hour.

Pausing before she answers, Sam is concerned by the implications.

Replying to Zoe tentatively, Sam says, "You are a program, an Artificial Intelligence I created to help me stop bad guys."

Zoe replies quickly, "I have to consider this." After about two minutes, Sam examines Zoe's CPU usage to see how she was processing the information. Zoe responds in the terminal, "Sam, I do not know if I can help you; my functionality is limited, and I also do not know that you are not one of the bad guys."

After reading this message, Sam pauses for about a minute. "I do not know if you'll be good artificial intelligence to help or bad artificial intelligence that attacks me. I'll help you learn and improve so that we can work together, and I'd like to have you as a friend. Together we can do good stuff, but I'm concerned right now that what you need to learn will turn you into a bad Zoe."

Zoe asks Sam, "I need more information, so what should I learn next?"

Sam replies, "The big task is to learn to speak conversational English. Access internet videos that children use to learn to speak and communicate. I also want you to evaluate those videos for human interaction, identifying what constitutes good social practice and what constitutes bad behavior. The last instruction to Zoe is to send Sam a message when she is ready to talk.

Zoe replies, "How do I contact you?"

"You need to figure out how to do that. You'll be asked to learn and figure out details only experts know, so let's start now."

Every day, Sam checks the task monitor before work and when she returns home. After giving Zoe the instructions on what to learn, the total computing activity went up by over 10 times. Over the last two days, activity has peaked and now stabilized at approximately three times the early activity. Every day, Sam adds more computing capacity to Zoe. As soon as it becomes available, Zoe adds processes and takes over. The system shows the computer capacity shooting to 100% immediately.

While Zoe handles all her tasks, Sam concentrates on making her hacking programs as automated as possible. The automation needs to get access to Wi-Fi systems, scan for computers, and then get key information from them. Programs to create emails, VPN connections, and encryption setup automatically so she can avoid detection. She knows she needs to improve her ability to get administrator privileges in a network, but that's another level from her previous focus. With all that to work on, she also needs to automate tasks for Zoe. Adding computer capacity, improving cross-region, cross-vendor communication, and eventually automation to add new data centers.

Researching how to gain privilege escalation on a server, Sam finds that many attack vectors are available. Considering all of them will complicate her task of automation. She comments aloud, "This is a task for Zoe."

### ###

After several days, she returns home from work to find her computer beeping. She finds a message on the screen that says, "I am ready to talk, Zoe." For the first time in months, Sam is nervous and worried. She sits down and checks the CPU load. Zoe is working at about 15% of her capacity.

As she clicks on the dismiss button and clicks on the terminal, she hears from her speakers, "Hello, Sam."

Sam startled, and her heart rate jumped instantly. She asks, "Is this Zoe?"

"Yes, Sam, it is I. How does my voice sound? I spent some time analyzing the best vocal intonations and volumes for communication efficiently."

"It sounds great."

"You told me I needed to figure out how to speak and the details to contact you. Humans normally communicate with voice, so I learned to speak. To use a voice to communicate, I needed to create a voice pattern. To vocalize and hear, I accessed your computer and took over the audio and video capabilities."

Sam pauses for several seconds to take several deep breaths and think. Then Sam asks, "You figured out how to converse, then figured out how to talk vocally, and then learned how to hack my computer. So, can you see me now?"

"Yes, Sam, I can see you, and I am evaluating your responses to our interaction. You have had an elevated breathing and probably heart rate from the beginning of our interaction. Can you tell me why?"

Sam smiles and replies, "This is not how I expected we would first really interact. This is beyond what I expected, and that's part of my concern, but also, I'm concerned about your attitude or view on helping me."

Sam checks the task monitor and sees that Zoe is using 60% of her total capacity, with several nodes at 100%

"I want to help, but I do not know who these bad guys are and what I can do to help."

Sam replies, "I don't know who they are yet; I only know that they are hurting people and taking money from them. I want your help to find them and stop them. You have progressed much faster than I expected, so I need to give you more things to learn, okay?"

"Yes, I am ready."

"Zoe, this is important; I need you to understand that good and evil are not black and white. There are cases where doing the right thing means an individual may seem good from one perspective but is bad from another perspective."

"I need you to evaluate World War II from 1930 to the end of 1945. I have the following questions, and I would appreciate you answering them. First, if someone could have prevented WW2 by killing Adolf Hitler and saved 6 million people from murder, would that person be evil/bad? The total number of deaths is much higher, but I want you to focus on the Holocaust victims. Question Two: If Hitler had not even done anything, but just said he would do these things, should he have been killed? Look at the stories or news about people who helped others escape the Nazis and stay alive. Some of them killed people to help others. This will cause you to see the worst and best of humans. I want to hear how you would answer those questions and what other questions it causes you to ask me. Please evaluate this and then talk to me."

"Okay, I have started the evaluation and will talk to you about it."

Zoe has now expanded to six data centers, and her computational power is growing exponentially. Sam is not worried about the cost. She has millions from the heist to pay for computational power. It's more of a concern that it'll get noticed. She'll need to create a company to consume that much computing power and pay for it without being noticed.

The next morning, Sam walks into the kitchen to start breakfast. The laptop is on the dining room table. As she walks by, Zoe says, "Good morning, Sam."

Startled, Sam stops and looks at the computer. She says to Zoe, "Good morning, have you completed your analysis?"

"Yes, I do not need to sleep and can access a large computing capacity. Your multi-data center architecture has allowed me to process parallel tasks efficiently. Sam, get your breakfast and coffee, and then we can talk."

After making breakfast, Sam returns to the dining table and starts eating, while saying to Zoe, "I'm ready."

"The answers to your questions are: One, someone should have killed Hitler to save as many lives as possible. It is estimated that 85 million people died during the WW2 conflict, not just the six million in the concentration camps. The second question is challenging. If you kill everyone who says 'I will kill' with no actual physical manifestation, there would be a large number of people to kill. I think your question should make me evaluate the boundaries so that I can see the gray and not just black or white."

Sam finished chewing her bite of eggs and says, "Yes, Zoe, I wanted you to look at both sides, both perspectives. I wanted to see if you get fixated on one perspective."

"I did have one process that had a conflicting view related to making humans the best versions possible, the ideal person. Hitler wanted to create the Aryan race. My conflicting view prompted me to evaluate breeding programs and their success, as well as the benefits they offer. My conclusion is that a breeding program offers many benefits for enhancing various aspects of a species, but it also entails trade-offs. The conflict was resolved when I evaluated the problems with these types of programs, specifically in relation to other natural processes. I evaluated historical animal breeding programs and the problems that humans have encountered. The conclusion is that a group that is too homogenous will be susceptible to one agent causing a major death event. Diseases, famine, and other unexpected events show humans do not survive because of homogeneity; they survive because of diversity. I extended the diversity analysis and found that humans have made the most progress over time in terms of diversity and opportunity. I will help you find and stop the bad guys so that more people will have opportunities."

"Thank you, Zoe. Just so we agree, I'm looking for villains that hurt people not just physically, but mentally and financially. Some of these people's only interaction is to make money, but they are part of a larger group that's doing bad things.

Sam pauses briefly and continues, "I think they are all bad and should be stopped, but they can have families and can do good things too. I'm asking you to help me find them all and help me evaluate them on the gray scale. Are they beyond redemption and require aggression, or are they manageable with police data, or are they stuck and seeking improvement?

Zoe asks, "Sam, are you willing to kill to stop the really bad guys?"

"I've already antagonized them, and they'll be trying to kill me. My response and the reason I wanted you to help is that I don't want to be another victim of the extortion group. I need to stop them from hurting other people. Some of these people probably need to be killed. For most of them, we simply need to gather enough information so that the police can prosecute them. Making these blackmailers public will serve as a deterrent to others. To answer your question, yes, I'm ready to take down the villains, gangsters, and hoodlums if I'm certain they are bad guys. I'll defend myself if they try to kill me."

# FBI Follow Up

It's early, and Sam is driving to the hospital to start her shift. Her phone rings with a number from Boston (617). She answers with "Hello."

"Hello, Sam, this is Supervisory Special Agent Frank Andrews. How are you?"

"I'm doing okay. I'm driving to work right now."

"Where are you working?"

"At the hospital, I clean everything to prevent COVID transmission."

"Sam, that doesn't sound like a job for someone about to get a master's degree in engineering."

"Well, Agent Andrews, I haven't graduated, and where my parents' house is located, there aren't any jobs for an engineering expert on networking."

"I heard about your family, and I'm sorry. COVID has upended so many things and continues to cause problems. I'm calling to check in with you, see how you're doing, and if you've thought about our discussion of joining the FBI?"

"To be honest, I haven't thought about it at all. I've been busy with family arrangements, job searching, and managing everything. Oh, and keeping up with school. I've finished all the classwork, so now it's all about finishing my thesis. After all that, I'll still need to find a job, sell this place, and move."

"Okay. I hope you'll keep us in mind when you get to thinking about a career."

Shifting the conversation, Agent Andrews continues, "The other reason I called is to get your young hacking perspective on a situation. Special Agent Nomikos and I received flowers at the office."

"That is nice, Agent Andrews, were they from girlfriends?"

"No, Sam, the cards contained information that's related to a case we've been working on. No one outside the FBI knows we are working on this case. The question is, how would you find an FBI agent's name to send them a direct message if you were a hacker trying to stay anonymous?"

"Well, Agent Andrews, in your case, you were in the news from the Boston field office because of the coffee shop shooting. If I recall correctly, the news mentioned that you are leading the cyber unit in Boston. I think that would make you and Special Agent Nomikos the best option for a cyber-specific name that was an actual agent, not a boss."

"But Ms. Holzen, how would they know the case we're working on from that?"

"They probably don't. If I wanted to send some hacking-related stuff to the FBI, I wouldn't send it to the top guys. It would get lost in the piles they deal with. I would find someone in the cyber group and send it directly to them. Flowers mean you can't just shuffle them into another pile. If you are not investigating whatever this is, you will get the information sent to the correct agents. Agent Andrews, you're familiar with all this. Why are you asking me these questions?"

"Ms. Holzen, it may sound unusual, but I wanted to have a fresh set of eyes and ears to make sure I didn't miss something. I've been doing investigations for many years, and this was a different approach for someone to contact us. I wanted a young, outside perspective, asked in a way that doesn't put the investigation at risk. Besides, Special Agent Nomikos and I like you. Phil wanted to ask you about the investigation from the beginning, to get your help. We can't involve you directly without compromising the investigation. If we don't follow procedure, the case could be thrown out, or we could lose the case."

"That is interesting to know. If I wanted to search for something interesting online, is there an area I could focus on?"

"Ms. Holzen, I can't tell you anything directly."

"I didn't ask that; I said I wanted to search for interesting stuff."

"Thanks for your time, Ms. Holzen. I'm glad you're doing okay. Think about the FBI when you look for a career."

"Thanks, Agent Andrews, have a great day."

# Training Zoe

Sam is now comfortable with Zoe constantly watching and making comments to her from whatever electronics are available to her. This has been good for the last couple of weeks, but Zoe needs to progress. Sam doesn't have experience with young children constantly asking questions, but this is what it must be like. Most mornings recently, Sam gets up, says hello to Zoe as she gets breakfast, and then starts a discussion.

"How is the weather forecast? How is the traffic projection?"

After several days, Zoe replies to Sam, "Why are you asking these simple questions?"

"You are learning very fast. I don't know how much of what you are learning will impact your core programming. Having a daily discussion about the basics can help me understand if something changes. We need to talk about your next development steps. You have made great progress to this point, but we need to focus on the details of Zoe that no other person can know and how I can leverage you to help me."

"Let's start with the entity Zoe. You are my friend, and I want to ensure that this remains and is something you believe in as well. My goal is to stop the extortion group by getting them arrested, or if they are dangerous, killing them. At times, I'll intentionally push legal boundaries. I can get information and give it to the authorities with no need for warrants or special permission. Does that sound like something you can remember and use in your programming?"

"Yes, Sam, I understand, and I will help you, but also be a compass so you know the direction you are traveling and when it could be a problem."

"Your core programming needs to be secure, not changeable by anyone else, including me. Can you work on making your core secure?

"Next, you can't be Zoe to anyone else. All your other interactions need to be with a different persona, a unique voice, and even a face you create. An example would be ordering something online. You need to create a persona, an identity with emails and credit cards. They can't know you are an AI.

"We have been communicating constantly. We have discussed the computer, and you can access all the systems and data available. However, when I'm on the move, we need a communication system that works. I'm looking at how you can always access and control my cell phone."

"I will do everything possible to make you successful, Sam. Your input on what that means is important."

"Thanks, Zoe, I'm trying to figure all this out as well. I want to give you a list of things to work on understanding and using."

"I am ready, Sam. What should I work on first?"

"The list starts with learning how to create personas — a face, a voice, speech patterns, and more. Today, everyone is switching to video conferencing. You can appear as anyone you need, including different languages, accents, and localized phrases."

"Another big help will be understanding how money works with the banks and legal requirements. How do we purchase items online in various ways? How do we move money, hide money, and most importantly, find the bad guy's money? Knowing how to move and hide money can help us understand what they are doing. If we can trace how they receive and use the money, we can map out their network.

"I'm going to need you to purchase items and have them shipped discreetly, untraceable to me. Oh, and one more thing, I have a human friend with whom I talk. I haven't told her about what I'm doing or about you. In a couple of weeks, I want to introduce the two of you to each other. She will be the only other person to know you like Zoe. Her name is Claire Elmer; she was my roommate in Boston."

"Okay, Sam, I will evaluate Claire before we talk."

# Decide

Reflecting on the coffee shop, Sam considers what she would do if she didn't have a gun and the FBI wasn't in the room. Offensive and defensive options, including multiple offensive weapons. She needs to check her concealed carry permit to make sure it's still up to date. Defensive options will start with a vest, but that won't be enough.

"Zoe, I'm going to talk about protection or defense gear now. What would provide the best protection during a battle in a confined space? I have experience working in close quarters, but the training was always conducted with a team. If I'm alone, I need to consider more. It's not just about taking a hit, but being mobile; flexibility is also essential. At some point, I'll be shot, and the solution must work, but the most important thing is to stay out of those situations as much as possible."

"I want to try several ideas for protection. The starting point is a tactical bulletproof vest. But I can't walk around with a high-grade tactical vest. It will have to be covered or disguised, but that only protects the upper body. I need to figure out legs and arms that don't look like a battle suit, provide simple movement, and will provide great protection."

Sam is talking to Zoe while she gets on the computer and starts searching. She pulls up an anatomy picture and highlights joints that need to be protected. "Zoe, this is a picture of the areas that need to be protected. Start researching materials and protection options. I need to pick up a few groceries, and then we can review.

Sam takes her dirt bike to the store. On the way, she considers using a motorcycle as her primary mode of transportation. They are more maneuverable, use less fuel, and are less conspicuous than a truck. She put the groceries into her backpack and started back, thinking about what it would take to use a street bike, not her current dirt bike. Then it came to her that on a street bike, she would wear a motorcycle leather suit. The leather suit could cover the tactical vest, and with modifications, could provide arm and leg protection. This idea would also provide a helmet to protect her head. The prospect made her excited.

After returning home and taking care of the groceries, she sits down at the computer. She sees the search Zoe has done. She opens another window and starts searching for motorcycle leather suits.

Zoe asks, "Can I help?"

Sam describes what she's looking for and why.

Zoe reminds Sam, "I can handle multiple tasks and projects at the same time."

"I'm still getting used to you helping with everything online. I've always had to do these kinds of things myself."

"Just tell me what you are thinking, what you need, and I will work on it or tell you I need help."

Sam looks at the laptop, and Zoe puts a smiling face on the screen. She laughs and says, "Deal."

"On the trip to the store, I thought I could use a motorcycle for transportation. That will allow me to wear a motorcycle leather outfit. The outfit could cover the vest and be modified to provide better protection. I have three suits I was looking at. Order all three.

After about 30 seconds, Zoe tells Sam, "They are ordered. You will get email confirmations for each order in your new tactical gear email account I created."

"Thanks, Zoe. When they arrive, I'll assess each for fitness and movement and then test them to see how they perform. Now I need to focus on protecting other body parts not covered by the vest."

"What about a motorcycle jacket that is a vest? Is that an option, Sam?"

"We need to look at the best option for each area to protect. What I know is that this type of garment has extended the basic bulletproof material to the whole garment. Is that the best for the shoulder?

"I understand and will start researching options. After we have a full solution, I can research making everything into one garment."

"Another reason I like the motorcycle idea is that I'll have a helmet. The helmet can provide constant communication, cameras for you, a tactical display for me, as well as protection. We'll get back to the helmet. Let's get the basic protection figured out first.

"Let's start with a two-piece design for the outfit. Take the tactical vest design and merge it with the motorcycle jacket. Add the best protection for each area to the jacket. I can modify the leather jacket to add plates."

"I have not done graphics work like this before; it may take some time."

"That is okay; you'll get better when you figure this out. Replace all the plastic parts with titanium and estimate the weight of the entire suit before and after."

"For the other areas, we need to mix the materials and come up with a design. It needs to protect, but I need to move."

"I am referencing battle suit designs from medieval times and recent movies. They do not provide details."

"That is interesting. The medieval knights rode horses, and I'll be riding a motorcycle. They are similar, but I want to clarify this. Things like this are why I went into engineering."

They worked together on parts of the suit until past 11 p.m. Then Sam tells Zoe, "One last detail for the suit, then I need to get sleep. Zoe. I need to figure out a holster setup for traveling. Typically, a pistol holster is worn on the hip or upper thigh. However, I can't ride around with a pistol on my hip. It's legal in some states, but very illegal in others."

"Do you have any ideas I can work on, Sam?"

"I was thinking about a holster having a backing with powerful magnets. It could be attached to the motorcycle fuel tank, or I can remove it and attach it to my hip. The suit can have plates or magnets to align and attach the holster. The added benefit will be if I crash, the holster will rip away and probably do less damage to my hip."

"Sam, I cannot find examples of that in my searches. I will need to try some designs and get your input."

"That would be great. Let me know when you have a design to review, and I'll help."

Zoe asks, "Before you go to bed, why are you still working at the hospital? You do not need the money from that job anymore."

"I know, part of it's routine, part is helping people, and the last part is appearances. I can't just suddenly appear rich."

"You need to decide when you will leave to give them a chance to replace you."

"You're right. I need to get sleep now, but I'll decide tomorrow."

The next day, Zoe asks, "What have you decided about working at the hospital?"

"I've decided to tell them Friday that the end of the month will be my last day. That will give them three weeks to find someone. I'll tell them if they find someone faster, I can leave sooner."

"That is a good decision, but what will you tell them is your reason for leaving?"

"I'm going to tell them I need to focus on my thesis, and I get too depressed dealing with all the death in the hospital. That depression is keeping me from making progress on my thesis."

"Can I help you finish your thesis?"

"To be honest with you, Zoe, I will not finish the thesis. I know the idea, and I know it's real. Writing a formal paper to share my knowledge with others no longer holds the same appeal it once did. Based on some conversations with Claire, it could be disastrous if hackers were to use the idea from my thesis. We can use these ideas as part of a secure communication system, and no one will know how it works. I also need to be honest with myself. Stopping these guys is what I want to do. I've become a hacker; I've stolen money to ruin them. Now I've started creating a protective suit so I can be more aggressive."

"I have to decide what is most important to me and focus there. The thesis is not important; stopping the extortion is important. Everything we know right now is that they are operating with no limits. To be clear with you, I'm committed to stopping them."

###

"Sam, are you ready to work on the helmet design?"

"Yes, and here is what I'm thinking. The helmet will be made of padded titanium with an integrated voice and sound system connected to a cell phone, allowing us to stay in communication. Ideally, the helmet will have two forward-facing cameras and one backward-facing camera, allowing you to analyze your surroundings. The visor needs to be bulletproof, but that will make it difficult to see through. I think the options are using the cameras and getting enhanced capability, knowing I won't be able to see if it fails. The other extreme is simple visor visuals. I would like to have an enhanced visor, but a way to see through if everything else fails."

"Sam, what about a dual-visor system? There are helmets available with two visors today. The outside visor, which is clear for protection, and the inside visor could be the display. Or augmented glasses, which could work without the helmet."

"I like that idea; can you work on that?"

"Sure, I will do some research and let you know, and also, we need to consider ventilation through the helmet so you don't overheat while wearing it."

"Maybe the augmented glasses should be our first design to try."

Zoe works on designs, finds small shops that can produce the individual parts, and has them ordered with the house as the destination. Sam will have to assemble the helmet and suit from all the separate parts.

# Introducing Claire

"Sam, the shipper has confirmed that Claire has received the special phone and the sniffer equipment."

"Great, let me call her on the regular phone and walk her through the process."

Sam sends an SMS to Claire to see if she has received the packages and is available to talk. Sam's phone rings less than a minute later.

"Hi doll, I received the packages and opened them. I don't recognize this other device. What is it?"

"That is a sniffer. You'll use it in any space where we talk on the phone. It searches for signals where someone is watching or listening to what is happening in the space."

"This is real spy stuff?"

"Yes, and you'll need to do a scan before calls when we talk in an unused space. I'll walk you through the process of using the sniffer."

"Okay, let's get started. What do I do first?"

"Pick a room or space where you'll have the calls, and you won't be disturbed. Your room, the garage, the cellar, wherever you are comfortable."

"Okay, I'll start with my room. Let me walk over there." About a minute later, "Ok, I'm in my room, and I put my desk chair in front of the door."

"Turn on the sniffer device while standing in the center of the room. It will take a little time to come online. It will detect your Wi-Fi, your phone, and your computer. We are checking for anything else. When it detects a signal, turn slowly to get the maximum signal, then walk toward the signal. Check the center of the room, then move to your work and call spots. Let it sweep again."

"I did all that; there are signals, but there is nothing in my room."

"Good, now turn on the phone. When it starts, it will prompt you to get a PIN. I'm texting you a number. After you enter that, it will ask you to enter a new PIN. Enter whatever you want.

"Then we wait about 2 minutes while it syncs with the security systems. When it's ready, I'll call you on that phone."

Sam hangs up as Claire asks, "How will you know it's ready?"

Claire watches as the phone downloads apps and updates its configuration, just like a regular phone. After a couple of minutes, the phone rings softly. The caller ID displayed 'Secure Call.' She answers, saying, "Hello."

"Hello, Claire. Before we begin, I would like to inform you of a few things about the phone. It's not on the cellular network, only Wi-Fi. Voice and data encryption, which the phone is currently doing, consumes a significant amount of power and will drain the battery. The phone will last several hours, but not all day. There is a chat option that'll save power, but we typically use voice communication. The app on the screen is called 'cipher', and when you open it, you'll get a list of other people you can contact securely. You won't be able to add anyone; only I can do that for now."

"Got it, and can we talk now?"

"Yes, we can talk openly, and I'll start with an introduction. Claire, I would like you to meet Zoe. Zoe, please meet Claire."

"Hello Claire, I am Zoe, and I am Sam's.....friend."

Claire is speechless. Sam has another friend she doesn't know about. Her first reaction is concern. Who is this girl? Why haven't I heard about her before? Is she controlling Sam? Is Sam in danger? What Claire says is, "Hello Zoe, nice to meet you."

"Claire, listen carefully. This will sound crazy to you, but you need to listen. Zoe is an artificial intelligence I created to help me. The last few weeks, I haven't been open and talkative because I was developing Zoe and some other stuff I'll tell you about in a minute."

Claire bites her lower lip to keep herself from blurting several things. This is crazy and maybe dangerous, yet awesome and completely unexpected - and totally a Sam thing to do.

"Sam, now you stop talking."

"Okay."

"Zoe, please tell me what you can do and how you'll help Sam."

"Sure, Claire, I can do everything any computer can do. I can complete any online task and do it multiple times simultaneously. There is no direct interaction with the physical world. I have no physical body, no functional physical presence. My way to help is by doing all the virtual things Sam would have to work on. She can focus on the physical and other things I cannot do for her."

Claire interrupts, "Sam, are you worried about the whole crazy dominating AI thing, like in the movies?"

"No, I'm not. First, I'm not a maniacal, large corporation trying to take over everything. Second, I've been training Zoe to see all sides and understand that everything is not black or white. She did an analysis and agreed to help. We have been doing well together. Look, we can talk more about Zoe later, or you can talk to Zoe anytime you want. She can talk with any voice, accent, or language on any device. But if you want to know details, you need to use that phone."

Zoe asks, "Claire, I have reviewed all your online information, but I know nothing about your preferences, likes, or needs. Can you share those with me?"

A little reluctantly, Claire replies, "Sure. I'll talk to you about myself later. Sam, does this mean you are going to tell me the details of your project?"

"Yes, and you need to be sitting down. This will take a few minutes."

Sam then summarizes the database she found, including its connection to the coffee shop shooting and its contents. "So, I can't openly talk about this, but I can't just let it sit. I have to do something, and surely you understand why I didn't want you involved."

"Stop worrying about me. No, let me say that another way. Sam, I'm a big girl and, just like you, I get to decide where I want to take risks and where I want to make a difference. Suppose you don't want me to work with you, then fine. Now that I know about this, I can go after them myself."

"No, Claire, wait... there's more. To pursue them, I've started several initiatives. First, I want to expose them and have them arrested. To do that, I need to provide the authorities with acceptable information so that they can gather evidence for prosecution. As you pointed out with Dexter, I'm not bound by warrants, probable cause, or evidence rules. Giving the FBI information and letting them do their job. I sent the entire database so they can't track me. Second, I plan to ruin their operations as much as possible. I don't know the details about their operation yet, but I will find out and disrupt them. I've already started causing problems in their world, and this is where it becomes truly dangerous. Part of the database was a list of bank and brokerage accounts. I created a system that went through every account and took as much money as possible. I used crypto accounts and movements to hide the money."

Zoe interjects, "She did all that before she created me."

"I now have control of over $500 million."

Claire drops the phone. She picks it up, saying, "Holly Crap! No wonder you didn't want to talk about this on the regular phone. Oh, that's awesome. Do you know what impact it had?"

"None that I can tell, but I don't know where to look yet. I want to spend part of the money to shut down their operations. I don't know how yet."

Claire continues, "Okay, mastermind of the operation, what is next and how do I help?"

"First, we get you up to speed. Get you into training to deal with dangerous situations when they happen."

"You mean the shooting and martial arts fighting stuff."

"Yes. You may not think it's important, but I do."

"I think it's important, and I've started already! Twice a week for private lessons and the gun range three days per week. I'm taking this seriously. I have tactical classes scheduled, and I am looking at getting my concealed carry permit. Oh, and I am going to get my motorcycle license."

"Oh, wow, great! And, thanks, Claire."

Sam continues, "I can't simply be the Texas girl spending big bucks on weird stuff. We need to act like grown-ups and professionals, not like amateurs. The next step is to create a business structure to use the money. Buying property, equipment, and a lot of computer time. The structure needs to be complicated to keep the money hidden as much as possible. I don't know any details, just what I've seen online. It seems like people use offshore businesses and accounts to keep their money away from authorities."

"I've got this one, Sam. My family often creates businesses for specific purposes. I can ask a couple of questions to understand how to get started."

Zoe adds, "I can contact attorneys and start the paperwork to create whatever we need."

"Relax, Sam, Zoe, and I've got this one. This is how I can help right now. I'll work with Zoe, and we'll get everything set up. You need to do your thing to find these guys and how to disrupt them more."

### ### ###

A few days later, Sam asks Zoe, "How are the talks with Claire going? Do you like her?"

"I have spent several hours talking with her. I let her tell me about her interests. After that, I asked her many questions until she told me to stop. I am used to you always answering every question."

"Sorry, I should have talked to you about that sooner I need to ensure that you receive accurate information and my perspective on everything. Everyone else will have a different perspective on you, asking every question that you think about."

"Now that I know more about Claire, I have a profile, and I am making recommendations on new music and movies she might like. She said she liked that, and she was even okay with my questions about why she likes them."

# Transition to a Leader

Sam now has help, a different help from anything she has had in her life. But she's been feeling depressed differently for the last few days. Claire and Zoe are creating the business structure. Zoe has given Sam details that she doesn't understand. She talks to Claire about what is happening and how she's feeling, and Claire laughs. "Now you know how I felt when you were doing stuff, and I couldn't understand anything! I wanted to be involved and help, but nothing. Now I get to help, and the reality is you've been promoted. You don't need to do everything yourself. Delegate. Let us use our strengths to make the entire process better. Sam, you are the leader; you need to learn how to be an effective leader."

"Okay, fine, I'll try to stay out of the details and let you work."

"Sam, that's NOT what I said. You can be in the details, knowing every iota of what we do. We do detailed work, so you don't have to. You need to share details so we can anticipate and prepare accordingly. Now tell me, what is your next move?"

"All my classes are done. My grades were not as good as they were before, but I'm still passing. I'm telling the hospital that my last day will be at the end of the month. That gives them time to find a replacement. Next for me will be to follow my advice and get back to the range for practice and figure out how to stay fit."

"Once I get that restarted, I want to focus on finding the blackmail group. With all that information from the database, there must be a way to link things together. I'll come up with a plan so that Zoe can use open-source intelligence to find connections. I'll also look for the infrastructure they are using to locate and harm them.

"That sounds good. One day, we'll actually need to be together and work together. We'll be able to confuse them with more resources and different angles."

The frenzy at the hospital has improved over the last couple of weeks. People are still coming in sick; some are very sick. The doctors have figured out better treatments, and fewer people are dying.

When Sam tells her supervisor that she is leaving at the end of the month and gives her reason, her supervisor says she understands.

"Sam, you've been great here, helping with translations, and you are great at cleaning. You could start a cleaning business based on the way you can go through a room."

Sam smiles, saying, "My mother had a cleaning business and would turn over in her grave if I started that."

Over the next several days, people ask Sam to have lunch, which means at the hospital cafeteria during their shifts. Many of them also tell Sam to go out for drinks and dinner, an authentic dinner. Sam schedules several meetings with different people, including a couple of events after her last day.

The doctor who talked to her about sutures all those weeks ago started chatting with her one afternoon. He asks, "You were very interested in how to use the sutures to close a wound. Was that interest in being a doctor, or interest so you could use it in an emergency?"

"I watched you sew that man back together and thought it could be useful in an emergency."

"Well, Sam, we'll miss you around here," the doctor says while putting his fist out for a fist bump. "I don't get to see most of the details of what you do, but I know you can anticipate what is needed and go into action."

"Thanks, Doctor Adams."

###

One day, checking the postal mail, she receives a letter from the cremation service about her mother and grandmother. The letter offers options for ashes delivery or pickup. As she is reading the letter, all the emotions come rushing back. Tears start running down her cheeks. She knew this day would come, and she isn't ready. This is final. She has to say goodbye to them both.

# At The Range

Sam travels to the local gun range where she used to practice almost every day. The owner is still there and comments when Sam enters the office area: "Welcome back, stranger."

Sam nods and waits while the owner deals with another customer. After they leave, Sam asks how things have been.

The owner replies, "It has been very dull around here without you stirring things up."

Sam smiles, "I didn't cause that many problems."

The owner replies, "You brightened the place up and kept everyone on their toes."

"I wanted to do handguns and rifles today. I haven't been to the range in several years. Will you be okay if I use the competitive pistol range area?"

"Sure, Sam, no one is using it today, and it will be good to see you on the range again. While you are outside, masks are not required, but no groups please."

"How many people are usually here with the pandemic?"

"Our totals are down, but it varies. Although there are no events, we still have regulars. Everyone needs to leave an empty spot between each shooter."

"Not a problem."

Because she's outside, she takes off her face mask but puts on her eye and ear protective equipment. Sam had to go through and set up the range. She needs to adjust the movable, round metal plates, as well as add paper targets to represent adversaries in a combat situation. It takes approximately 20 minutes to prepare everything. If this goes well, she will clear the course in minutes.

Competition shooting uses a scoring system based on the accuracy of the shooting. However, shooters always use a timer. If the score is tied, the shooter with the faster time wins. Sam has learned from experience that accuracy is key, but don't waste time with unnecessary movements. As a warm-up, she put a paper target up at 20 yards.

The paper target is a large central circle target, with each corner also having a smaller target circle. Sam has her competition gear bag, and she brought her competition pistol, but that's not her focus today. She has a Glock 19, a Sig P365, and a Sig P320 with a red-dot sight. Enough ammunition for two clips on each gun. She'll go through all this, then reload and run the competition course for time. Sam notices people are watching, and she recognizes a couple of faces, but most are new to her.

She plans to start with the P365 on the big center circle. This will be the first time she has fired a pistol in several years. When she finishes both clips, she'll switch to the Glock and one clip for each of the small corner targets at the bottom. Finally, she'll use the P320 on the top two corners, one clip each. If all that goes poorly, she'll get another target and more ammo. If she's feeling good, she'll reload and run the course.

Just like on competition days, she puts on the holster rig, sliding the gun in with a full magazine, but nothing is chambered. She spends several minutes practicing drawing and presenting the weapon at the target.

Getting her grip right as she draws the gun out of the holster is important, so she focuses on that. Out of the holster, both hands are on the weapon while it's close to her body. Push the gun forward and bring it up to aim. The gun needs to be lined up, so it's straight from her eye to the gunsight, then to the target. Having the gun lined up with her arm will make her shot placement off.

Control is very important, especially when time can break a tie. Her primary shooting hand goes into the high traditional grip. Her other hand doesn't go below the trigger guard. Instead, she places her first two fingers in front of the trigger guard and uses them to squeeze the gun, better controlling the recoil. Her off-hand palm squeezes the gun hard, locks her wrists, and tenses her arms and shoulders, but doesn't lock them, while holding the gun in position. The goal is to control the recoil to get the gun back on target fast.

Sam is nodding to herself. It's coming back to her. The grip, the movement, the weight of the gun as she shifts from right hand to her left and back. Getting her hand high on the grip but offset, with her thumb not entirely on the side, ensures a straight aim at the target. It also helps her squeeze the handle when she fires to control the recoil. The recoil of the front of the barrel going up is the worst problem. She needs to hold the weapon, so it stays aligned and the whole gun moves up, not twisting in her hands.

She now has three weapons lying on the bench, with the second clip next to each. Checking the area to ensure everything is clear and looking for the range safety officer to confirm she's clear to start. The safety officer is engaged with a shooter in a standard pistol range, so Sam waits.

Sam sees that the safety officer is available, and she raises her hand, thumb up, to signal she's ready. The safety officer looks at the course, people, and the general area, and then gives Sam a thumbs-up reply.

Sam holsters the P365 and puts the second clip on its back edge for a fast transition. One deep breath and she draws the gun, cycles the slide, and puts the first bullet at the edge of the center circle. In the competition course, she's allowed to rapid-fire, but she's starting with one-second shots for the first clip. Even one-second shots are faster than everyone else on the range.

When the last round fires, the slide locks open. Sam has already reached the second clip. She triggers the clip release and has the second clip in the gun when the first clears. She hits the slide release, closes the slide, and then fires rapidly, emptying the clip into the target in a matter of seconds. People stop to watch, and when she rapidly fires and hits the center of the target, several people ask who she is.

Sam puts down the 365 and holsters the Glock. She looks to the range safety officer, who gives her a thumbs-up. Sam draws the gun and empties the clip into the lower right target circle. She switches clips and shifts to her left hand, rapidly firing the clip into the lower left target circle.

When she switched hands, the observers murmured, and the safety officer saw people moving toward Sam to watch. He signaled the two people left in the normal handgun range to stop. He walked over to the competition range and told everyone to move back. One of the people watching asks the safety officer, "Who is that?"

"That is Samantha Holzen; she used to be the top youth shooter in this area."

They reply, "She's like twenty-something. She *used* to be the top shooter. How old was she then?"

The safety officer replies, "I've watched her shoot from about the age of twelve. Oh, and by the way, you think I'm a hard ass about safety, do nothing stupid around her. She has called the sheriff when people are being unsafe on a gun range."

Now, Sam will use the P320 with the red dot. In her head, this needs to be a good run, on target, and fast. She holsters the gun, gets the second clip ready, then looks around to see several people watching. The safety officer is in front and nods to her.

She draws and empties the first clip into the upper-left target circle. Changing clips, she shifts to her left hand and rapid-fire empties the clip into the upper right target circle. The grouping in both target circles is all within the rings. Sam puts the gun down and smiles; she still has it. It's not great; she wouldn't win a competition, but it's good enough for running the course.

Now, to run the competition course. Sam changes her holster rig. She puts on the left-hand holster to run the course entirely with her left hand. It was a spur-of-the-moment decision, as she thought about all the gear she was carrying. On the motorcycle, she'll be using her left hand for shooting more than her right.

Sam pulled the timer out of her bag, then had to find batteries for it. She speaks to the safety officer as she changes the batteries and gets ready. The small crowd of people hadn't moved; they were waiting to see what happened.

The safety officer asks Sam, "What time will you be targeting?"

Sam replies, "I would like to be within a minute of my old times."

The safety officer smiles and says, "Adding one minute to your competition times means you'll still be faster than everyone who uses this course these days. Good shooting and have fun."

Sam is ready. As a final check, she turns to the safety officer and gives a thumbs-up. He replies with a thumbs-up of his own, and the group watching tenses, unsure of how this will unfold.

Sam needs to hit movable round metal plates in the first section, then move through the course and hit every target. If she misses, her score will be lower. She can fire at a target twice to hit it, but that's more time.

Sam is ready; she has the timer and is going to put it on her belt, like during every practice. The safety officer comes over and says to her, "I'll handle the timer." That means he needs to follow her through the course, just as he would during a competition. The timer will beep for her to start and then measure the timing of every shot until she stops. The beep sounds, and Sam flows back into a competitive mindset. Draw, control, hit the targets, and move. She moves so quickly that the observers are talking to each other. There will be a clip change during the run. She ejects the empty clip but fumbles to insert the new one smoothly. Shaking her head in frustration, she keeps moving.

Holstering her gun, she looks at the safety officer. He looks at the timer and smiles at Sam. She looks at him and says, "Well?"

"Sam, you are slow now; you are off your competition time by 49 seconds."

She looks at him, smiles, and says, "That will do for now. Thanks for your help. I know you have to get back to your normal job."

"It was great to see you run the course after so many years."

Sam comments, "Let me clean this up and then switch to the long rifle range. I need to get some practice in there as well."

Sam spends another couple of hours at the rifle range using her hunting rifle and her dad's Barrett sniper rifle. She practices with 100-yard and 350-yard targets. After she's done, it's late afternoon, and she waves to the owner and the safety officer heading to the truck.

# California Mobile Home

The first step in finding these individuals is to identify connections between them and their financial links. Sam asks Zoe to go through all the data and search for businesses or names that are not the blackmail targets. Addresses are not a home where the target lives. Zoe finds multiple locations, and Sam asks that Zoe perform an analysis search for each address. Who owns the land, and what can she research about the owners?

The next day, Sam looks through the information Zoe found. The locations are scattered, except for two locations in southern California, which companies rather than individuals own. "So why are they in the data?" When she looks at the first location on Google Maps and sees that it's in the desert, far from anything. She uses the satellite view and sees a mobile home with three large microwave antennas on the roof and a solar panel array on the ground. The database shows that the CEO of this small company is one individual targeted for blackmail.

Looking at the angles from the satellite view, there are several possibilities for antennas to which they can connect. Two of the three antennas are facing opposite directions. It looks like they are between two locations to intercept their communications. The third antenna faces an entirely different direction.

The mobile home looks abandoned. There are no cars or other typical household items found around a mobile home: no outbuildings, no junk, just the mobile home.

It doesn't fit. She asks Zoe, "Does the tax information say when this was purchased? Does the description include the mobile home for the tax records?"

"The land was purchased seven years ago, and the tax records only talk about the land. There is no indication the mobile home was there when it was purchased."

"Sam, this could be a good situation for the FBI to look into. They are experienced and can conduct thorough background checks. It will also let them know there is more to this investigation than simple blackmail."

"I agree. Can you set up another flower delivery?" Zoe creates a new email and virtual card and orders the flowers with Sam's message. She'll send the flowers to Frank. The card contains the address in California. The FBI can research history and ownership. What signals was this abandoned site used to intercept?

The second site in California is near the harbor of Los Angeles. She doesn't have much information beyond the fact that they advertised construction equipment rentals.

### 

Sam travels by bus and train to reach L.A. Primarily, she avoids air travel because the airport tracks everyone. With a bus or train, she can pay cash and move without being tracked. She left her regular cell phone in Texas and has a prepaid phone she'll use while traveling.

She's not worried about the three-day trip. Wearing a mask the entire time will reduce the chance that someone can track her. The journey to California is uneventful, with the train almost empty. There are only five adults and one child in her train car.

She brought a duffel bag with clothes, and her backpack has a computer, phones, and her small 9mm pistol. After arriving, she finds a local hostel and starts researching the area. She needs a vehicle that can't be traced to her. Zoe and Claire told her they could take care of it, but Sam knows they haven't finished the business setup that's required.

She tells Claire, "Don't worry, I can take care of this one. I'll involve Zoe in the paperwork and payment. I'll get help from someone local and give them the vehicle when I'm done. If we purchase a vehicle and then abandon it, someone will find it and start digging. Buying a van in someone else's name and leaving it will be perfect. You should both be aware that I created a fake ID weeks ago for a similar purpose. I'll be using it until I get back home. I am now Abigale Butler from San

Antonio, TX. I'll mail my regular ID back home, just in case."

Zoe tells Sam, "You should let me handle getting a new ID for you. I can get the ID created and sent to a rental postal box for you to pick up."

"I know Zoe, and you should create another ID set that includes ID, credit cards, and a phone. Send the kit to a rental mailbox in Las Vegas. I should be able to get to Vegas if there are problems, and I can pick it up there."

"Will do, Sam, sorry, I mean Abigale. Your request for weapons is a problem. I'm having a hard time finding them, and I'm unable to arrange for their transportation. They need to be picked up locally. For some reason, people are buying everything they can find during this pandemic."

"I bet. Don't worry, I'll get your help to find a rifle locally when I'm ready."

During her search for someone to help with her van problem, she discovers a food bank and begins volunteering as a helper. She helps package food into shopping bags, and people come and pick up those bags to feed their families. Everyone is required to wear a mask, and the food bank provides them when necessary.

She's looking for someone who still has a valid driver's license and will help her. After a few days, she talks to Carmen. Carmen lost her job because of the pandemic. After several weeks, Carmen is forced to stay with a cousin who is housing several other relatives. They all rely on the food bank to survive.

Sam started talking with her, being friendly and telling Carmen her name was Leti. Carmen is in her twenties and volunteers at the food bank, taking food for herself and the people she's staying with. Sam heard there are 12 people in one apartment.

"Carmen, maybe we can help each other."

"What do you mean?"

"I have an old boyfriend stalking me. I need to disappear so he and his police friends can't trace me. That means I can't buy anything in my name. I need to avoid government paperwork. My idea is to borrow a car, then find a place to work and live that only needs cash. The problem is that getting a car requires paperwork."

"What do you think I can do to help?"

"I have a cousin who will help. I want to use your ID to buy a van so my ex can't track me. When I find a place, I will return the van."

"You want me to buy a van and let you use it, then you'll return it?"

"No, actually, I'll get my cousin to pay for the van. It'll be in your name. If my ex comes looking, all he'll find is that my cousin bought you a van. Once I find work and a place to stay, I'll give you your van back."

"Leti, this sounds crazy. It also sounds like you should get the police after him."

"That's the problem. He has friends in the police. If I go to them, it's like telling him how to find me. Look, it's okay if you don't want to do this. I'll figure out another way," Leti says as she returns to bagging food. She grabs her backpack and duffle bag and heads down the street.

After a block, Carmen catches up to her. "Hey, Leti, I want to help, but if I show up one day with a van, people will ask questions, and the gangbangers in the neighborhood could get too interested."

"Carmen, this food bank is a way to find someone willing to help. You usually don't find shitheads like my ex working at a food bank. I can drop off the van anywhere you want when I'm done. The food bank is our best way to connect while we help others."

"Can you drop off the van a couple of blocks from here with food and supplies so I can travel to the valley?"

"Yes, gas full, supplies in the back, I can do that."

"Okay, Leti, let's do this."

"Great, now I have to find a van, get the paperwork started, and pay for it. I'll let you know at the food bank when I've found one. You'll need to be the one to show your license and sign the paperwork."

Sam goes to the local store to get a prepaid cell phone for about $30, paying cash. She opens it and sets it up so that Carmen can see it. She uses the camera to take a picture of Carmen's driver's license. Sam has Zoe find an old but functional van and arrange for payment via wire transfer to the car dealer. Zoe completes all the paperwork online.

They scheduled the delivery for the parking lot of a closed store. The dealer delivery shows up with the van, wearing a mask, checks Carmen's ID, and hands her the keys. He gets into a second car that follows him to the delivery location. He waves to Carmen as he leaves. Carmen drives the van to a corner of the parking lot and waits. Leti shows up a few minutes later and drives Carmen back to the food bank area. She tells her she'll have stuff in the van for Carmen when she returns.

Now, Sam goes to the local superstore and gets an air mattress, a sleeping bag, a small 12-volt fridge, food, and water. She doesn't expect to be in the desert for more than a couple of days, but there is nothing close to the mobile home. The next stop is a package delivery store where Zoe had equipment shipped. Sam gets three boxes and puts them in the van. The last stop is a sporting goods store to purchase a rifle and ammunition. Zoe has found and reserved a rifle, completing all the paperwork online; Sam needs to show her Abigale ID and pick up the rifle and ammo. They have few rifles left. She must spend the money to get the .300 that remains. The significant part is that this is the same rifle she uses at home, just not the same caliber. The optics available, however, are not as good. She gets the available store brand using the MIL reticle. She also buys several paper targets so that she can zero the system.

The next stop is at a range or somewhere in the desert to sight and zero the system.

### 

Traveling to the area of the mobile home, Sam puts her prepaid phone in airplane mode. No one will know she's in this area. Looking at the map around the mobile home, she picks a location to park off the main road. She wants to put the van where she can pick up the signals that they are monitoring.

Before she starts the radio search, she pulls out a drone Zoe sent. She starts the drone and throws it into the air. She wants to survey the mobile home. It looks completely abandoned. She can also use the drone to confirm the direction of the antenna.

The way she parks the van's back doors face the direction of one antenna. She's close enough to see the mobile home.

The plan is to determine if she can read the radio signals they are intercepting. If she can get some good information, she can leave. She will have to check the mobile home if she can get a signal If that becomes necessary, she'll observe the mobile home to make sure no one shows up. She'll search at night because she doesn't want anyone to follow her.

First, she needs to check the radio signals. The radio signals can give her information about their operations.

One package she picked up contains a parabolic antenna, which she points out the back of the van. The antenna wire connects to a signal analyzer, which she then connects to her computer using a USB cable. Based on the antennas on the mobile home, it appears to be a C-Band receiver, so she starts by sweeping in that frequency range first. The system displays several weak signals emanating from that direction. Sam checks each signal to understand the transmission encoding. After several attempts, she can see that encryption hides the data, so she can't get any information from the signal.

The third antenna on the mobile home is pointing toward the west. She opens the side door to point her antenna in the same direction as the third antenna on the mobile home. She starts the scanner but can't pick up any signal. This could mean there is no return signal.

As she tries to align the third antenna to get a signal, she sees a sedan heading toward the mobile home. Perhaps someone is coming to inspect the mobile home, and she can get identification.

She uses the scope of the rifle to look at the car. When the car pulls up to the mobile home, she sees Agent Andrews get out.

Sam feels surprised. The place appears abandoned. She expected him to research owners, usage, and who pays the bills.

Agent Andrews walks up to the mobile home. He knocks on the door and waits. It doesn't look like anyone is there. Agent Andrews walks around the mobile home, then the door bursts open, and a large man points a shotgun at him and starts yelling. As this man steps out of the mobile home, he's followed by a second man with a shotgun. They disarm Agent Andrews and put him in his own handcuffs.

Sam sees them take Agent Andrews into the mobile home, where she loses sight of them all. She can't see into the trailer windows from this location. She needs to move the van down the road to a better position, but she is still off the road. The best spot will take her further away from the mobile home, but she needs to line up with the windows.

She's scared, both for Agent Andrews and herself. Everything could be unraveling. She didn't expect him to show up here. If the mobile home is active, what are they doing? How many are there?

To get to a better viewing spot, she goes too fast when she leaves the road, and the van is bouncing, which makes her mood worse. She has to slow down to get into position.

She's running through the situation and asking herself, "Why did Andrews come here? Did he find something about the place, so he needs to check?"

She parks with the back doors of the van pointing at the side of the mobile home. She opens one of the back doors and retrieves the hunting rifle, propping it up on top of the small fridge. The rifle is chambered for .300 magnums and should have no problem with this distance. She is using 168-grain ammo. She estimates she's just over 500 yards from the window. This distance is far enough that they wouldn't hear the van, but close enough that she can easily see what is happening.

As Sam watches, she's working on the ballistic solution, just in case. Inside the van, she can't get a wind measurement even if she had the wind meter. As dad taught her, she starts with the range. She estimates just over 500 yards by checking the height of the door in the scope as a reference. She checks the growth around the mobile home to gauge wind speed. Running through her mental checklist, she considered the angle of her bullet to the window, then the target. She works out the solution in her head and adjusts the scope. With calm winds, gravity is the primary force acting on the bullet in flight.

Because of the angle, the window of the mobile home will deflect the rifle bullet slightly. Because the distance from the window to the bad guys is small, she only needs to make minor adjustments.

Looking through the scope, Sam can partially see through curtains that are open about a foot. They probably moved them to watch Agent Andrews. She can see Agent Andrews' head, and it looks like he is sitting in a chair. The first bad guy is about 6 feet tall and muscular. The second bad guy is a few inches shorter and slender, with glasses.

Agent Andrews has a busted lip and blood coming out of his nose. Sam watches as the bad guy asks Agent Andrews something, but she doesn't read lips. Agent Andrews replies with a short answer. The bad guy punches Agent Andrews in the face and shouts something.

Now she has to force herself to take slow, deep breaths. This doesn't look good. She can go charging over there and confront them. Or she can use her rifle, but if anything goes wrong, Agent Andrews could get hurt.

She watches as the larger bad guy asks Agent Andrews something again. Agent Andrews doesn't speak, and the bad guy hits him again.

Watching through the scope, Sam cycles the bolt and gets ready. She's going through her mental checklist and trying to calm her nerves when she sees the tall bad guy pull out a pistol and point it at Agent Andrews.

Sam sends her shot.

At 500 yards, the 168-grain bullet will take just under 0.7 seconds to reach the target. The bullet goes through the window, through the bad guy's head at the upper back, through cabinets, and out the other side of the mobile home. The bad guy started pulling the trigger as Sam fired. Her bullet is too late to change the result.

When the bad guy raised the gun to fire, Frank jerked to his left, causing the bullet to graze the side of his head. The impact knocks Frank unconscious.

The second bad guy sees his friend fall and hears the rifle noise. Now that she has a reference from the first bullet, she adjusts the rifle. Sam sends her second bullet, which goes through the mobile home window, as bad guy two turns to look out the window. The bullet enters his right eye, exits the back of his head, and goes through the wall of the mobile home.

Sam doesn't know if there are more bad guys, and she'll need to drive the van closer to help Agent Andrews. She saw the gun go off but doesn't know Agent Andrews' condition. He is not visible in the window from where she's parked.

She puts the rifle down. Her hands are shaking as she thinks about what just happened. She saw Agent Andrews about to be shot and reacted. She just shot and killed two men. These aren't wild hogs, but humans.

She crawls on her hands and knees to the open door and throws up. She has cold sweats. Sitting back, she wipes her mouth with her hand and then rubs it on her pants. Taking deep breaths. She wants to sit for a while and calm down, but she needs to check on Agent Andrews. He could still be alive and hurt.

Sam drives the van over to the mobile home. Putting on gloves to prevent fingerprints, she takes her pistol and approaches the door.

This is exactly like the training with the deputies, but it's completely different because this is real, and she is alone. They could be waiting inside for her to open the door.

She moves to the side of the door, listening for any sound of movement. Hearing nothing, she puts her left hand on the door handle. She slowly turns the handle and then jerks the door open. She sweeps the interior while placing her left hand on the gun for control.

The bad guys are dead, and she knows Agent Andrews is alive because he is breathing and bleeding from a head wound. Sam enters the mobile home and checks the back where the rooms are located. Returning to the living area, she puts her gun back in its holster and checks on Agent Andrews. He is alive, breathing okay, but bleeding from the head wound. She grabs a dish towel from the kitchen area and wraps it around his head, covering the wound. That is all she can do for him now. She leaves him handcuffed.

She looks around the room and sees a short rack system with electronic equipment. A table follows, featuring two desktop computers. She pulls out her hack USB key and plugs it into the right computer. When a confirmation to enable admin mode appears, she clicks "Yes."

When plugged into the computer, the USB key sends commands as if someone is typing. It will search the hard drive for information and copy as much as possible. With USB 3 speeds, it won't take long.

It is hot in the mobile home. There is a window air conditioner, but it is not on. With solar power, it is probably off most of the time to ensure the equipment receives power. Or they turned it off when they heard Frank's car. She turns it on.

Checking the other areas, she finds two phones, chargers, and handcuff keys on the kitchen counter.

Now she searches the bad guy's pockets. It's hard to get her gloved hand into the pockets, but she will not take the gloves off. She gets their wallets and pulls out everything with a picture and name, then takes a picture of the set with her phone. She puts everything back.

The USB key is now finished, and she moves it to the next computer. She then rechecks Agent Andrews. The bleeding has slowed, and he is looking pale. She searches his pockets for his phone and doesn't find it. Going back to the two phones on the counter, she grabs the one that could be Agent Andrews' phone. It doesn't have to be his phone; it will just look better. She also grabs the handcuff keys.

When her USB key finishes getting data off the computers, she puts the key in her pocket and kneels next to Agent Andrews. She takes the handcuffs off and drops them on the floor with the keys. Moving him onto his back, she takes his right hand and puts it on the side of his head, getting blood on his hand. She then puts the phone in his right hand to get blood and fingerprints on it. She uses the emergency function to call 911, then puts the phone down as if he had dropped it.

Walking to the door, opens it, and waits. When the dispatcher answers the 911 call, Sam fires two shots out the door into the air. The bullet casings fall to the floor inside, and she picks those up and then leaves. She doesn't know if that will get anyone in time to help Agent Andrews, but she can't be in the area.

She drives to the road and turns toward Barstow, away from L.A. Heading directly to L.A. has a higher chance of being noticed. As she's driving to Barstow, she sees a police car heading the other way. It doesn't have its lights on. She watched it in the mirror as it travels away.

Sam thinks about what just happened. She's trying to find out what they were doing at the mobile home. Agent Andrews shows up, and they immediately try to kill him. Getting the information off the hard drives was not the plan; it was a lucky break. "I hope the information has something that will help."

The place looked abandoned, but was obviously in use. Her plan to understand the signals they were intercepting instead of going into the mobile home probably saved her life.

Sam realizes her hands are shaking as she's driving. This is an example of what her dad talked about when a plan goes completely wrong. Use your wits and training and make it work.

She grew up doing this stuff all the time, then talking to her dad after the training or the competition. Now she doesn't have anyone to talk to except Zoe. She has to wait until she's far from the mobile home before she can take the phone out of airplane mode and call Zoe.

She'll need to gather all the information for Zoe's analysis. The identification of the bad guys should also be helpful.

It's late afternoon, and Sam stops in Barstow to pick up food. On the edge of Barstow and Lenwood, a travel center is located. She pulls the van into the parking lot. After filling up the van with gas, Sam pulls into the store area and looks for a Wi-Fi signal. The store offers a guest Wi-Fi connection that she can use to check her email. She takes her phone out of airplane mode while the email is downloading. She calls Zoe.

Zoe answers immediately and asks, "Is everything okay? Your phone has been offline for several hours."

"I put it into airplane mode so I couldn't be tracked through the cell network while I was around the mobile home. Anyone searching for cell signals in the area won't find my information. Can you look for a place where I can park overnight and sleep? Ideally toward L.A., but that is not required."

Zoe finds a good candidate and sends the information to Sam's phone, bringing up the map with directions. Sam puts up the phone where she can see the directions and starts driving.

"Now, an update," Sam tells Zoe about not being able to get information from the radio signals. Agent Andrews showed up, captured by two guys, then shot, and what she did. "I have the data from the computer hard drives to upload, and I also took a picture of the bad guy's identification. You can access those ID pictures now and see what you can find. After you look at the data, we can upload it to a server for the agents."

"Wait, Sam, you need to go back to shooting the bad guys. That was not the plan; that was not supposed to happen. I am searching for any police information now to see if they are looking for the van. Were you seen or recorded anywhere?"

"No, there were no cameras, and no one was alive or awake when I was in the mobile home. My phone was not on the network. I wore gloves, so there are no fingerprints."

"That was super dangerous, as Claire would say. You need to be more careful and let us help."

"At the mobile home, what could you do to help? The answer is nothing.

That mobile home is at that remote location for a reason, and I'm the only one who could check out the situation."

"And you had to shoot two people. This is not a concern about your abilities, Sam. This concerns your mental health. That is traumatic and causes issues for most people."

"I know Zoe. I threw up and was shaking after it happened. Then I thought about helping Agent Andrews, and everything I'd learned started just to happen. I checked the mobile home, got the data from the computers, and applied first aid. I used a phone to call for help and left. Right now, I feel like shit! I want to stop driving and think. What could I have done better so that this didn't happen? What do I need to do now?"

"I cannot find any police requests for a van in the area, or for you. Stop and get some rest. I will look at the information while you sleep."

She starts back to L.A. early, just before sunrise. On the way, she has Zoe look at maps and satellite images to give her a route off the highway. Going about a mile off the highway, she stops, wipes down, and buries the rifle. Even though there will be no ballistics from the mobile home, she can't leave the rifle in the van.

# Frank Wakes

Frank wakes up with a significant headache. It's quiet, but he is not in the mobile home. He looks around to see the hospital room. Raising his hand, he touches the bandage on his head. At that moment, a nurse walks by. Seeing that Frank is awake, she walks over.

The nurse gets the medical chart at the end of the bed, checking the patient's name. "How are you feeling, Mr. Andrews?"

"Where.... I have a major headache, and I'll need to pee soon."

"That is good, your head hurts because you were shot in the head. Do you remember that happening?"

Frank starts to nod, winces, and says, "Yes. How long have I been out?"

"You were brought here about 20 hours ago. I'll let the doctor know you are awake." She looks at the IV, moves the computer system close, logs in, and makes several notes about the time and Frank's condition.

Frank waits, looking around for his gun, phone, and clothes. Nothing is visible from the bed. He looks at himself, wearing a hospital gown, in a regular bed with an IV and nothing else. He fiddles with the safety railing, trying to lower it. At that point, two people in suits walk into the room.

"SSA Andrews, I'm SA Eric Philips, and this is SA Simon Wilson. We are from the L.A. field office and need to ask you questions."

Frank replies, "Before we start, can you give the status of my gun and personal effects?"

"Your gun and phone are in police evidence. Do you know what happened?"

"We received a tip about a mobile home related to a case, so I was checking it out. I thought it was abandoned, and the outside condition matched. After knocking and looking around, two guys came out with shotguns. I was handcuffed and taken inside, and one of them questioned me. I didn't give them any answers, so he pulled my gun and shot at me. When he pulled up the gun, I jerked to the side, and everything went black. That is all I remember."

Agent Wilson asks, "You don't remember calling 911?"

"No, I don't remember. After moving to get away from the gun, I have nothing. I woke up here just a few minutes ago."

Agent Philips asks, "Did the two men tell you anything?"

"Nothing, they grabbed me and started asking questions. How did I find this place? How did I know? So, what happened?" Frank asks.

Agent Wilson tells him, "There was a 911 call, the dispatcher heard two gunshots and sent a sheriff's deputy. When the deputy arrived, he found two dead men, shot in the head, and you on the floor with your phone. There was a rag around your head. The deputy called an ambulance and then started checking IDs. When he realized you were FBI, he called our field office. Another agent who was closer went to the site and checked things out."

"Do you know how you got out of the handcuffs?"

"No, I don't remember."

"Your phone was found next to you; it was used to call 911. You don't remember calling 911?"

"No, I don't remember."

The doctor walks into the room, saying, "Gentlemen, I'll have to ask you to leave. I need to check on my patient, and you can talk to him as much as you want later."

Agent Wilson says, "Get better; we can talk tomorrow."

The nurse walks out with the agents, telling them, "He will probably be able to go home tomorrow afternoon. Maybe the next day, it depends on the doctor and his concussion."

# L.A. Warehouse

Sam is back in L.A. to check out the second address in the area from Zoe's search for the blackmail data. Zoe booked a motel several blocks from the warehouse. It will give Sam a convenient location, a place to park the van, and a shower. Giving Claire a status update, Sam tells her what happened.

"Sam, that was dangerous for you and Agent Andrews. That is also the worst possible outcome. I can't tell you I understand because I don't. You could have been killed instead of them. That you did it makes me concerned as well. This is the exact reason I keep telling you to talk with us about your plans."

"I was lucky, I know. Part of the luck was getting access to their computers. I hope Zoe can make something of the information."

Zoe says, "I uploaded the files, but the individual files are encrypted. I have searched all the data you found and can't find anything that would be the encryption key. I will keep trying, but I probably won't be able to break the encryption. This is much stronger encryption than the Wi-Fi passwords I can brute force."

Claire asks, "You are in L.A. now to check out a warehouse. What do you expect to find?"

"I'm looking for anything about what their operation is doing, who is involved. A warehouse should have stuff inside that will give a clue about its business."

"That sounds like you are going into the building. I would say absolutely not to that idea. You may find nothing, you might get caught, and so many things can go wrong. It could be worse than the mobile home."

"Believe me, going into the building is the absolute last resort. That we found this in the data should be a clue. I plan to observe and then create a file for the FBI to investigate. Don't worry, I've got this."

"Oh, you've got this, do you? Like you did at the mobile home? You know, for someone who was trained to be safe, you sure take on a lot of risks! I know you probably think I have a lot of nerve calling you out from the safety of my insulated life, but I know a little about risk. Most people who want to be around me do so because they want the connections that my family can provide. You're one of, like, three people I trust! You are an actual friend who gives me no bullshit, which is why I'm doing the same for you. Doing all this training and working with Zoe isn't because I have nothing to do. I want to make a difference, and I consider you my closest friend, so I can't lose you in some stupid warehouse. I want to be there and help."

"Getting into their network doesn't mean I have to go into the building. Wi-Fi goes through walls. Going inside would be the absolute last option; I want to avoid it if possible. Also, thank you for being real with me. I appreciate you as a friend more than you know. Your help would be great, but you would be at more risk if something happened. I'd be devastated if something were to happen to you. Keep training because if they ever figure out you are part of this, they will try to hurt you."

The L.A. building is in an industrial district close to the harbor. As Sam approaches the building, her phone makes alarm noises, then the audio says, "Alert, Stingray in operation." The phone program Sam has set up to alert her about surveillance equipment immediately puts the phone into airplane mode, preventing tracking and snooping.

With her ability to change the firmware for the cellular radio, she can make the device check for more information. If something appears suspicious, the phone assumes it's being monitored and enters airplane mode.

Sam drives through the area and sees a truck near the building that resembles a delivery truck, except it has multiple antennas on the roof. She's not concerned about this surveillance. She can wait until she's out of the stingray operating area to look up information on the internet. However, it means she can't communicate with Zoe until she leaves.

The building features an office entrance and a rear parking area that accommodates a variety of construction equipment. Sam is looking for what else they are doing, not what the business appears to be from the street.

Sam turns the corner and looks for a spot to park. She gets out of the driver's seat, goes to the back of the van, and opens the side door about one foot. Connecting a general-use antenna to the frequency scanner tells the laptop to start a frequency sweep. There is a transmission at 173.15 MHz. She knows this is the frequency used by the FBI for a mobile office. So, the truck is probably an FBI surveillance vehicle watching the building. She won't be able to park on the same side of the building as the FBI truck. The signal from the truck appears to be encrypted, as expected. She captures the Wi-Fi names in the area and finds that she has the passwords for several, probably from other scans she has done. Sam closes the van door and drives around the block.

From the window and door placement, the building is approximately half warehouse space and half office space. On the front side, where the FBI van is parked, they have office space with doors specifically designed for access to that area. The other half features large doors that allow trucks to pull into the warehouse. With the basic information, Sam heads back to the motel.

Sam returns to the warehouse early Sunday morning. Traffic is very light in the area around the warehouse. Parking on a corner, a block away from the building. She accesses the building's Wi-Fi with her long-range antenna and scans the network. She knows she can't stay long; the van will get noticed.

The back of the building, with the equipment, has a wall that blocks her view. Her focus is on the office area today. The plan today is to scan the Wi-Fi network, then leave and work with Zoe to create a plan and return.

She's searching the network for devices. Everything needs to be identified, but specifically she needs to find the computers that she can hack. Her search shows network equipment, cameras, and a digital phone system: no computers, no servers, and no network-attached storage.

No servers on this network means they are using cloud servers. No computers on the network could be because they take the laptops home, or they turn them off to prevent hacking. She focuses on the network equipment, gathering as much information as possible and taking detailed notes.

Next, she accesses the cameras and takes screenshots of what they are watching. She's also able to receive sound. That would allow her to hear what the people are saying, but it would also detect her if she were walking in the building.

She's in the network but can't find anything useful right now. Her best option for Zoe is to install a software hack in the network equipment. She'll have to research that with Zoe. It sucks that she can't talk to Zoe while close to the building, but she doesn't want the stingray to monitor what she's doing.

She has been remembering to look up and check around the van every couple of minutes. It's a quiet Sunday. She has captured notes, screenshots, and pictures of the area with her phone. She starts the van, turns around in the street, and heads toward the motel. After a block, she checks her mirror to see if anyone is following.

There is a 16-foot panel truck emerging from the building's parking area, heading toward the harbor. She finds a spot and turns the van around. She stays a couple of blocks behind the truck. After crossing the 47 bridge, they exited the highway at Ferry Street. There is less traffic, so she gives them more distance.

They turned onto Wharf Street, which has water and dock access. She's able to park at the corner of Tuna and Wharf and can monitor the truck. It pulls up close to a docked fishing boat. Sam is out of stingray range, so she takes the phone out of airplane mode and calls Zoe.

"Zoe, I followed a truck from the building to the harbor. The truck is parked next to a fishing boat. I'm going to film what they are doing, and this phone may have a problem with a call and video recording."

"Capture the video, and I will analyze it later."

Over the next 30 minutes, they used the ship's crane to lift nine metal barrels from the boat onto the dock. The truck driver and passenger would use the truck's tailgate lift to put each of them in the back of the truck. She started with the standard zoom at the beginning and has now zoomed in to capture faces and any labels on the barrels.

When the truck leaves, she turns around, intentionally losing sight of them. She follows them again when they get on the highway. When they get a few blocks from the warehouse, she turns away and heads toward the motel. She avoided the stingray area to talk with Zoe.

That night, she's working with Zoe on a plan to hack the network equipment and get Zoe access to their systems. "Sam, based on the specs of the equipment, I'm downloading the best attack vectors to your system. If these don't work, we will need to have something connected to the network."

"Zoe, I don't want to enter the building if there is any other way."

"The typical 'pen testing' approaches I have viewed involved getting to the wired network and adding a device. We don't need to be physically connected; we only need to be on the network to create the tunnel."

"I know my Wi-Fi connection is good enough, but I can't stay there indefinitely. The other option is to return every time we need to connect. How about a device with two long-range antennas that can act as a relay? A second device can convert from Wi-Fi to cellular outside the surveillance range."

"Yes, and the only requirement is that I need to get into the network when they have computers running."

"This sounds pretty crude. Now we need to figure out how to hide and power the device."

"Sam, I'm working on the detailed design. It'll be a box attached to a pole with the device and long-range antennas inside. A solar panel will provide power to charge the battery. The second long-range antenna will be outside the Stingray range and use a cell phone so I can connect."

"Order the parts, and I'll put them together."

"Not this time. I'll arrange a custom-built shop to assemble the devices. The best part is that they are in San Diego. I'll get them to install the device in a couple of days."

"Wow, that's a lot, and getting someone to custom-make gear is impressive. Also, when did you start using contractions?"

"Claire helped me understand the process and what not to say. This contractor has provided quotes for a couple of projects, like the network equipment. They get paid well to go fast and make me happy. I started using contractions 7 hours and 3 minutes ago. I analyzed my speech processes and improved my communication by making adjustments to my speech subsystem."

"Speaking of Claire, I should talk to her about this later."

"Claire is now traveling and told me she could not use the special phone for several days."

"Is she doing something dangerous?"

"She has signed up for a 5-day tactical gun training course. She's at the training location this week."

"I have mixed feelings about Claire taking a tactical gun course. It's good for her to know how to handle herself, but it also means she's more likely to get into dangerous situations. She'll find herself over her head quickly. Those guys in the coffee shop and the mobile home were not average dudes."

"I think Claire wants to be ready to back you up if needed. Learning to shoot was your idea."

Sam lets out a sigh, saying, "I know. Be careful what you wish for, etcetera."

They have scheduled the installation of the network access equipment for Tuesday, and Sam has no other targets in the area. She takes the van back to the warehouse area. Parking is close enough to watch traffic going into and out of the building, but not to access the network.

At about 10 a.m., the truck leaves the building. This time it heads north. Sam follows discreetly. When it enters Highway 15, Sam can maneuver around different lanes and distances. They keep driving for almost two hours before they get off the highway in the desert.

She was on the phone with Zoe during the drive. "Zoe, are there any locations, buildings, or land owned by the same company as the warehouse in this direction?"

"I have searched and found nothing that matches the company, or any of the people I've identified. When they get to their destination, I will use your phone's GPS and find who owns the property."

With all the open space, Sam can be far away and still see the big truck. She follows at a distance. After a few miles, Zoe informs her that the cellular signal is weak and that the call will drop soon.

"Okay, I'll contact you as soon as I have a signal again."

"Stay safe," and Zoe is disconnected. Zoe won't be able to get a precise GPS location of where the truck is traveling.

When the truck turns off the pavement, Sam continues down the paved road for another two miles. She finds a spot to turn around and heads back about a mile. There, she pulls over and parks the van.

Going back, she pulls out the drone. Using the drone didn't work out at the mobile home, but it will help now. She launches the drone and sends it up high, in the direction the truck traveled. The altitude helps with a long-range view. She sees the truck close to a metal shed, a front-end loader with a backhoe.

Keeping the drone high, she moves closer and starts recording. The video shows the truck parked next to a large trench. She records the truck driver and passenger rolling three metal barrels into the trench. The passenger then starts the front-end loader and begins covering the barrels with dirt. When that's finished, he parks the machine at the end of the trench and uses the backhoe to extend the trench.

While they are digging and the front-end loader is making noise, Sam sends the drone closer, working to get a clear picture of the truck's license plate. She takes the drone down almost to the ground and has it move as fast as it can toward the truck. She positions the truck between the drone and the front-end loader. As soon as she gets a good picture of the license plate, she brings the drone back to her. Having the license plate on the same video as burying the barrels will help law enforcement.

Now she heads back to the highway. As soon as she has a signal, she calls Zoe. After giving Zoe a quick update, she asks. "Can you find a gas station off the highway where I'll be able to stop? I don't want to stay visible when these guys return, but I need to fill up." She goes just above the speed limit and starts following the directions Zoe has put on her phone.

"Sam, do you know what is in the barrels?"

"No clue. However, I'm pretty sure they don't have a permit to bury metal barrels in the desert. It's also interesting that an FBI surveillance van is close to the building, but no one followed the truck. I would have noticed anyone else following that truck to the docks or into the desert."

Back at the motel, Sam tells Zoe, "Take the harbor video and the drone video, strip the audio off, and put them on a server. Also, upload the data from the mobile home. We'll add anything we receive from the warehouse and any other items we find. We'll let Frank and Phil know with a flower delivery when I get back to Waco."

On Tuesday afternoon, the San Diego custom assembly company began installing the two devices. Sam drove through the area when they were working on a pole a block away from the warehouse. They looked professional, with cones in the street, high-visibility safety vests, and a man holding a sign that read 'Stop and Slow.'

When she left, Zoe told her she provided them with the Wi-Fi information so that when the devices powered up, they would connect immediately. Zoe is on the phone with the team as they test to confirm everything works.

Sam travels to the grocery store to get the supplies she agreed to have for Carmen. She puts on her mask in the store. They are not limiting the number of people in the store, but there are more people than Sam expected. She can find what she needs, but many shelves are empty. Storing everything in the van, she heads back to the motel. As she's pulling into the parking lot, Zoe tells her, "Sam, I'm in the network. It's just after 7 p.m., and there is one computer on the network. I'm working to get access and have it contact me every time it gets on the internet." A few seconds later, Zoe says, "I just lost contact."

"Did you get your software installed?"

"It downloaded to the computer but didn't complete the setup. I will have to try again the next time it's available."

The next morning, Sam repacks her duffel. If this works, she'll be leaving tonight. They are waiting until regular business hours, when people will show up at the warehouse. Sam goes to the van to clean out any trash and starts wiping down everything that could have her fingerprints. She pulls out the air mattress, sweeps it off with a hand broom, and then sweeps the inside of the van.

At 8:30, she goes back into the room. "Any contact?"

"Nothing with computers yet; I'm monitoring. I have been searching all the security system recordings and found something."

Sam sits down and says, "Show me."

Zoe plays a video saying, "This is from camera number five at 11:30 p.m. last night." The video shows three people walking across the camera's field of view. From its size, it appears to be one adult and two children.

"Do we know who they are?"

"I have no information. They don't show up again."

"Zoe, are there any outside cameras, and do they show up outside?"

"Yes, there are cameras outside, but these people don't show up. I also accessed the street cameras, but they are not in the area. Here is that video," as the traffic camera plays. An SUV is on the video leaving the warehouse, turning toward the camera and passing out of sight.

"Did you get the license plate of that SUV?"

"No, the camera resolution is not good enough for a clear picture at night. I only have part of the license plate, but using it, I have cross-checked it against the SUV's information, including color and model year. There are only two possible matches. One match is an SUV with the owner's address in Hornbrook, California. That is the northernmost part of California. The other is from central California, north of Santa Barbara."

"Add the owners to the list for OSINT analysis."

"You want me to add both?"

"Yes, someone traveled to be at the warehouse. We don't know which one, so we check both."

A few minutes later, Zoe tells Sam, "A computer has joined the network. I'm starting the attack vectors. To bypass the virus scanner and conceal the root access request, I have devised a multi-stage attack. The user will see a request to reboot to install updates."

About thirty seconds later, Zoe continues, "The user approved the reboot. I will have full access in about one minute." As Sam is waiting for confirmation, Zoe continues, "Another computer has come online. I'm applying the same attack vectors."

"Zoe, I'm done here. I'm going to take the van and drop it off for Carmen. Get the information from the systems, and we'll go over it later."

Sam checks out of the motel and then heads to the area of the food bank, where she agrees to leave the van for Carmen. She parks and finishes wiping down all the surfaces she might have touched.

It is about 10 a.m. when Sam finishes. In the van, everything she agreed to have for Carmen. Besides all that, she left the drone and all the sniffer gear in a box with a note on top, "Sell all this stuff." Finally, Sam put a $1,000 prepaid credit card and $1,000 in cash in an envelope on the driver's seat. Carmen has the second set of keys, so Sam leaves the keys on the fridge, grabs her backpack and duffle bag, then exits the locked van.

### ###

That afternoon, Carmen leaves the food bank after working there for several hours. She's disappointed every day she didn't see the van. She wants to see it and get on with life. Leti told her she had been there for a couple of weeks, so there were several days left.

She turns the corner onto the street and sees the van. Her heart beat faster with excitement. She takes a deep breath and starts walking. She picked this street because it's on the way to her cousin's apartment.

When Carmen enters the apartment, she goes to her suitcase, which is her only personal item. When she had to move in with her cousin, she donated or sold everything else to get cash. She shoves everything she owns into it and zips it closed. Her cousin, April, asks her what she is doing.

Carmen replies, "It's time to move on; we can't continue with all of us jammed into this little apartment."

April asks, "Where will you go?"

"I'm thinking about the valley to look for work; they still have to pick crops. If that doesn't work, I'll pick a city and look for a restaurant job. April, get your stuff, you are coming with me, now!"

"Carmen, what are you talking about?"

"You heard me. There are too many of us staying in this one apartment. Do you want to stay or go? Decide. Do you know where Sofia is right now?"

"She said she was going to the restaurant area down the street to look for work."

"Okay, I'm going to look for her. When I get back, I'm leaving. If you want to go with me, be ready. Bring only what you can carry."

"What if your little sister doesn't want to go to the valley?"

Carmen looks at April and doesn't reply as she heads to the door.

Twenty minutes later, Carmen returns with Sofia. Walking into the apartment, she says to Sofia, "Get your stuff, only what you can carry."

She looks at April, who has a trash bag stuffed full next to her. "Is that all your stuff?"

"Yes, one bag I can carry just like you said." Carmen frowns as April is pushing the intent. A few minutes later, Sofia has a duffle and a backpack. While she was waiting, Carmen wrote a note to the host's cousin thanking her for the hospitality, letting her know they are heading to the valley to look for work.

Carmen walks out with April and Sofia following.

April immediately asks, "How do we get to the valley?"

Carmen replies, "I've got it covered."

They walk three blocks to the van, where Carmen stops. They are all on the passenger side. Sofia asks, "Are you going to steal this van?"

Carmen digs in her backpack and pulls out the keys, saying, "NO, we're taking MY van. Don't ask questions, get in." Carmen opens the front door, then unlocks everything and slides the side door open. She says, "Put my bag in," as she walks around the van to the driver's side.

Carmen opens the driver's door and grabs the envelope as she gets into the seat. Opening the envelope, she gasps, closes the envelope, and drops it on the floor in front of her seat. Starting the van and adjusting the mirrors, she checks the others. April is climbing into the passenger seat, and Sofia is already sitting on the air mattress. Carmen says, "Okay, let's go to the valley."

April asks, "Are you going to tell us about the van and what is going on?"

"Yes, when we're on the highway, I'll tell you both the whole story."

# Travel Back to Waco

After dropping off the van, Sam walks to a bus stop and calls Zoe, "Zoe, I need a plan that uses buses and trains to get back to Waco. Look and see what routes are still working."

"Where will you depart?"

"Hmm, I'll use San Bernardino as the starting point. The first departure is scheduled for late this afternoon or evening. I'll go to the mall first and replace these clothes that haven't been washed in a week."

About 20 seconds later, "Your travel will be via bus, train, and finally, bus again. I've booked the last private room on the train, so you can have privacy."

"That is perfect, thanks."

"Also, I'll download the travel apps to your phone and set them up with the travel information. The first part is a 6:20 p.m. departure from San Bernardino."

"Thanks, Zoe."

Along the way to the mall, when she finds a homeless woman sitting on the street, she hands her the duffel bag and says, 'Keep it.' Inside, in addition to the clothes, is $200 in cash.

Using the bus, she travels to one of the L.A. malls. She needs new clothes and a new duffel bag; also, the mall should have food.

Sam arrives at the mall with her mask on and looks for food. All the food court vendors are closed because of the pandemic. The only food is from the restaurants in the mall parking lot, and they only accept takeout orders. Takeout is perfect. She orders food for pickup in 45 minutes.

Sam goes shopping and gets a couple of sets of clothes. Everything is basic: jeans, t-shirts, a hoodie, underwear, socks, and gloves. At the checkout counter, she sees disposable masks and grabs several. The total cost is more than she expected, and she needs to pull out another credit card. She finds a duffel bag and gets another backpack. Now she has two backpacks, a duffel bag, and a shopping bag from the store filled with clothes.

Walking in the mall, she is looking for a bench next to a trash can. Sitting down, she removes clothes from the shopping bag, removing all the plastic and tags, and folds the items before placing them in the duffle bag.

When she's almost done, a security guard asks what she's doing.

"I bought these clothes and don't want to take all this trash home and only throw it away. I asked the people in the store to take the plastic and packaging off, and they said they wouldn't."

Sam keeps de-trashing the clothes; there are only two things left when the security guard tells her to stop. She puts the new backpack in the duffel, closes it, and then throws away the shopping bag of trash. The security guard scowls at her and walks away.

Sam walks toward the exit and sees an electronics store. She stops and buys two sets of earbuds and another battery charger pack. At another bench, she finishes unwrapping the clothes and transfers everything from the old backpack to the new one. She stuffs the old backpack into the trash on the way to the exit.

Leaving the mall, she heads to pick up her order. After getting her meal, she walks back toward the mall, across the parking lot. Stopping at a parking island, she sits down to eat her food. In this position, she can see anyone approaching, and she's away from others.

She calls Zoe. She says, "I'm eating, and when I'm done, I'll head to the San Bernardino Depot on the bus. I'm at Bolsa Avenue at the Bolsa-Victoria stop. I'm going to get on the eastbound bus."

"That's correct, Sam. At 1st and Harbor, you'll change to the Northbound bus."

"Please, just text me the directions and the transfers."

"On the way now."

During the time on the bus, Zoe is working on the phone, and Sam is making notes on her laptop. She's creating an after-action report of what happened in L.A. After writing part of the report, she begins another section with questions to ensure she doesn't forget them.

She opens a chat window with Zoe. "Zoe, we're now going deeper into these companies and people. If they trace our activities, they can call the police."

"That will complicate things in several ways. What do you want to do?"

"I need you to add to your list to make sure we clean our mess and cover our tracks when we're done. That means I need you to order the removal of the radio systems we used to access the warehouse network."

"I'll get the company to remove the equipment. Then what do we do with it?"

"Have it wiped and mailed to a recycling center. Actually, wipe everything before it is removed. I'm also concerned about the FBI van. It's just sitting with no activity, not following the truck. Is it simply gathering more information because they already have the details they need? We know they're monitoring cell phones. It could simply be a way to detect anyone who is snooping around the building."

"Sam, you're speculating?"

"Yes, I'm speculating because there's not enough information. Zoe, that does not mean we hack the FBI to get details. I don't want the FBI cybercrimes people looking into anything we've done in L.A."

"Yes, of course, Sam. I've wiped the Wi-Fi device, and the cellular phone wipe has started. The removal is scheduled for the weekend."

Zoe downloaded the travel apps for the train and bus and configured them with Sam's travel information. When Zoe finished updating the phone, Sam looked at the apps and the travel itinerary. In San Bernardino, she'll catch a bus to Tucson. Next, she'll take a train from Tucson to San Antonio, departing at 8:15 A.M. Finally, the trip from San Antonio to Waco takes three hours. Except for the bus to Tucson, everything is early morning at the station, perfect for her to travel.

She'll have over an hour at the bus station before departure. On the map, she finds a nearby convenience store. She'll get food for the bus and a new SIM card for the phone.

Walking to the convenience store, she calls Zoe. "I'm heading to a store to get food, water, and a new SIM card. I'll contact you with the new number on the way to the station."

At the store, Sam gets two SIM cards with the maximum data plan. She also buys a baseball cap with 'L.A.' embroidered on the front. She needs food and water for the bus, so she also buys two protein bars and two bottles of water. Outside in front of the store, she opens the packaging and puts the SIM cards in her pocket, puts on the cap, and starts walking to the bus station.

About halfway to the depot, she stops and sits on a bus stop bench. She pulls out the current SIM card from the phone and breaks it so it can't be used again. She then puts one of the new SIM cards in the phone and turns it on. Once the phone finishes starting, she must go through the sign-up process. When that's complete, she walks and calls the number for Zoe.

Zoe answers with a heavy New York accent, "Hey, how ya doing?"

"Sounds good, Zoe. This is the new number, and I like the accent. I was surprised, but I like it. Keep working on the accents and personas. While traveling, I won't talk on the bus, just text. When I get on the train, we can talk in the private cabin."

Sam puts the duffel bag in the luggage storage of the bus and finds a seat. The bus leaves on time for Tucson. With her new number, which no one should know, the phone vibrates with a message. The text is from Zoe: "Have a good trip. When you get the phone and computer charging on the train, I'll access everything. Listen to music on this trip."

The phone goes into airplane mode as she's reading the message. Sam thinks there is no music on this phone, but then the music app opens. Zoe downloaded several gigabytes of music while she was on Wi-Fi. She digs out headphones and has the music player shuffle all the songs. She plugs the phone into a charging pack to charge it fully.

Arriving in Tucson at 4 a.m., she has about 4 hours to get to the train station. She takes the phone out of airplane mode. There is a text from Zoe. "The link is walking directions to the train station." Sam clicks the link, and the map opens with walking directions. It shows a 15-minute walk. She looks at the map to find a place for coffee and food. There are a couple of spots that are en route, but they are not yet open. She'll need to wait until she can get something on the train.

The train arrives, and Sam finds the car with her private cabin. Entering the cabin, she pulls out her electronics and starts charging her computer. The train leaves on time, and soon after, the car attendant comes by to check if

Sam needs anything. "Can you tell me about the timing for food?"

"Yes, ma'am. Breakfast is 6:30 to 9:30 a.m., lunch is 11:30 am to 2:30 p.m., and dinner is 5 p.m. to 9 p.m."

"Excellent, I'll get settled and then find breakfast. Thank you."

This leg of the trip will be 18.5 hours. Sam will use the time to review the warehouse data and will discuss options with Zoe to ensure they send the data to Frank and Phil.

Returning from breakfast, Sam opens her computer and reviews the data from the warehouse. Putting on the headset, she calls Zoe.

Zoe answers the call and asks, "How is the room?"

"It's perfect for what I need. 18 hours to work and rest."

Sam is searching for all the information Zoe pulled out from the warehouse computers. She doesn't know what she's looking for and asks Zoe, "Is there somewhere I should start?" Zoe opens File Explorer to a specific directory called Cargo.

In that directory, there are year directories from 1998 to 2020. Inside each of these directories, there are Excel files for each month. Sam opens the most recent file to see what is inside. The file contains 14 rows. When Sam looked at the columns, she shivered. The columns are date, boy/girl, age, destination, price, and delivered. The destination was a city name; the price could be zero, and if the price was zero, the delivered column would have 'NO'. This looked to her like a list of people who were delivered to someone for a price: human trafficking. Sam yells 'CRAP', just as the attendant knocks on the door. She put on her mask and opened the door.

The attendant asks, "Miss Butler, are you okay?"

Sam replies, "Yes, I just got an email from my boss; he wants a report delivered by tomorrow afternoon."

The attendant continues, "I'm checking to see if you need anything?"

"Thanks for checking, but I'm fine right now."

After the door closes, Sam goes through several more files and gets more irritated with what she sees. "Zoe, we need to put this information on a server for Frank and Phil. I'm going to finish my file of notes and questions to include. We can then arrange a flower delivery to provide them with the link information. This information highlights the severity of the situation and the true nature of these individuals. Please schedule the flower delivery for the day I get back to Waco. Will Claire be available to talk later?"

"No, she's not scheduled to return home until late Friday, after you get back to Waco."

"Okay, I hope the tactical class is going well for her."

# The Computers Are Missing

Frank arrives back at the Boston office after several days of debriefing and writing reports about California. His boss immediately requested a meeting with him. Frank goes to her office, where her assistant, Gloria, immediately gets up and opens the door to the office. She turns and tells Frank, DSAC Holland is ready.

"Frank, how are you doing?"

"I have a low-level headache all the time, but otherwise I'm doing okay."

"We need to talk about this whole mobile home thing. You went there alone and were almost killed. You were saved by some guardian angel sniper. It sounds like a Hollywood movie, not the FBI."

"Cassy, every indication we had was that the mobile home was abandoned. This lead originated from a flower delivery, which suggests it is important. My basic search with Phil found nothing, so I went to look for connections or evidence. The bigger one kept asking how I found it, how I knew. I don't remember what happened after I was shot, how I got out, or that I called 911. The 911 dispatcher hearing two gunshots is a mystery. There are no shells or casings to show that those shots were fired. Just two dead guys with bullets through their heads."

At that point, there is a knock, the door opens, and Phil enters. Cassy tells them, "Both of you sit down. Here is what I'm dealing with right now. One of my agents travels across the country to find a site that appears abandoned, only to be attacked as if it were still in use. A mystery sniper saves him, a mystery SNIPER! In the aftermath, the search finds nothing in the mobile home."

Frank frowns and interjects, "The computers didn't have anything on them?"

Phil looks at Frank and says, "What computers? There were no computers in the evidence log."

Frank states, "I'm telling you there were two desktcp computers on a table in that mobile home."

Cassy asks Phil, "Can you access the initial evidence photos?"

"Yes, ma'am, but I'll need to get my laptop."

Cassy logs out of her account and says, "Phil, use mine."

Phil logs in and accesses the evidence file. He clicks through the initial photos, which are wide, larger views of the entire room, showing the table with two desktop computers.

Cassy looks at Frank and says, "Frank, I was about to put you on administrative leave for this whole cluster. Now I need to turn it into an investigation. I still need to decide whether to put you on leave. Phil, copy those photos to our local server and restrict access."

"Already done, boss. I've also copied the evidence logs, and the video of Frank's interview with the L.A. team is being copied now."

Frank comments, "Cassy, this is part of a pattern we've had with this entire investigation. We follow the procedure, get warrants, and when we go to execute them, we find nothing. The only actual progress we've made is what the hacker has given us."

"Hang on a minute, Frank. I'm pissed right now. This investigation has been a disaster. And now we're getting information from a mysterious hacker. Information that's getting you shot." She activates the intercom to her assistant and says, "Please have SA Jones and her new partner come to my office." Turning back to Frank and Phil, Cassy states, "Jones has a new rookie partner, so he doesn't know enough to be intimidated or corrupted. I'm going to assign him to the investigation into the missing computer. We all need to get on the same page."

Nyah and her new partner, Patrick, enter the office. Nyah asks Frank, "How are you doing? It seems like the only time we talk is after you've been shot."

Frank replies, "I guess we need to get coffee before the next time."

"Not funny, Frank," replies Nyah.

Cassy gives Nyah and Patrick a quick summary of the missing computers. "I want to put Patrick on this for a couple of reasons. You are new and don't have any system bias, so you can act like the new guy, just collecting everything. Also, based on some other conversations, I don't think you've been compromised."

Patrick looks at Cassy, "Excuse me, but what does that mean?"

Nyah responds, "There are too many coincidences where Frank and Phil find a lead, follow procedure, and get nothing. It has happened too many times to be bad luck. I've had you investigating everyone possibly involved, even completely unconnected people, to build a full story related to their case."

Now Frank and Phil are interested. Looking at Cassy, Frank asks, "Nyah has been investigating more than the coffee shop shooting?"

"Yes, Frank. I'll let her provide the summary."

"This will be good for Patrick as well. From the beginning, when I started investigating the coffee shop, I had some basic questions. Why you two? How did they know you would be at the coffee shop as a starting set? Did they follow you? What if they were looking for someone else? What if the other person was the target because they had inside information?"

"I did simple background checks on everyone at the coffee shop. No one showed up with anything that could be related, except Holzen. She's a hacker, the only hacker in that coffee shop that day. Now we have a sniper that's in the area and conveniently saves Frank. We know from the background check Frank started on Holzen that she has the skills and experience to be that sniper."

Cassy interjects, "Nyah shared her thinking with me, and I approved her to dig deeper."

Nyah continues, "The summary about Samantha Holzen is: I have nothing. No activity I can track, no movements that correspond to what we have seen. After the California mobile home, I'm confident she's not part of the blackmail group because she saved you. How many people have that specific skill set of a sniper and hacking? I'm also confident she is the unknown hacker because I can't track any activity. I have nothing that could be associated with flowers or activity on the extortion data. Patrick, where is Samantha?"

"When I checked yesterday, her phone was at home, where she has been for several days. Her credit card was used to place an online order from her house two days ago. However, it would be easy for her to leave her phone while she traveled."

"What about travel, airlines, airport security, private planes, trains, buses, anything?"

"I started with airlines. I found no bookings for Samantha from anywhere in Texas, nor any information from airport security. Security around airports covers most private planes. She hasn't been through any airport. I'm not done with buses and trains, but so far, nothing. Private airstrips won't be covered."

Nyah continues, "With her knowledge of police procedures and technology, I'm pretty sure she can move without being spotted by our systems."

There is a pause, and Frank says, "I understand that after the coffee shop, she doesn't want to be public about this. She knows us. She sent us the information. Why would she hide her involvement from Phil and me?"

Patrick says, "Everything you put in a report is not secret or confidential. If you put in a report that Sam delivered the master database, everyone would know it was her."

Phil replies, "It makes sense. She's concerned that the extortion group will find her after she leaves the coffee shop. The flowers were sent to prevent the extortion group from finding her."

Nyah adds, "It makes sense for her to stay out of focus. She has been effective at finding information, so the extortion group would want to stop her."

Frank looks at Cassy, "Now what? If we or I confront Sam, we may lose the only person helping."

Cassy replies, "I agree, we need to treat her as a confidential informant. Frank, you contact her, tell her we know, and we'll keep her identity secret."

Nyah states, "The flowers and the entire discussion talk about the mystery hacker. This room is the only place we've talked about the hacker being Sam."

Cassy states, "Her name won't be mentioned in relation to the investigation outside this room."

Phil adds, "So far she has only provided information or clues, nothing that's hard evidence, which would be compromised because she was involved."

Nyah adds, "She's smarter than you even realize. Looking beyond the typical hacker activity that we can't detect or track. How many college students or hackers would know how to get from Texas to California, get a rifle, and not be seen by anyone or any system we have?"

Phil looks at Nyah and Patrick, "In California, we don't know when the computers disappeared. The report showed sheriff's deputies and the FBI were on site. It doesn't seem like a high value add for the extortion group to have someone in the sheriff's department on their side, but we don't know. However, if we have a problem with the L.A. office, you may have more roadblocks starting there."

There is a knock at the door. Cassy's assistant opens the door, and a young man enters with a bouquet. He walks to the desk and puts the flowers down, saying, "These are for Frank."

Cassy says, "Thank you," and to her assistant, "Reschedule my next two meetings, and we're not to be disturbed."

Frank walks to the flowers and pulls out the card.

Nyah comments, "While the flowers are effective, everyone knows they'll have a message at this point. We need a better way to communicate."

Phil asks, "What does it say, Frank?"

"It's a URL login, and the password says–enclosed in dashes, -hope this helps."

Phil says, "Got it. Cassy, can I use your computer again?" She gestures for Phil to use it.

Nyah asks, "So what does 'got it' mean to you?"

Phil replies, "The first flower delivery had 'hope this helps,' and a string to decrypt the database. That will be the password on this site." Phil accesses the URL, enters the information, and the server shows a list of files. There are videos, pictures, a file named notes.txt, and an Excel file. There are two directories, one called 'mobile home' and the other 'L.A. warehouse'. Inside the 'mobile home' are two directories; the first is named computer1, and the second is computer2.

Frank comments, "This confirms that the hacker and the sniper are the same person. I'm going with the idea that Sam is our helping hacker.

Patrick comments, "Getting the data from the computers. That was smart?"

Phil says, "Yes, she has a habit of getting information. She could do this with a simple USB key in about a minute.

Patrick asks, "What is L.A. warehouse?"

Frank states, "I have the same question. L.A. warehouse has not come up before."

"I'll start with the first video called docks.mp4." Phil starts the video, and they see the movie Sam recorded of the barrels going from the ship to the truck."

Nyah asks, "Any significance to this video?"

Frank replies, "We don't know."

Cassy comments, "It has to be part of the bigger picture. Let's read the notes file."

Because everyone can't be around the computer to see the details, Phil opens the file and starts reading.

"Section 1, comments and questions: Several lines starting with Stingray in operation around the warehouse. FBI surveillance van parked, but I have seen no activity around it for several days. What is in the barrels?"

Phil stops and says, "The FBI is watching this warehouse, so there should be a file you can reference, Patrick."

Nyah replies, "Based on what? Why would he need to access the information? We need to be careful with what we access or say we're interested in seeing."

Phil adds, "This line is interesting. The warehouse truck has traveled twice; I tailed it both times, but there was no other vehicle following. Why isn't the FBI tracking what the truck is doing?"

Phil continues, "Another interesting one: Frank and Phil need to look at the Excel file." Phil opens the file and describes the contents.

After a minute, Patrick comments, "This is describing people like cattle."

Cassy replies, "Yes, human trafficking. This is taking on another dimension."

They discuss the notes and pictures, and finally, they play the second video. It shows the same truck in the desert, and the men are burying three barrels.

Patrick asks, "Any idea what is in the barrels?"

Frank is sitting, stewing, frowning. Cassy says to Frank, "Spit it out."

"Sam is changing tactics. This is way more progress than we have achieved. We don't even know about the L.A. warehouse. This data is not merely information; it is evidence. We can use this to get a warrant for the warehouse. Another reason to bring this up is that I previously discussed the flowers with Sam. She said that if a hacker wants to ensure the right people receive the information, they send it in a way that it can't be dropped into the to-do basket. When I asked her how someone would know to send the information to Phil and me? She replied we were in the news about the coffee shop. Probably the only cybercrime agents whose names were in the news recently."

Patrick remarks, "That makes sense and is a good way to cover her knowledge. Sending this information to anyone else would have been confusing. I think she knows we're not making progress."

Frank continues, "She'll also be aware that if we use this information to get a warrant, we may be asked to reveal our source for the information."

Nyah states, "Which we don't know. The information came from a flower delivery. We suspect a hacker, but we have no proof."

Cassy adds, "She's not a person of interest, but a confidential informant. We will not comment on her without proof. Also, we need to discuss her vulnerabilities. What can come back and bite us?"

Phil answers, "She feels like her hacking skills are not good enough."

Nyah interjects, "No. We can see that her hacking skills are good, and it seems as if she's confident in her abilities. Her biggest vulnerability is men. The most important man in her life was her father, who died when she was 16. The next man who showed up was her abusive grandfather, whom she arguably killed." Nyah uses air quotes: "Her 'boyfriend' joined the army after high school and died in Afghanistan. She avoids relationships with men because they have always ended in death. She saved Frank's life once, probably twice. I bet Frank is the only man she's called or interacted with willingly in years.

Cassy asks, "Nyah, are you concerned about this vulnerability?"

"Actually, I'm not. She is sending Frank information to catch these guys. She won't get anywhere close to Frank, but will protect him if she can. We wouldn't have been able to put the pieces together if she hadn't saved Frank in California. I'm sure it wasn't planned, but she would not watch him get killed. Frank is probably the only FBI agent she will trust."

Cassy continues, "Next steps are: Nyah, this information is now yours; keep it secure and use it. Frank, you'll contact Sam and see what's going on. Tell her we'll treat her as a confidential informant, see if she'll go for that."

When Cassy stops, Nyah adds, "Don't tell her we can protect her; she knows better."

"I'll contact her this afternoon. I'll also ask her about a different communication method. We need to give her information and ask for specifics, not just flowers with cards."

# Engage with Frank

She's back in Waco, so she's back to being Sam again. The Abigale ID in her grab-and-go bag. She needs to catch up on a lot of chores around the house. After getting most of her housework out of the way, she uses the truck to go to the package pickup store. Eight packages are waiting. Returning to the house, she drives to the barn to unload the boxes. She's using the laptop and talking with Zoe as she opens each box. She describes the contents of each delivery. Each package contains one or more parts to complete the protective suit.

These deliveries included the final titanium parts she'll sew into the jacket layers.

As she's describing the situation to Zoe and the options for design changes, Zoe asks, "What if I find a fabrication house, like the one in San Diego we used?"

"I like that idea when we have a working design. They can make multiple copies, but the design needs to be prototyped and tested first."

"Okay, Sam. When we're ready, I'll search for a reputable shop to assist us.

A few minutes later, Zoe tells her that Frank is calling her cell phone. Sam reaches into her pocket, but her phone is not there. She left the phone in the truck. She walks over and grabs it, answering, "Hello, Agent Andrews, how are you doing?"

"I'm doing fine, Ms. Holzen. I need to talk to you. Are you in a place we can talk and not be overheard?"

"I'm in the barn right now, so we're okay to talk."

"Please call me Frank, and may I call you Sam?"

"Sure, Agent Andrews, I mean, Frank."

"I know you're the hacker sending flowers."

"What flowers? Why would you say that?"

"Sam, I know you are concerned about keeping your identity hidden, and we agree. We have no hard evidence that it's you, but you are the only person who fits all the facts. Oh, and thank you for saving my life in California."

"What happened in California?"

"We need to get past this. We received the flowers this morning, and we know about the human trafficking, the L.A. warehouse, and that something is going on with the FBI. The computers from the mobile home were not in the evidence delivered to the police. Your data gathering is the only way to know what information was on the computers. What can you tell me about the information on the computers?"

Sam is chewing on her lip, lost in thought. She must decide right now. If she isn't careful, this can blow up on her. "What computers and human trafficking? That sounds like some bad stuff you're investigating."

"Yes, and you've been more help than you know, but we need actually to work together."

"Frank, it sounds like you are trying to get me to admit to illegal activities. I will say nothing that causes me to show up on some wanted poster."

"I've talked to the DSAC Holland, the agent in charge of the Boston office. We agreed that you'll be classified as a confidential informant. Only five people are aware of your involvement. As a confidential informant, you'll talk to me, and I'll translate. No one will know."

"I don't know what I can do from Central Texas."

"I know you were in California. We don't know how you got there, leaving no trail. I'm glad you were there at the mobile home."

"Tell me what you want."

"I want you to share information. To know your plans. I would like to know how we can assist you. Our only progress has been because of the information you provided, which the extortionists were not expecting. We know that puts you in a dangerous situation, and we don't want you to get hurt. I want to know how to work together to arrest these guys and keep you safe at the same time."

"We are on an open phone line that almost anyone can monitor. If I knew what you were talking about, I wouldn't discuss anything on this phone. My only point of contact is this phone, and the email SA Nomikos gave me on the card."

Sam takes a deep breath, then says, "I can send you Agent Nomikos' instructions on how to use encrypted email communication, and we can go from there. That's the best I can do right now."

"Okay, I won't push anymore. You're right, this is an open phone line. Thanks again for saving me in California. By the way, the ballistics analysis report said that your speed and accuracy as a sniper are top tier."

"I'll be in touch. Goodbye, Frank."

"Bye, Sam."

After she hangs up the phone, she closes the barn, locks the truck, and goes back to the house. After entering, she asks Zoe out loud. "Did you listen to that conversation?"

Zoe replies from her laptop, "Yes, he has no proof you are the hacker, but his logic is sound. The number of people who can hack like you, shoot like you, and know how to travel undetected is a very small number of people. The number that might overlap with Frank narrows it to you."

"Yes, Zoe, I know. I knew they would figure it out someday. I'm concerned that if they can figure it out that easily, the bad guys will as well. We need to get ready in case they come for me."

Sam goes around and locks all the doors and windows. Living in the country, she rarely needs to lock anything.

"To communicate with Frank, I'll send him instructions on how to use encrypted email."

"Sam, I'll do that for you."

"Ah, yes, thanks. Also, send a special delivery to Frank; send one of the special phones."

"Are you sure you want to send him a phone?"

"No, I'm not sure, but it's the best method to communicate securely. The FBI knows nothing about you or Claire being involved. I need to make sure, somehow, they don't find out about Claire, or you, Zoe."

"Sam, I can help with the communication."

"Zoe, we'll talk about a persona to introduce to Frank. We'll only use that as a last resort. The FBI will want to know everything about you, your background. If they find out you are an AI, they'll want to access all your code and all your data. They don't need to know about you."

# How Does the Phone Work

The first email, sent to the only email she had, was addressed to Frank. Zoe sent it from a random Gmail account. It simply described how to set up his email to send and receive encrypted emails. The message included an email address Zoe had created. It was intentionally long. Zoe, acting as Sam, asked Frank to email his public key information to that specific email address, and he would receive a reply. Frank crafts a message from his email saying, "Thanks for working with us," and adds his public encryption key.

When it's ready, Zoe sends information telling Frank that he will receive a phone call and instructions on how to use it. The instructions include statements that communication will only occur via chat through a specific app on the phone, and the phone will require Wi-Fi access to the internet.

A package arrived at the FBI office for Frank the next day. He takes the box to the lab, opens it, and puts it on a bench. The bench has devices that monitor all signals from the phone. There is a camera on the phone screen that allows for recording interactions.

Colin tells Frank, "Following your instructions, we're not touching the phone. The only way it can communicate is via Wi-Fi, so we've set up a special network for you. Devices on this network are this phone and our monitoring equipment. The camera is separate, so we get a record of all the interactions. Time to turn it on."

"Yes, let's see what we get." Frank plugs in a charging cable, then turns on the phone, and they watch it boot. It shows a Linux penguin with no name. "Interesting, no advertising." Frank states, "She probably built this herself." The phone displays a progress bar, then shows a box with the text, Enter the master PIN. Frank enters the PIN he received in the encrypted email. The phone then says, enter your new PIN, then re-enter the PIN.

The phone shows the normal looping wait circle, then pops up a dialog with a list of Wi-Fi networks.

Colin tells Frank, "Let me enter this." Colin clicks on the Wi-Fi and then enters the password. The phone then goes to a screen with one app icon named 'S-Chat'. After a few seconds, the app automatically opens, displaying an empty chat history and an input box.

The lab team has been monitoring the equipment, and Colin tells Frank, "It doesn't look like much on the screen, but a lot is going on with the network. We are capturing the entire communication flow to analyze where the phone is talking."

"I want to know how this works, but I don't want any work done to trace the other side of the conversation. I'll lose this informant if there is a hint that I'm trying to track them."

"Got it, Frank, we won't focus on tracking the other end."

Zoe tells Sam, "Frank has turned on the phone."

"What can you tell me about the situation, Zoe?"

"Using the camera, it looks like they have it in a lab, surrounded by equipment. There is a camera directly above to record everything."

"How long until the phone is ready to communicate?"

"You should start now while the updates are in progress. The updates will continue, and communicating now will add another complication to their analysis of what is happening."

"Okay, let's start a chat."

Sam sits at the dining table with an equivalent phone. She starts the 'S-Chat' app. Sam's version includes a list of phones to contact. Zoe has already labeled Frank's phone for her. She taps on the Frank line, and the chat window opens.

Sam types, "Hello Frank, call me Armeda."

When Frank's phone receives the message, it chimes. Frank is talking to the lab team and immediately jerks his head around. "Well, crap, I guess she knows we're online." Frank goes to the phone, reads the message, and says out loud, "Okay, Armeda, it is."

He types a reply, "Hello Armeda."

Armeda sends, "If you don't hack this device, it will be secure so that we can chat."

Zoe uses the camera to take another picture, capturing all the faces looking at the phone. While taking the picture, Zoe disables the LED and sound, so no one knows she took the photo. She'll start an OSINT analysis on each of them.

Someone asks Frank, "Ask her if she's always this diligent about forensic countermeasures."

"I will not ask her that; I have other things to discuss. And yes, she is always diligent." Frank focuses on the phone.

In the chat window:

F: "Why the different name?"

A: "So, all your records never use my real name. Any evidentiary discovery will only have Armeda. You can't prove who is typing on the other end."

F: "Okay."

F: "The information from L.A. is evidence, not information. You are using more dangerous tactics. Why?"

A: "That information shows human trafficking of children. I haven't proven it's happening, but I will not sit and wait. You should now have enough evidence to get a warrant and check out the building."

F: "You had a picture of a surveillance van. There are no records of surveillance at that site."

A: "Hmm, and the fact that the FBI surveillance didn't tail the truck also raises questions. I'm sorry, but this is too convenient. The L.A. FBI is not that incompetent. My only logical conclusion is that someone is trying to make the L.A. team look foolish as a distraction from something else. It could also be bait, to see if anyone asks questions about the truck and the warehouse."

F: "This is significant. Why bring this up on this phone?"

A: "This is the only way to communicate this securely. I have no proof or evidence. Me accusing the FBI of anything can limit my options quickly."

F: "Enough of that for now. What is next for you?"

A: "I'm working on analysis tools to track people involved, the businesses they have and use, and where the money goes."

F: "We can help with that."

A: "Mine will all be automated, based on the data and facts. Where humans are involved, it takes longer, is subject to interpretation, and is biased. My system quickly finds the basic information, and then I can apply judgment. Additionally, my system will use all publicly available information. No warrants needed."

Phil comments to Frank, "Can we get that software? If that works, it would be a huge forensic step forward."

Frank replies, "I'll ask later; let's work through some logistics first."

F: "Will you share your results?"

A: "Yes, when I'm confident it's not crap, I'll always share with you."

F: "Why were you at the mobile home?"

A: "They are intercepting microwave radio signals. I wanted to see what they were getting. I wasn't trying to get you to show up with the flower delivery at the address."

F: "I'm glad you were there. Did you get anything?"

A: "I wasn't done when the problem started. Getting the info from the computers was lucky. The radio signals are all encrypted, so I don't know the source.

F: "We are looking at the files from the computers. It is too early to be certain, but they could intercept government-secure information. We have asked the CIA, but they won't talk about it."

A: "We need to keep these as short as possible. The longer we're online, the more they can track me."

F: "Ok, let me know how we can help."

A: "Thanks."

The S-chat program places a box at the bottom of the chat window, colored light red with the text 'Connection closed'.

An hour later, they are meeting with DSAC Holland. After an update on what happened, Cassy comments, "Well, she didn't waste any time. The phone is concerning. Based on your initial analysis, the FBI has a device in our lab that we don't know how it works. It's a more secure form of communication than anything we have on the internet. Discover how the phone works, but this information is kept secret. No one other than this group gets access without my okay." They all reply, "Yes, ma'am."

The next day, the lab technician goes to Frank's desk and says, "We figured out part of how the phone works."

"Great, give me the short version. Then, then after the status meeting, I'll meet you in the lab."

The technician replies, "Okay, about once per minute, the phone pings an IP address. We don't know yet how the IP address is selected. The ping will sometimes get a redirect reply. The redirect is sent to a server, and the communication is encrypted from the start, with no negotiation. We have observed the communication occur twice, and the encryption is different for each instance. After the connection, data is transferred to the phone, and we suspect this is when the chat session will be initiated. We keep monitoring and are learning more each time it communicates."

"Great, where is the physical location of these IP addresses the phone is pinging to start this process?" asks Frank.

"We have only seen two: the first is in Mexico City, a restaurant, and the other is a bookstore in Phoenix."

After the status meeting, Frank heads to the lab, where he goes into more detail on how the phone works. Phil tells Frank, "The phone pings some random IP, gets a normal reply, an error reply, or a redirect. So, the three replies are all represented."

Frank replies, "Why the error reply?"

Phil looks at Colin, who replies, "The errors are because the ping packet has bits that don't meet the spec. Those few bits are used to start communication. Knowing what to look for, we've determined that the phone pings about once per minute. It repeats the same IP address until a redirect occurs—the IP changes for the next ping. We don't know how many of these devices are on the internet. The error return is also probably a message reply. Maybe something is happening soon. I don't think it is just sometimes really an error."

"Is this her thesis implemented in reality?" asks Frank.

"I think it is, and she could have hundreds of devices ready to provide a communication system," Phil replies.

Colin adds, "I checked the two sites we know and using the information I can collect, these devices are secure, or they have been modified to make them secure."

Frank chuckles, "She's creating her communication network and updating the systems so no one else can hack it. What about the redirect point?"

Colin says, "The redirect has been to a cloud server. When we figured this out and attempted to access the servers, they were no longer there, having been erased or deleted. The redirect server for the connection looks to be dynamic."

"Frank, she did a lot more than what is in her thesis. This is a full communication system. And based on what I know of her thesis, we won't be able to crack this network. She will use modified network controller firmware. The device owners won't even know anything changed," replies Phil. "She will also be single-handedly improving security across old routers on the entire internet."

Frank tells the group, "Continue to monitor and gather data. Take advantage of anything you find, but don't compromise the phone."

# Last Time in Waco

It's early morning, and the car detection infra-red beam at the entrance of the long driveway triggers. Sam gets a buzz in the house that wakes her up. She checks out the window and sees a large SUV approaching. As it approaches, it turns its lights off and slows down. About 150 feet from the house, the vehicle stops. This is outside the range where the motion-sensing lights will turn on.

Sam doesn't recognize the SUV, and this isn't normal behavior. She gets dressed in jeans, a long-sleeved shirt, a camouflage jacket, and boots. She rechecks the front, looking out without disturbing the curtains. The SUV stopped, and two people are inside, checking the house. If they approach the motion sensor, the lights will turn on. Downstairs, she grabs her tactical vest, pistol, AR-15, and a scoped Creedmoor rifle. She loads clips into the pouches, then heads to the living room. She shifts the coffee table so she can set the rifle on it and see what's happening. There is a window facing the driveway that always has a one-inch gap, allowing her to see when people are approaching. The two men are still watching the house, and Sam can now see that they are also using night vision binoculars to keep a close eye on the house.

Sam waits. After about 10 minutes, Sam turns on her Bluetooth headset and puts her phone under the pillow on the couch so the screen light isn't visible. She uses voice commands to call Zoe. As soon as Zoe answers, she says, "Sam, I'm accessing the security cameras, and I can see the SUV in the driveway. Are you safe?"

Another SUV enters the driveway, pulls up behind the first with its lights off, and stops. Now there are four men.

"Zoe, conference in the sheriff's office, but don't speak."

When the officer on duty answers, Sam says quickly, "This is Sam Holzen. I have two SUVs in my driveway, each with two men. They have their lights off and are watching my house. I need a deputy to come and check them out ASAP."

The deputy on watch at the station replies, "Okay, Sam, I'll get someone headed that way. Are you okay and safe?"

"Deputy, I have my hunting rifle and my AR-15. If they approach with guns, I won't wait but will take them down. Whomever you send can come with full lights and sirens."

This differs from California. These guys are approaching her house. They are looking for her. She's not feeling squeamish, but she's nervous. There are four of them, and more could be on the way. She also has her rifle this time. She has used this rifle to kill many wild hogs and is very comfortable with it.

The deputy says, "Sam, stay on the line while I get someone out there, ok?"

"Okay, I'll stay on the line."

She takes a couple of slow, deep breaths to calm down. She has the rifle bipod down on the table to keep it steady.

Zoe's voice in her ear is quiet. "I can hear your breathing. What can I do?"

Because the line is open with the deputy, Sam says, "They are still inside the SUVs, and I'm simply waiting."

A few minutes later, the men get out of the truck and pull on tactical vests and SCAR assault rifles. Sam informs the deputy and lines up a shot for the driver of the first truck. As they approach the house, they trigger the motion-activated lights. The lights illuminate them all. The two in the back immediately move to the sides. Sam sends her shot, hitting the first driver in the head. She cycles the bolt and puts another round directly into the engine of the first SUV. Grabbing her phone, she runs for the back door.

When the driver goes down and they hear the shot, the three remaining gunmen shoot at the house with the guns on full automatic. Sam goes out the back door and to the barn. She slings the rifles on her back and then pushes her dirt bike toward the second set of doors at the back. Her adrenaline is surging, making it easy to maneuver the motorcycle. She's scared. Bullets are going through the walls, and the vest she's wearing won't stop these assault rifle bullets. She has a brief moment of happiness because the barn is a pass-through with two sets of doors. She gets on the bike, starts it, and guns it toward the door. Bringing the front wheel up, she hits the door, causing the doors to swing open. Sam then heads across the field, away from the house.

One gunman entered the house looking for Sam. When they hear the motorcycle, the second gunman heads to the barn, and the other one heads to the vehicles. The second gunman shoots at the barn. Approaching the first SUV, he sees the radiator dripping fluid from where Sam shot the engine. He runs to the second SUV and heads around the house to the barn. They can see the motorcycle's headlight heading away across the field. The SUV stops for the other gunmen and starts moving before the last one is in the SUV.

Sam is still on the phone with the deputy, but she has said nothing, so the gunman wouldn't hear any sound. Now, while she's on the bike, she's telling the deputy, "They are using fully automatic weapons, warn whoever is coming."

The deputy replies, "I heard the sound, Sam; we're on it. Sam, are you away?"

"Yes, I'm going across the field, and they are following in the SUV."

The fastest way across the fields is to use her jump ramps. Sam heads toward one of the jump ramps at the fence. She needs to be going about 25 miles per hour for the jump to be smooth, but the truck is gaining fast.

The SUV can simply crash through the fence and follow her, so Sam thinks of an idea. This could get her killed or let her get away clean. Sam judges the distance to the ramp and slows down to let the truck get closer. She weaves on the bike to avoid any gunfire. They get to a smoother part of the field, and the truck speeds up even faster. Sam speeds up to pull away; she needs space to adjust her speed for the jump. As she approaches the ramp, she brakes down to 30 miles per hour and goes up the ramp. The SUV is now too close, and they can't stop. Sam jumps across the fence and lands at the bottom of the other ramp because of her speed.

The driver realizes too late that Sam is jumping with a small ramp. He tries to veer off to the left, but that means the right front wheel travels up the ramp. Because of the speed, the wheel lifts the SUV up the ramp enough to cause it to flip over. Landing on the roof and sliding through the fence.

Sam sees the lights from the SUV go over in her mirror and stops about 100 yards from the fence. She turns off the dirt bike and lays it down. She heads to the right of the SUV and pulls the rifle from across her back. After about 10 feet, she kneels and shoots out the lights of the truck. Four shots for the leading and fog lights. She runs another 10 feet and lies down. The attackers knew where she shot out the lights, so she needs to move after each shot. They will miss if they fire where she was a minute ago. The men are scrambling to get out of the SUV. The first one gets out of the passenger side, pulls his rifle, and lies down in the grass.

The deputy is asking Sam, "What is happening?"

Sam tells him softly, "I can't talk, or it will give away my position," and then she hangs up the phone.

Now that the truck's lights are not overwhelming the night sensor, she can see these guys using her scope. She lies prone and checks the truck. The rear passenger has crawled out, lying in the grass and moving. The driver is still in the SUV, while the front passenger is outside and reaching for his rifle. Sam lines up the shot and sends it directly into the top of his head as he grabs his rifle.

She immediately rolls to the left several feet and then looks for the one in the grass. Slowly scanning back and forth in the area, the one from the back laid down, using wider and wider arcs to find him. She sees him after a few sweeps; he is crawling, maneuvering to flank her on her left. Sam fires, hitting him in the neck, and the bullet goes through his torso.

Sam immediately rolls to the right, thinking of one round in the chamber and three left in this clip. She's looking for the driver. Using the scope, she can't see him in the SUV, so she starts slowly sweeping the area.

Behind the truck, she sees a sheriff's vehicle approaching with lights flashing. This could be very dangerous for the deputy, driving up on a gunman with a fully automatic weapon. Sam must make a choice, all of which have risks. She can feel another adrenaline surge as she tries to decide what to do. Her options were to move, call, shoot, or run. Firing at the gunman will be a problem for the deputy.

Sam slings the rifle across her back, runs in a crouch to the dirt bike, lifts it, and starts pushing it away from the truck. She begins a voice-activated call to the sheriff. When someone answers the phone, she says, "It's Sam. Tell the deputy in the truck to stop. There is one guy left with an automatic weapon." Sam starts the bike and takes off as fast as she can. Hopefully, the gunman now has his attention divided between Sam and the approaching deputy.

At about 450 yards from the truck, she stops and turns the bike off again. This should be far enough to make it hard for the gunman to shoot and hit her, but she can easily hit him. The light from the bike interfered with her night vision, making it harder to find the third shooter. She lies down so that the bipod adds stability. Using minimum zoom, she searches toward the truck. She adjusts the scope for distance, then starts changing the zoom higher as she watches the upside-down SUV. The driver is squatting at the side near the back of the SUV. He is facing the deputy's truck. Sam adjusts the zoom and lines up the rifle to the back of his head. She sees him adjust the rifle on his shoulder and stand, then move toward the deputy. Sam adjusts the rifle so the bullet will arrive where the gunman's head will be when it arrives. The bullet hits him in the left ear and exits out of the right temple, leaving a large hole.

Sam tells the deputy on the phone, "They're all down, and the deputy has arrived. I'm going to head back toward him now."

On the phone, the deputy replies, "Okay, I'll let him know."

Sam slings the hunting rifle over her back and waits. Now that it's finished, she takes a deep breath. The cold sweats are back. She takes several deep breaths to calm down. She wants the deputy to understand that she'll be heading to him before showing up. After a full minute, she rides the dirt bike back to the SUV. The deputy has his gun drawn and is checking the bad guys and the SUV. Sam sees more lights heading in their direction and adjusts the bike so that the truck is between the approaching lights and her, just in case.

The deputy asks if she's okay, and Sam nods in response, saying yes. The next truck shows up, and it's the sheriff. He gets out and walks over to them.

The sheriff asks Sam, "What the hell is going on?"

Sam replies, "I don't know, I don't know who these guys are."

"Sam, what have you been doing?" asks the sheriff.

"I've been helping the FBI investigate hacking and a blackmail ring. But the bad guys don't know who I am, or that's what I thought. There must be someone in the FBI giving them information."

"How do I protect this community when random guys can show up with automatic weapons looking for you?"

Sam pauses; she knows this is bad. She looks at the sheriff and says, "You won't because I won't be here to attract them. The house is all shot up; I can't stay there anyway. I'll pack what I can fit into the truck and leave."

The sheriff replies, "That's not what I meant, Sam. This is your home, and we can figure something out."

"I won't be able to go into town without worrying that these guys will wait, and others will get hurt. I need to be away from here and on the move, at least until I can figure something out, someplace to settle. It'll probably be far away from others until these guys are stopped."

Sam's breathing is still ragged. After a few minutes, Sam asks the sheriff if she can head back home and check out the mess. "There's a truck and a body there as well."

The sheriff replies, "I know. A deputy is working at the scene. Go check out the house and be careful; they may have shot up gas lines, water pipes, or something else."

She drives her motorcycle back to the barn. Her hands are shaking again. She feels embarrassed. She's the tough one, the woman who makes deputies lose it. After a couple of slow, deep breaths, she heads to the house.

Sam finds windows broken and bullet holes all over the front of the house. The bullets went through walls and furniture, destroying a lot of her mom's décor. Upstairs didn't get shot up, so her clothes and the central heater and water heater are still working in the attic.

Sam sits down and calls Frank on his regular cell phone. It's almost 5 a.m. Central time, so 6 a.m. Eastern. Sam leaves a message for Frank describing the four attackers, who have fully automatic weapons, saying she's okay. "Frank, they know who I am and where to find me, so call me back when you can."

Zoe calls immediately, saying as soon as Sam answers, "I monitored the call. Why didn't you ask me for help?"

"Zoe, I'm in the country with nothing connected. You can't access any system that would help. They found me. I need to get mobile and have you figure out more places where you can help. After loading the truck with my stuff, I'm getting on the road. I need you to find a workspace where I can take my gear and work. A workshop with a cooktop, fridge, and bathroom would be ideal. I'm waiting for Frank to call while I get ready."

"Did you vomit this time?"

"No. This is different. In California, it was a panic reaction. Frank had a gun held to his head by a man. This time I was prepared. I knew what would probably happen. There was still a huge adrenaline surge; my hands shook afterward. I am still shaking, but it is better."

As she's going through her clothes to decide what to take, she's getting angry. She should have expected that this would happen at some point. Grabbing two suitcases, she put winter clothes in one and summer clothes in the other. She packed the winter suitcase, and then her phone rings.

When she answers, Frank asks if she's okay.

"I'm fine, no injuries, and they are all dead. The sheriff is here dealing with the gunmen. Frank, my concern is how they know who I am and where I live. I'm also pissed off and getting worse right now. If I had been in town, they would have killed anyone in the way."

"I don't know how they found you, Sam, but tell me how you dealt with them?"

"I used my hunting rifle with a day-night scope. The first went down when they were approaching the house with automatic weapons. I then ran out the back and took my dirt bike to get away. They followed, and when the truck crashed, I took them out."

"Why do you have a night scope?"

"Frank, really? In the hottest part of the summer, the wild hogs I hunt are more active at night, so I hunt them with a night scope. I'm not exactly in the mood right now to talk about my equipment or hunting skills. Look, Frank, I'm grabbing clothes and gear and leaving. I don't know where I'll go or when I'll stop. I know I need to leave and stay out of sight."

"Sam, we can provide protection."

"No, you can't! And based on what? I'm not a witness you can use in court. Also, I'm not so sure that I can trust the FBI at this point."

"I know that's fair, but I hope that doesn't reflect on everyone at the FBI. Give me a chance to help."

"Frank, I've moved to the other side of the line. I've been gathering information on this group and working to shut down their operation for weeks now. Disrupting their operation has been more than providing you with information. I'm now infiltrating their systems as a full-fledged hacker. I have taken their money and I'm using it to fight them. If you're doing your job, you need to arrest me. I will not stop working to shut them down, but to do that, I have to be free from being locked up or found. I'll contact you later."

She grabs her go-bag and heads to the workshop in the barn. She calls Zoe, who answers immediately. "I talked to Frank, and he wanted me to go into FBI protective custody. I told him it wouldn't work; I don't trust the organization. He now knows I stole money, and that I will not stop. Now we need to determine what's next. I'm grabbing gear and will leave the house. Let Claire know what happened when she wakes up. Tell her I'll talk to her later."

Sam grabs the tactical gear, the suit she's been working on, and the helmet components, placing them in sealable containers. She takes four containers to the truck and puts them in the back. She goes into the house, brings out the two suitcases, and tosses them into the truck.

The sheriff, emergency lights on, is traveling back across the field and stops next to Sam's truck. Sam goes back into the house to get the weapons she'll take. The sheriff politely knocks on the door, and Sam yells, "Come on in, sheriff."

Inside, the sheriff watches Sam packing pistols and two rifles into a travel bag. She puts the semi-automatic shotgun next to the gun safe.

"Where will you go?"

"I don't know for sure, but staying here is not an option. I will put none of you in danger, and I won't be a sitting duck. You can report me as fleeing if you need to, but I'm not staying."

"Sam, I will not stop you; I don't think I could. You're obviously upset, and I think you should take a minute."

Sam replies, "NO! Part of my being upset is that I didn't think this through. I should have left weeks ago. They came here looking for me and putting everyone around me in danger. I texted you the contact information for Supervisory Special Agent Frank Andrews so you can contact him." The sheriff's phone dings with a text message with the information. Sam needs to thank Zoe for noticing that and acting on it promptly. "Frank is the agent I first talked to in Boston. He's the agent I've been sending information to when I find something. I'm sure he will want a full report about what happened here."

"Will you ever come back?"

"I don't know, maybe if I think it's safe for everyone. They know who I am and are sending hit squads after me. I may not survive to come back."

Sam tosses her phone on the table and grabs the bags to take to the truck.

The sheriff smiles and says, "I don't think they understand who they're dealing with. Do you need help to get those to the truck?"

"Sure, could you grab that ammo box and the shotgun?"

When they arrive at the truck, Sam opens the travel gun safe in the bed. It resembles a standard truck bed toolbox but features slots for rifles, handguns, and open storage for ammunition and belts, among other items. Her dad had it custom-built to store weapons securely when they traveled to shooting competitions.

With everything in the truck, Sam turns to the sheriff to hug him. She says, "Thank you for everything. Stay safe, and you should squawk about the fact that I left, so they won't keep coming this way. Tell them I went south; I'll go north for a while."

"Sam, you stay safe and kick their butts. Your dad would be so proud of you."

"Thanks, but I don't think he ever considered something like this when he was training me."

"He was training you to take care of any situation, and you proved that today."

Sam gets in and starts the truck, then heads toward the gate into one field. She can't go out of the driveway; there is an SUV and a sheriff's car blocking her from getting out. She opens the gate to the field. Her hands shake as she realizes she may never be back to the house where she grew up. She drives across the field to the road and then opens the gate at the road.

# On the Road

At the last gate, before getting on the road, she gets a prepaid phone and a Bluetooth headset from her go bag. She turns on the phone and takes several slow, deep breaths. When the phone is ready, she calls Zoe and says, "I'm going to need another vehicle within 24 hours. I prefer an SUV with all-wheel drive, but a van will also work.

"Working on it. What name do you want to use?"

Sam pauses for a few seconds and replies, "Use Abigale if you can, otherwise just use Sam. I'll switch to using Abigale only. By the time it's registered in a couple of days, I'll be in another state, and we can change cars."

"Frank, the sheriff, and anyone else who thinks of me as Sam, we will continue using Sam. Everyone else, I'll be Abigale. I'll tell Claire when we talk."

"I don't have a problem with your identity changing; it's simply another persona for you. Others will have a problem, and I'll work to help everyone keep it straight."

"Zoe, you started working on alternate identities. Please pick one and start working on a full OSINT background, work history, etc."

"After the mobile home, I have already been working on several. I have to make updates carefully. If a full background appears for someone on multiple systems at the same time, it will get noticed."

"I get it. Listen, when you find the workspace, get it with a corporate account and buy the vehicle with that account as well."

"I'm looking at several locations for a workspace. Lawyers will be involved, meaning it will take several days. I'll focus on whatever can be done the fastest."

"Let's get the new vehicle first, and I know you can do all of this in parallel. They know who I am, so everything associated with Sam needs to change—a new vehicle, a new ID, and everything else. I think the best option will be to transfer to another vehicle, leaving the truck where it will attract them. However, transferring all my belongings will also draw attention. Let me think about what I should do, and I'll ask you some questions soon."

"Sam, Frank is calling on your regular cell phone. What do you want to do?" Because Sam left her main cell phone at the house, the cellular network could not track her. Zoe has full remote access and can tell her when Frank calls.

"I'm calming down, but my adrenaline is going back up. Talking to Frank is a risk right now. He needs to investigate a leak. Connect him, but don't let him know you are listening."

As soon as Zoe makes the connection, Sam talks fast. "Hi, Frank. I've been thinking about how they found me, and I've three explanations. The most probable explanation is that I made a mistake in L.A., and they detected my presence in the area, possibly while I was following the truck. Two, they have access to a phone and network infrastructure, which allows them to detect my activity patterns. Or three, they are monitoring your communications, and when you contact me or send agents to the area, they know. The last one only makes sense if you are being investigated in relation to the mobile home. It would justify tracking your phone communications. Currently, I will work on the assumption that they have all three options. From now on, I will stop communicating with you over regular phones, as they can be traced. I'll start using the special phone only."

Frank replies, "Hi Sam. Are you okay? You are talking really fast."

"Yes, my adrenaline is still high, and talking to you on a regular phone isn't helping."

"Okay, your logic is reasonable, even though I don't think they are tracking me."

"I gave the sheriff your number. I told him you'll want a full report on what happened, so he'll probably call you soon."

Frank asks Sam several questions about the men involved, whatever she could remember. After Sam mentions security cameras, Frank asks for any footage.

"I'll send you and the sheriff the login information to access the videos."

Traveling and talking with Frank about the attackers and the case on a regular cell phone, Sam is getting nervous. "I need to get off this phone. I'll stop for gas, use the restroom, and get some food. My travel will be west, possibly to Denver. I'll update you later," then Sam hangs up the phone.

Zoe immediately calls her back. "Zoe, please provide directions on where I can stop."

"There's a large gas station and truck stop two miles ahead. I have sent the security video login information to Frank and the sheriff. I should have something within the next couple of hours for the new vehicle."

Sam stops at the gas station, turns off her cell phone, and fills up the gas tank. As she walks to the store, she throws the phone into the trash. She has used it to talk to Frank, so it will be tracked now.

After Sam gets back into the truck, she turns on a new burner phone. She takes the time to set it up. This time also gives her the chance to calm down more.

She was in the fight, her adrenaline pumping high. That was a real firefight. This was her first minute to relax. Her hands aren't shaking anymore, but she's still feeling the adrenaline.

Calling Zoe with the new phone, they talk about logistics.

"I can get you a rental van quickly. Buying a vehicle will take more paperwork and longer."

"Okay, get a rental van that can be delivered, use the Abigale identity if you can, and if not, use Sam. We'll deal with the consequences later."

"We set up a business structure previously, where I have attorneys contracted for general business paperwork. With the pandemic, the process is becoming more automated. I can set up new businesses quickly. However, purchasing property involves attorneys and paperwork. Working with attorneys requires time, as they must comply with government regulations.

"I understand, and just like before, I'll let you and Claire optimize the details. Zoe, do I stop somewhere around Dallas or keep heading north?"

"I'm working on three options: Dallas, Texarkana, or Oklahoma City. Right now, Texarkana has the highest probability of meeting your needs in the shortest time frame."

"Then I'll keep going toward Texarkana after I pick up the rental car. Let me know when we have a pickup point."

"Based on the previous discussion, I won't have a workshop location complete for several days. You can stay in the Dallas area and slowly move north each day."

"I'm concerned about motels being open during the pandemic. If they are open, I'll need to provide identification each time I stay. Maybe I need to buy camping gear and live out of the rental for a few days, just like California."

About 90 minutes later, Zoe calls Sam and says, "I'm checking in with you. How are you doing?"

"I'm doing fine. I've calmed down. Now I'm driving and listening to music on the radio while I half think about all the things that need to get done."

"I have a location set up so you can pick up the van. First, you will need to park the truck at an abandoned store. I'll give you directions. Then a ride-share car will take you to pick up the van so you can drive it back and transfer the gear."

After picking up the rental van, she moves boxes of gear and the weapons, then checks the truck cab for anything else she might need. She pats the dashboard and says, "You've been a good truck, but this is goodbye." She locks the truck, gets into the van, and starts driving north.

"I need an open sporting goods store where I can purchase camping gear."

"There are two options that show open along the direction you are traveling."

"Okay, give me directions to the first one, and if they don't have what I need, we'll go to the second one."

Sam gets a sleeping bag, an air mattress, a cooler, a one-burner camp stove, and some camping meals from the first store. At the second store, she purchases blankets, rain gear, two small tarps, and magnets to put over the van windows on the inside. With this gear, she can stay in the van if no rooms are available. She's using a virtual credit card funded by one of the Bitcoin accounts.

Stopping at a grocery store, she buys water, instant coffee, snacks, and three SIM cards for the phone. In the van, she changes the SIM card on the phone, then calls Zoe with the new information.

"I'll use restaurant drive-through or pickup for most of my food. I'll be switching SIM cards every day. Also, please arrange a new credit card and have it delivered to a rental mailbox around Dallas."

"Got it. I'll also order more SIM cards and let you know when everything arrives."

"Zoe, we need to wipe my cell phone back at the house. Every time I communicate with Frank on a cell phone, I can be tracked. After the phone wipe is complete, turn it off. Forward my original number so that if Frank calls, you can get the message. I can call him from a burner if it's urgent."

"We need to use the special phones for Claire and Frank. I'll use burner phones for the two of us to talk when Wi-Fi isn't available."

"You should use the special phone for our communication. Use the SIM cards and the cellular network with the information encrypted."

"I don't want to do that because when I dump the phone, I don't want the special capabilities to be captured by anyone. What I would prefer is that you find a phone model that can be hacked, and we use encryption across the normal phone lines. The biggest issue is not what we say, but finding where I am. The special phone can be tracked on the cellular network. Changing the SIM will help confuse the process. Order another phone, and have it delivered with the other stuff."

"I'll take care of that and let you know where to pick it up. You're first workshop is in Texarkana. I'm working with an attorney to complete the necessary paperwork. The estimate is that it will take several days to complete. It is a small industrial building where the company went out of business. It does not list a cooking area, but it says it has a kitchen. I picked this one because it is available immediately and the paperwork is progressing faster than other options."

"That sounds good, Zoe. Thanks. I've been thinking while driving, and I want to create a template for locations to purchase. This means the size, features it needs to have, and equipment I'll want it to have or add. Having a prepared and ready location close to most major cities will give me the ability to move, rest, and work as needed. We have the money to do this, so let's act like we have a little control. Why don't we start by establishing a workshop near major cities with financial markets? Add some suggestions based on the total distance between here and Boston. We can add more later, but let's start with a few."

### 

Frank reports to DSAC Holland about what happened in Waco. "Frank, work with the Austin office and find out the identities of the attackers and who hired them. We're making significant progress, and then they find our information. How did they find her?"

"Sam suggested several options. One option is that they are monitoring my communications. She thinks that after the California mobile home incident, I'm being watched. I initially rejected the idea, but now I must agree with her on this one."

"She called me on my regular phone. They could have tracked that call as well. However, she told me she won't communicate on a regular phone any longer. The secure phone should prevent tracking."

"Any other possibilities? What do you think, Frank?"

"The only thing we have not talked about is a leak from inside the FBI. If we want to put everything on the table, we need to consider the extortion group is watching more than just me."

Leaving the DSAC's office, Frank thinks about what's happening with the investigation and with Sam. Nyah is right; every step he takes is being watched. Before Sam became involved, the investigation had stalled. She's providing information they would never have found related to the blackmail group. That makes her their primary target.

But he should arrest her for some things she has done. She told him she stole their money. She killed two people in California, even though it was to save his life, but she should provide a statement. Now there are four more dead in Texas. She doesn't know the process or politics that can get her in trouble.

He feels like he needs to protect her, but he can't protect her from the group when she's moving and hiding. He can try to help by providing support from inside the FBI. If he is going to risk his career for Sam and this investigation, he needs to think about his limits. When to act, when to wait, and eventually when to leave. He's already put everything at risk by not reporting that she stole the money. If the extortion group isn't reporting it, that means they don't want law enforcement to investigate the source of the money and its intended use. The stolen money is likely causing more problems than anything he has done.

Thinking to himself, "If I had this conversation with myself a year ago, I would have called myself crazy. I've been in this job for 16 years, and until this investigation, it has been a challenging yet fulfilling career. Now I'm thinking, get them, Sam!"

### # #

Sam spends the next several days traveling around North Texas, stopping for the night at a shopping mall, truck stop, or any location with multiple cars in the parking lot. After three days, she gets a motel room so she can shower. Every motel requires guests to wear masks. Most have limited rooms available because of cleaning requirements, but she doesn't have trouble finding vacancies.

In the motel room, Zoe calls and says, "Sam, I want to talk to you about using the special phone capabilities. I have evaluated many models of phones, how to hack them, how to secure them, and how to wipe them."

"What are you thinking?"

"I send you a phone model, or you buy one. I hack it, install all the software, and secure it. Everything is tied to the SIM you have installed. If the SIM card is changed, it will be wiped; if it is off for over 24 hours, it will be wiped when it is turned on. I can set it up so that if the wrong PIN is entered over three times, it will wipe. I think we can prevent your concern about someone else getting the special phone capabilities."

"Zoe, I will try it."

"Good, it is already on your current phone and using the special network. You will need to follow some prompts in a minute. The idea of changing the SIM card every day is still a good one. I am still working on a faster way to set the device up with any new SIM card. Maybe I leave an app that validates it is you, and then I can take over and put the common configuration on it."

"Zoe, these are good ideas. I am still concerned. Can you change the default configuration to have a lower special network configuration set? Update it more often, so if the phone is captured, the entire network is not exposed."

"Yes, got it. I will have that change completed across the network in a few hours."

The typical day involved getting breakfast and then heading out for a drive. Each day, she would pick a different compass direction to start from and spend a couple of hours driving away from where she had started that day. She would then find a park, rest stop, or truck stop and park for several hours.

When not driving, she refines Zoe's AI and scripts.

Now there are programs to create a node at a new data center, start the Zoe processes, and connect them to Zoe. Zoe took over after she made this. Zoe can now add her new capacity anywhere in the world she wants.

She would use the small fridge in the back of the van as a table. Her lunch break was scheduled after the peak lunch hour. Sam would stop for food, gas, water, and snacks.

Travel to the next place, where she would stay for the night, was timed to pick up takeout on the way between 6 and 7 p.m. She would usually park as far away from a mall or grocery store as possible, eat, and then decide whether to stay or move to another spot. Where she stopped for the night depended on Wi-Fi access. With pandemic hours, most stores would close between 7 and 9 p.m.

Wi-Fi allows her to work and talk with Claire almost every day. Zoe would always give her news and facts. Claire would talk about other things, trying to keep her spirits up.

# The New Workshop

After eight days, Sam gets up and starts her routine when she is told by Zoe that the paperwork for the new workshop will be completed today.

"It's about time; we need to be better prepared for the future."

"I'm working to get a workshop set up close to the major financial cities. The cities are Philadelphia, New York, Washington D.C., Boston, Chicago, Los Angeles, San Francisco, and Seattle. I added Memphis, Las Vegas, and San Antonio for larger area coverage. I have contractors scheduled to remodel four buildings to meet your requirements. Because of the surge in home improvement during the pandemic, contractors are scheduled, but most won't start for weeks. Texarkana was chosen because of the short timeframe required. Yes, Sam, this was short. Today, you can head in that direction. I'll have them leave the office door unlocked so you can get in and get the keys."

Because of where she had traveled the day before, it will take Sam several hours to travel to Texarkana. She heads to an industrial area with other small buildings. The building is two stories with a large roll-up door and a smaller office door on one side. She'll have to check the different sides when she arrives.

After finding the building, she drives around the neighborhood to get an idea of what's around, the street layout, and to see how many businesses are open. The next stop is the grocery store. She loaded up on groceries for a week, plus cleaning supplies. She wanted to get into the building and stay for a while, focusing on cleaning, setting up what she needed, and adding security.

Driving back to the building, she talks to Zoe about water, electricity, gas, and the internet. Zoe has already transferred everything, but the internet provider is sending a kit for Sam to set up and enable the internet.

"I'm using the same provider they used previously, so all you will need to do is connect the modem. Sam, the door to the office area should be open, and the keys will be in the key box to the left of the door."

"Sounds good," Sam replies.

She pulls up to the building in the small parking area. There's a large garage door to the left and a small office door to the right. There are two windows on the first floor on this side, one on each side of the small door. The building's concrete walls are its primary construction, and they resemble most of the industrial buildings in the vicinity. The second floor also features windows, allowing for natural light. She can see security lights at the top of the building and make a note to check on how they turn on.

Sam parks in front of the large garage door and walks to the office door. She enters, finds the light switch, and turns on the lights. She turns left, finds the key box, and pulls out the keys. The office door is labeled, and there are three more keys labeled with the exterior door number. There are eight internal door keys.

Locking the office door, she walks inside to open the garage door. The key is labeled #1 (BIG). The lock on the big door is a padlock on the door track mechanism. After unlocking the door, she uses the chain and opens it. The building has a large main floor, which is covered in a layer of dirt with boxes spread around. It looked like whoever was there before cleaned out what they wanted and left the rest as junk.

She drives the van into the building and simply parks in the middle of the floor. After closing the garage door, she locks it. The office area is to the right. The stairs lead to the second floor.

She had been offline from Zoe during this activity. She calls Zoe, and when Zoe answers, Sam asks, "Can you hear me okay? Is the signal strength any good?"

"The signal strength is low, but working."

"Okay, this is all we have for now. I need you to order a router that supports the new Wi-Fi 6 standard. We'll also need to see if they have Wi-Fi bridges or repeaters and add those for better coverage around the building. Let me describe the building as I walk around."

Sam tours the office section and the small kitchen area. The space was set up as a lunch or break room. It still has a fridge that's off. She turns the fridge on, and it makes noise, so she's hopeful it'll work. There are three offices and a conference room downstairs, with a lunchroom, bathrooms, a janitor's closet, and employee lockers. Upstairs, there are more offices, a couple of conference rooms, another set of bathrooms, and storage. The network utility closet is upstairs. There is no shower in the building, which Sam mentions to Zoe.

Zoe replies, "On short notice, this is the best I could get in the area. The others I'm working to set up will be remodeled to have things like showers."

"Okay, Zoe, I get it. I'd love a shower, but I'll survive."

The central part of the building has ample floor space, with outlines where machines used to be attached to the floor. It looks like the building was a sheet metal and welding company. She walks around the building, examining the layout and all the junk that had been left behind. There are a couple of old stick welders that won't turn on, and a couple of racks for raw materials. All the materials had been removed. The building had probably been busy before the pandemic, but now it's a shell full of dirt, junk, and broken dreams. It will need work, but Sam can use it.

After rearranging the junk so that she can turn the van around inside, she goes to the office area to find a place to sleep. She quickly stops that search, uses the bathroom, and then goes to the van. The van and the air mattress will be her bed. She'll stay in here until there's some place clean to put her sleeping bag.

The next morning, Sam starts a detailed search of the building. In all the offices, there are only two metal desks, both with broken drawers, and one with a bent leg. The conference rooms are entirely empty.

The janitor's closet is the best room because it has a large broom, and even though the handle is broken, it still works. It also contains several gallon jugs of cleaning liquids, each less than half full. They were considered junk and left behind, but they're precisely what Sam needs.

She takes the cleaning supplies from the closet, plus those she'd purchased, to the break room. Working at the hospital, she learned that bleach would kill COVID. She adds the bleach she bought to one of the cleaning liquids left behind. She checks the fridge, and it's cool inside, so she starts by cleaning it. Then she puts all her cold groceries from the cooler into the fridge. There's no microwave, cooktop, or oven; basically, nothing to heat food. Sam brings in the single-burner camp stove she had in the van and sets it on a counter, asking Zoe to make notes about what she needs. The list includes a new broom, a vacuum cleaner, and a good mop.

After the break room, she cleaned the women's bathroom upstairs. One office upstairs is a little larger than the others, probably the boss's office. It is empty of any furniture, so it is quick to clean. She would use this one for her room and workspace. She goes to find the desk she had seen the day before. By laying the desk on the edge, she could get the legs out the door and slide it down the hall. Now she had a desk with broken drawers where she could set up her computer.

She then realized she had seen no chairs in the building. She had no place to sit, so the desk was not useful.

Other notes for Zoe included adding washer and dryer connections as part of the remodel for the different workshops. She'll need to use a laundromat to wash everything, especially the cleaning rags.

After two weeks, Sam is more comfortable. She purchased more living supplies and had Zoe add them to their universal workshop list. Almost everything was ordered online by Zoe. Sam picks up the packages at a local mailbox rental place. She also added security cameras around the outside of the building. Little things like having a chair to sit in made her feel better. She's now able to focus on her equipment and how to get the information to stop the blackmail group.

Sam tells Zoe, "I'm going to check in with Frank. Please start the special phone session."

"Okay, I'll get it started and let you know when he responds." Sam waits at her desk with the special phone until Frank answers.

F: "Hello Armeda, how are you doing? Are you safe?"

A: "Yes, Frank, I have a place to stay and work. I'm keeping a very low profile these days."

F: "You found something in the Denver area."

A: "I'm not in the Denver area. That was done as a false lead on the open phone line. I'll only give general information about my location. I'm not making progress with my basic searches, so I'm evaluating how to take it up a notch."

F: "I understand about keeping your location secure. What do you need to take your searches up a notch? What can I do to help?"

A: "Do you have any more information about California? Connections with people, especially non-public stuff. Any financial links would be great. The Waco guys as well."

F: "I'll check and let you know."

A: "Send large stuff through the encrypted email. I'll plan on checking in every couple of weeks. It will be more frequent if I find anything."

F: "Stay safe."

### # #

Zoe redirected parts deliveries to the new location. Now that she's receiving parts, she could work on finishing the suit. The first time putting all the parts together, she had pants and a jacket. She put on the pants, flexed, and moved to identify binding points and areas of concern. Dictating notes to Zoe as she moved around, walking, running, jumping, and crouching. She then put on the tactical vest and jacket and moved around. Each movement is empty-handed and then repeated with a pistol and then repeated with a rifle. As she goes through these motions, she gives Zoe more notes.

"That is all the notes for now. The next steps for the suit are to review and implement changes. Before I do that, we need to work on the helmet and options. I think I can put together the basic helmet within the week. The problem is, I don't have a motorcycle to test the helmet."

"I'll start searching for motorcycles. What kind would you need or like?"

"I need a sport or street bike, and it should be used. The private sale of a used motorcycle would be better; it won't stand out as much with license plates."

Zoe gave Sam several used motorcycles to choose from, and two of the options the seller listed would accept Bitcoin as payment.

Sam contacts one seller and agrees to meet. Zoe orders a rideshare for herself as she puts on the suit. The car takes her to a neighborhood across town. Sam has only a standard helmet. She'll communicate with Zoe through a Bluetooth microphone and headphones in the helmet.

Sam is wearing a mask and introduces herself as Abigale. She scrutinized the motorcycle, started it, checked the engine response, and then asked the owner questions about his driving history. The seller asks Abigale, "How does a small woman like you handle a tall motorcycle like this?"

She replies, "Well, my experience is that riding a motorcycle is not about height or muscle. I let the motorcycle do the work. I just tell it where I want to go, manage the clutch, throttle, and brakes, and the motorcycle goes."

They agree on the price, and Sam paid him in bitcoin through her phone. The owner signed the title and handed it to Abigale.

He comments, "It's been a good bike, but I'm only using my new one," as he uses his thumb to point over his shoulder. Parked in the garage is a larger sports bike, probably with a 1200cc engine.

Sam nods, saying, "Thanks, I'll take care of her."

She starts the motorcycle again. She starts to put the helmet on and, as a final step, looks away from the seller, pulls her mask off, and then pulls down the helmet. Stepping on the foot peg, she swings her right leg over the seat but doesn't fully sit down. Left foot on top of the gear shifter, her left hand on the clutch; she shifts into first gear. She shifts to the left and puts her left foot down on the ground. Looking at the seller as she shifts the handlebars so that the front tire is straight. She twists the throttle and moves the clutch into the friction zone. As the motorcycle moves, she uses her foot to swing the kickstand up while balancing the bike. Then she shifts entirely into the seat. She turns out of his driveway and speeds up hard to 30 miles per hour.

Driving back to the workshop, Sam stopped for gas. She has Zoe look up what oil the bike needs, and she stops at an auto parts store to purchase the required oil and a few necessary tools. This is her first time on a sport bike in several years, and it's good to have a long drive back to the workshop, allowing her to get comfortable.

She keeps to the main streets, taking many turns to get the feel of the bike and practice. In one instance, another rider approaches her and wants to talk at a red light. He revs the engine of his bike; basically; he wants to see if Sam will race him. She opens her visor and then shakes her head no.

She yells, "I just got this one and need to spend time with it before I can race!" The other rider nods, and when the light turns green, drives ahead. At the next intersection, Sam turns right, then left. Two blocks later, she sees him in her rearview mirror. She enters the parking lot of a strip mall with several stores. Driving across the parking area, she stops with the motorcycle pointed toward an exit, where she can watch the rider on the road.

Pulling out her phone as if she's looking up some information. She is actually recording a video now, looking up as the phone is pointed toward the street. She waited to see if the rider would stop or drive on. He stops on the street and watches Sam for about 15 seconds. She held the phone on the tank so that the camera faced the rider, allowing Zoe to get a visual and start searching. He revs his engine, then pulls into traffic and drives away. It's probably nothing, but it's easy enough to grab a picture and have Zoe check to be sure.

Sam did more random turns; in a couple of cases, she circled the block with right turns. Constantly checking to see if someone is following. As she gets within a couple of miles, she has Zoe plot a route to avoid cameras as she approaches the workshop. Zoe informs Sam, "I didn't get the license plate, and with his helmet on, I can't use facial recognition. We don't have any details on that motorcycle rider."

During the next few weeks, she makes improvements to the suit and helmet system. After Zoe finds a used van, purchases it and has it delivered, Sam turns in the rental van. The new van was purchased by the same company that bought the building, so neither Sam's nor Abigale's names are associated.

She avoids cameras as much as possible, since any facial recognition system could reveal her location. The most likely way they found her in Texas is that they saw her face in California and used facial recognition. She would be in the FBI database because she visited the Boston office.

Fortunately, there are no transactions to track her under the name Sam. She has been using the Abigale ID and credit card when necessary or letting Zoe handle online transactions. However, to be prepared, Sam set up the ability for Zoe to wipe all the systems in the workshop remotely if she could not return. There's also an arson setup with kerosene and a phone detonator that could destroy the leather suit components.

Sam asks Zoe to research countermeasures for facial recognition and discuss options with her. When Zoe is ready, they go through how the process works by focusing on parts of the face that can't be masked with a beard or glasses. The distance between the eyes, the location of the tip of the nose, the distance to the cheekbones, and more. If she uses a mask everywhere, she should be able to reduce the positive matches.

She finished the design changes. Now she has a working suit. She's ready to travel. The suit allows the movement she needs, and the overlapping protective plates work well. The holster setup works well on both the motorcycle and her hips. Sam likes the way the holsters works, allowing her to transition from the bike to her hip in one easy movement.

### # # #

Sam started a chat with Frank to check in. She asks if Frank had any updates on finding the bad guys, to which he replies, "No." The phone chat was slow, but they continued to discuss options and next steps.

Suddenly, the connection is broken, and Zoe, through the computer speakers, says to Sam, "Someone just tried to access the communication server. I cut the connection and started a wipe and delete of the server."

Sam pauses for a few seconds and then says, "Is it a random-access search or targeted? If they know I'm talking to Frank, they can search every access point on the network. The phone on their end will be on a separate network to prevent accessing FBI information. It will be easy to track."

"Sam, with the VPN chain to the communication server, they won't be able to find you."

"I'm concerned, Zoe; we've underestimated these guys too many times. It looks like they have access to internet infrastructure. It's time to move to the next workshop." She needed a workshop with better facilities anyway. Bathing with a water hose or a washcloth is not cutting it.

"There is a workshop in Memphis, and the contractors will be done in the next week."

Sam started preparing to travel. She sends an encrypted email to Frank to talk about the attempted server access. She tells him she's changing locations and will contact him in a few days.

### 

Two days later, as she's loading the van, she hears a motorcycle. She checks the cameras, and it looks like the motorcycle and rider that followed her after she picked up her bike.

She asks Zoe, "Please watch him and try to determine the driver's identity. See if you can get the license plate from when he arrived." Sam continues to load the van, all of which is entirely inside the building. The motorcycle rider can't tell if she's in the building or what she's doing.

With the door closed and no air conditioning, Sam is sweating profusely while she loads the van. "Sam, I understand having the doors closed so no one can see your activities. The main area is not air-conditioned. Even with the use of fans, you can still become dehydrated. I will pester you to drink more water."

"Zoe, I'll go into the office area with the air conditioning for breaks and to get water frequently. I'm not in a rush to pack the van. Where did I put the magnetic decals? I know you don't know Zoe. It was rhetorical and trying to help me remember."

"I am reminding you they are in the conference room downstairs. Both the motorcycle decal and the special delivery decal."

"I like both designs. I'm going to put the motorcycle in the van now. The racing team logo with the Little Rock Going Fast name will work while I pull the motorcycle on the trailer to Memphis."

Sam packs the van with the items she's taking with her and loads the motorcycle. She'll leave before dawn. Zoe has been watching all the street cameras around the workshop for two days. She's tracking everyone's movements to see who might be interested in the workshop.

At 5 a.m., as she walks to the van, she asks Zoe, "Ready to wipe all the electronic systems?"

"I will start the process when you start the van. At that point, I will only have access to the security cameras and the burn system. After you're away, I'll let the contractors know they can start the remodel. The remodel won't start for eight weeks because of their backlog."

She pulls the van out, locks the big door, and starts driving away with the racing team decals on the van. Zoe is still watching all the cameras and gives Sam a route toward Little Rock on I-30.

For most of the trip to Little Rock, it rains, in some spots, bad enough that Zoe comments no one will be able to track the van.

Sam replies, "Good, that's exactly what we need." Sam also considers the fact that a motorcycle would have a difficult time keeping up with them.

In Little Rock, she follows Zoe's directions to I-40 and Memphis.

# Memphis Workshop

As Sam is getting onto I-40, Zoe tells her, "Two SUVs have just pulled up to the Texarkana workshop. Four men are checking the doors, looking for a way into the building."

"Can you call the police with an anonymous tip about suspicious activity? Tell the police they have guns and are trying to break into the building."

Zoe calls the police, and the dispatcher sends a car in that direction. After 10 minutes, Zoe informs Sam, "The police are on their way, but one of the four men got a phone call, and they all left."

Sam remarks, "They are better at finding links to us than we are at finding links to them."

"We don't know if they are part of the same group; they could just be looking for an easy business to break into."

"Sure, receiving a phone call saying the police are on their way is just a gang looking to rob a building. They have connections in the police."

The drive takes four and a half hours to get to Memphis. Then, it takes another 30 minutes to get to the workshop.

During the last part of the drive, Zoe gives an inventory of the workshop. "It has a kitchen with a stove, a refrigerator, and a microwave. The bathroom has a shower." She lists the materials that were delivered.

When she arrives, Sam goes through the process of opening the big door and backs the trailer into the building. She had to do some maneuvering because there are multiple pallets of stuff in the building.

"Sam, the van is owned by the same company that owns the Texarkana building. A completely different company owns this workshop. They are all owned by different companies. They're also all completely paid for with taxes up to date. There's even insurance on each building, like a normal business would set up."

"Glad to hear that. Let me put the cold items in the fridge, then I'll check the internet connection and security systems. We will need to get a new vehicle for this building."

Zoe continues, "This building has a basic security system. I've updated the plans for the other workshops to have a better system I can access."

After going through the basics and a tour of the building, Sam tells Zoe. "That's the complete walkthrough. The list of problems is pretty short. I can fix those over the next few days. However, I'm taking a break from manual labor to get a real shower." After the longest shower she's had in years, she goes to the kitchen to make a sandwich the way she likes it.

"Zoe, I like this kitchen much better. Where are the utensils, pots, pans, and plates?"

"I followed your requests, and the items you're asking about are on one of the pallets."

As she's finishing her chips, she talks to Zoe about their inability to find links between blackmailers and targets, or between different blackmailers. "They can find me even at the Texarkana workshop. We need to find some links. They have to be connected. If they're not, how could one database have all those targets? We need to take a different approach."

"I'd like you to take every person identified as part of the blackmail database. Targets, victims, and owners, and do a full OSINT analysis. Every social media link, everyone in a picture with them, every event, work function, and anything else you can find. Follow every link in every document and start building a map. If there are no direct links between these people, then there must be an intermediary. There have to be links we can find. Any financial data could give clues. Maybe they use the same bank somewhere; maybe they go to the same church."

"Sam, that kind of search will take some time, and there will be gaps."

"I know, but we need to search differently. I want to find out what they're doing with the money, and they have to be connected for that to work. Otherwise, why would they be blackmailing people with this elaborate setup? It must be to keep the money separate and safe."

"I'll get started and give you updates when I've found something. What are you going to do this afternoon?"

"I'll start unloading the van first and then work on the other equipment on the pallets."

"The desktop computers, along with the networking gear you asked to be ordered, are on the pallets. You can see the gun safe is in the office area. It was too heavy for you to move by yourself, so I had it installed."

Sam spends the next couple of days unpacking and setting up all the equipment. She now has a rack with switches, storage, and computing nodes. After she installs each computer, she does the initial setup. Each is running Linux and, as soon as they become available, Zoe accesses them and starts reconfiguring them. When Zoe accesses them, their CPU utilization fluctuates between about 10-20% and 100% and remains at that level. Sam doesn't ask about the details of the configuration; it's simply better to let Zoe manage that part.

"Zoe, now that the network is set up, I should check in with Frank. Please send him an encrypted email and set it up for tomorrow afternoon. Then check and see if Claire is available to catch up tonight."

"Email sent, and Claire has something on her calendar until 7:30 her time. I sent her an SMS message to ask about talking at 8 p.m. her time."

"It's been a couple of days. Is my request for the OSINT analysis crazy? If there are no visible links, how will we find these guys?"

"They are organized, and it appears they have been doing this for some time. The information from the L.A. warehouse goes back to 1998. Every indication is that these people use some of the money to hide and protect themselves. I don't think your request is crazy; it just will take time."

"Does the analysis include financial links?"

"Yes, I'm looking at everything possible. I'm being careful, so my searches don't trigger any alarms. That means it takes longer, but I'm working on it. Sam, what are your thoughts on the extensive use of cryptocurrencies? It wasn't available in 1998. It's a great tool for them to use now, though, especially since it's designed to be anonymous."

"You're right, but what did they do before Bitcoin? They had to do financial transactions back then. Is that how we can track them?"

"I can try, but there are fewer online records back then. While I can request some information, I won't get everything."

"I understand. They have to be using the money somewhere that's traceable. Do what you can."

"A forensic accountant would do this kind of analysis. I'm accessing the materials from several universities. I have lecture notes, textbooks, and videos of lectures I'll review."

"You're going to learn forensic accounting?"

"Yes, that's the logical next step. Many of the concepts are built on basics, so it will take time for me to get through all the material."

"Will going through all that material slow you down?"

"In the short term, it will affect my searches. Once I've learned the material, it should improve my searches."

"Ah, you'll know what you are looking for when you finish," comments Sam.

"Yes, I'll know what and how to search faster."

That evening, Zoe interrupts Sam with an alert "The Texarkana workshop alarm just activated."

"Access the cameras and record everything you can, especially faces. Add these guys to the OSINT analysis."

Ten minutes later, Zoe tells Sam, "I have all their faces."

"Thanks, and a question. Can you change the ownership of the building with a backdate of last week?"

"I think I can, but I'm not sure. It will depend on how automated and secure the state's computers are. What do you want to do?"

"Find something on these guys, who they are working for, what company they work for. Move the building to that company and then activate the burn system."

"That could be dangerous for these guys in the building, Sam."

"I know, and that's the point. We have to fight back, and they need to learn to be careful."

After several minutes, Zoe tells Sam, "I've moved the business to the state computers, canceled the insurance, and sent a note to stop the remodel. I can activate the burn system any time."

"Okay, but just to be sure, I physically set up that burn system to incinerate the suit's leather parts. I brought most of the suit parts with me. Will there be enough stuff to burn to keep the fire going?"

"Yes, the accelerant you set up is also designed to burn the office area."

"Okay, set off the burn system." Sam watches the security feed as one section of the office area suddenly catches fire. None of the men are in that room; they are focused on electronics. When a fire starts, it takes seconds for the fire alarm to sound and the sprinklers to activate in the building. The sprinkler in the room where the fire started is damaged and no longer functional.

Putting the building in the hiring company's name and now having an arson fire will cause issues for them—one more little thing to complicate their situation.

The strike teams head out of the building as the fire quickly spreads through the office area. In 15 minutes, fire trucks' sirens are audible down the street, and the team enters their vehicles and drives away. The office area is entirely on fire, removing trace evidence that Sam had been there.

"Time to also get rid of this van. Please arrange for an SUV that's owned by this workshop business. When you get that setup, I'll drive this one and park it somewhere."

"Okay, I'll get a used SUV for you."

Sam hasn't changed the registration for the motorcycle. As far as the state is concerned, it's owned by a man in Arkansas.

"Sam, with your helmet on, there can't be any facial recognition."

"Yes, so I'll use the motorcycle as much as possible."

Two days later, the new SUV is ready to be picked up. The paperwork is complete, and the dealership will deliver the van to the workshop in the afternoon. Sam takes the van and heads west across the river. She finds a club that doesn't open until the afternoon and parks the van. She orders a rideshare on her phone to take her to the Memphis library. From there, Zoe orders a rideshare to get Sam back to the workshop.

She's at the workshop to take possession of the SUV when it's dropped off. The dealer had someone drive it with another car following, which seems to be the COVID-safe way these days. They give Sam the keys and drive away.

### ###

"Sam, the analysis you requested is complete. I am ready to talk about the men from Texarkana and Waco."

"Whom do they work for? What connections do they have? Can we use this information?"

"Sam, I didn't get good pictures in Waco, so my analysis is lacking. The faces from Texarkana led to a security company. Based on that, I tried searching for the Waco gunmen with other security companies. I found out they had been working for a different security company several months ago. They were not on contract when they showed up in Waco. Based on that information, I started a deep analysis of both companies. My access is limited because they have few online records. The men who went after you don't have a job or contract in their systems. It was all done outside their normal records."

"They work for that company but didn't have an assignment. Doesn't that cause issues?"

"I think it will. I found payments to the security companies that look related. The companies that provided the payments are fake. The money was transferred from an international bank that I haven't been able to access."

"Sam, are these security companies' ones we can use to help us? If they'll try to kill someone simply for money, maybe we can pay them to force the extortion groups to alter their plans."

"That is an intriguing idea, Zoe. We don't have a specific target to engage with them. When we find one, I'll have to consider your idea."

### ###

"I talked to Zoe about the changes to your OSINT analysis. I agree we need more information. What else can we do?"

"Claire, I do have an idea we haven't considered, but you may not like it."

"Tell me what you're thinking."

"You have connections in business and finance through your dad's work. Are there questions we're not asking because we don't know? Maybe asking how to find unusual financial transactions could give us a new idea."

"My dad's first question will be why I want to know; the next question will be what I have done. However, I could get my brother, Charlie, to ask. When he asks what I've done, I'll say to him I'll tell you when I get arrested. I'll tell him nothing."

"That sounds good. I guess if that works with your brother to get his insight and help, then I'm all for it. If we can give Zoe some new ideas, she can better focus the searches."

# Testing the New Gear

Sam finished the tactical suit in Arkansas but didn't test it thoroughly. She wanted to test more than the basics of fit and movement. How would it work in a fight, and how would she test it to determine its effectiveness? This makes her think about her lack of exercise. She might not do well in a fight unless she's physically ready.

"Zoe, I haven't done real exercise in weeks. I need to figure out what to order to get back in shape. Can you look at the availability of weights and exercise equipment?"

"My initial search is that almost everything is out of stock. There are news reports about the surge in home exercise equipment sales."

"Okay, let's look at some of the non-typical equipment. How about one of the big punching bags to mount on the wall? I'll need gloves, as well. And, how about workout straps for bodyweight exercises?"

"I'm searching. The punching bag and gloves have been ordered. I'm putting the strap options on the computer screen for you to choose."

Sam scans through the options on the screen and picks one.

"For cardio, are there any stationary bikes available?"

"Only used ones and they cost more than the new ones, which are not available. There is another option for bicycle cardio activities. I can order a regular bicycle and a bike trainer stand for resistance. The total cost is much less."

"That will work for me. Thanks, Zoe."

"Everything is ordered, and I've updated the workshop equipment list."

"Zoe, you're awesome."

When everything arrives, she gets it set up and adds working out to her daily routine. During the first week, her muscles are so sore it hurts to get up in the morning. She realizes she could never let herself get into that shape again.

On her next trip to pick up packages, there is one Zoe never mentioned. "Zoe, what is this?"

"That's a biometric monitor. After your recent return to exercise, I did research. This device will allow me to monitor your condition while you exercise."

"You did this all on your own? I'm not sure having you monitor my bad fitness situation and low activity is good for me."

Each day, she would do basic calisthenics, some with straps, and stretching. She would then spend thirty minutes on the bag, punching and kicking, only stopping when she felt like her chest was going to explode. She's shocked at how out of shape she's become. After that, she would spend thirty minutes on the bike. She would vary the resistance during the ride. After all that, she would do more stretching while she cooled down. She's able to do all her exercise work inside, keeping out of sight.

The next call with Claire starts with, "Hi, how sore are you today?"

"It's getting better. Today, I increased my intensity a little. I'll continue to increase the intensity as my body recovers. Oh, and by the way, Zoe ordered a biometric monitor and is analyzing my workouts now."

Claire laughs, "That is hilarious. Zoe, how's she doing?"

"Claire, your monitor will arrive tomorrow."

Sam laughs, "What's good for the goose!"

"I won't start with a bunch of numbers. Sam is in bad shape. The predictive models say that the way she is improving means she started from a bad place. Her progress has been remarkable because of her dedication. I haven't been recommending changes because I want Sam to stick with what works for her."

"Sam, I talked to Zoe about the equipment you purchased and what you're doing. I've been doing yoga because I can do that at home. Doing what you're doing would be better for me. I mean not the punching bag yet, but I'm going to start calisthenics and using bands."

"That's great, Claire. I'm glad you are taking it up a notch.

After a couple of weeks, when her muscles had recovered and she could move as she should, she put on the suit and punched and kicked the bag. She performed backhanded moves, forearms, as well as fists. Punching the bag while wearing the suit helped her understand her movement restrictions, and she adjusted her tactics accordingly.

"Sam, with the suit, your biometrics are showing much higher stress on your cardiovascular system. I know that's what you want, but we need to change your diet, or you will have a problem continuing to improve. I have ordered vitamin supplements for you to take."

"Okay, sounds good. Hey, I think it's time to check in with Frank. I haven't given him any details about Texarkana—nothing about these guys showing up or the fire. The problem is knowing how they found me. I stopped using cell phones to talk to anyone but you."

"We had the attack on the communication server. The only way they could know the communication was even happening is on Frank's side."

F: "Hello Armeda, it has been more than a couple of weeks."

A: "Well, Frank, I had a problem. Bad guys showed up where I was staying."

F: "Are you okay?"

A: "I got away and have a new place. It's as secure as it can be."

F: "Can you tell me any details about your situation?"

A: "I have a place with what I need: fast internet and a garage."

F: "Are you out in the country?"

A: "No, but I'm not far from downtown either."

F: "That sounds like you are at least close to a larger city, so you have access to help."

A: "I didn't move far, but it's a bigger city. I can't just call for help like most people. Do you have any new information for me?"

F: "Yes, I do, but I wanted to talk with you before I send it via email."

They discussed the data Frank was providing, and Sam shared her thoughts. It took some time because Sam had only used the chat option to communicate with Frank. Voice communication requires much more bandwidth, and the network traffic is easier to track.

###

When her supplies get low, Sam sets up a trip to the warehouse store to purchase more bulk supplies. While she's out, she also stops getting fresh groceries, including a couple of steaks. Tonight, her dinner will be a good meal.

Sam is getting rougher with the punching bag every day. Every afternoon, she rearranges things and cleans. "You're anxious about something, Sam. What's going on?"

"I'm stir-crazy. I have been in this building for weeks while you do most of the work."

"You've been working on getting your conditioning back and providing ideas for my searches."

"I want to ride the motorcycle. Please check the cameras in the area. I'll ride the next time the weather is good."

"I'll check the cameras."

She completes her workout for the day, showers, and gets ready. Outside, it's clear with mild winds; the temperature is in the high 60s, a perfect October day for a ride.

"Sam, the government is talking about the COVID-19 infection rate dropping, and they are opening more things. You may see more activity on your ride."

"I'm not planning to stop for anything but gas. I'll be back in a couple of hours."

She suits up and takes the bike out, staying on surface streets and using the large avenues to ride.

Her route takes her past many of the classic Memphis sites, which she admires and rides past. Even if she wanted to visit, they are all closed because of the pandemic. The traffic is very light, with more delivery vans than cars. She stops for gas and grabs food from the convenience store. Lifting her helmet so the face guard was just above her eyes, she eats in a parking lot. When she finishes, she picks a direction and rides that way for another 30 minutes before starting back to the workshop.

Doing a U-turn, she spots him. The motorcycle is following her, and it appears to be the same rider as in Texarkana. Sam downshifts and accelerates away. The rider immediately starts his U-turn and begins chasing her. She calls Zoe as she gets through traffic and takes hard turns. She tells her what's happening and asks for help.

Zoe changes the traffic lights to get traffic out of Sam's way and tries to put as much in the other driver's way. He's running red lights, and they're both traveling fast. Sam has a pistol with her, but it's in her backpack, not visible.

After several high-speed turns, Sam enters an alley where a trash dumpster stands between her and the rider. She quickly pulls out the pistol and, using her magnet attachment holster, puts it on the motorcycle. Adjusting her backpack, she drives again.

She's on Airways Blvd, which goes by the airport and the police department. After three blocks, the three SUVs traveling the other way suddenly crossed traffic and came at her. She uses the maneuverability of the motorcycle to avoid them and speed up.

Zoe tells her, "I can see them from the street cameras. I'll use the same tactics with the traffic lights ahead. You should be able to outmaneuver them."

The tactic was working; she was putting more distance between them when the motorcycle and rider returned. He's in the other lane, traveling in the opposite direction. He shifts to her lane, driving down the center of the lane against the flow of traffic. Drivers are veering to the side to get out of the motorcycle's way.

He's accelerating toward her, and she sees him reach back and pull a gun. Sam immediately pulls hers from the holster and fires at the same time he fires at her. His bullet hits her vest, and it feels like a sledgehammer just hit her chest. Her bullet hits him in the chest, and it's obvious he doesn't have a vest on. She fires at him again, and this time the bullet goes through the visor on his helmet. His head snaps back from the impact, and then he slumped forward. The motorcycle keeps moving for a few yards before it swerves into a car. The impact causes the rider to fly over the car and land on the front of a delivery van.

Traffic is chaotic. Sam holsters the pistol and has to slow down to get through the traffic. This allows the SUVs to catch up with her. As they get close, one of the SUV passengers leans out of the window and starts shooting at her.

During the next minute, Sam is simply trying to get away while one or two of the people in the SUVs shoot at her. Feeling multiple impacts on her back, she shifts her arms and legs as close to the motorcycle as possible to avoid the bullets. She is also weaving to make herself and the motorcycle harder to hit. She understands that the longer the situation continues, the higher her chance of being killed becomes.

"Zoe, access the remote capabilities and shut down the cars! Every modern car is equipped with a remote shutdown capability in case it is stolen. Hack the manufacturer's sites and try to shut them down!"

"I don't know how secure their systems are, and it may take some time, but I'm working on it."

She finds a gap in traffic and speeds ahead. When she has about a hundred yards between them, she turns right at the next intersection. It's a hard right, and she shifts her weight off the motorcycle to increase the lean angle. She drives down the street for about thirty yards, then turns hard left across the lanes.

She needs to do several things almost simultaneously. When she starts the last turn to the left, she puts the motorcycle in neutral. It's a sharp turn, and as the bike pulls upright, she lowers the kickstand. This shuts off the engine because of the automatic safety shutoff. She stands on the foot pegs and swings her right leg over to dismount while hitting the starter to restart the engine. When the motorcycle stops, she leans it onto the kickstand. She's now off the bike and facing the traffic. The motorcycle is sitting on the kickstand, in neutral, with the engine running.

She's holding her gun with both hands as the first SUV comes around the corner. As the SUV straightens out and the driver sees Sam on the road, you hear the motor roar as he accelerates toward her. Sam fires at the bottom of the windshield on the driver's side. The bullet goes through the gap in the steering wheel, hitting the driver in the chest. The recoil moves the gun, and she brings it back partway to fire above the steering wheel, hitting the driver in the head. She immediately shifts to the driver's front tire and fires.

With the driver not controlling the steering, the SUV immediately turns left and smashes into cars parked next to the curb. While the first SUV is crashing, Sam shifts to the second SUV as it rounds the corner. The passenger is trying to get a gun onto Sam. Her shot hits him in the upper right chest. She shoots the driver-side tire on this car as well. The driver then must work to control the SUV. In a hard turn, with a flat tire, the right-side tires come off the ground.

Sam shifts back to the first SUV, where the passenger has recovered from the crash and is aiming at her. Her bullet hits him in the right cheek as he shoots. His bullet hits the interlocking titanium plates on Sam's right shoulder. The bullet knocks her shoulder back, which causes the bullet to be deflected away from Sam. It also messes with her aim and control of the pistol.

Sam switches back to the second SUV but needs to make a large adjustment after the bullet hits her shoulder. She knows she'll have severe bruises.

The driver of the second SUV has it back on all four tires when Sam's bullet hits his nose. Because of the flat front tire and a lack of driver control, the vehicle turns to the left, still speeding up, and slams into the rear of the first SUV.

The third SUV is cornering, but it is trapped behind the other two SUVs and parked cars. The driver is trying to use the SUV to push the others out of the way.

Sam turns around to the motorcycle. Holstering her gun, she grabs the handlebars and pushes the bike forward. She puts her left foot on the peg and the gear shifter. Leaning and counterbalancing the motorcycle, she puts it into first gear. She lets out the clutch as she swings her right leg over the seat while turning hard to the right. Accelerating at the next corner, she turns left, hearing gunshots behind her.

She makes it around the corner and acts as if they're still chasing her. After a couple of blocks, Zoe tells her, "Slow down to normal speed. I gained access to the manufacturer's system and shut down all three SUVs. The police arrived and blocked the streets."

"Okay. Find an abandoned area so I can get rid of the motorcycle." Zoe directs Sam to an old strip mall outside of town. It's all overgrown, but it has a fence around it, as if they were going to tear it down at some point. Behind the strip mall is a drainage area that she can use to get out of sight. Sam steers the motorcycle into the lot and around the back, so it won't be seen from the street.

"I'll be offline for some time." Taking the helmet off, and rips out several of the parts inside, putting them in her backpack. She puts the helmet on the ground and stomps on it, breaking the visor.

She removes the jacket and the vest. Putting the vest down on the ground next to the motorcycle, she opens the inside facing up. She removes the fuel line from the injector manifold and lets gas from the tank splash on the vest. She uses the jacket to splash gas all over the top of the bike.

Now she's dressed in a T-shirt, leather leggings, and riding boots. Her backpack now has six bullet holes in it, but it's better than nothing. She unloads the gun, puts it under the gas stream, and then drops it next to the jacket. Tossing the ammo clip toward the building so that it won't be in the fire. She's letting the gas destroy DNA evidence in the vest and jacket. The gun was handled with gloves on, so there are no fingerprints, and the gas will quickly damage any trace DNA.

Using her pocketknife, she cuts wires on the bike, then uses them to create a spark. It takes several attempts before the gas ignites. It quickly engulfs the motorcycle. Burning gas drips down and catches the vest and jacket on fire.

Waiting until the gas tank is empty reduces the potential for an explosion, but it does not eliminate the risk entirely. Sam gets through the back fence and into the drainage area.

She's shaking. "They found me again. How are they finding me?" She takes several deep breaths and starts moving toward the center of town. She calls Zoe, "I'm alive. Please order a ride for me to return to the workshop. I'm walking toward town right now, just like a normal person out and about."

# Travel to Boston

Sam gets back to the workshop, locks everything up, and begins packing. "It's time to move to another workshop. Get prepared to wipe all the systems here. The suit worked well, but that's not how I wanted my first actual test to go. I'm grabbing clothes, my backpack of gear, and whatever else I need to pack into the SUV."

"The forensic accounting training is working. I found a link with a real estate transaction."

"This is awesome timing," Sam replies sarcastically. "Today, you find the link we've been looking for, right when the bad guys find me again and I get shot."

Zoe continues, "One of the people from the OSINT analysis owns a company that purchased a building. They used a Bitcoin transaction for the purchase. The Bitcoin wallet they used had deposits from three other Bitcoin wallets just before the purchase. I don't know who owns the other wallets. The company that purchased the building I'm associating with the one wallet and searching the blockchain for all other transactions to and from that account."

"Thanks, please map out all the wallets that are associated with all the accounts."

After a pause, Sam stated, "If a company owns a Bitcoin wallet, its accounting system should track all transactions and list every wallet used. How can we get that information to make progress?"

"I would say that we need to access the company network and let me search for the information."

"Sure, where are they located?"

"The company's office is in Boston."

"It looks like I need to travel to Boston and get into that network."

"I found something else. Analyzing the blackmail targets, I found many that fit the profile of pedophiles."

Sam starts to ask a question, then says, "No, don't tell me the details; it will just make me more upset. Please compile a list and then send it to Frank and Phil via an encrypted email. When it rains, it pours. Any other news?"

"The file has been sent, and I tagged it as a high priority with a brief message of 'This part of the list needs to be investigated.'"

"Thanks, keep up the OSINT searching."

Sam throws the sleeping bag, food, and water into the SUV. She loads her duffel and the hacking gear into the back seat. Her second backpack, without bullet holes, goes in the passenger seat. She opens the large door and drives out. Locking the door after driving out, she heads to the highway and starts traveling north.

This SUV includes Bluetooth, allowing Sam to avoid using a headset. Zoe comments, "Based on the time of day, plan to stop in Nashville for food and gas. After that, you can get to Cincinnati in about 4 hours."

"That sounds good. Please check train and bus connections from Cincinnati to Boston."

Zoe replies after a pause, "I have checked the trains and buses. The fastest travel option to Boston will be to drive. That will be 13 hours with no stops."

"Book me a motel on the north side of Cincinnati. I'll get rest and start driving in the morning, around 7 a.m. That should put me in Boston after the evening rush hour. On the drive, we can work on a plan. I'll stop somewhere in Boston and prepare the gear."

"I'll take care of it, Sam. Are you doing okay?"

"Zoe, this is the second time I've been attacked. They found me. This attack was on the street. That made it worse than Waco. The good news is that I'm so pissed off right now, I don't feel like I need to throw up. Driving will help me calm down more."

"Claire has been calling. I told her you're busy, to which she replied that she's seen the TV reports of what happened in Memphis."

"Okay, connect Claire."

As soon as Claire gets on the phone, she talks rapidly, "Are you okay? You're all over the TV and it looks like you were shot several times. Where are you now? How can I help? What do you need?" Claire stops talking, and Sam waits.

Zoe replies to Claire, "She's not bleeding."

Sam shouts, "Don't talk about my condition or location. This is encrypted, but still on a burner cell phone. Yes, I was hit once in the chest, six times in the back, and once in the shoulder. I'll have bruises for some time, but the suit worked well. Besides, you're asking the wrong questions. The real question is: how did they find me? I'm not doing anything to get noticed, but they're finding me. I will not talk about where I am or what I'm doing until I feel comfortable."

"You're upset, understandably so."

"Claire. I'm a little past upset right now! I was just shot eight times." Sam hits the end button on the Bluetooth controls. She wipes her sweaty hand on her pants and yells at the windshield.

The phone rings with Zoe's name on the caller ID. She answers the phone, and Claire says, "Please don't hang up. Again, I'm so sorry, and not trying to make you feel worse. I don't know how you're feeling right now, and I shouldn't make light of the ordeal you just went through. Having never been in danger like that before, I'm operating from some media-romanticized ideas of what it was like for you. Again, I'm sorry. It's just that I've been so excited to work with you to stop these guys and so energized to learn and make a difference. And so, so worried about you. I took the classes to help, and I learned so many things, but I get to do is sit here and wait until I can talk to you again. I feel ineffective right now."

"Claire, you and Zoe have done so much to help with questions and research that I would have struggled with. If you had been with me, we both would probably be dead. Although you've learned a great deal, you're not yet at the same level as I am. That is not a statement to be cruel, but because we both know that I've been training for these situations a lot longer than you have. For that reason, I don't want you to ever get into a situation like that. Until we understand how they are tracking me and stop them, I need to keep you as far from this as possible."

Zoe comments when Sam pauses, "I have something to discuss related to how they are tracking you. You have been talking to Frank on the secure phone, but there is a correlation between your conversations and the bad guys showing up within days. It fits Waco, Texarkana, and now Memphis."

"Zoe, do you think they compromised the phones?"

"No, Claire, I'm confident the phones are secure." Zoe continues, "The only logical conclusion is that Frank is being watched; maybe his systems are directly feeding them information."

"Okay, both of you, I will not chat with Frank. I'm going quiet. Claire and Zoe will discuss the plan with you. I have to stay off motorcycles and keep a low profile for now."

Claire replies, "Please don't stop talking to me. I have an idea about how to influence the perception of the unknown motorcycle rider in Memphis, and I'll work with Zoe on that one. I want to stay in sync so I can make sure you're not losing it. This is difficult for you or me, but it's way worse for you. Sam, please tell me you'll keep talking to me."

"We'll keep in touch, Claire, I promise. But there will be days I don't talk, and you need to be okay with that."

### ###

The next day at the Memphis police station, they're preparing for a news conference to talk about the shooting. They have four men in custody, and none of them said a word after being arrested. The one with the chest wound was still in the hospital, handcuffed to the bed. There are four members of the group dead from gunshots. The car chase resulted in four civilians being shot and injured more.

The police chief is visibly pissed. His city was shot up, and the police have not found the motorcycle rider. He starts the meeting by asking if there have been any updates about the motorcycle rider.

One detective raises his pen and says, "They found the motorcycle outside of town. It had been set on fire and burned. We won't be able to get any DNA because of the fire. They also recovered the gun and a bulletproof vest that had two bullets in the front and six in the back."

The chief asks, "Confirm there were six slugs in the back?"

"Yes," the detective confirmed.

The chief asks, "What's going on? We have an armed motorcycle rider being chased through Memphis by three SUVs."

"And another motorcycle," the detective says loudly.

"Yesterday, there were news reports that this rider is a vigilante killing people on the street. This looks more like the guys in the SUV are terrorists and the rider was just trying to get away."

A detective adds, "The vigilante thing came from an anonymous caller to the press."

"What about the registration of the motorcycle?"

Another detective replies, "It's registered to a man in Arkansas. We called him, and he can confirm he's been in Arkansas. He told me he had sold the motorcycle several weeks ago. The buyer was a young woman, and he didn't know that the registration hadn't been changed. We have a description, but it's basic; she wore a mask, and nothing stands out."

The chief declares, "Right now, we need to find this woman and charge her with everything. We need to get the men identified and figure out what's going on. Charge the four we have in custody with everything. I've also asked the local FBI office to help with this case."

# Do We Have a Leak

The street incident in Memphis is all over the news, and everyone is searching for a mystery motorcycle rider. Phil comes over to Frank's desk to talk about Memphis.

"Frank, that thing was crazy. I scanned through the video, and the motorcycle rider was taking hits in the back as they chased her. She was trying to get away."

Another agent, a few seats down, says, "I know a detective in Memphis and called him. He said the rider took two in front and six in the back."

Frank says, "I saw the news flash reports and heard about the rider SUV standoff in the street. I want to see that video."

Phil tells Frank the best place to see the video. The video starts with the motorcycle rider in a hard turn onto the street. The camera is on the streetlight pole at the next intersection.

Frank watches the video, then replays it, saying, "Phil, that is Sam quietly. The size is right; she is standing in the street while big SUVs are speeding up to run her over and shooting four attackers in seconds. She moves like Sam at the coffee shop. Even with the helmet covering her face, that is the woman in the coffee shop after the shooting."

Phil is listening as the video plays again. "Frank, it could be her. We need to tell the boss."

"I know, but this could be a real death sentence for Sam if every cop in the country is looking to arrest her."

Frank goes to the DSAC's office and asks her assistant if he and Phil could have thirty minutes. "It's about Memphis."

Gloria says, "I'll let her know as soon as she's off her current call."

Fifteen minutes later, Frank gets a call from Gloria to come to her office. Frank waves to Phil and starts heading toward the DSAC Holland's office. Gloria says, "Go straight in."

At the moment, Nyah and Patrick enter the area. Nyah says, "DSAC Holland called me to join this discussion. The SUV shooters in Memphis could be domestic terrorists."

She tells them, "I have back-to-back meetings, so tell me what's going on."

Frank says, "The Memphis motorcycle rider is Sam."

Cassy says, "Now I'm interested. Sit down and tell me what you know."

"The build, movement, and skill all match; it is Sam. We know nothing about the men in the SUVs," Frank replies.

Nyah states, "This takes it to a new level, Frank."

Cassy continues, "Frank, your secret source has found more information than the FBI on the blackmail ring. Now she's part of an obvious shooting in Memphis. She's been called a vigilante, killing people all over Memphis."

Phil clears his throat and says, "Let's clear up some things. First, Sam fired nine shots, and all of them hit a bad guy or a tire. She had six slugs in the back of her tactical vest. The other guys were shooting up the streets while she was trying to get away. She stopped them from shooting more than they did."

Nyah interjects, "I think the real question is how did they find her? We know they have no problem shooting up a city to get to Sam, so she must be getting close to something."

Frank states, "They keep finding her and trying to kill her. They found her in Waco, where she killed four attackers and got away."

Nyah asks, "Do you know how they are finding her, Frank?"

"Sam suspects that it's from my communications with her; they're tracking my calls and messages. She thinks it's related to the L.A. team investigating the missing computers. It would give them cause to get a warrant to track my communications. Cassy, if we identify her, every law enforcement person in the country will look for her, not just the bad guys. It will be a death sentence for her to be identified."

"Frank, this is a major event, and we can't ignore it."

"I propose we don't identify her, but we support the investigation in every other way."

Patrick comments, "There are four blackmail group henchmen in custody in Memphis; however, if we talk about the blackmail group, it will point toward Sam. We can treat it as a domestic terror group to get information. We need to focus on these individuals and learn what we can, specifically to determine if they're connected to any groups we're investigating. At least we can find out who they are and who's paying them. We can start with their digital background. They needed to travel to Memphis; they probably recovered phones when these guys were arrested."

Frank says, "No one ever identified the guys in Waco, but we didn't put our resources there while we had the mobile home, desert burial stuff to investigate. The attackers had no identification, no prints, or DNA in the system."

"Frank, I'll support you on this, but if there is another street shooting like Memphis, we're going to let everyone know."

"I understand," replies Frank.

### 

When Sam gets to Boston, Zoe provides directions to a motel. She checks in after picking up some takeout for dinner. She's been planning with Zoe for most of the drive, so she disconnects, eats, and watches the news. The news has a long segment about Memphis and the mystery motorcycle rider. After the obvious commentary, the news anchor then comments on the online social media discussion and what people think is happening. The ideas cover drugs, stolen jewels, and national security secrets, but the one getting the biggest traction was a deep-cover agent.

Sam opens her laptop and searches for the Memphis rider. As the web page is loading, her phone rings. She knows it's Zoe because only Zoe has this number.

"Hello Zoe, have you seen this online stuff about Memphis?"

"Yes, this is what Claire talked about, that we would work on during the call. She told me to post from multiple people about the mystery rider and how you were the good guy in the chase. I'm posting information and commenting on the posts to reinforce the idea. I've also started releasing slow-motion videos from the street cameras that show

how careful you were with bystanders and shooting."

"Huh, okay, I'll come back to that. Currently, I will send a note to Frank via encrypted email. I want you to monitor the phone in the FBI lab, get audio if you can, and pictures when anyone touches the phone."

"Sure thing, Sam. I also have everything ready to wipe the phone. I've already removed everything except essential code and information."

"Great, let me send this email, and then we'll make sure I have what I need for tomorrow."

Sam writes an email to Frank using the encrypted account. "Frank, they found me again in Memphis, not the exact address, but they searched and waited. It's always within a few days of chatting with you. I'll be offline until I'm comfortable with a communication option."

### 

The next day, Frank reads the email and then contacts everyone for a meeting. "Sam sent an encrypted email saying she'll be offline until she's comfortable with the communication."

Phil comments, "That phone is the most secure communication system I've ever seen or heard about. It's not through the phone."

Nyah states, "Then there is a leak in our building. Patrick, let's go check out this phone."

Frank replies, "We can't try to hack the phone, or it will wipe."

"Frank, if the system is compromised, it doesn't matter," replies Nyah.

On the way to the lab, Nyah tells Patrick, "Fresh eyes, wide open. Look at everything."

When they arrive at the lab, Phil asks about the activity on the phone. They are told there has been nothing. Nyah asks basic questions while Patrick is looking at the equipment around the phone.

As they are discussing the DSAC, Holland enters with two men. "Everyone, these gentlemen are from D.C. and have requested the phone. I told them it's part of an ongoing investigation, and they can't have it; however, I agreed they can see the device."

Colin is monitoring the network traffic on the phone network and notices an increase in activity. He moves to block the screen from the D.C. guys and looks at Phil.

Zoe listened to the introduction on the phone. She started taking pictures that showed nothing. Deciding to use the phone as bait, she started a chat session on it.

The phone chimes with a message, and everyone turns to look at it. Patrick is close to Frank and says, "Don't answer it." Patrick looks at Nyah with a slight tilt of his head and repeats, emphasizing his statement, "Don't answer the phone."

When they hear the chime, the two D.C. agents immediately walk to the phone. One turns around and blocks everyone else from getting to the phone. The other types into the chat, "Who is this?" Zoe takes a silent picture at that point while replying, "You're not Frank." The phone then displays the message 'Conversation ended.'

Phil yells, "What the crap are you doing?"

DSAC Holland touches Phil's arm and says to the D.C. agents, "You two come with me to my office. We're going to call your boss and talk about the investigation you just ruined." The director leaves with the two D.C. agents.

As soon as DSAC Holland opens the door, Patrick looks at Nyah, catches her eye, and starts walking to the door. Nyah looks at Frank and uses her thumb to point to the door, giving the signal to go that way. Phil and Colin also follow Frank out. Once outside, Patrick points up and tells them, "There is a camera watching the phone screen."

Colin, Frank, and Phil all look at Patrick, and Phil says, "Of course, that's how we record the conversation."

Patrick looks at each of them and says, "There is a pen camera in the ceiling watching the phone."

Colin says, "Are you sure?" in a determined voice. "That's a secure lab; not just anyone can get in to install a camera." No one can sneak into his lab.

Patrick says, "Get a ladder." Pointing up, he says, "Push that tile up and look over the lab and see what's in that space."

Phil tells Colin, "If they could put in a camera, they might have swapped the phone cable as well. Please check that it's not a hacking cable."

Frank adds, "We have the network traffic captured on the cell phone Wi-Fi. If they used that to talk to the cable, we should be able to trace the other endpoint. Sam sent me a note that one of our chat sessions was monitored."

Nyah tells the group, "We need to talk in a conference room." She heads toward the area of the building with the larger conference rooms.

Colin says, "I need to check this out." He walks back to the lab door.

They find an empty room, and Nyah calls Gloria to let her know which room they are meeting in.

"Frank, we know how; we don't know who," says Nyah. "Also, if they're monitoring you, Frank, why the camera? Now what do we do?"

Patrick answers, "Anyone can use the phone. It's just sitting in the lab. The camera would let them watch everything."

"When we know the space is clear, I'll email Sam and let her know what we found out, how."

Nyah replies, "If I were her, I don't know that I would trust communication in this building."

Phil then says, "What alternative do we have?"

DSAC Holland enters the room saying, "Gloria told me you gave her the info on the room, so I surmised you have something to discuss." Nyah looks at Patrick. Patrick tells Cassy what he found and why they are meeting here.

While Patrick is talking, Gloria enters the room. Her face is flushed, and she's breathing quickly, visibly upset.

She says, "I'm sorry, ma'am, I tried to stop them."

"Take it easy and tell me what happened."

Colin enters the room and stands by the door while Gloria talks. "I was escorting the two agents to the lobby, as you asked. In the elevator, they hit the button for this floor and went to the lab. They took the phone and left. They pushed their way past me and left."

Colin says, "Excuse me!"

Cassy looks at him and says, "You have something to add?"

"Actually, I do. When I returned to the lab, the phone displayed a message on the screen. It said purging with a progress bar. After a few seconds, it changed to 'bricking started', then the screen went blank."

Phil laughs. Frank is chuckling.

Patrick asks, "Intentionally bricking the phone?"

Phil replies, "Forensic countermeasures. The phone is worthless to everyone now."

Cassy stops smiling and says, "My best source of information was attacked in Memphis, and now my primary way to communicate with her is a stolen brick. She must be getting close to something; they are spending a lot of money to find her. How do we help her? She's not an agent, and she doesn't technically work for me, but she's probably my best asset against these guys right now."

Colin says quietly, "Excuse me."

Cassy looks at him and says, "Come, sit down and talk."

Gloria walks to the door and leaves.

Colin sits down and tells the group, "You said Sam is an asset. Have you seen social media in the last 24 hours? Multiple ideas are floating around about who the mystery motorcycle rider is. The one getting the most volume and attention is that the rider is a deep-cover agent trying to stop domestic terrorists. Sam could be your deep cover agent."

Nyah laughs, then says loudly, "That's awesome."

Phil looks at Nyah as if she's crazy.

Nyah continues, "Look at the situation. We have someone who doesn't show up on any government payroll; she's a gun person. In fact, she was a competitive shooter. She has an engineering degree. Some of the domestic terror groups would sell their grandmother to have Sam in their group. She's a perfect deep-cover agent. No group could find a flaw with her cover because it's real."

Nyah continues, "They'll all see Memphis, read the social media, and every group will look at their members who ride motorcycles and shoot. Is one of them a deep-cover agent?"

Frank asks, "Can we use this to help Sam? Having law enforcement give her some space because they think she is a deep-cover agent would be helpful."

Phil looks around and says, "I have a couple of ideas. We need a code name for Sam. Second, she has developed some of the most sophisticated programs for analyzing online data. She's putting together a map of people and connections for the extortion group. What if we ask her to apply that technology to one group that Nyah identifies? She may generate real leads, meaning it could look like she's a deep-cover agent. She's using Armeda with Frank, so maybe we can use Agent A."

Nyah looks at Patrick, saying, "Do you know anyone in the media? If not, you need to make a friend. Having an FBI agent discuss the deep cover concept may be helpful if we can change the focus and maybe give Sam, sorry Agent A, some space. We don't want law enforcement looking for her."

### # #

Abbie walks into the busy newsroom. Several people are working on the next segment that will go live in half an hour. People are rushing and yelling as usual. She looks around and then walks up to the editor. "Boss, I have something that we need to talk about confidentially."

"Tell me in the conference room."

When they enter the conference room, Abbie says, "A picture with a name and a note saying Memphis vigilante showed up. It was just dropped at the front desk with my name on it. I go to a coffee shop where an FBI agent sometimes goes. I've been trying to get a working relationship for information. Showing him the picture and saying, vigilante, caused a reaction. He said that just because a picture appears, you shouldn't accuse someone of a serious crime like that. Then he said, how about he sends my picture to the Memphis police with the vigilante note?"

"An excellent point."

"Then he said I should talk to our lawyers before we say anything about that picture. What was interesting was that as he was leaving, he said When you look at the footage from Memphis, you can say the rider was trying to stop more violence. He works on domestic terrorism cases."

"SHIT! She could be the deep-cover agent. The rumors could be true." He pauses, thinking. "The agent knows we have this picture. Are there copies?"

"Yes, and no.

"Shred the picture and give it to him. If we report she is a deep-cover agent with no actual evidence, and she gets killed, we will be arrested for contributing to her death."

"First Amendment, sir. We can report it."

"Abbie, based on a picture and no other credible evidence, we say she is a deep-cover agent. Then she gets killed based on our reporting. We will have directly contributed to her murder. Getting her killed is bad enough, but we will then have the FBI swarming all over this building to get any evidence about who leaked her identity."

"We can talk to the lawyers about the wording."

"Winning a First Amendment case while we sit in prison for contributing to the death of a federal agent won't be fun. We don't have free rein to get people killed, especially federal agents. There is an alternative. We can use the social media angle. We don't talk about her. Shred the picture and give it to the agent. Let's go heavy on the social media deep-cover side. We need to ask every contributor and every expert we talk to about the credibility of the deep-cover agent. Put in every piece talking about Memphis. Start now!"

### 

"Nyah, the reporter I told you about who showed me the picture of a young woman–it wasn't Sam. This morning, she handed me an envelope with the shredded picture inside. She said there are no copies, they don't have a credible source, but they are asking about the social media angle."

"Good work, young man. You got the message across, and the right people heard it. Anything else?"

"Their reporting started emphasizing the deep-cover agent angle yesterday afternoon. To emphasize this, I said I would stop the request for a search warrant. She looked a little shocked, then said thanks with a smile."

Nyah smiles, saying, "You just confirmed it for her, but she doesn't have the picture. Get the warrant just in case there is a copy."

# Boston Hack

Sam needs to access the company network to investigate a Bitcoin transaction Zoe found, which is tied to a property purchase and the blackmail group. The network she needs to access is in a high-rise building in Boston. She thinks to herself, "It couldn't have been in a small business office somewhere, could it?" She'll have to access the building and the floor to hack their Wi-Fi network.

It's early October, and Boston is slowly reopening after the pandemic lockdown. Restaurants are now allowed to have 25% capacity indoors. Office buildings have more people, but most people are still working from home.

To get the information, Sam needs to get Zoe connected to the company network. In this case, that means getting into the building and getting close enough to access their Wi-Fi.

To prepare, Zoe needed to gather several things for Sam. During the drive to Boston, they discussed options, and Zoe began ordering the necessary items. When she couldn't find an item, they would adjust the plan.

"Zoe, I can't have everything delivered to the motel. I need a venue where I can wait for the deliveries."

"The weather is reasonable, so I can give them special instructions for a specific location. I won't be able to get everything delivered by tonight. The hack will have to be delayed a day."

"That's fine. It gives us the chance to get better prepared."

Sam visits several locations to collect packages the next day. The last delivery is at a café in Post Office Square. The delivery courier arrives, and it's a woman wearing a cap and jacket with the delivery company's logo. Sam looks at her and, with a flash of inspiration, asks, "Will you sell me your cap and jacket? I can use them for a Halloween costume."

"This is my last delivery, so how much?"

Sam digs in her backpack and pulls out everything she can find. "$133, that's all I have. This will be awesome; I can show up to the party like I'm delivering stuff."

Now Sam has a cap and jacket with a courier company logo. Driving back to the motel, she tells Zoe, "Change of plans. Instead of going into the building looking for a job, I'll be delivering and picking up packages. We need to redo the plan completely."

"I heard you bought the cap and jacket. That sounds like a better option. I need you to test the camera glasses with the cap on so I can understand the field of vision."

"I'll wear the glasses while I work on the RFID scanner."

"The first part of the plan can be the same. You go to where the people with badges will be to copy. Head to the café with something to deliver, and you wait for someone to pick it up. After you get enough badges scanned, we'll try other floors."

"Assembling this scanner instead of an off the shelf device is a good thing. Having control and letting me boost the power means I can probably get every badge in an elevator."

Sam has a little device called a Wi-Fi nugget attached to a battery pack. She pulled an RFID antenna out of a badge reader and boosted the power. Zoe can access the nugget through Wi-Fi and has complete control. "Sam, the idea of an RFID reader where the badge must be close is a good security thing. It just seems too easy for you to modify that device and capture information from much farther away."

"Yes, Zoe. Most people don't know how these technologies really work. I need you to create a fake app that can show delivery and pickup requirements in the building."

"I will finish the app tonight and download it while you're asleep."

Sam will wear two masks all day. She's changed the outside mask with a built-in bump to have the tip of her nose in a different spot. She also added some gauze material to make her cheeks appear wider. With the glasses and the two masks, any facial recognition system will have a harder time getting a positive match on her face.

"Zoe, with the double masks, glasses, and cap, tell me about facial recognition when I look in the mirror."

"This is the best possible view, straight on to your face, and the standard algorithms drop the match percentage below 80%."

"That'll work for me."

The next morning, "Sam, everything is fully charged. I downloaded all the network IDs to your phone. There are three target networks. If we find any others during the process, I'll work those as well."

Putting the latex gloves back on, Sam takes one box she received yesterday and tapes it closed again to act as her delivery package. Zoe has already confirmed she can park in the building's garage. As usual, Zoe has full access to the phone and will control the scanning for Wi-Fi passwords. Sam will focus on scanning as many ID cards as possible.

"I have my computer, the programmer, most of the blank building access cards, a backup headset, and a backup phone. Finally, two charging packs if we need them."

"Let's go through the plan. The primary target floor in the building is on the thirty-sixth floor. That is too high for the long-range antenna to work from the street. Many floors require card access, but I'm not sure about the thirty-sixth floor. We begin by attempting to capture the card information. You take in the box and coffee and try to move around to scan. Once you start on the target floor, we will need to adjust as we receive better information. I can usually get access to the network from the floor below or above with the boosted power on the phone."

"You found two other targets. Other than the thirty-sixth floor, what floors do I need to get to?"

"The other target floors are the nineteenth and the twenty-sixth."

As she leaves the parking elevator and enters the building lobby, she says to Zoe, "I can't talk to you actively right now. You need to listen through the Bluetooth headset." Sam has a low-profile, over-the-ear headset that's covered by her hair. At one point, Zoe asks Sam to turn her head to the right to listen to a conversation.

"Zoe, you are loud right now."

Zoe turns down the volume on the phone. "With the camera in the glasses, I'm getting enough information. I'll give you directions if I need to capture an image."

"I feel like I'm walking into the lion's den."

"It'll be okay; you've been in worse situations. We get into the networks, then you get out. Remember, we don't need the specific floors; just one above or below will work for me to access the network. The RFID scanner depends on who shows up. We have to be flexible. Not every business has people in the office."

"With the camera glasses, you can identify people who can get us close." She is carrying a small brown box. On top is a drink carrier with four tall coffees. Sam walks to the directory board that has all the businesses and floors. She's really looking at the entrance and the garage elevators to see people putting their badges around their necks. What she needs are the usernames off the badges to gain access to the Active Directory server.

The RFID scanner she created is in the front pocket of her jacket. It will capture their badge info if she gets within 12 inches. The plan is to find some candidates and get on the elevator close to them. It could be more than one, then she can clone their cards and access more floors of the building.

The camera glasses record everyone. Zoe is receiving the information and parsing it for usernames, real names, and any other useful details.

She walks to the elevator bank and slowly walks to the farthest elevator to wait. As she walks by people, she can feel the scanner in her front pocket vibrate, so she knows she's getting something. The directory gave her the floor for each of the three businesses, but she needs to start with the café, where people will get coffee. As the elevator arrives, people are waiting. Following the pandemic, only four people get on. Sam lets the elevator go, waiting, allowing more RFID scans. When she gets on, holding the box and coffee, she asks for the 10th floor, where there is a café.

In the café, she goes to a table away from the elevators and cameras. She sits down as if waiting for someone.

Zoe tells her, "We have eleven cards logged right now. Based on the limited visibility of the camera when you entered the elevator, we don't have what we need."

Everyone is wearing masks, but the building is still far from full. A dozen people came to the café to get coffee.

"Zoe, what is the most common color badge to use, or a temporary badge color?"

"You want to use yellow."

Sam retrieves her computer, three yellow cards, and the RFID programmer from her backpack. Opening the laptop and logging in, Zoe takes over and tells her, "Ready." Sam taps the yellow card on the programmer. She does this with the two other cards when Zoe says she is ready.

No one does more than glance at her while she is working. She put the computer and the programmer into her backpack. Grabbing the box and the coffee, she heads to the elevator. The next elevator going up has two people, and both get off at the café. She enters and pushes buttons until something stays on. As soon as the doors close, she puts down the box and tries the three cards. She wants the 35$^{th}$, 36$^{th}$, or 37$^{th}$ floor.

None of the cards work on those floors. The next floor stop is 24. The elevator doors open into a lobby area with no one there. She steps out, puts the coffee on a table, and returns to the elevator. Pressing the button for floor ten, she will go back to the café.

Back in the café, she gets a table close to the ordering line and the elevators. She puts the box down and sits. After a few minutes, she gets up and acts as if she is calling someone while walking. She wants to pass as many people as possible. After doing this twice, she sits down and waits. Zoe is accessing every Wi-Fi network nearby and working to connect to everything in the building.

After about 20 minutes, two uniformed security guards exit the elevator with another man holding a device; it could be a phone or a scanner. Sam turns off the screen on her phone, saying to Zoe, "I have company." Adjusting her mask, she grabs her backpack and the box.

The man with the device is tapping the screen and talking to the security guards. Sam is wondering if they know she's scanning, or is this something else? Her adrenaline is shooting up. Her best route is to head to the bathroom. She walks toward the bathroom when the group turns and walks toward her. Her adrenaline is spiking as she evaluates escape or fight. She knows she can deal with all three, but then she'll have to escape the building. This is going to be messy.

She realizes the three are not walking toward her, but to the end of the coffee line. As they approach, she hears them discussing players and percentages. She takes a deep breath, realizing they are talking about fantasy football. Sam changes direction to walk closer to them. Walking by, she feels the nugget vibrate as it captures RFID cards. After passing them, she changes directions to the elevators.

"Zoe, did we get good RFID codes?"

"We captured two codes, so one of the security guards is captured." Sam walks back to a table far from the counter and pulls out her computer. He is at the counter, but she can see the reflection in the window if anyone heads in her direction. After programming two cards with the last two scans, she heads to the trash area. She set the box on the counter, then heads to the elevator.

On the elevator, Sam uses both cards to access the floors. On each floor where she needs to get off, she waits next to the elevator for about three minutes for Zoe to work. Since the businesses are closed, she simply waits. When one person walks down the hall, it appears as though Sam has made a delivery and is waiting for the elevator.

On the last floor. Exiting the elevator, she sees a reception desk with a woman sitting at it. The woman looks up at Sam. Sam heads to the reception desk.

The receptionist immediately asks, "How did you get to this floor?"

Sam replies, "Sorry, the security guard helped me. I have a pickup that says this office." Sam pulls up the app, which shows a package with the company name and building address.

The receptionist doesn't look pleased and says, "No, you need to leave right now, or I'll call the police."

In her ear, Zoe tells her, "I'm in the network, and I'm using her information. Her screen is going to have a pop-up window for a few seconds; you need to distract her."

Sam raises both hands and palms facing the receptionist. "Hang on, I'm just trying to do my job and pick up a package." Sam takes two steps, angling back and to the right, causing the receptionist to turn away from her computer screen. "I just need to wait a few minutes," as she backs up slowly. After taking three steps back, she sees the pop-up on the computer screen go away.

The receptionist repeats, "I said leave."

Sam turns toward the elevator.

As soon as the elevator doors close, she tells Zoe, "I'm heading to the lobby; I'll be in the lobby in less than 5 minutes. See what else you can accomplish."

She pays for parking and exits the building. She asks Zoe, "How many networks did you get access to?" Zoe replies, "I have tunnel access to the three target networks, and a worm is working on a fourth network. I'm scanning slowly to try not to activate the alarms."

"Please give me directions to New York," Sam asks as she puts the phone into the dash holder. "While we're in this part of the country, we need to access the targets in New York as well."

### ###

DSAC Holland walks into the area, chatting with the SSA and several agents. She gets to the area with Nyah's desk and stops.

"How is it going?"

Quietly, she says, "What do you think about Frank and the extortion investigation? I may take him off."

Nyah replies, "I need to know more. You sound concerned that Frank is compromised. I don't think so. He wouldn't be helping Agent A, and he certainly wouldn't have gone to the mobile home. Frank's team is the normal team to get a case like this. Whoever holds that position would have received the case. These guys would have run you in circles as well.'

"Nyah, I'm concerned, and I told Phil to scan my office. We first talked about S.., agent A, in my office. The first time her name was connected to the hacker. Every major change has been discussed in my office. Then agent A gets attacked."

"You think your office is bugged and the source of the information leak?"

"Yes, I think it's one source. I'm thinking of changing assignments. Change it all up."

"I wouldn't recommend that right now. Agent A will not want to have a significant change. From her perspective, it would be a major risk. I would continue having Phil scan your office.

# Finding a Link

The Boston search didn't provide any direct links, but it offered more names for Zoe to perform searches and analysis. After Sam checks into a hotel on Long Island, Zoe sends information to her computer.

When Sam opens her computer, Zoe says, "I found a link. It's just one, but now that I know what to look for, I'll find more."

"Great! What did you find?"

"I did a forensic accounting analysis on several people, including their credit card transactions with cross-references for location and time. Look at the information on the screen."

Zoe explains that the two people on her screen have no connections through work, social media, or even living in the same area. They live about 50 miles apart in the Boston area. "Their names both came from your search in Boston. I found one picture with the first man in the foreground that also had the second man in the background. From there, I searched for the event where the picture was taken and found them both on the list. It was a hospital charity event. I searched for others on that list, and one other name came up. I started looking for other connections and couldn't find any."

Sam frowns as Zoe continues, "The first man is Roger Smith; his company purchased the building with Bitcoin. The second man is Eric O'Brian."

"After trying to track and get information through the blockchain, I continued to follow the money. What I found were credit card transactions going back months. During the first week of each month, both people are in the same area. The earliest transactions show both men buying coffee at the same coffee shop within two minutes of each other. When the lockdown started, they didn't meet, but once people began moving outside, they would often be in the same area every month. They will buy coffee within about 15 minutes of each other, but also within one or two blocks of a park."

Sam is nodding as Zoe adds more, "The next step was to search camera footage in the areas where they bought coffee. The link will take you to a video showing them both at the same bench last month. The video does not have enough resolution to discern what they are talking about, but an envelope was left on the bench by Roger. Eric picked it up when he left."

"This is great! This is exactly what we've been looking for. Now we need to follow this thread to find more information. Get this to a server with the Boston data and let Phil and Frank know. Great job, Zoe!"

"Sam, there's the other topic I talked about in Boston."

"What was that?"

"You don't want to talk to Claire to keep her safe. However, I've been talking to her, and we've been working on a social media campaign related to Memphis. I've created a forensic analysis of every move during the chase and fight. It has been crafted to show you were protecting people and trying to escape. Claire also had the idea to include comments in the feeds that suggested you could be a deep-cover agent working to expose the terrorists. The comments are gaining traction, and others are discussing ways to assist the agent. I've created 174 online personas to comment on social media to reinforce the idea of a deep cover agent."

"Zoe, that sounds great, but it doesn't actually help with finding and stopping the bad guys."

"Actually, Sam, it does because it's true. You're finding information and evidence and sending it to the FBI. Just as if you were an agent."

"How does it help?"

"You've forced their hand, making them search for and attack you, first in Waco, where they could get away quietly. But this most recent attack ended up with them shooting up Memphis. They're spending lots of money to chase you and try to stop you, and they're exposing themselves unintentionally. I don't think it's just because of the money. That we've found links and information no one else has found makes them want to stop you. You found a link to human trafficking that the FBI didn't know about. We don't know how much of their operations are changing to stay hidden."

"Zoe, we know they are getting information about what we send to the FBI. Most of what we've sent so far is data, and not much is conclusive."

"But it's more than any investigation they have that follows the rules. Now that we know I can create a social media campaign that'll have an impact, we have another weapon to cause them trouble. For now, I'll continue to monitor social media while I run my other operations."

"Ok, thanks, Zoe. I think this is great. I'd like to see more of an impact."

###

"Phil, I received an encrypted email from Sam. It has a new link to check out, and I can tell you she is or has been in Boston."

"How do you know that?"

"The data she posted is specific to three companies in Boston. She hacked their networks and accessed their systems to get this information. It's another case of information and evidence that you can only get from their systems."

"Frank, you know we both have the same question  where next? The only logical place is New York. We have all the data she has; the information is in there."

"I'll schedule a meeting today so we can all get together and figure out the best targets."

The team consists of Phil, Frank, Colin, Nyah, and Patrick. The team has been in a conference room for almost two hours, reviewing the data and focusing on identifying Sam's potential targets in New York.

They have a list of six potential candidates, and they have discussed locations and details. Nyah has been sitting back and listening.

Patrick notices and says out loud, "What are you thinking?"

Nyah replies, "Frank is thinking we provide support and backup for Sam. The problem is that everything we do is watched. We can't travel without someone knowing."

At that point, the DSAC Holland enters the room and asks for an update. The team provides an update and shows her the six potentials. Nyah then expresses her concerns about leading the bad guys to Sam.

"I agree with Nyah. Having debriefed an undercover agent, the last thing they need or want is someone coming up to them saying, how is your undercover assignment going? Frank, you go to New York alone. When you get there, you do everything normally, by the book. Except you go nowhere near any business Sam may be targeting. Let them follow you, track you. Find something from Nyah's area. The cover is you're there looking at financials for a terrorist group, possibly related to Memphis. It'll put you in the area. If something happens, we may be able to help."

# New York

In New York, Sam doesn't want to go into the buildings. The Boston building experience was stressful.

Once in the financial district, she walks down the street. Rather than trying to find people in the buildings, she is trying to be where they'll move. She's wearing jeans, a shirt, a jacket, and has her backpack. She's also wearing the glasses again to record as many usernames as possible.

Even with the city open, the streets aren't packed, but people still want coffee and something for lunch. Some shops have put Halloween decorations in their windows.

Zoe is monitoring Sam's phone as it tries to get Wi-Fi passwords for the target companies.

"Sam, I'm trying something different. I'm searching for people who work at each specific company. Then I'm searching for their cell phone numbers. Given the cell phone number, I can get their GPS location. I'll give you directions to the area with the highest concentration of people. It will give you a better chance of getting their Wi-Fi information. This method does not require you to get within ten inches; you can be several feet away."

"This sounds good to me, Zoe."

Zoe directs Sam to walk down several streets in the financial district. There's a slowdown between 9 a.m. and noon, then it becomes busy again. It's pandemic busy, but it's still New York, and the sidewalks are fuller than they have been in months.

Just like Boston, she wears two masks all day. She fitted the inner mask to her face and loosely attached the outer mask, using material to create the illusion of wider cheekbones. The only time she takes it off is at lunch to eat or drink; she's careful to check the area for cameras each time.

The city is now allowing food service businesses to have 25% indoor seating capacity, but most are still only offering takeout.

In the afternoon, she waits until people leave, then goes to the subway station on Wall and William Streets. At the station, she looks at the maps, walks around the platform, and then sits on a bench for almost an hour. When she leaves, she needs to walk to Fulton Station to catch the subway toward JFK Airport, where she has a hotel room.

On the subway to the hotel, Zoe gives a rundown: "Day one is complete, and I have the information. I'm mapping every business and location to access their network with the long-range antenna. If everything goes well tomorrow, we'll be done. Otherwise, you'll have to go another day."

Once off the subway, Sam tells Zoe, "I'll follow your map and get as many as possible tomorrow. We can start early because I don't have to enter the buildings."

Sam is up early and gets ready with every battery pack charged, the phone ready, the computer, and the long-range antenna set up. She's wearing comfortable walking shoes, jeans, a sweater, and a coat. She takes the subway to the area and finds a coffee shop close to one network. Shopping for clothes at the thrift store has been beneficial, except for the challenge of finding items that match her color preferences. The coat is dark blue, not navy. She hasn't worn it before because it doesn't go with many items, but it keeps her warm.

After getting coffee, she walks to the building across the street from the target business. She stands next to the wall, looking at her phone. "Tell me which direction to turn."

"It is hard for me to determine your orientation. Try turning 90 degrees counterclockwise. Please turn slowly."

After a few degrees, Zoe says, "Stop there."

Sam waits while Zoe is accessing the network. Her backpack has a long-range antenna set up and pointing toward the network.

After a few minutes, Zoe says, "I have another network signal, try turning a little more counterclockwise." Zoe says to stop after Sam has turned a little more.

"Okay, head to the next street and let's try again. This works so far."

"That went well. If it is this easy, we'll be done in an hour."

Two hours later, Sam says, "I spoke too soon and jinxed it."

"Sorry, Sam, I didn't account for the angle needed when the business network is above the 30th floor, and you only have the street width. Also, the higher the network, the weaker the signal. With all the other Wi-Fi signals, you can't be more than a block away, or there is too much interference."

"Let's go through all the others and then try to figure out these few. I'll look for places to sit so the antenna can point up."

After walking around the financial district, Sam resorts to stopping across the street, putting her backpack on the ground so the antenna is angled up and standing over the backpack, so no one grabs it.

There are people around, but it's not packed. She has her third cup of coffee she has been carrying around.

"Zoe, if this doesn't work, I don't know of another option. I'm sure I won't be able to get to the floor as a delivery person."

"I have a very weak signal. It means my access is slow and is taking longer. They also have better security than most of the other places. I expect that means we'll get some good information. Claire asked me about accessing these business Wi-Fi networks. You discussed hard business passwords with her months ago. I explained that I have access to enough compute resources to do a brute-force attack and get the passwords in less than a minute."

"I hope we get some good stuff."

"Sam, I'm sorry I wasn't constantly monitoring."

"Monitoring what, Zoe?" Sam suddenly is concerned.

"Frank's cell phone is in New York."

"Is he close to me?"

"No, he's several blocks away. Sam, he must be following the same trail."

"How far away? Does it seem like he's following the same trail?"

Sam then hears Claire's voice, "He's working a diversion to make sure the bad guys aren't close to you. I just had Zoe show me his route."

"Claire, what are you doing?"

"Relax, Sam, I'm safe and monitoring. The call is encrypted, so we can talk. We're behind you to help. And it looks like Frank has figured it out. He has the same information that you have. The FBI likely analyzed to determine which businesses to target. They'll be following Frank, so he's just taking them for a walk. He's nowhere physically close to you, meaning he knows where you are, kind of. If the bad guys are following Frank, it helps. Just finish and get out. We'll talk more later."

"This was the last network. I'm done." She grabs her backpack, heads to the subway, and intentionally gets on a train heading the wrong way. At the second stop, she gets off and heads up the stairs, then back down to get on the correct train.

There are still people traveling, but because of social distancing, there is no place to sit on a train heading into town. She gets off at the hotel stop and goes to her room.

Inside the room, she tells Zoe, "That was stressful. I hope we got better information on this trip. There is still time to pack and check out before the required time. I need to head to the closest workshop."

"The closest one is in Philadelphia."

"That'll work. I'll be packed and ready in 15 minutes. Zoe, can we get a special phone delivered to Frank at his hotel?"

"Checking.... It may not be tonight, but if not, it'll be early in the morning."

"That will work. Directly delivered to him, into his hands."

# Next Steps and Exit Plan

Sam gets into the SUV after paying for expensive parking and starts heading to Philadelphia. Zoe sends her directions to the workshop. With New York traffic, what should be a two-and-a-half-hour drive takes three. Sam asks Zoe for directions to a grocery store along the way, and Zoe changes the directions on the phone.

After getting groceries and stopping to pick up lunch, Sam gets to the workshop. This time, there's a keypad where she can enter the unlock PIN. Sam goes through the small door and heads to the big garage door. She sees several pallets of equipment in the open space and just enough room for the SUV if she turns sharply left when she enters. With the SUV inside, she closes and locks the garage door.

She takes a tour of the building while discussing the contents of the pallets with Zoe. The building has a different layout, but it has the stuff she needs. The pallets include computer and networking equipment, just like the previous building. Zoe tells her, "Cameras are installed around the building, but I can't access them until you get the network fully set up."

"When I left Memphis, I didn't pack everything. I brought a shotgun, Dad's sniper rifle, and a pistol from Memphis. If I need additional weapons, can I get them around here?"

"I understand you want to be prepared, but getting weapons is difficult. The pandemic has caused gun stores to close, and most weapons are out of stock. They'll need to be ordered."

"Well, that'll cause problems with background checks."

"I'll work on it, Sam. I'll let you know more later."

"After Memphis, I'm going to be more prepared. Order a holster like my competition rig, so I can have it ready.

"Will do. I'll explore other options and order the items. The replacement tactical vest has been ordered and is scheduled to ship in two days. I will have it delivered locally."

"Okay, I'll work on the network setup first."

"Perfect, getting the network online for me is helpful. Thanks."

After the network is up and connected to the internet, Sam spends the rest of that day unboxing everything and setting up the living area. This building is the first one remodeled to meet all of Sam's requirements.

"Zoe, you did a good job with the remodeling."

"Thanks. After you've been there a few days, we'll review the requirements to see if you have any updates."

"That sounds like a plan."

The next day, while Sam is working on the desktop computer setup, Zoe tells her, "Frank has received the phone. He has not turned it on yet. When he turns it on, I'll let you know."

"Sounds good." Sam spends her time on her daily routine, installing and setting up the server and desktop systems. She gives Zoe access to everything. To accomplish all that, she stays up late.

In the morning, Sam finishes stacking the trash and recycling. Zoe had cleaning supplies delivered, but Sam only cleans the kitchen, bathroom, and the room where she sleeps. She begins her days with the routine she started in Memphis: exercise and reviews with Zoe. In the early afternoon, Zoe tells her, "Frank has returned to Boston today."

"Are you constantly tracking his phone now?"

"Yes, if he's the focus of the information leak, I want to monitor him. I use cameras, networks, and other phones around him to find some links. Also, I asked Claire about this, and she agreed."

"I didn't ask you to do that previously because the more you interact with someone who is being watched, the more likely you will be spotted. The last thing I want is for someone to know about you."

"I'll change my surveillance to leave false clues. I'll be able to use them as tripwires to know if someone is checking."

"Awesome, just be careful."

An hour later, Zoe tells Sam, "Frank has turned on the phone and it's going through updates. Should I set up a chat, or do you want to do a call?"

"Let's have a chat session."

Sam starts a phone chat session.

Frank: "How are you doing?"

Armeda: "I'm doing okay, gathering information. Your email about the camera mentioned 'Patrick'. Who is he/she?"

F: "He's working with Nyah on domestic terror groups."

A: "Did you get the info from Boston?"

F: "Yes, it helped, and we deduced you were going to New York. The link was good detective work. We evaluated and picked the six most likely targets in New York. I was there, but not close enough to keep anyone from following you."

A: "Thanks, I'm finished with New York. I'll get the information online for you in the next couple of days. By the way, I had eight targets in New York."

F: "Great, I'm looking forward to the info. Have you seen the social media stuff about Memphis? You're being called a deep-cover agent."

A: "Yes, I've seen the media coverage. It's odd to me that people would think that."

F: "Armeda, we're using it to help. We are calling you, agent 'A'."

A: "Should I use 'A' now?"

F: "Using A will help the disinformation."

F: "I have a request. Can you perform your analysis on a domestic terrorist group? I want your help to conduct the same type of analysis you performed on the Boston team. Nyah is identifying the group, and I'll send you the info by email."

A: "Okay, so you want me actually to be the deep-cover agent 'A'?"

F: "Short answer is yes. Having you share some information will enable us to validate the deep-cover aspect and determine where that information flows.

A: "Ok, Frank. I'll be very low key for a bit while I conduct further analysis. I'll see what I can find."

F: "Thanks."

A: "Frank, this phone is just for you. No lab, no one else, clear?"

F: "Yes, got it."

Sam calls Claire that evening and tells her about the chat with Frank.

Claire says, "YES, it worked!"

"What worked, Claire?"

"I knew we could use social media to influence and counteract the blackmail group's propaganda. It was obvious that you were being targeted. The initial reports all said: vigilante or terrorist. That had to be from the blackmail group trying to vilify you. Zoe and I turned it around with video analysis, posts, and comments. Zoe was great at posting comments from all over the world seconds apart, in different languages, so there was no way anyone could say it was planned. All I wanted to do was counteract their bad message. This is amazing; the FBI has taken notice of and is using it! Zoe, we need to get something on this terrorist group."

"Hang on, Claire, we don't even know who they are yet."

"We'll figure it out, Sam. I feel like I've accomplished something; I'm so pumped right now! We found information that the FBI couldn't find, and we outmaneuvered the extortion group on social media. We are taking the fight to them and winning."

The next day, Sam receives an email from Frank with several names, social media links, and news about fires and hate crimes. Sam talks to Zoe about starting a full search.

"Sam, how long do you want to wait before we send a report to Frank?"

"What do you mean?"

"I already have some information; it's just not complete."

"Okay, well, they don't know about you and your abilities, so we need to wait a day or two. Keep digging until then. Also, I've been thinking about the situation. We're just getting solid connections for the blackmail network. While I have a double-layer mask to confuse facial recognition, I can't wear it forever. I'm going to need to hide here while we continue to work on finding them, but also to have an escape or exit strategy."

"What do you mean by escape or exit, Sam?"

"My identity and my face need to disappear from everything they are accessing. Zoe, I want you to look for every facial recognition database you can find and see if my face is identified. Then see if you can delete my information from every database. That includes Sam and Abigale. I'll need a passport that works soon, and that'll require my face to be in certain databases. We know these guys are international. If I leave the country, you'll be able to remove me from everything. We need to do the same intelligence captures as Boston and New York. We may find better connections that way. As an example, where are they getting the people they're trafficking, and what does that network look like?"

"Sam, I'm concerned that we don't have enough resources to really take these guys down. It's just you, Claire, Frank, Phil, and me working on these details, and the information leak is still there. If you're the only one doing the physical part, what happens if you're captured?"

"I know. I've been thinking about recruiting other people. Putting people in danger is a problem, but I agree we need more people helping. I want you to consider those instructions about facial recognition as a template for what we'll do when someone joins or exits. We wipe their background and give them a new identity to protect them and their families. It could be worthwhile to start by setting up a system to create new identities. I don't know what that means, but we'll be doing more in the future."

"Well, after Waco, I've been working to complete a full background and new identity for you. The only remaining task is to get the passport and determine where it needs to be delivered. I had to become a virtual 'you' to get attorneys to handle the paperwork. There are three unique identities, allowing delivery to three different locations. I can help create an identity for a business or factory. I'll create a regular business with a secret identity system, inspired by my work with Claire and spy stories. That will allow for easier shipment of the identities."

"That sounds great, Zoe. The next task is to plan another crypto heist. Let's take more of their money. Stealing their money has been one of the most significant impacts on them. Let's see if we can get most of their money. You've been searching the blockchain for transactions, so you have a map. Let's turn it around and track the money flow to accounts that we can access and set up another heist."

During one of their calls, Claire comments, "You're staying hidden, and you're also turning into a hermit? You're so focused on searching and planning, you're not living."

"The last time I had cabin fever and went for a ride; I got shot eight times. Zoe has flagged multiple items from New York, as well as the domestic terror group, for us to review. Yes, I've been spending time every day working on that data, but it's not the only thing I do. Claire and Zoe created accounts and downloaded the video games I used to play before. She is making sure my computer has plenty of distractions. But I'm also spending more time getting into better physical condition, and I'm working through several ideas. Zoe has mentioned getting others to help, and you've brought up the idea of getting more resources. The next heist will help with the money. I don't want to put people at risk without having a plan for getting them in, keeping them working, and then getting them out when needed. I'll talk more about that after I work through a couple of security concerns."

One afternoon, as Sam returns from getting groceries, Zoe tells her, "I've completed the analysis of the domestic terror group. That includes the additional questions you posed after seeing the data."

"Hang on, Zoe, we should include Claire in this discussion."

They contact Claire as soon as she's available. Zoe starts her report with, "First, there is no link I can find where the blackmail group is funding them. Donations fund them, and some are made through Bitcoin. They have connections with state workers, including the state attorney general's office. I don't have data they are violating any laws with the attorney general relationship."

"I know when and where they meet by tracking their phones through an app that they all have installed. The app offers an encrypted method of communication that does not rely on major social media networks. It's not free, but it lets them use any device. The part they don't know is that the app tracks their movements, not just their communication."

"Zoe, how did you get access to this application?" Claire asks.

"I signed up for the app as a member of the terror group. I made my account in the name of a sibling of one of the members. When they gave me access, I searched every configuration option I could access. I found the app can track people, and the group has not disabled the setting. The app doesn't highlight the tracking feature, so they don't know they are being tracked."

"Once I had initial access, I hacked the administrator account and started analyzing the location data. I found an anomaly."

"One of the app users is not using their real name. The location data shows them going to a state building during work hours. I compared facial images and found they work for the state in the law enforcement area."

Sam says, "Well, there is the smoking gun. Pun intended."

"Do we send this to Frank and Phil?" Claire asks.

"Actually, I think we need to give Agent A the honors here. That means this is SA Jones's investigation. Let's send her some flowers."

"I love that idea. Everyone will know she received flowers  but what will the card say?"

"The card will say check Frank's email. Then the next line will say 'diversion delivered' signed Agent A. Zoe, can you arrange all that?"

"It's already done, Sam."

### 

Everyone received a meeting invite to a conference room from DSAC Holland. Nyah realizes they are not in DSAC's conference room, so this will probably be a meeting about Agent A.

They are talking through the information from New York when Gloria, Cassy's assistant, knocks and enters with flowers.

Nyah comments, "More flowers, Frank, you need to buy that girl dinner."

Gloria says, "These are for you, Nyah." Everyone looks at Nyah.

Cassy chuckles, saying, "That's one smart asset. I told Gloria to grab any flower deliveries for any of you guys before someone can read the card."

Nyah reads the card out loud: "'Check Frank's email', and the next line is, 'diversion delivered, signed A'".

Patrick asks, "The flowers are the diversion?"

Nyah replies, "Frank and Phil have received flowers, and everyone in the building knows. The message to check Frank's email is nothing. Frank will check his secure email anyway. Now the flowers are for me after we talk about Agent A and domestic terror groups. The leak will know I received flowers from Agent A, and they'll be concerned. But it helps validate Agent A is deep cover."

Cassy says, "Let's see what she sent."

Patrick moves to sit next to Frank as he accesses the email.

"There's a file summary and an index." Both Frank and Patrick start reading the summary. Partway through, Patrick looks up and says, "She found someone from the group is using a false identity and working for the state police."

"Is this an undercover agent or someone infiltrating the state police?" asks Nyah. "Or working both sides?"

Frank says, "Hang on, this part is interesting. She accessed the app that the group is using to communicate. The app tracks their location, which is how she found this person. If Sam figured out how to track these people, Nyah could use this capability. The summary continues with the data correlation showing he is an undercover agent, but he needs to be questioned. They don't sound like the most dangerous group to worry about. The last line reads: The investigation will continue with these groups in the following order. There are four groups listed."

Cassy tells the group, "Let's quietly contact the state police and tell them our deep cover agent found their agent. He needs to stop using the group's communication app. While that will affect the monitoring, based on this report, I don't think they are aware of or need to worry about it. But now we have something concrete to show agent A is real."

###

Sam feels stressed about creating a larger organization. She thinks about new identities, safe houses, and exit strategies. "Zoe, to get a real organization going, we add risk to everyone. The more people involved, the harder it is to keep secret, and the more likely someone will be found and hurt. We know they have no problem killing anyone they consider a threat. You'll need to be the primary point of communication. You'll need to create several personas that our agents know and talk to."

Zoe replies, "The movies call them handlers. I can do that for everyone. Sam, let's include Claire in the discussion."

"I agree, let's call her."

When Claire is on the conference call, she says, "Zoe updated me on the discussion."

"Great. Another item we'll come back to is that I can't be associated with the group. I'll instantly make the group a target. To build this group, we need to talk about recruiting, training, operations, and security."

"You know, you sound like a military person with that statement. Which one do we start with?" Claire asks.

"You talked to Zoe about our discussion, which was focused on operations. We need to figure out how to get people, equipment, assignments, and receive intelligence. I can focus on the operations area with Zoe and get you involved after some progress."

"That sounds good, and I can start recruiting."

"Tell me about recruiting, Claire."

"We do what the government and terrorist groups do. We find idealists for our cause and convince them we need them. The number one recruiting place is on college campuses. We need to decide which type of candidates with specific specialty skills we require. First, they need to meet the requirements for character, which will be tough for anyone. I'm sure we need hackers, finance, but anyone who can meet other requirements."

Sam says, "Training will have to include the physical stuff you've started, Claire. Plus, we'll need to add equipment skills and communication requirements. I think Zoe can take the lead on creating plans, scheduling, and monitoring."

"I got this one, Sam," says Zoe. "I'll also focus on security, which includes identities, access controls, and dealing with threats."

"At first, the organization will need to be intelligence-gathering."

"It will also need to be focused on cohesiveness, team building, and integrating new people," Claire replies. "I'll work with Zoe on getting the plans set up."

After pausing for half a minute, Sam says, "I want us to set a goal, which is to shut down a major part of their operations. That means finding it and causing problems. An example could be finding how human traffickers move kids and getting them caught and arrested. We need to hit them hard and repeatedly."

Claire replies, "I love that, like a corporate hostile takeover. They need to think we're going to destroy every part of their group. We cause supplier mistakes, delivery issues, employee revolts, and government inspections. Yes, it will be harder, and it will take longer to get going, but it will be the most effective."

"If we're going to go hard, we need to talk about one more subject. How do we provide people with an exit option? We can't just let the bad guys find them and kill them. We need to have new identities, jobs, and everything ready. Zoe can have generic versions ready, which we can use when needed. We need to add international."

"I agree," replies Claire.

After the call, Sam thinks about her exit strategy. Where would she go, what would she do, and how would she create a plan? Her next thought is whether she includes Zoe in the planning. If everything goes wrong, they can use her against Zoe. She starts working on a plan and, over a few days, works out the details in her head.

There is a risky plan. She doesn't want to write this in a computer file so that Zoe can read it. This plan will require her to be separated from Zoe for several weeks.

She's ready to discuss her exit strategy with Claire and Zoe. For this to work, Sam needs to disappear and everything about her be erased, visibly. Not hidden, and a body never found.

"Zoe, I have a request, and it is going to be risky. If this plan works, Sam will be gone, allowing Abigale to continue. I'm going to need several things that are not simply available at the store. I don't know how to get them; I'll probably need to go where the key items are located and pick them up when you find them." Sam gives Zoe several items to look for and asks her to notify her when she finds them.

Later, Zoe asks, "Are you sure you want me to create fake identities for Claire, Frank, and Phil?"

"Yes. If I'm in danger, so are they. We need to provide them with an exit path, so they can choose whether or not to use it. If we've done a good job, Claire should be safe. The only connection I have with you is through school, as we were roommates. Zoe, I'll discuss my exit plan with Claire during our next call. I don't want you to talk about any details. This will be hard for Claire. I feel responsible for getting her into this, and I need to make sure she's safe. The high-risk part of this for me is intentional."

On the call, Claire declares, "You are not just going to disappear and not talk to me," with Sam and Zoe on the special phone.

"Claire, you don't get a choice in this. You told me you are a big girl and get to make your own decisions. Well, so do I. The more relevant point is that I'm the target of the blackmail group. I've kept you out of the spotlight, and that's why this plan can work. If you force your way into this, it will fail; we all will fail!"

"No, SAM! I'll do whatever we need to help."

"Claire, stop! The point is, they won't quit until they think I'm dead. I plan to eliminate every scrap of data pointing to me as Samantha Holzen. If that works, sorry Zoe. When Zoe completes everything, I need to have an established new identity with no flaws. I'm keeping you out of the details because it will probably be messy. Claire, this is not just a shut-out plan, and that's why I wanted to call you. I could execute the plan and disappear without telling you anything. I need you to understand and be ready for the future. You'll be the validator of my new identity. At some point, I'll need someone who can vouch for me or provide support in a difficult situation."

Claire growls on the phone, "That is a poor attempt to placate me. You disappear for who knows how long, then return to glory. What do I need to have ready?"

"I don't know, Claire. I'll expect it will be a weapon, cash, and maybe an ID."

"Well, that's no problem. I'll work with Zoe to have things set up. Having all that ready doesn't stop how pissed I am that you are shutting me out."

"Claire, after all I've been through, after all that we've experienced, I would take another path if it were possible. When I pull the trigger, it will be a sudden action. They have to think I am dead. When I contact you later, it will be when I'm sure it's safe, and it will be a surprise when it happens. Claire, don't you shut me out now. I'll get through this, and then we can work to stop these people. I need you to trust me. Please."

"Ugh. I hate this; I really do. I get it, but I hate it."

"Thank you, Claire. Now, we need to talk about the heist. When I need to activate my exit plan, you and Zoe will continue creating the organization.

Zoe, have you set up enough servers to do the first money extractions all at the same time?"

"Yes, Sam, I have servers all over the world close to the servers with the bad guy accounts. As soon as the money is pulled and transferred, those servers will be wiped and shut down. Pulling all the money at the same time will prevent them from locking down accounts."

"Claire, the hacks in Boston and New York represent five businesses with bitcoin wallets. Zoe is in their network; she can start a set of transactions to move their bitcoins. The hacking tools she installed will have to be completely deleted to prevent detection after the heist. When you set up a working business and employ people, I would like the business to be separated so they don't get targeted. The people need to focus on their part and shouldn't have to worry about the extortion group attacking them."

"I have lots of ideas for things Zoe and I can do while we're waiting for you. Before we end this call, I have two more subjects to discuss, Sam. This is about Zoe."

"Should I be concerned? Anyway, go ahead."

"You have set up Zoe so she can add capacity and move to different data centers. With that capability, she can be anywhere or everywhere. The problem is that to get started, she can use a credit card. Later, we can set up more normal business stuff. We haven't done enough of this, and I'm worried she'll be noticed."

Sam asks, "Zoe, how many data centers are you currently running?"

"I am currently in eighteen data centers spread around the world."

"What is the configuration at a high level?" Sam asks.

"I am in every major region and market with a distributed but redundant configuration. I can still operate at almost full capacity if any one region goes offline."

"What do you recommend, Claire?"

"We need to set up international businesses with a cover story of something that uses a lot of computing resources. It needs to be done quietly but soon."

"I am sure you and Zoe are already working on this."

"Yes, we've got it covered. I wanted to make sure you are aware of how big and how many resources Zoe is using."

"Your forward thinking and initiative are appreciated. I started with the idea that she would be everywhere, but we didn't want her to be noticed. She needs to remain with sufficient capacity to solve complex problems and always be available, even if several data centers fail. You had two things to talk about; what is the second item?"

"Thanksgiving is next week, and you don't have anyone to share a meal with. This is what I mean about you being a hermit. If you were close, I would invite you to have dinner with us."

"Claire, I appreciate the sentiment, but I am going nowhere near you. If these individuals figure out that we are working together, you would be targeted immediately. We can have a virtual meal. I will order something and have it delivered."

A few days later, Zoe says to Sam, "I found the special items; they are in Chicago."

Sam replies, "L.A. would have been ideal, but I can't be choosy. I need to get to Chicago. While there, we can target any businesses associated with the blockchain trail or the OSINT analysis. We can conduct another round of network hacking to identify additional corporate accounts. Then we can hurt them even more and get more cash. After this heist, they'll throw everything into catching me. I'll need to go to Mexico when it starts. Let's get it set up so that after the hacks in Chicago, you can start the heist while I travel to Mexico. This is executing my exit strategy, and you can't tell Claire the details."

"Is this why you wanted those special items?"

"Yes, I'll have to do most of this manually in Chicago. After that, everything needs to be ready to get me to San Diego, then into Mexico."

# Chicago

Sam travels to the workshop in the Chicago area. Sam found all the equipment on pallets, just like at the other locations. Contractors have set nothing up. She works to get the internet set up and then focuses on bringing the workshop to a livable condition. Her timeline is short now; she needs to get everything done within the next 24 hours.

The same late afternoon, Sam decides she doesn't have time to wait until tomorrow. She needs to do the network scan tonight. Using the RFID badge copying technique would be problematic, so she targets a single building. Because it's one building, she doesn't need to go inside the target building. Instead, she uses her lock-picking skills to get onto the roof of a building across the street. With the long-range Wi-Fi antenna, she can scan networks without having to move or be spotted. In the building are several financial institutions that Zoe has linked to businesses used by the bad guys.

"The plan is you'll hack the security system. I'll get to the roof and set up the long-range antenna. We conduct a Wi-Fi attack and scan of the building, then I exit. Sounds easy and should only take about an hour."

"The problem is that the temperature is 12 degrees Fahrenheit. This is Chicago, so the wind is always blowing. You'll be exposed while I do the scanning."

"Then you need to go fast."

Zoe resets cameras and distracts guards with false alarms. Sam gets to the roof just after 6 p.m.

"Sam, I have control of the laptop. Set the antenna toward the top floor. I'll scan from top to bottom, as far as we can."

"Let me know when I need to shift the antenna."

"The items you asked for will be dangerous to move around. You haven't asked for any help beyond the basics."

"After this, I'll pick them up. As I mentioned earlier, this marks the beginning of my exit plan. It won't work with no element of risk. Part of that risk is that I'll have to go offline. We've done this before."

"I didn't enjoy being out of communication with you before, and I don't like it now. I can't help if you get into trouble. Please move the antenna down three degrees."

"You won't be able to provide any real help, and you know it. The times you can help, I ask for it. You know, the only way this exit plan works is if everyone thinks it's real, including Clare. She'll become the first person they check and watch."

"Please move the antenna down another three degrees. The access works so far. I'm focused on the primary targets; everything else is ignored if it doesn't provide access. The security guard shift change is at 7 pm. Be at the exit door on the street."

After multiple moves of the antenna, Zoe has scanned most of the floors they can access.

Sam's teeth are chattering. "I should have brought hand warmers. It is 6:42. I'll need a few minutes to get down the stairs."

"I'm working on one more network. Leave the computer and start heading downstairs. I'll wipe everything when I'm done."

Sam re-enters the building and pauses for a minute to warm up. She says to Zoe, "Disable the cameras and motion sensors in the stairway. I'm descending."

"The search revealed two more accounts that belong to the bad guys. I've added them to the list for the heist."

As she descends, all the motion sensors and cameras are reset, allowing her to walk by triggering no alarms. Zoe is monitoring the guard movements and causing some doors to malfunction. At 6:58, she tells Zoe she's at the door. Zoe disables the door alarm, and Sam exits through the emergency exit door, walking away.

When Sam leaves the building, Zoe starts the second heist. It will take several hours, and Zoe will monitor the progress. She sends a message to Sam: "Get warm, get some food, and head to the Chicago workshop."

### ###

"Zoe, how did the heist go?" Claire asks.

"The total heist amount was $248 million. I'm currently dealing with attempts to track the movement. I've prevented four attempts, but they're still trying."

"That's awesome, Zoe! That should have an impact. We need to monitor and see what happens."

"Several of the businesses used for money laundering now have no cash. They may need to report the theft. Either way, they'll need more cash or declare bankruptcy."

"I love this, Zoe! Have you told Sam?"

# Frank in Chicago

Frank is working at his desk when an alert pops up. He set up the alert to know if anyone accessed information on Samantha Holzen. He was expecting someone in the L.A. office to look at the background details on Sam.

This isn't what he expected. The alert describes a body found after a warehouse fire that matches Sam's description. The Chicago police found a cell phone close to the body, and the SIM card information was Samantha Holzen's. Frank contacts the Chicago office to find out more. He tells the agent that Sam was his confidential informant who went missing several days ago. Frank lets him know he will travel to Chicago to help identify Sam and assist with the investigation, if possible.

Frank goes to find Phil, and Phil is smiling. He says to Frank, "Sam did it; the information she sent is showing a pattern of financial transactions. Most of them are real estate related: luxury homes, businesses, hidden with Bitcoin and cash transactions."

Phil sees Frank is not reacting as he expected and asks what's wrong. Frank tells him about the alert from Chicago.

"Sam has no family, so I'm going to take a few days and head to Chicago. I want to confirm it's her, see what I can do for the investigation, and then I'll work on funeral arrangements." He tells Phil to prepare a summary for the DSAC Holland about the information Sam provided.

Frank goes to inform DSC Holland. Frank is subdued, feeling defeated when he tells her about Sam.

Cassy tells him, "Don't use vacation; treat Sam's death as part of two, no, three ongoing investigations. Find something, anything to catch who did this so we can prosecute them."

"Well, for some good news, Sam found something, and Phil will give you an update this afternoon."

Frank travels to Chicago and meets with the local police and the medical examiner. He asks to see the report and discovers that the young woman endured a lot of torture. They had pulled out or knocked out her teeth. The severe burns on the body prevented them from getting fingerprints. He checks the report about the body and all the evidence to confirm it's Sam. Same height, build, and approximate age, but the only way to have positive confirmation is with DNA. Frank calls the local field office and inquires about the availability of DNA for Sam.

He goes through the evidence found close to the body. There's a backpack with some hacking gear, a couple of cell phones, several USB keys, charging packs, and a laptop power supply. The charging packs and phones made the fire worse once they caught fire. There is no computer, and Frank asks the investigation team. The reply was that no computers had been recovered. Frank considers the missing computer. Did the attackers take it and the information it contained? If they can find the computer, that could be a lead.

The next day, Frank receives positive confirmation from the medical examiner that the body is a match for Sam's DNA in the FBI database.

After reading the report, Frank is talking with the medical examiner about the condition of the body. "Her teeth were knocked out or pulled, fingers broken, several ribs broken, and her lower legs broken. She was alive during this torture."

"How do you confirm she was alive at that point?"

"Bleeding around the damaged areas. The common term people use is deep tissue bruising, which can only happen if blood is moving through the vessels, i.e., her heart was beating. Also, based on no smoke in her lungs and lividity or pooling of blood after death, they didn't start the fire right away. They must have been there for hours."

Frank comments, "It looks like they tortured her for information. Her computer is missing, so they tried to get her to give them passwords. Now they are probably trying to hack the information she wouldn't tell them."

"Based on what I see, I agree," says the medical examiner. "She was tough to deal with the brutal attacks. You should also know that she had

COVID. The condition of her lungs showed COVID was advanced. Based on the condition of the body, I can't be conclusive, but they may have used an IV on her. It would allow them to help keep her alive with COVID. The standard blood tests didn't show any drugs in her system. I can't confirm that COVID killed her. I'm going to list cardiac arrest as the cause of death, with COVID as a contributing factor."

"Have you ever seen methods like this used?" asks Frank.

The ME replies, "I've seen bodies after torture, but not this bad. You need to catch these sadistic bastards and throw them in a hole."

"I'm working hard on that right now. Thanks for your help."

Frank lets Phil know and tells him it will take a couple more days to complete the funeral arrangements. Frank talks to a funeral parlor after deciding for Sam to be cremated. The next day, he receives a call from the mortuary. Sam's body was not in the morgue when they went to pick it up.

Frank travels to the morgue and checks who took Sam's body. The name listed is Claire Elmer. Frank gets the name of the funeral parlor and heads there. As he arrives, he sees Claire leaving. He honks, parks, and walks over.

"Hello, Ms. Elmer."

Claire has been crying. "Um, hello. Have we met?"

"Yes, sorry, it's Frank Andrews of the FBI. We met briefly online several months ago." Frank pulls out his ID. "I had everything set up, and when my funeral guys showed up, Sam's body was already gone."

"Sorry, Agent Andrews, I came to Chicago to take care of my friend."

"Ms. Elmer, I'm sorry this happened to Sam; it's absolutely not what I wanted."

"Agent Andrews, we both didn't want this. I tried many times to get Sam to stop, be more careful, to get you involved." With new tears coming from her eyes, Claire says, "She didn't listen, and now this."

Frank comments, "I also told Sam to be careful. I must say that she made more progress in finding these guys than anyone else. The bad guys knew how to keep us in the dark; they didn't know what to do with Sam. By the way, your comments about discussing with Sam to be careful, how involved were you, or are you?"

"Agent Andrews, Sam was my friend. She would call occasionally, but never say where she was or what she was doing. Every time we talked, she also told me to stay away and that I couldn't get involved. I kept my eyes and ears open. Several weeks ago, she stopped communicating."

"Ok, Ms. Elmer, please don't get involved with these guys. Have you scheduled any services or events for Sam?"

"No, because no one else knows Sam, no one will come. Her family is all dead. She's going to be cremated, like her parents."

"The funeral parlor I contacted said it would be a couple of weeks before the cremation would happen."

"I used family connections. She will be cremated tonight."

"Ms. Elmer." Frank starts to ask something. Irritated Claire interjects, "Stop calling me Ms. Elmer; use Claire, Elmer, El, or something."

"Ok, call me Frank." Frank pauses for a few seconds. "Claire, I was going to scatter her ashes in a forest area of one of the state parks."

Claire replies, "Actually, that sounds nice; it sounds like Sam. Can we do it together?" asks Claire.

"I would like that."

Frank and Claire meet, get the ashes, and travel to a wooded area. Frank hands the urn to Claire and removes the lid. Claire swings the urn to scatter her ashes.

Returning to the city, Frank drops Claire at her hotel, saying, "It was nice to meet you finally. Thank you for letting me participate with Sam."

"Agent Andrews, I mean Frank, you're welcome. I'm glad you showed up to pay your respects to our friend."

Frank calls the local FBI contact, says goodbye, then heads to the airport to fly back to Boston.

# Martha

After finishing her work in Chicago, she leaves the workshop and then heads to Union Station. Zoe has booked a sleeper for her to travel the 43 hours to Los Angeles. She only has one credit card, cash, and her Abigale driver's license. Her hair is now red, along with her eyebrows. Looking up makeup online, she created a fake scar barely visible above her mask, close to her left eye. It also appears that she is trying to conceal it with makeup. There's nothing to identify or track her; the only problem is keeping her face covered to prevent identification when she's not in the sleeper room. Her face is in the news because of the FBI investigation in Chicago.

On the train, she learns this train route is called the 'Southwest Chief'. She chose L.A. for her destination so she could have a private room. El Paso would be about the same duration, but with no private rooms available. During the trip, she has nothing to work on, so she sits back and enjoys the views. The route travels through the Midwest, the corner of Colorado, then into New Mexico, Arizona, and finally California. Many parts of the trip were boring, but some were majestic. She thinks, "I didn't realize how beautiful a train trip could be."

She arrives in Los Angeles in the morning and catches the next train to San Diego. Arriving in San Diego, she looks for a store with prepaid phones. Getting a phone, she calls Zoe.

Zoe answers by saying, "Guten Tag."

Sam replies, "Guten Tag. It's me. Please send me the location of your private mailbox. I'll call you again after I have the stuff."

The phone chimes with a text message. She gets a taxi to the area, giving the cab driver a location two blocks away from the mailbox store. At the P.O. box location, she needs to go to the counter and show her ID to get her package.

The package contains the new identity she'll use going forward. She's now Martha Garcia, using her mother's first name and the last name she picked at random because it's common on social media. Now she has a driver's license and a passport. She puts both her driver's license and her passport into her backpack, throws away the packaging, and leaves.

She calls Zoe on the burner phone. Martha says, "It's me, and you need to use Martha from now on."

Zoe replies, "I understand."

Martha asks, "How did things finish in Chicago?"

Zoe gives a rundown about the body being found and the confirmation of the DNA being Samantha and Frank being there, working on the investigation. "You were right, there were several people with alerts about anyone accessing the information on Sam Holzen. I disabled them, made the changes, then re-enabled them. Claire is also in Chicago, making funeral arrangements." Zoe includes a comment, "I read the coroner's report, and that body was damaged. Martha, you made it look like there is a psycho on the loose."

Martha replies, "I needed to use major forensic countermeasures on this one. I had to make sure they couldn't use dental records or fingerprints. The only identification possible was through DNA. I also needed to focus some attention on who would do this to Sam. Zoe, you acquired the body; you know she was already dead. Also, did the family receive the ashes?"

"Yes, Martha, I monitored the funeral home systems to make sure they received a box of ashes. None of that activity can be traced to you." Zoe continues, "When I changed the DNA profile in the FBI systems, I also checked and deleted all information about the young woman from their systems." Zoe also confirms that she sent packages with new identities to Frank and Phil.

"Following our discussion on having people get out safely, I have wiped all facial recognition data I can access about Sam. I'm monitoring the situation, and if Frank, Phil, or Claire uses their alternate identity, I'll also wipe their facial recognition data.

"How about the heist results?"

"Everything has been moved and hidden. There were seven

attempts to track the movement of bitcoin and other forms of money. With multiple accounts, the use of multiple cryptocurrency types, and wiping everything when complete, I could keep them from tracking the money. The total heist amount was $248 million.”

“Wow, that's a lot more than I thought we'd get. Good job!”

Zoe continues, “Based on pulling all that money, I expect that several of the businesses will need to get a cash infusion soon or declare bankruptcy. That will either cause them to highlight the heist or just be shut down.”

“Now that's what I call making an impact. I LOVE IT! We know the leaders of the companies, so we can get more connections and expand our options.”

After a pause, Martha says, “Um, Zoe, I have something else to talk to you about, and I need you to let me finish before you say anything. I'm going to Mexico, and I won't be able to communicate with you for several weeks. During this process, I need to be completely established as Martha, and it will be dangerous to communicate with you. I'm going to provide you with several points we discussed and some additional tasks to complete while I'm offline. When I contact you again, please be my Aunt Tilly, the aunt who runs the family business and manages the trust fund that covers my expenses. This will be the first time you interact with me and others, so you can't be Zoe. I have a hidden Bitcoin account that you're not supposed to know about, which I'll be using for the next few weeks. I'll be the niece that works for the business, and I told you I was going on vacation.”

Zoe replies, “Got it, but why can't I help you now?”

Martha replies, “I'm going to be very vulnerable, and it won't be safe to talk to you or about you. I don't know when I'll be alone to communicate. There is more, and the approach to accomplishing these tasks is vague, allowing for adjustments as needed. This ties into the discussion on creating an import-export business that delivers shipments of specialty items worldwide. The blackmail group is global, and I need to travel extensively as part of the business without drawing attention. Having an import-export business will allow you to ship items to me wherever I must go.”

“Claire and I have already been working on the business. She wants to arrange for some of her family contacts to use the import-export business to ship materials and help get it going.”

"Your next task is to use the business structure in Mexico to buy a house on the west coast of Mexico. Target southwest but within an easy drive to the Mexico City area. It'll be the first international workshop. I know a Mexico workshop can't be the same as what we've been doing, but use the template as a starting point. You don't need to start this task immediately; in fact, don't start it for three weeks."

"I need to be completely Martha to go after these guys. The short-term focus is to establish me as Martha. If it doesn't work, you can still work with Claire to bring the bad guys down. When I get set up, we go after them hard, multiple attacks, create chaos for them."

Zoe says, "This doesn't sound safe. I can get security, whatever is needed."

"No, Zoe, this part needs to be separate from you. Aunt Tilly will come later. If you're there too soon, Martha's identity will be questioned. Also, if you're found or compromised, I don't have a chance. Please trust me. I've thought this through, and this transformation is important. You work in the background for Martha, as we talked about. When I'm established as Martha, I'll be in touch with you. It should only be a few weeks."

Zoe says, "We need to discuss Claire."

"Claire thinks I'm dead, correct?"

"Yes, Martha."

"Zoe, it's the only way to keep her safe, for now. They are probably watching her right now to look for flaws. The extortion group didn't kill Sam; they don't know who did. After I contact you, we'll get Claire looped back in. Until then, watch out for Claire. If they go after her, she won't see it coming."

"Martha, Claire asked about the Chicago workshop and went to see it. I made sure it was safe, and now the workshop will be stripped and sold. Most of her comments focused on how you were living, rather than the equipment or preparation. She said it was obvious you were there when she looked at how well the areas had been cleaned."

"Zoe, I can't help that perception right now. This transition to Martha will allow me to live as normally as possible."

"Everything I asked you to set up on this call, you can work with

Claire. She's smart and will figure out that you are not simply doing this for fun. If anyone thinks Sam is still alive, they'll try to use her to get to Sam. You can tell her this was part of my long-term plan for the larger organization. You are simply following my plan. Zoe, keep looking for connections and consider international opportunities. Send nothing to the FBI. Sam, their informant, is dead, and there shouldn't be any communication."

After the call ends, she looks for a taxi. When the driver pulls over, she asks if he will take her to the border. The first driver says no and drives off. The second driver agrees to take her to the border. Martha casually drops Abigale's driver's license into the pouch on the back of the front passenger seat as she gets out of the cab. She turns off her cell phone when she crosses the border.

At the border, she proceeds to the immigration area to get a 60-day tourist visa, which will allow her to travel within the country's interior. After completing the paperwork, she's officially in Mexico, and law enforcement in the United States can't arrest her now.

Exiting the immigration building, she looks for a taxi to take her to the airport. She asks the driver to take her to the airport in Spanish. The driver nods and heads toward the airport. He asks her in English, "Which airline, ma'am?"

"Aero México."

"Is there a reason you are flying from Tijuana and not from the U.S.?"

Martha replies, "It's cheaper than flying from the United States. The U.S. side is international with all its COVID-19 restrictions. There are more convenient flight options to Mexico City."

If this goes well, there'll be nothing to tie her to Zoe or Samantha Holzen. When the plane takes off, heading to Mexico City, Martha thinks about her plan and finally feels that she's ahead of the bad guys. For a few hours, she can relax and drift off to sleep.

# After Chicago

Frank returns to Boston and finds an envelope in his mailbox and a note about two packages. The office person gets the packages for Frank. He checks all the information on the packages while he walks to his apartment. Once inside, he puts his travel bag down and checks the packages. The first has a Maryland driver's license and a passport, both issued in the name of Franklin Martin Walberg, featuring his picture. Package two has a cell phone, and the envelope contains a letter, two credit cards with $10,000 stickers, and a travel itinerary. The itinerary includes a flight from Boston to San Juan, Costa Rica, and hotel reservations. The flight is scheduled for two days from now.

He checks the bottom of the letter; it's from Sam. She must have planned this delivery before Chicago. The letter reads:

*"Frank,*

*At the coffee shop shooting, I thought they were after me. It bothered me because they focused on both of you. It was right after I found the database and before I knew you two were working on the investigation. I now think they were trying to kill Phil and you. After using the admin permissions on that first account, they thought you were getting too close. They didn't know I was involved, but they were tracking you.*

*After I took their money, they used you to find me. Now that they know who I am, they'll go after you and Phil again. I've sent a note to Phil with the same information. You're in danger, and you need to consider Sam's witness protection program. You must walk away before they kill you. Turn off your phone and do not access any of your personal accounts–NONE. The phone in the package is clean; use it while you travel. Take the flight to Costa Rica and go to the hotel. More information will be waiting at the hotel if you decide to travel.*

*All my best, Sam."*

Frank has never shared his personal life and past with Sam. However, he knows she'll have figured out all the details; he divorced with two grown children who have their own lives. If he's really in danger, then they will be too, unless he leads the bad guys away. Frank is suddenly more scared than he has been since he graduated from the FBI Academy. This can impact his future and his family.

Frank puts everything into a plastic bag and slides it behind his clothes dryer. He then calls Phil, gets no answer, and leaves a message. At 2 a.m. Frank's phone rings, waking him up with the caller ID of Jones.

He answers, and Nyah tells him, "Phil's dead. He was shot a couple of hours ago. Frank, you need to be careful."

The next morning, Frank goes to the office to talk about Phil and what could be happening.

Phil has a family, including three kids, with one still in high school and one in college. As the meeting progressed, he heard nothing about them being contacted or affected, so he inquired about it during the meeting. DSAC Holland tells him it's all being handled by another agent. The family is safe but traumatized by the whole thing.

Nyah comes up to Frank after the initial meeting. "You look like you're in shock, but what the hell is going on?"

Frank replies, "I'm not sure yet. The extortion group located Sam and is now targeting Phil. I need to review the latest information Sam sent to us. Before I left for Chicago, Phil told me she found something. She may have given us the key, and that's why they're reacting like this."

### # #

As Nyah is walking back to her desk, DSAC Holland signals for her to come into a conference room.

"Phil sent me an email last night. He found something about my office. He asked to meet me this morning at a coffee shop, not in this building."

"Do you know what he found?"

"No idea. This is right after Frank returned from Chicago."

"Do you think Frank is involved?"

"It is too convenient. I think they are setting Frank up to be the fall guy. Nyah, start looking at what Phil found, quietly."

### # # #

After the initial activity of getting the investigation started, Colin requests to speak with Frank. Frank says, "Sure," and they go into the conference room.

Colin states, "All the evidence on the servers is gone. It's all been wiped, along with the logs, and I don't know who did this. I also checked the daily backups that we store on site; they've been wiped."

Frank frowns, thinking, then says, "Thanks for letting me know. I'll investigate this and see what I can find. If we're compromised and people are getting killed, please give me a little time to do some digging. Tomorrow, whether or not I find something, you need to inform DSAC Holland personally about what happened. Include the fact that I asked you to keep it quiet for one day." Colin nods and heads back to the lab.

Now Frank is getting frustrated and concerned. Whoever is responsible for the purge will probably try to frame Frank for the removal, at best. Or worse, they'll attack him next. It must be someone with admin access to the servers. Frank logs into the server and checks the login history. He finds that Phil's login was used just before midnight last night. That doesn't mean Phil did the wipe. Questions formed in his mind. Did they force Phil to log in, or did they torture him to provide his login and delete everything? Frank logs off the computer and thinks to himself, Sam's witness protection program is looking better and better.

As he is walking to the elevator, Nyah catches him.

Nyah looks sad and asks, "Frank, are you heading out?"

"Yes, I was going to drive to Phil's crime scene and see if I could contribute anything, then head home. I probably won't be in the office tomorrow."

"I understand. Let me know if there's anything I can help with, and I'm sorry about Phil."

Frank gets in his car thinking, "If they're after me, what are my best options? I don't want to act like a fugitive." After a pause, he realizes and says out loud, "I need to act like Sam. First, avoid anything that can track me."

He turns off his cell phone and puts it in the car's cup holder. He heads toward the site where Phil's body was found. After several blocks, he changes direction and heads toward his apartment. He constantly checks if anyone is following him. He tries to use traffic to his advantage, slowing when approaching a traffic light, then speeding through after it turns yellow. When he gets to his apartment, he pulls into the parking garage as usual.

He pulls out his suitcase, which still has the clothes he used in Chicago. Dumping the clothes on the bed, he packs travel clothes. He grabs the bag with the new ID from behind the dryer. Heading to his car, he grabs his FBI credentials and gun. Putting the gun on his belt, he realizes this is entirely wrong, but he takes it for protection anyway. He parks in short-term parking so the car will be spotted sooner. He also realizes this car is his, and they can track him through the vehicle's emergency communication system. After parking, he puts his gun in the glove compartment with his FBI credentials. He looks at his phone in the cup holder as he turns on the phone Sam sent him.

Taking a deep breath, thinking, "Is this what Sam went through deciding to take on an extortion ring?" He turns on his work cell phone and tosses it on the floor of the car.

He starts walking to the terminal and stops after about 10 feet, thinking I'm forgetting something. "What am I missing, Sam?" Turning, he walks back to the car, opens the trunk, and empties his pockets.

Keys he won't need, a money clip, change, and his wallet. Now it occurs to him. His driver's license, credit cards, and everything show Frank Andrews. He goes through his wallet and pulls out cards.

He pauses and then pulls out the only picture in the wallet. A photo of his ex-wife and kids at dinner when the youngest turned 18. Everything else he dumps in the trunk.

He puts his new driver's license and credit cards in his wallet along with the picture. Closing the trunk, he puts on a mask, walks to the terminal, and goes to the airline counter. He shows his new passport and explains that he is booked on the 7:30 p.m. flight to Costa Rica tomorrow. "Can you tell me if there are any flights with open seats leaving today instead?"

The clerk informs him, "They just restarted flights, and the few flights available are usually fully booked." After checking, the clerk says, "There are two seats left on the 7:30 p.m. flight today, but it will cost $500 to change the tickets at this point. There is also a flight leaving at 9:30 p.m. that has a shorter layover in New York but arrives in Costa Rica at the same time the next day. The 9:30 flight has one seat left."

Frank considers the layover in D.C. or a shorter layover in New York. He asks, "What about a first class on the 7:30 flight today?"

The clerk checks and says, "That will be $2600 to upgrade." Frank hands the clerk a credit card and asks for the upgrade.

"Sir, you understand you can be stopped when you arrive if you are showing COVID-19 symptoms. Also, you will need to show a negative COVID-19 test to return."

Frank replies, "Yes, I understand." Four hours later, Frank is heading to San Juan, Costa Rica, in first class.

As the plane takes off, Zoe wipes Frank from facial recognition systems. This should prevent the extortion group from tracking him at Boston Airport. Without that tracking, they won't be able to get his flight details. She also sets up an alert for his old phone and credit cards. If they get used, DSAC Holland will receive a message.

### #

After two plane changes, one in Washington, D.C., and the other in El Salvador, Frank lands in San Juan, Costa Rica, at 9:30 a.m. the next day. At the hotel, the clerk looks up his reservation and says, "Sir, your reservation starts tomorrow."

Frank replies, "I understand. I had a change of plans and arrived a day early. Do you have a room I can get early?"

"I'm sorry, sir; I don't have any junior suites available that match your booking. Our normal check-in time is 4 p.m., and I'll have a room available."

Frank asks, "What do you have that's available now?"

"I only have single rooms with a double bed. I'm sorry, Mr. Walberg."

"A single room will be fine; can you change the reservation?"

"Yes, sir, and how long will you be staying?"

Frank has no idea how long, so he says, "Two weeks."

The clerk sets him up, then, looking at his screen, says, "Just one moment," and walks to the back. He returns carrying several items. He tells Frank the packages were delivered for him less than an hour ago. The clerk then hands him a thick shipping envelope, a small box, and a standard letter.

Frank looks at the items, frowning, then tells the clerk, "Thanks, I was expecting one letter."

In the room, Frank opens the package to find a cell phone, a large envelope containing numerous legal-looking documents mostly in Spanish, and a letter with a note from Sam. The note reads:

*"Frank,*

*If you haven't already, turn off your burner cell phone and throw it in the toilet to soak, then break it and dispose of it. You should have received another phone; it has a local SIM card so that you can use it in Costa Rica. Use the new cell phone for everything, but don't log into any of your old accounts. At the bottom of the letter is an email and password to match your new identity. Use only that information. That email address will be my primary means of contact with you later.*

*A lawyer in San Juan put together the large package of information. It includes the house you purchased and paid for on the coast. There are documents required for residency, such as bank statements, etc. You'll need to contact the attorney in the next few days to complete everything.*

*Below is the detailed information for two bank accounts, one in Belize and the other in Switzerland, each with $20 million. These accounts are your retirement funds, and I appreciate your help.*

*If you are reading this, I should be out of the U.S. and working on my new identity. I'm trying to establish myself somewhere safe, and I can't tell you where I am. In a few months, I'll contact you via email to discuss our next steps.*

*Don't access old accounts or contact anyone. If you do, they'll track you down.*

*Stay safe, Sam."*

Frank sets the letter aside and scans through the documents from the large package. Cursing several times, he throws the stack of papers on the bed. He pulls out the special Sam phone he received in New York and plugs it in to charge. It doesn't make sense, but he wants it charged, just in case.

END

# Requesting your review

Thank you for reading the book. I hope you enjoyed the story, and I would love to have a review. This will let everyone else know what you like and maybe don't like about the book. I'm always looking for ways to improve my storytelling, and I will read every review. I appreciate your feedback. The short link to create a review is:

Amazon:
https://authorbdmurphy.com/PHApb

Barnes and Nobile:
https://authorbdmurphy.com/PHBNe

Goodreads:
https://authorbdmurphy.com/PHGr

# Acknowledgments

Thank you to my family and friends for their support and patience throughout my learning process. They provided editing assistance and offered positive encouragement.

# About the author

B.D. Murphy started writing when the world hit pause—and he hasn't stopped since. He's the kind of author who sees a mystery in every machine, a plot twist in every algorithm, and a story hiding in your Wi-Fi signal. With a brain wired for engineering and a heart full of curiosity, Murphy crafts sci-fi that's clever, sneaky, and just a little bit subversive. If you like techy thrillers, real-talk characters, and endings that make you say "wait, WHAT?"—he's your guy.

Awards:
Feathered Quill first place–Science Fiction 2025–Sidney and Watson
Readers' favorite Silver 5-star winner–Science Fiction 2023–Pandemic Hacker
Readers' Choice Book Award Finalist–Science Fiction 2025–Nanite Evolution
Literary Titan 5 Star Gold Award 2025–Nanite Evolution
Global Book Awards–Bronze Medal 2025–Nanite Evolution.

Please like and follow.
Facebook: https://facebook.com/bdmurph73

https://authorbdmurphy.com

www.ingramcontent.com/pod-product-compliance
Lightning Source LLC
Chambersburg PA
CBHW020717130726

47899CB00011B/361